PRAISE FOR *SHADES OF RESIST*

"*Shades of Resistance* is neither wholly about
about despotism. But it draws very finel,
localized and felt reality of both. In its treatment of those
unexceptional humans who make the exceptional decision
to risk and resist, it succeeds splendidly in illuminating the
discovery that resistance is not so much a choice as a necessity."
—Christopher Hitchens, author of *Hostage to History*

"*Shades of Resistance* is beautiful and richly evocative, but underneath
the surface is an inventive and skilled use of metaphor and careful
control of meaning. Jonas Korda is a complex character in self-exile
among a varied lineup of strange and colorful characters. In an
almost Kafkaesque labyrinth of politics, power and alienation, the
reassembling of his perceptions is a rich and complicated metaphor for
all human struggle to connect, and to know the truth about the self."
—Ian MacMillan, author of *Village of a Million Spirits*

"*Shades of Resistance* is a deeply moving story about exile, danger, love,
fear and, though unsought, commitment. Set in the 1970s in vividly
rendered Greek islands under a dictatorship, the novel also inevitably
becomes a parable speaking to the reader's own place and time."
—Thomas Farber, author of *Acting My Age*

"*Shades of Resistance* deftly juggles political terror and the natural
beauty of Greek island life, where the senses come alive. Wandering
disillusioned in Greece during the dark regime of the Colonels,
Jonas Korda finds himself repeatedly in jeopardy but is buoyed by
strong women who appear as the spirited undercurrent of rebellion.
Shades of Resistance is a journey into a grim recent history, a magical
tour of place, and a study of human fortitude and survival."
—Summer Brenner, author of *The Missing Lover*

Shades of Resistance

a novel

Joseph Matthews

Also by Joseph Matthews

The Blast

Everyone Has Their Reasons

The Lawyer Who Blew Up His Desk

Afflicted Powers: Capital and Spectacle in a New Age of War
(with I. Boal, T.J. Clark and M. Watts)

Shades of Resistance
© Joseph Matthews 2023
This edition © 2023 PM Press

ISBN: 978-1-62963-342-8 (paperback)
ISBN: 978-1-62963-304-6 (hardcover)
ISBN: 978-1-62963-670-2 (ebook)

Library of Congress Control Number: 2022942366

Cover and interior design by briandesign

10 9 8 7 6 5 4 3 2 1

PM Press
PO Box 23912
Oakland, CA 94623
www.pmpress.org

Printed in the USA.

For Sanjyot

and

For Lia Yoka, Nikos Nikolaidis and Sokratis Papazoglou

PROLOGUE

The third morning after his release, Jonas leaned on Liana's arm and struggled through the Old Town's whitewashed passageways. Within a row of stately if slightly peeling Italianate buildings along one side of a central *platea* they found the address to which he had been instructed to report. The buffed brass sign in Greek and English read "Nikolaios Skilopsos, Solicitor." Liana said she would wait at a nearby *kafeneion*. Jonas dragged himself into the building and up a flight of marble stairs.

Behind high white Mediterranean walls, the second-floor anteroom to Skilopsos's office was dark and anomalously appointed in heavy wood and overstuffed upholstery. A young male assistant gave a start at the sight of Jonas's battered, tottering presence, but when Jonas gave his name it was apparent that he was expected. The assistant disappeared through another door, returned in a moment and showed Jonas in.

"How do you do, Mr. Korda," said Skilopsos in vowel-enamored Oxbridge tones without rising from behind a vast desk. "Do sit down, won't you?"

Jonas took the chair but was careful not to lean his galled and ragged flesh against a carved oak back designed to remonstrate pointedly with the least lapse in posture. He peered at Skilopsos first with his green eye, then with the blue: both were still partly closed, and since being exposed again to the light he had been uncertain which one was seeing more surely. What both eyes could agree on now was a slight man in his fifties wearing a thick wool three-piece suit, heavily starched white shirt and regimental tie. The outfit seemed decidedly cumbrous given the Ionian heat, but the lawyer's cultivated pallor suggested that the sun was to him no more than a parochial truth he had decided completely to dismiss. Skilopsos settled thin, manicured hands over a file folder on the desk and smiled wanly. Each of the few glossy black hairs on his head was arranged to cover as much expanse of white scalp as possible, and for a moment Jonas was transfixed by how well each strand minded its place as Skilopsos spoke. Skilopsos's own gaze had shifted up from Jonas's massively bruised and swollen jaw and now jumped disconcertedly between one color eye and the other. It was a puzzled first reaction to which Jonas was so long accustomed that normally he barely noticed. But this was the first person other than Liana whom Jonas had faced since he'd come out of the cells, and now he felt a sudden chill at Skilopsos's failure—or refusal—to settle on one view of him or another.

"I must say I don't see too terribly many Americans in such . . . circumstances." Skilopsos pressed his fingers together in front of his chin and with an impressive display of euphemism began to explain that he was to assist Mr. Korda—he referred to Jonas in the third person—in sorting out the recent, ah, unpleasantness occasioned by certain absurd but nonetheless provocative anti-Greek activities to which Mr. Korda, most unfortunately, had been a percipient witness.

"Anti-Greek?" Jonas managed without moving his battered mouth.

Skilopsos responded with professional equanimity that discussion of details was not within his brief but that there would be proceedings against the transgressors which would assuredly and in due course sort out such matters. The process, however, was apt to be long and tedious. And although the Greek government certainly would be pleased if Mr. Korda were to return . . . someday—Skilopsos spun a hand in the air—to testify against those responsible, the decision about whether to do so would be completely Mr. Korda's. "Once you are out of Greece, you see, you will be free to do as you choose."

To emphasize the relationship between "out of Greece" and "free to do," Skilopsos now reiterated less obliquely that Jonas was to leave Greece immediately: "You have been our guest, Mr. Korda. But then, an overlong visit can easily become unseemly. Don't you agree?"

Jonas shifted his weight but despite an extreme effort at masking them, the howls from his body were beginning to show on his face. Skilopsos noticed the deepening grimace and asked how Jonas was feeling after the "discommodious circumstances" occasioned by the "regrettable instance" of his "mistaken identity." A new rush of pain served momentarily to blot out Jonas's trepidations, and unthinkingly he blurted: "What about the ones you didn't mistake?"

From Jonas's still-healing mouth these words emerged stunted and muffled. The emotion, however, was clear enough, and with it Skilopsos's painted smile darted away: "I am authorized to accept formal complaints regarding any discomforts you may have suffered as a result of the, ah, accident."

"Accident?"

"Or the conditions of your . . . protective recuperation." Skilopsos ran a fingertip along the thin edge of the folder on the desk as if seeking a physical pleasure there, then allowed himself a different smile, a dog's smile: "I understand Americans are quite partial to such complaints."

When Jonas said nothing more, Skilopsos drew a small blue booklet out of the file and shifted it from hand to hand while informing that ferries left daily for Italy, as did a small plane for Athens where Korda could catch a flight to America without even having to leave the airport. Skilopsos would be happy to arrange things. As the lawyer spoke, Jonas alternately squinted each eye until he realized that the booklet in Skilopsos's hands was a US passport. Jonas's passport.

The blood was draining now from the top of Jonas's head. His jaw brayed insistently. The room was becoming unbearably hot yet his brow had gone cool and clammy. Suddenly his stomach was churning, his bowels twisting, and from the past days and nights Jonas knew that he had only moments before the paroxysms would once again thrash his body. Skilopsos was in midsentence, waving the passport like a bone, when he saw the rapid change on Jonas's face. He began to rise from his desk just as Jonas lurched to the door, through the anteroom and down the bone-jarring stairs.

At the street door, Jonas stopped. Unwilling to face the harsh light and humans outside but unable to hold off the wrack of his innards, he stepped back toward the stairs, dropped to his knees and retched onto the smooth white floor. His inability to eat, plus two attacks during the night, had left nothing to come up but bile and pain. And noise: the sounds of humiliation, which echoed off the walls and careered up the marble stairs to the office above.

After his body had quieted, Jonas remained on the floor. The undamaged side of his face was resting against the staircase cool. It was peaceful here. Quiet. No people. And a door—an unlocked door—only a few steps away. There wasn't any hurry. He'd rest a bit, just a bit . . .

A scraping sound roused him. Opening an eye, he peered upward: two shoes, two hands, directly above. A toe scratched along the baseboard but the hands remained still, perched on the banister. It was the green eye that Jonas had opened, so details remained vague. But that was the eye that knew color well, and the deep olive skin of the hands told him that whoever was waiting and watching above, it was not the sallow Skilopsos. Jonas inched his head around and looked up with his blue eye. The face above remained in the shadows but Jonas could now see the outline of the dark hands clearly: resting on the railing, they formed the shape of a steeple.

Jonas got slowly to his feet and hauled himself up the stairs. By the time he reached the second-floor summit of his Calvary, the person who had been watching from the banister was no longer in sight. In the anteroom, the assistant stood quite still as Jonas moved by him to the inner office.

Skilopsos was sitting unperturbed behind his desk: "You are better, I trust?"

"Something I ate," Jonas mumbled.

"Mm. Well, of course you are at liberty to remain here in Corfu until you are somewhat more rested. That is, until you are fit to travel." Skilopsos held up the passport. "However, I would advise—*strongly* advise—against your returning to that . . . unsavory little village."

"New York?"

"I beg your pardon?"

"Oh. You mean Glaros. . . . I'll do my best."

"We are counting on that, Mr. Korda." He let the words settle, then handed Jonas the passport. "*All* of us."

PART ONE

Running from the Minotaur

*This tribute consisted of seven youths and seven
maidens, who were sent every year to be devoured
by the Minotaur, a monster with a bull's body and a
human head. It was exceedingly strong and fierce, and
was kept in a labyrinth constructed by Daedalus, so
artfully contrived that whoever was enclosed in it
could by no means find his way out unassisted.*

—Bulfinch, *The Age of Fable*

I

Jonas didn't so much awaken as simply realize his eyes were open; where he'd been didn't deserve the word *sleep*. He blinked and instantly regretted it. Instead of clearing his sight, the reflex unleashed his other senses, pushing and shoving into focus. Shoes soaked, feet frozen on the rough iron floor, long legs jammed up stiff under his chin. There was no feeling in his rear end, sunk into his canvas bag, but he knew that the next message there would be pain. His mouth was dry, throat sending signals it would soon be raw. He swallowed and was forced to taste again the sour sliver of mortadella and stale roll he had tried to eat at the station in Padua while waiting for a train heading south.

The clack and whine of the wheels and the ceaseless rattle of the door latch just above him entered Jonas's head directly through the temples. His neck muscles clenched against blasts of cold wind from a corner where the walls were supposed to meet the floor. And something on the wall jabbed his back. The jostle of the train plus his damp shirt and jacket made the poking more insidious, a slow and subtle torment: just enough that he couldn't ignore it, never so much that he could ignore everything else. His hair and moustache were still wet, though he managed to position himself so the rain dripping through the roof fell on no exposed skin. And his nose was running.

A tobacco smell—strong, almost sweet, curious—widened his circle of awareness by a few feet. A haze filled the butt end of the third-class car, like the coat a night's drinking lays over the morning. Directly across from Jonas were the two toilet stalls, each with a primitive pot and long-dysfunctional corner sink. Five feet of corrugated rust floor separated the stalls from the car's end wall against which Jonas was wedged. The stall doors were open; in each cubicle sat a thick-set, dark-haired man. Though they could not see each other, the two men held exactly the same position: elbows on knees, cigarette in right fist, head down and fixed on a small, cheap magazine. Jonas had seen these comic-book soap operas all over Italy the past couple of weeks, but these two were somehow different. The print was blurred. Or the type off-center. It was as if Jonas had something in his eye which he only noticed when he tried to read. He closed his green eye and squinted through the darkness but still couldn't make out the script.

He was reproached once again by the poking at his back. Edging away from it, Jonas inadvertently threatened the precarious balance of bodies pressed together on the floor: his foot nudged the man inches to his right; that man moved his leg, causing the next to move slightly and then two more to readjust themselves.

Jonas stared at the pile of bodies pinning him in the corner of the tiny passageway. He could remember nothing since he'd straggled at the back of the crowded platform, squeezed himself onto the last packed car and joined a clump of dark young men dropping themselves onto the entryway floor. He had an impulse now to check the time, as if that could tell him something about where he was. But reaching for the bandless watch in his pants pocket, he realized, might cause waves of realignment in every direction. And the attention that could bring was the last thing Jonas wanted. Anonymity had been his sanctuary since setting adrift in Bologna a week before. If he didn't know what he was doing, how explain himself to anyone else?

Ten men, he counted, in a space no more than five feet by eight. Plus the pair in the toilet stalls. And baggage: battered valises, mushy cardboard boxes held together with rope, plastic bags announcing stores in which their current contents had certainly not been purchased. Most of the men were dozing. Several arms and legs appeared unconnected to the main layer of bodies, giving Jonas the impression of another stratum beneath what was visible. Yet the men seemed accommodated to their extremely awkward positions. No agitation in the air. No faces aggrieved or bodies tense. Jonas was soothed by the men's composure, their tranquility even.

But it didn't stop his nose from running. And surreptitious hand swipes just weren't enough anymore. He had to go for his handkerchief;

he just had to. Very carefully he shifted his weight and slid his hand down, but the corner of the handkerchief was stuck under his hip. He tilted farther and pulled again. The handkerchief let go but, as it did, his feet jutted into the man he had nudged a few minutes before. Jonas tried to speak, to apologize, but mortification made Italian impossible while the impulse for anonymity halted his English. A slight gasp was all that emerged.

His neighbor had been asleep. Yet Jonas's kick produced only a flutter of the man's lips. Through a half-open eye he looked at Jonas's expectant face, muttered in a benign tone something that sounded like "Taxi" and went back to sleep. Jonas glanced around; no one else seemed to have noticed. The men in the toilets never looked up from their magazines.

Jonas now examined the tiny passageway as if it were one of those children's puzzles that asks, "What's wrong with this picture?" The men were dressed simply but not peculiarly, except perhaps with less style than Jonas had become used to seeing on Italians, even poor ones. Coats bulkier. Pants baggier. And it was years since he'd seen so many square black tie shoes: "biscuit-toes," they'd called them in the housing projects of Jonas's Brooklyn childhood. Several of the men had long, full moustaches, not at all the fashion of the moment in Italy. And their hair, though neither very long nor short, was clipped exceedingly close on the sides, as if the top had been saved only by sudden flight from the barber chair. One of the men lit a cigarette. The smoke was harsh yet aromatic and unlike any other Jonas had smelled in Italy. He looked in vain for a packet to identify the brand.

The men shifted themselves and their bags, adjusted clothing against the cold, and offered, reached for, smoked and extinguished cigarettes, all without strain or disruption. Once in a while a quiet word was exchanged. Jonas tried to pick up fragments of conversation, but the sounds always fled before he could find any words with which to connect them. There was a throaty quality to the voices, guttural and rich. Without actually shaping it into thought, Jonas sensed a relation between the voices and the singular scent of the cigarettes. A relation that bound these men together and set them apart.

≮←

The men were trying to create some space on the floor while looking apprehensively into the netherworld of the train's interior. The source of their anxiety soon showed itself to Jonas: a huge leg encased in black cotton stocking poked into the entryway and hung in the air as if trying to decide if the water were too cold. Then the rest of an enormous woman in black lurched through the doorway, only the men's collective arms preventing her from toppling into their midst. A face like bad Chianti, her eyes went wide when she saw the toilets occupied. The man in the stall nearest her divined the woman's need and raised his head. Only then did Jonas realize that this man in the stall was, rather, a woman in the stall: black hair only slightly longer than the men's, same olive skin, high cheeks, blocky clothes. She was about the same age as the others—late twenties, early thirties, it seemed—and shared their countenance of equanimity and good humor in the face of this long night's wet, miserable ride. There was one difference, however, which Jonas only noticed with second sight: the deep black centers of the woman's eyes were wrapped in scarves of rich violet.

The woman rose to vacate the stall in favor of the large woman in black. But how to get herself out and the other woman in without trampling anyone on the floor?

"*Madonna!*" the large woman called for heavenly intervention.

The woman in the stall closed her eyes in commiseration. The men, too, showed compassion, despite the woman-in-black's disruption of their tenuous comfort: they shrugged, clucked, and made undeniably sympathetic noises with teeth and tongue. None, however, made any moves sufficient to end the woman's distress. Jonas watched and tried to pose logistic solutions to himself. The men on the floor were now gradually pressing farther back from the stall but they were not clearing enough space for the necessary exchange of positions, and soon their movements were threatening Jonas's meager supply of air.

"*Madonna putana!*" the woman screeched, rocking on her heels. The men tightened another notch and Jonas could envision himself squeezed down and under the bodies now pressing him against the wall. Although he had no feeling below the waist, he pushed hard and managed to stand. This allowed the men on the floor to make room for the woman in the stall, which in turn permitted the woman-in-black to lunge into the vacated compartment. "Aieee!" she gasped, darted roughly equivalent glances of gratitude toward Jonas and heaven, and slammed the door shut.

Jonas stood facing the woman with violet eyes. Facing the top of her head, actually. She smiled up at him: "*Bravo.*"

Jonas smiled back and shrugged. The same shrug, he realized, as the men had offered the distressed woman-in-black. The two stood stranded above the others. Jonas slouched to avoid seeming too tall.

"*Posso avere questo ballo?*" the woman asked, bowing in mock politeness. Her gesturing hand accidentally struck a head below.

"*Sigha, sigha!*" the man on the floor complained.

"Oh, *sighnomi, kirio,*" the woman seemed to apologize with a heavy brush of sarcasm.

To Jonas this was an odd exchange, strange words formed more in the throat than the mouth. He tried to locate the dialect: Calabria? Sicily? The woman with violet eyes faced him again.

She's waiting for an answer, Jonas thought. Something about a *ballo . . . Posso avere*—Can I have . . . Can I have a ball? . . . What ball? . . . What the hell is she talking about?

He smiled weakly, hoping to be saved somehow from having to reveal that, despite their common plight, he wasn't truly one of them.

"I . . . *Io non . . . ,*" Jonas stuttered.

"I ask if you want to dance," the woman said kindly in a curious accent.

Jonas was embarrassed to be addressed in English but relieved to find that nothing real was being asked of him.

"Ah . . . *grazie.*" Jonas gave a bow of thanks.

The stall door opened. The men on the floor now shifted more easily and the woman-in-black tiptoed back into the car. When she had gone, there seemed a spaciousness unknown before her arrival. One of the men stood and sought a stall. The man in the second toilet squeezed into the entryway. And when all the adjustments had been made, one compartment stood empty. Jonas was closest. The seat looked beautiful, beckoned to him. But he didn't move. He was unsure of the proprieties: Does the previous occupant have the right to reclaim the seat? Or does already having had a turn militate in Jonas's favor? Or perhaps, as with other thrones, the old ruler determines the right of succession? After a minute or so, when no one else made any move, Jonas finally took the stall. He lit a cigarette and leaned forward, elbows resting on knees. But with the bit of comfort came a twinge of self-consciousness. He peeked around the entryway: the others were adjusting to their new positions, paying him no heed.

A final drag on the cigarette. As he'd seen the others do, Jonas let it drop between his feet onto the wet metal floor, then crossed his arms and leaned back. The last thing he noticed was the face of the violet-eyed woman who had asked him to dance. Wedged against the wall, she was already asleep. And she was smiling.

The train would slow, speed up, sometimes stop for a minute or two, all without apparent reason. At the first few breaks in the rhythm of the ride, Jonas opened his eyes to try to see where he was. After a while he no longer bothered.

He must have been asleep for some time when he next raised his head; his neck and back had stiffened in place. It was the quiet that had wakened him—the train stood panting softly in the darkness. The outside door opened and into the entryway stepped two middle-aged men with shiny dark suits and cheap attaché cases on which their names and that of their company were embossed. Above their soft chins were fearful, ill-fitting faces, mouths turned down at the corners; faces shaped by lives of goading people to buy things they didn't need. The newcomers barely disguised their disdain at the men on the floor but were stymied by the impassible inside corridor and so were stuck in the entryway. They edged to the rear wall and remained standing.

The train was rolling again. Jonas's erstwhile dancing partner reached into the chaos of bags, produced a nameless bottle of clear liquid and pulled the cork. A rough-edged alcohol odor filled the passageway and several men stirred on the floor. The woman pronounced a strange benediction—"*Yia mas!*"—tapped the bottle once on her knee and took a swig, then passed the bottle to the man next to her, who drank and passed it on. The woman fumbled in a plastic bag and pulled out a hunk of bread and some olives the colors of her eyes. As she settled back to enjoy her meal she noticed Jonas watching and, when the bottle returned, offered it to him. An ingenuous smile and an open-palm gesture encouraged him, so he reached for the bottle and took a drink.

Fire and fumes filled his head. Tears in his eyes. He gasped, snorted, saw nothing, felt nothing.

"*Raki*," the woman explained. "Good, eh?" When Jonas clung to the bottle and did not, could not, reply, the woman assumed he wanted more. "Sure-sure," she said. "Good for you. Very special."

The woman refused the bottle's return until Jonas drank again, so he pressed his tongue tightly to the opening and dissembled another gulp. A small amount of liquor slipped through and to his surprise he found a bit of pleasure in the hidden anise taste, though the afterburn suggested licorice-flavored lighter fluid. Jonas regained some of the feeling in his mouth and most of his breath, then handed back the bottle. "Thanks," he managed. ". . . Ah, *grazie*."

"*Ela*," one of the men called softly to the woman, "*eladho*."

She passed the bottle, then settled back to her meal. Jonas watched as she ate, the surges of a supple neck above square broad shoulders, muscular thighs easily supporting an awkward crouch, strong arms, blunt rough hands. And a smile that anchored the wide-open face of someone who knew who she was. The woman again offered the bottle to Jonas. He declined. Raising her eyebrows, the woman shrugged and tucked the bottle away, then nestled back into the baggage. The entryway became still again. Jonas retreated into the stall and soon he was asleep.

Deep in the night, the train made another stop. Jonas opened his eyes to the two men in shiny suits being nudged along the wall by new passengers. The violet-eyed woman shifted on the floor and bumped her head accidentally on one of the attaché cases; the suited man clutched the case tightly to his chest as if protecting a holy artifact from the grasp of an infidel. The woman looked to Jonas for support of her innocence and they both shrugged. Jonas stretched and adjusted himself on the toilet, then noticed the briefcase men staring with a mixture of disapprobation and envy at his unconventional seat.

"*Per favore*," Jonas said, rising from the toilet and offering his place. In unison the men in suits quickly looked away, as if the very idea of taking refuge there were inconceivable to them. Jonas's violet-eyed friend looked at him and just shook her head.

The train slowed almost to a stop, then lurched ahead. One of the suit men lost his balance and fell over the woman, dropping his case into Jonas's stall. It popped open and before the man could grab it and snap it shut, Jonas saw that it was completely empty except for half a salami and a chunk of cheese partially wrapped in newspaper. The woman saw into the case, too, and she and Jonas exchanged a smirk.

The fallen briefcase man righted himself and inched farther away from the woman, unblocking a sign on the wall behind him:

VIETATO TENERSI IN PASSAGIO
(No Standing in Passageway)

The woman noticed the sign and tried to suppress a grin, but when she glanced at Jonas they both began to cackle. Others on the floor now looked up at the sign and the entryway began to bubble with quiet laughter. The men in suits turned and saw the sign, then quickly conspired to the pretense that they had seen nothing.

This last pose did it. Jonas and the violet-eyed woman exploded in laughter. And in a moment all the men on the floor had erupted, shaking and rolling against each other. Every look, every expression made them roar. At the next station, the mortified briefcase men fled while the train was still moving. The woman and men on the floor barely noticed. They laughed on and Jonas laughed with them. Laughed until it hurt, until joyous tears came finally to release them and they all sat quietly, smiling, waiting for daylight. When morning came, the train reached the sea.

2

There is no light more barren and grievous than the glare of a cold March sun over a dying port city gray and tired with winter. It obscures what it's meant to illuminate. The world hangs suspended in its grainy vapors.

Jonas stood at the window, stupefied. The light was mean, confusing: morning, midday or late afternoon it was impossible to tell. He tried each eye alone, but even to his blue eye the outlines of streets and buildings remained blurred, to his green eye the colors mottled and faded. There were no shadows. Through an opening between buildings, Jonas glimpsed a corner of the sea, but it, too, was the color of nothing—he couldn't tell where the city ended and the water began, where water ended and sky began. But the sea was there. He could smell it. He could feel it moving.

Jonas knew nothing about the town. It was the end of the line, he got off the train. Wandered the rainy streets, bag banging his hip. For a while he sat in a neglected park, under a tree, mostly out of the rain. Several times he found himself by the water.

Finally to a room in a cheap *pensione*, four flights up a narrow stairway, peel off soaking clothes, drop on the bed. Hours he lay there unable to sleep, unwilling to get up. Couldn't think, couldn't not. An overloaded barge of memories cut loose from its flimsy mooring and coursed through his bloodstream, sharp-edged, gouging and distending as it forced its way along: his wife's tearful face, such sadness as she turned away from him in the room her relatives had given them in Bologna . . . the pained looks of her aunts and cousins as he lurched out the door . . . the friends who would say with a shake of the head, "Jonas? Who knows?" . . . his wife's face again . . . their plans for his birthday, his thirty-first.

His birthday, alone in a *pensione*, in bed, wet clothes, nowhere, nothing. It made him sweat. The pills. He leaned over and rummaged his bag: antihistamine, antibiotic, anti-seasick—all the antis. Hadn't looked at them before. Wasn't sure which was which. Took two of each.

Now he stood at the window, groggy, unable to focus. The light, that miserable light—it made his teeth ache. The pills had put him out, but the sleep had merely altered the shape and shade of his stupor. He staggered down to the street, headed for the harbor. Reached a seawall. The water's quiet undulations were hypnotic, lenitive. His shallow breathing became deeper. The world came slowly back to him.

But this wasn't much of a world. A gritty, uninspiring harbor dominated by land creatures: trucks, cranes and hoists that poked and prodded a few ships at dock. A place that evoked words like *drayage, dross, dredge*. It could have been any port in Italy. Any port in the world. When you're not really there, "there" could be anywhere.

It began to drizzle, a sickly mist too weak to clear the air. Jonas walked by a forlorn pier and through the dampness saw unaccountably familiar outlines: figures clumped together under a shelter, gathered close around their bags to ward off the chill. One of the figures rose, jaw set and face expressionless as if committed to a long struggle with Time. She saw Jonas and smiled. "Hello, my friend," she called. "You come to dance?"

Jonas couldn't speak. They looked at each other stupidly.

"No Standing in Harbor," the violet-eyed woman read from an imaginary sign. Jonas managed a smile, shifted his weight.

Someone came along the pier and opened a gate. The woman watched Jonas for a moment, then picked up her things. Jonas stood rooted to the spot as the woman and men from the train moved through the gate. At the end of the pier, a rusted old ferry waited patiently, squat, homely, a pack animal that knows its route without human direction. A slate board on the fence read in faint chalk: "Corfu/Patras—25/3/73—17:30."

The woman and men lined up at the foot of the gangplank. Jonas's heart pumped hard. One by one they showed their papers at a folding table in the cargo hatch. Other passengers trickled through the gate and joined the queue. Jonas pulled out his watch: 16:45. His mouth was dry. The line became shorter, the travelers disappearing into the boat. Jonas's stomach was churning, then his legs were churning, he was running through the dreary streets, into the *pensione*, up the stairs. He stuffed his jacket, still wet, into his bag and bolted out the door.

Racing headlong toward the water, he got lost in the misty back streets, then found the harbor and pounded to the dock. The woman and men were no longer in sight but the boat was still there. Nothing moved on deck and the table was gone from the hatchway but the plank was still down, the cargo bay open. It was dark inside. Too dark to see in from the pier.

⚓

Jonas moved through the ferry looking for a likely place to spend the night. He found a small lounge open to deck-class passengers but kept moving, hoping to find not just a comfortable place but the right place. Up a narrow ladder to the top deck, and there was the group from the train, flopped among wooden benches under a fiberglass awning. Jonas sat nearby, close enough to be included if invited but far enough to avoid awkwardness if not.

The violet-eyed woman spotted Jonas and nodded. After a few minutes she came over, slid onto the bench and offered a cigarette from a flat, white cardboard box. They lit up—again that curious tobacco smell from the train—and smoked in silence; the woman seemed to feel no need to speak. Jonas shivered: two days in the same wet clothes.

"Maybe you need to be drinking something."

"Maybe so." Jonas thought back to the train. "Like *raki*?"

"Sure *raki*." The woman laughed and called to one of the others: "*Ola, Aleko. To raki . . .*"

The bottle was passed; Jonas and the woman shared it.

"You coming from Padua?"

"Yes, that's right, Padua."

"Hmm. You don't sound like you coming from Padua."

"No. I mean, I'm not *from* Padua. I'm just . . . coming from Padua."

"Oh," the woman said without the distinction seeming to have registered. "Where you are learning English?"

"New York. That's where I live. New York."

"Ahh, New York. Very special."

"You've been to New York."

"Been? Mm, no, never been. . . . But Alekos been. And he's telling me everyplace: Big Apple, the Queens, Brooklyn."

"I live in Brooklyn."

"Ahh, a Brooklys. You Greek?"

"Greek? No. Czech and Polish, or, really, Silesian."

"Eh?"

"Czech. Czechoslovakia. My father. And Polish, my mother. From Silesia."

"So, you coming from . . . Czechoslovakia?"

"No, New York. My father was from Czechoslovakia. And I'm part Polish. Not really *from* there; not from either place."

The woman was puzzled and said something, indecipherable by Jonas, to one of her companions.

"Hey, man, where you comin' from?" the other called to Jonas in a heavily accented version of American Black patois.

"Hard to say," Jonas replied, laughing.

"Alekos." The woman indicated her friend with the American slang. "He was to New York. Also, he was working at the US Army, in Germany. He's talking pretty good, eh?" The woman considered Jonas for a moment. "You know, no difference where you are, you always coming from someplace. Me, from Kriti—Crete, you say." She straightened up. "Kalliope Savakis," she introduced herself and held out her hand.

"Jonas Korda."

The woman grinned, then tried not to laugh.

"Sorry," Kalliope said. "I don't mean nothing. Only, your name. In Greek it's meaning 'covered by garlics'—*Tzones skorda*. It's a good name! Very special. . . . You know"—Kalliope took a drink—"I was working two years in Sweden. Two years never smelling garlic. *Tzk.* I was almost dead!"

The awning provided little protection now against a thickening chill mist. A few of the men drifted down the ladder. Kalliope crossed her arms for warmth.

"Ah, there is, ah, room inside," Jonas ventured.

"Yes . . . inside." Kalliope pronounced the word as if it made her very tired. But it got steadily wetter and colder, and soon all of them gathered their things and went down.

There were twenty or so rows of airline seats in the deck-class lounge and at one end a small coffee bar. Two dozen people were scattered about. Jonas and Kalliope put their bags on seats and went up to the counter. Kalliope ordered coffees and pointed at two woeful pastries.

"*Quanto e tra tutto?*" Kalliope asked. She was buying.

The barman added it up and Kalliope clucked with disgust.

"Inflation," Jonas said.

"Bah. If you make labor, then what you don't afford today for a dollar, tomorrow you don't afford for two." They sat down. "Inflations just means whatever it cost, you don't afford it.... You coming before to Greece?"

"No. First time."

"Ah, where you are going then? Athens, eh? Acropolis. Maybe, too, you are coming to Kriti. It's very beautiful, Kriti. Very special. My village is Martissa, a small place by the south. And always there is a place you can be staying. In Martissa, *O xenos einai xenos*—A stranger is a guest."

"Is that where you're headed?"

"Well, first I'm making some stops. Seeing...how things are. I'm gone a long time.... You know?"

She seemed to look for Jonas to acknowledge something but he didn't know what.

"I been all over. Italia, Sweden, Germany. Since six years."

"Six years? And you haven't been back?"

Kalliope clicked her tongue, tilted her head and raised her brow while briefly closing her eyes. "We stay outside," she said and nodded toward the men from the train. "All of us." She hesitated a moment. "You know, it's maybe a little more time before I'm coming again to Kriti. So...first you are looking around to other places, yes? Maybe Delphi. Very beautiful, Delphi. And old.... How long you visit to Greece?"

"How long...?"

Kalliope waited, and when Jonas did not answer, she shrugged. "Well, when you coming to Martissa you ask for Nemosia Savakis. My mother. And she's speaking very perfect her English." Kalliope looked away, adding quietly: "She...was teacher in the village."

Kalliope sank back and said no more, was lost in thought. The lounge was hot and stuffy; Jonas went on deck for some air.

Greece. Jonas let his mind's eye wander over the word: classical columns; ancient statuary; whitewashed walls. But Greeks? Well, there was Mike's diner, a joint down the street back in Brooklyn: breakfast ninety-nine cents, talking, smoking, arguing, lots of arguing.... But actual Greece? Modern, real-life Greece? There'd been something about the military, he recalled, but he wasn't sure. He no longer paid much attention to the flip-flops of governments. And things must have settled down, he guessed, whatever it had been...

Too cold and wet again; he went back inside. Alekos was holding a fiddle, his lanky legs draped over two chairs, the bow an extension of his long, lean arm. He touched it to the strings absentmindedly, then gently began to play. Kalliope sat next to him and hummed along from deep in her throat. A bottle of wine moved around. Their music was soft and slow and sweet and added to the torpor of the overheated room. Jonas had a few sips of the wine and settled low into a chair, lulled by the music and the ship's throbbing engines.

"Some reason you didn't call?" he was asking his wife as unconcernedly as he could manage.

"What do you mean?"

"What do you mean, what do I mean? You didn't call last night."

"I didn't?"

"Any particular reason?"

"An awful lot of questions."

"No questions. Just how come you didn't call?"

"That's a question."

"Yeah, okay, it's a question, *mea culpa.*... You usually call, that's all."

"Usually.... I was at my studio, where do you think?"

"I don't think anything."

They were sitting at the kitchen table of their Bushwick apartment. The slanting light said autumn, but the weight of the air was still miserable Brooklyn summer. A sneering sun pushed through two layers of unwashed windows, one opened over the other, and glared onto their coffee cups.

"So what's the big deal, then?" Jonas asked.

"*I'm* not making the big deal."

A moment's truce, then one more remark squirmed its way out of Jonas: "And you didn't answer the phone."

His stomach did a somersault and immediately he regretted not having settled for the truce.

"What is this?" she demanded. "Am I supposed to check in with you all of a sudden? I mean, that's why I keep the studio, right? That's what we wanted.... That's what you agreed."

After their impulse marriage they had decided for a second time to try to live together. Jonas gave up his apartment and they rented a flat. But his wife had kept her studio—rent-controlled, a waste to give it up, she'd said, and Jonas had nodded. She kept her piano there. Spent two or three nights a week.

In describing the arrangement, they disdained magazine phrases like "separate identities" or "independent lives." When pressed, they would simply say, "We're together when it counts." And initially Jonas had relished the extra time alone. As months became years, though, he found himself appreciating the idea of the studio more than its realities. Increasingly he felt that the gains didn't match the loss.

"Come on," she said, "this is old stuff."

"I know. But you do always call if you're not coming home."

"I *was* home."

"You know what I mean."

They allowed some tension to escape.

"Let's go in the other room, huh?" his wife suggested.

"You know," Jonas said as they got up, "lately it seems wherever you are, you always want to go in the other room."

They settled at opposite ends of the sofa. "So, someone with you?" he asked as casually as he could manage.

"What does that have to do with anything? Shit!"

"You tell me."

"Since when would it matter?"

"No, it wouldn't matter. Only... maybe sometimes it would," he said with a conviction that surprised them both.

"I know it matters." She softened. "But it doesn't make any difference, right? Anyway," she teased gently, "what are we talking here, jealousy?"

"You know I don't believe in jealousy." Jonas looked away.

She smiled, enjoying his spill of emotion.

"Anyway," he went on, "I didn't say there was anything wrong. I just want to know, that's all. We've always said we want to know."

"Yeah, that's what we've always said. . . . But I mean, it wouldn't have anything to do with how you and I feel about each other."

"Or how we don't?" Jonas did not so much speak the words as let them escape.

"I was alone," she finally said. "Which is mostly why I keep the place, remember?"

"Mostly, yeah. . . . So, why didn't you say so?"

"Why should I have to? I'm supposed to call or something now? Just to say there's no one with me? After all this time?"

"After all this time," Jonas echoed softly. He was sweating, though the sun did not reach this room.

"I'm not used to this possessiveness," his wife said with some pleasure at the notion. "It's just that we have . . ."—she sought a phrase—"a good balance, you and I."

"Balance? Yeah, I guess we do. We do have that."

"I mean, five years," she continued from a distance. "We haven't made each other . . . give up anything."

"No, we haven't, have we. Not giving up anything . . ."

"We never fell into those traps." She leaned back against the arm of the sofa. "Other people's mistakes."

"That's right." He also leaned back. "There is something in that. Not making their mistakes."

Jonas's eye drifted over her shoulder: her books in one bookcase, his books in another, nothing on the wall.

"Brooklyn, huh?"

Jonas woke to Kalliope on one side, Alekos speaking to him from the other: "You know Spiros's joint? On Washington Street?"

"Ah, no. I mean, I'm not sure."

Alekos gave Kalliope a quizzical look, then turned back to Jonas. "Best gyros in Brooklyn. I worked there two years."

"Ah, yeah." Jonas tried to clear his head. "Yeah . . . but what about Mike's, in Bushwick? You know Mike's? Mike's X-Lint Food?"

"Oh, come on, man. Mike does rats and pigeons. Course, some people like that kinda thing. So, from Brooklyn, huh? . . . Listen, we're coming up to Corfu pretty soon, now. You . . . gonna be stoppin'?"

"Corfu? I don't know. Haven't really thought about it."

"Oh, you gotta check out Corfu. Beautiful island, man. Most beautiful place you ever seen. Even more than Miami Beach."

"That's right, my friend," Kalliope added dutifully. "Very special."

"Kalliope here's gonna check it out, too," Alekos went on. "She ain't never seen Corfu neither. Me, I'm a homeboy there. Glaros, a little village up in the hills. So, maybe we'll get somethin' goin' there, huh? You make sure to check this place out, man, okay? . . . Okay."

Alekos moved off, satisfied that things had been settled. Kalliope, though, seemed uncomfortable.

"Corfu I think is very special." Kalliope hesitated. "But . . . you go where you got to, yes?"

"Yeah, sure. Of course."

"Good." Kalliope was relieved. "We got no problem."

Jonas went on deck again. The wet, cool air was refreshing.

Corfu? he spoke inside his head. . . . Well, why not? No reason why not. No reason at all. An emptiness welled up in him but he stifled it at his throat: Well, why the hell not?

His nose was running again. As he blew, someone at the dark railing turned toward the sound. She stood alone, shadowed against the gray night sky. Despite the light rain, she wore no jacket, her hair wet, a green silken shirt damp against her skin. Her solitude broken, she headed toward the lounge. Faded jeans and scuffed boots came into the light. As she passed, she gave Jonas a glance— not hostile, not exactly cold, but from somewhere a long ways away.

⚓

Oh, that runny, troublesome nose. It had long been the center of more than just his face. Bony and prominent, it might have grown into something one could describe as aquiline had it not been rearranged several times in his youth. Broken four times, officially. Unofficially, another three or four. (In the Brooklyn neighborhood of Jonas's youth, a nose had to be displaced to qualify as broken. Mere cracks deserved neither treatment nor comment and were, therefore, not worth counting.) Two of the official breaks had come in his early adolescence and both could be thought of as the inevitable wages of sin. The first, from a hopeless lunge on an icy street to catch the wind-blown scarf of stuck-up Agnes Mulka, which had won him naught but a collision with a parked Chevrolet. And the second when he was startled by a noise and turned suddenly into a low-hanging pipe during an ill-fated break-in at what turned out to be an empty warehouse. Unavoidable.

But the next two broken noses, as well as a couple of unofficial cracks, had made him think. One could say he got them playing basketball. But the larger truth was that Jonas got his third and fourth broken noses not exactly playing basketball but in fights while playing basketball.

Having reached an athletic, sinewy six-foot-two by age fourteen, Jonas and basketball were a natural pair. But Jonas was suited to basketball not only by size and skill but also by temperament. Pickup ball—the classic city game—fed simultaneously into each of the major competing elements of Jonas's emerging character. On one hand it presented clear evidence of the potential in collective endeavor: intelligent cooperation overcoming even significant disadvantages in naked power. At the same time, the game was also a revolving showcase of individual confrontations in which posturing—of which there was plenty—and the arts of the hustle had to be both learned and overcome.

The serious pickup game also provided Jonas with extraordinary visceral release. He could let out all his raw, undigested emotion, let it out leaping, banging, sweating and . . . fighting. The organized basketball world, however, did not fully appreciate this aspect of Jonas's love for the game. His high school coach finally decided that Jonas's compulsion for disruption was a fatal weak spot in his considerable talent. Breaking his clipboard over Jonas's head one day had served to confirm Jonas's developing view of authority and had signaled the end of Jonas's formal basketball career.

But no matter. There was still the pickup game. To the teenage Jonas, Brooklyn was the world that counted, and an extremely high percentage of young and no-longer-young males in that world played, had played, or had always wished they could play serious pickup ball. The very best players in this world were known simply as "players" and were accorded an unbegrudged respect. At an unusually young age, Jonas had become a player. He loved the game. And the game, the real city game, loved him.

Ah, but those broken noses. In a sense, the genesis of Jonas's basketball life prefigured his impending adulthood. Through basketball, Jonas first made relative judgments about emotion and calculation, beginning to mistrust the former in favor of the latter. After his fourth broken nose, Jonas cogitated on the fact that, for him, serious basketball inevitably meant fights. And putting his fingers gingerly to his nose, he considered the incontrovertible proof that the bigger the player, the more damage he did when he hit you. Jonas was now playing with increasingly large humans, and his proboscic condition attested that the price of his emotions was becoming far too high. So, as he had done earlier with regard to his fledgling attempts at petty burglary, he now calculated that fighting paid poorly for the risk.

However, Jonas's recognition of this direct line from emotions to damage led him not to examination of the source of his angers but to an attempt at their categorical restraint. He cultivated a thoroughgoing, unflinching version of what his contemporaries referred to as Cool, which on the basketball court meant shooting the ball from the outside, from a distance, and avoiding the violent inside maneuvers which were a player's greater test of virtuosity and pluck. In his new incarnation, Jonas still had great success: he scored well, his teams won, he continued to garner respect. But something essential had changed. The world might still think of him as a player. But for Jonas the game was no longer the same.

⚓

It was getting light. Jonas pulled himself up and out on deck. Through the gray and wet, he could just make out the nearby shapes of land on both sides of the ferry. To the east, purple mountains—massive, looming. To the west, the outlines of an island's coastal hills covered with trees and backed by the shadowy ridges of an inland range. Jonas looked at a map affixed to the deck housing: east, the mountains of Albania; west, the northern tip of Corfu.

He went to the rail to get a better view of the island. The sun broke through and lit up a white pebble cove tucked between two thickly wooded promontories. Splinters of gorse showed among pine and cypress, framing the cove in yellows and greens, and a cascade of olive trees flowed down to the very edge of the crescent beach, their silver leaves reflecting glints of early morning light.

"Corfu," Kalliope said softly, coming up behind Jonas. They stood quietly as the sky brightened and the colors of the sea awoke in brilliant patches—deep violets, aquamarine, turquoise—which varied with the depths and currents between ship and shore. Alekos the fiddler joined them.

"Hey, big-time. What d'ya say 'bout my island?"

"Gorgeous. . . . Very special," he added Kalliope's phrase.

"So, you gonna check it out, right?"

"I guess so."

"Way to go." Alekos exchanged a quick look with Kalliope, then slipped back into the lounge.

The ferry slid along the coast, and Jonas and Kalliope watched the sun finish burning off the mist, setting the island aglow. An occasional small house appeared nestled among the trees and rock: white walls, brightly painted doors and windows, tile roof.

"How about some coffee?" Jonas said.

"No, no!" Kalliope grabbed Jonas's sleeve and glanced over her shoulder into the lounge. "I mean, wait one time." She steered Jonas down the rail and after an awkward moment pointed: "Look there."

Something moving on a hill: animals, on a cliff.

"*Katsikes,*" Kalliope said. "Ahh, *katsikaki.*" She swayed and closed her eyes in rapture.

"Goats." Alekos reappeared. "Roasted goat. Almost Easter, see, when everybody does this big barbecue scene. And Kalliope, she thinks with her stomach. Poets are like that, know what I mean?"

Alekos said something in Greek to Kalliope, who nodded.

"Okay, now it's time," Kalliope told Jonas. "You want coffee?"

✦

The boat drew near Corfu Town, the ferry's first port of call on Greek soil. Kalliope and the men from the train became silent, almost grim. Not at all what Jonas would have expected of vibrant people returning home after a long absence. Announcements in Greek and Italian came over the intercom. Kalliope and Alekos bade quiet goodbyes to their fellow train travelers and joined other debarking passengers on the aft deck. Jonas moved along silently behind.

"I got a place for you to stay, man." Alekos turned to Jonas. "Nice joint, and cheap. At the Old Port. Hotel Brooklys. Hah, like Brooklyn, you'll feel like home. So, see you there later. A deal?"

Kalliope watched Jonas closely as he nodded agreement. She whispered to Alekos, who shook his head firmly then stared straight ahead. Kalliope set her jaw. There was no more talk.

The ferry glided by small harbors ringed with houses, then a stretch of low buildings, fishing boats, a few cars. They moved past a massive rock topped by a Venetian fortress and there, just beyond it, Corfu Town jutting into the sea. It was like sailing back in time. Back three hundred years, arriving to meet the Doge: tall and stately Venetian-style buildings with white and pastel faces peering over the port, shuttered window eyes and ornate balcony lashes, morning sun brushing their stone and plaster cheeks with gold.

On the new cement wharf, disembarking passengers were shunted toward a large metal shed. Frowning men in uniforms gave orders. Soldiers posed around the walls as other men, in mufti, loitered in twos and threes, oozing Police from every pore. At the entrance to the shed hung a large sign in Greek and English proclaiming "A Greece of Christian Greeks." Below it, a shield with a huge bird, a phoenix rising from flames. And superimposed over the phoenix, the shadow of a soldier with fixed bayonet. Jonas felt a shiver.

Just as they all reached the shed, Kalliope spoke quietly to Jonas: "We see you very soon. Don't be worrying." Her face was drawn; a muscle twitched in her cheek.

Inside the shed, Greek passengers were herded behind a partition; men, women and children alike looked apprehensive. Non-Greeks were passed along tables at which passports were scrutinized, questions asked and bags examined. The questioning was gruff and menacing or polite and solicitous depending on appearance and credentials. Well-to-do vacationers were passed along quickly and a small tour group was waved through with no formalities at all. Two young Italians with long hair and backpacks, however, were abruptly pulled out of line and interrogated in a corner, their bags ransacked on the floor; they were still surrounded when Jonas reached the first table.

The official scowled at Jonas's scruffy looks: three days' beard, grubby jeans and badly rumpled shirt, cheap canvas bag. Two men against the wall stopped talking and stood alert. When Jonas showed his US passport, though, the official's countenance softened. And when Jonas produced traveler's checks in dollars, the man passed him through with only a few perfunctory questions. He chalk-marked a cross on Jonas's bag. The man at the next table passed the bag without opening it and Jonas moved toward the light at the far end of the shed. He half expected an arm to reach out of the shadows and grab him, but he emerged unscathed into the sunlight.

An old man shambled up the dusty wharf: "Room? *Zimmer?* Room?" Jonas shook his head, remembering the Hotel Brooklys, and started to walk toward the Old Port a few hundred yards away. After a couple of steps something made him stop and look back. A cluster of men stood by two cars next to the shed; the car doors were open. Several other men in and out of uniform hustled four people from the shed and shoved them roughly into the back seats, the doors slamming shut behind them. Of the four, Jonas recognized Kalliope and Alekos. One of the men by the cars saw Jonas watching and took a step toward him. Jonas turned quickly and walked away.

3

Dirty Dick was born Nathaniel Butley, eighteenth-century scion of wealthy English gentry. After years of cynical dandyism, Butley inexplicably fell in love, his passion as extreme as had been the dispassion of his philandering. His beloved came from exceedingly respectable family. So, to overcome his history as a rake, Butley embarked on an impeccably restrained yet dogged courtship which in two years rewarded his labors: Butley and his love were betrothed.

To commemorate fittingly the demise of his profligacy, Butley planned an elaborate engagement celebration. Fashionable London buzzed for weeks in anticipation. On the glorious day, Butley dressed in an outfit of blue velvet and lace that reached a new height in his flamboyant sartorial career. A hall in Bishopsgate, splendidly decorated and stocked with vast quantities of food and drink, filled with excited revelers waiting for the beautiful bride-to-be . . . who never arrived. On the way into London her carriage was set upon by highwaymen, and the struggle over her betrothal ring ended with a fatal pistol shot.

When word reached the banquet, Butley uttered a single long anguished cry, then ordered everyone out of the hall. He emerged three days later, instructing that the rooms be sealed, nothing touched: each chair, each cup, each plate and scrap of food was to remain exactly as it had been at the fateful moment the news arrived. And for the next twenty years until his death, Butley neither spoke nor took off the suit of velvet and lace. Nightly he wandered the streets of London, silent and aimless, his ragged, odiferous presence earning him the sobriquet Dirty Dick.

On Butley's death, the hall was reopened. Two decades of dust and spiderwebs coated the rooms, a sea of white over the foundered hulls of glasses and platters, moth-ravaged cloths, shredded decorations and the skeletons of rats. The remarkable scene was left intact and a pub built alongside. The hall is still a minor London tourist attraction. And the pub does very well.

Jonas heard this odd tale from gravel-voiced Nosey, the afternoon counter man at the derivatively named Cafe Dirty Dick's, next door to the Hotel Brooklys. Nosey was a slight, delicately featured, extremely short man about Jonas's age, with a shock of sandy curls and twinkling, darting blue eyes in which Jonas noticed every turn of emotion by a slight change in depth or fleck of color. Olive skin contrasted handsomely with Nosey's fair hair and eyes, and a stupendous dark moustache—seemingly the result of some faulty experiment in transplant technology—completed a strikingly singular appearance. Nosey finished the story by taking Jonas into the back room of the little cafe: overturned chairs, shattered plates and glasses, and fossilized traces of food and wine, all covered by a thick layer of dust.

"Six years back, yah see, the blokes who was runnin' this place got, ah, took out of commission, like." Nosey had spent two years in England and another three in Australia, during which he had watched too many American movies, the result being a Greek-tinted Cockney-Merseyside-Aussie spiced with Hollywood gangster-talk which mangled each of its components into a remarkable language all Nosey's own. "So me cousin buys out the joint, but then up and decides he ain't gonna touch this room here 'til the blokes what got nicked is let out of stir. Course, the heavy muscle boys, you know, the security types, that lot, they might get right stroppy 'bout him keepin' the room like this."

Jonas tried to sort out a connection between the blokes getting "took out of commission" and "the heavy muscle boys" not being happy about the room being preserved, but he made no progress.

"Me cousin, though, he hears tell of this Dirty Dick's in London I were clockin' you about. So, he takes it on for the new name of the caff here, and tells the security lot that he's done up the room special like this for the Brit tourist trade. He knowed anything's jake 'round here nowdays if they think it's for tourists."

Tourists? Jonas had seen no sign of them, British or otherwise, at the tiny port cafe.

"What a waste." Nosey looked disgustedly about the dusty room. "Could have made this into a right smart kit. Get the Surrey package crowd in here and all that lager money they fling about. But now what's he got? His bleedin' politics . . . and an empty room."

Jonas had spent his first few days on Corfu wandering the narrow cobbled lanes that wend through the Old Town, an amalgam of marks left by successive cultures of occupation: Byzantine churches; Venetian forts and narrow, four-story Italianate buildings with molting pastel paint; Napoleonic houses with wrought-iron balconies and folding-shutter windows; a handful of Georgian mansions; even a copy of the Rue de Rivoli, its archways running beside a grassy esplanade on which the British had manicured a cricket pitch. Jonas walked and sat. Had a coffee, walked, had an ouzo, and sat. Had a cheap Greek brandy, a coffee, more brandy, and walked. In a *kafeneion* or *taverna* he read his pocket Greek phrase book, looked at a map of the island. Then moved along the cobbled lanes again, circling, circling. It would have been difficult for him to reconstruct much of those days: he spent them in a haze, vaguely aware that a past had ended but without the faintest vision of a future. At night he did not dream.

When able to focus on the world around him, Jonas became further disoriented. He wasn't a tourist: tourists have an image of where they're going, even if it bears little relation to anyplace real; they have a sense of what they're after, even if they settle for just having been away; and they know how long they'll be gone, even if it's barely long enough to feel they've left. Nor was Jonas a "traveler": too weighty a notion, connoting far more awareness than Jonas could muster. Even "wanderer" implies someone with his eyes open.

The only places he managed to be at rest during these days were the Hotel Brooklys and Cafe Dirty Dick's. His hotel room was tiny and bare but gave him that sense of calm which comes when you return someplace, anyplace, where you have already spent a night. And at the cafe he could be nearly alone and invisible without having to feel that he was entirely so.

The hotel and Dick's were on a rise at one side of the Old Port, the cafe's four outside tables overlooking the *platea*—a wide, open plaza ringed with broad leafy trees. From here each morning Jonas would watch Corfu Town come slowly to life: mule-drawn vegetable carts coming in from the countryside; men on bicycles and motor scooters on their way in to work; here and there a donkey laden with mountain goods; town women stopping to chat as they made purchases for the midday meal; doors opening, gutters being swept. Ferries and boats of various sizes made ready—often in a welter of chaos and disputations, a distracting entertainment for which Jonas was grateful—for neighboring islands and the mainland while incoming boats unloaded passengers and cargo. Although Nosey often waxed rhapsodic about his village and its countryside, Jonas couldn't get himself to move outside the town. In part he was holding on to Kalliope's promise that she and Alekos would meet him at the Brooklys. But what truly held Jonas in place was that irresolution and languor that so often accompany the lower registers of fear.

On the morning of Jonas's fourth day, Nosey sat outside Dick's soaking up the gentle sun like a reptile, barely seeing or hearing, barely breathing, his expression placidly content.

"What are you thinking about, Nosey?"

"Thinkin'? Why thinkin'? Lovely day. Makin' me shekels. No one tellin' me what I got to do . . ." He squinted at Jonas. "Sometimes it's best to do a bit of not-thinkin', innit?"

Obvious wisdom, Jonas thought, then caught himself thinking. So, with Nosey's countenance for support, Jonas settled back to see if he could manage some not-thinking of his own. And he continued his quest for not-thinking during his walking, sitting and drinking around Corfu Town. And soon found that not-doing and not-thinking worked well together. Better by far than the former without the latter. And seeing very little. Choosing not to see. Which he also found soothing.

Later that afternoon, however, while sitting outside Dick's, Jonas noticed a group of men in suits—itself somewhat unusual—having coffee on the far side of the *platea*. Two waiters scurried back and forth to their table faster than Jonas had seen anyone move at that normally somnolent time of day. No one sat near the men; no one stopped to talk; it seemed that no one even looked in their direction.

"Nosey, can I ask you something?"

"Sure thing, guv." Nosey slipped into a seat.

"Who are those guys over there? In the blue chairs."

Nosey sat up: "Why d'you want to bother 'bout that lot?"

"I don't know. Just something about them. I don't know."

Nosey took a long look at Jonas before quietly answering. "Them blokes is *Asfalia*, mate. Security coppers. And that's all you'll want to know." Nosey shifted in his seat. "But anyway they ain't no trouble for you. You ain't local."

"Huh. I haven't seen them around before."

"Nah. Mostly they work . . . inside, like. See that place over the road?" A thick block building squatted on the far side of the port. "Well, that's where they, ah, do what they do."

"So, what kind of 'security'—"

Nosey cut him off. "Give it a rest, mate. What you don't bother 'bout, don't bother you, ay? And that's the way to get on." Nosey got up abruptly and went inside.

Jonas returned to Dick's that evening and took up his usual spot. The men in the suits were gone. He positioned himself so that he could watch the *platea* without seeing their block building, but his eyes kept returning to it involuntarily.

The next day, the men in suits were back under the trees.

⚬

"It's the eyes of the world you've got on you."

The words of Father Janusz, his mother's priest. An oblique comment on Jonas's less-than-reverent attitude as much as a literal reference to his remarkable visual orbs; a way for the priest to say that he had major doubts about the boy. Because by the time Jonas was nine or ten—before he refused Communion outright but had already begun to roll his eyes disdainfully as the Host approached his tongue—Father Janusz had sensed that it was his late father's militancy rather than his mother's piety that had made the most lasting impression on the son. Among other places, the priest had seen it in those upturned eyes.

They were a startling, iridescent green, the eyes. A mesmerizing combination of color and brightness that during the social and sexual tumult of young manhood Jonas found to be his most affecting attribute. But well before their looks began to serve his libido, Jonas had realized something remarkable in how the eyes saw. Early in childhood, doctors had spotted a preternatural visual acuity to which they were reluctant even to assign any of the standard twenty-something measures. Jonas's eyes saw things extraordinarily clearly and from great distances; he could assess a visual field more quickly and completely than anyone around him. And since the world of children is so much ruled by what they can see, from his early years Jonas described things to his peers with such conviction that they—and he—readily came to accept his impressions as the most accurate picture of what was there.

But telescopic acuity alone was not what made the green eyes special. These visual organs also "felt strongly." At least, that was how the young Jonas translated the startled doctors' conclusions after a round of special optometric examinations. More than merely seeing clearly, the doctors confirmed that his eyes also differentiated color saturation and hue to the finest degrees. This actually explained a lot, and relieved a worry long suffered in silence by Jonas's parents: since he had been a baby, they had been concerned at how arrangements and movements of color could transfix Jonas for long stretches of time. Indeed, if either his parents or Father Janusz had asked, Jonas could have told them that it was only his fascination with the unwashed and, to others, utterly unremarkable stained-glass church windows that for several years had fooled the priest into thinking that Jonas might one day have a calling. When at about age ten the vision-blessed Jonas stumbled onto the world of fine art, he began slipping away from his friends in Brooklyn and riding the subway into Manhattan, there to spend an entire ecstatically stunned afternoon in but a single room of one or another museum. Conversely, however, when the Sixties arrived Jonas found its kaleidoscopic fashion miserably overwhelming and the light and color offered up by psychedelics far more than he needed to see, thank you very much.

Moreover, since shade and texture rather than sharp outline most often serve to separate an object from its surroundings, Jonas's heightened color differentiation also afforded him an extraordinary capacity to focus: that is, to see one form, one shape, one object, to the exclusion of all else. When added to his sheer optic power, this "color consciousness" permitted Jonas to see any given thing with exquisite—or excruciating—clarity. And capable of such fine gradations, Jonas's receptors could register in particular the merest change in tone or character of human light. For example, that blush of embarrassment you feel but safely know no one can actually see; well, Jonas could see it. Or an invisible flush of anger, which would warn Jonas of dangerous ground. Or a blanch, telling him he had the upper hand.

Of all Jonas's ocular talents, this was the one which had the most profound social resonance: this ability to read what he called—when on rare occasion he'd mention it at all—a person's "field of light." His capacity to follow normally invisible fluctuations in the light each of us reflects permitted Jonas to see when such changes failed to match what a person simultaneously registered in some other way—with words or movements. That is, like some listeners on the autism spectrum who hear beyond language to the undisguisable messages of tenor and timbre, Jonas could actually see—or, at least, believed he could see—whether someone was telling the truth.

⚕

Once the view from Dirty Dick's had lost its innocence, Corfu Town became for Jonas just another human agglomeration going about its aimless business. The cafes and *tavernas* and scrabblings at the port ceased to distract him; the circle of his walks became tighter and tighter.

Nosey had suggested that Jonas come to Glaros, Nosey's village in the hills. But Jonas thought that was the village name Alekos had mentioned. And if so, he was uncomfortable at the prospect of running into Kalliope and Alekos after they had stood him up at the Brooklys. Still, Glaros was, if not an actual destination, at least someplace different. A reason to move.

As the rickety bus made its way around a last dusty mountain curve, Jonas sensed a change in the texture of the air: it was heavy with the voluptuous smell of freshly pressed olive oil and seemed to envelop the cluster of small stone houses, sealing it away. As the bus departed, Jonas found himself standing at the edge of the village square, squinting from the glare of noon into the dark of a three-sided shed where a donkey and a rye-brown man with glistening arms steadily turned a creaking wooden olive press, the viscous, translucent oil surging into a trough below. Jonas was transfixed: by the oil's bright green color, by the murmur of the liquid and the groaning of old wood, by the waves of crushed-olive scent which rolled out of the shed on the breeze. The bus driver's son was waiting for Jonas under a huge plane tree that shaded one side of the square, but the boy made no effort to move Jonas along toward his house, where Jonas had arranged for a bed. There seemed to be plenty of time.

Jonas ate dinner under the trees at the village's only *taverna*, just up the hill from the square. Nosey was there, helping to cook, discussing the contents of the pots, taking and serving the orders for a half dozen locals and tapping a barrel of island wine with a flavor that hinted at thistles and low stone walls. After the meal, Nosey took Jonas down to what he called The Bad, one of three small cafes on the square. Several homemade brandies later, Jonas headed for bed. Nosey wished him a good night but warned of the accommodations at the bus driver's house: "I know them beds, mate. You see me tomorrow and I'll fix you right up."

The next morning Jonas was surprised to find a taciturn, almost grumpy version of Nosey. Then he learned that despite their late-night drinking, Nosey had been up at first light to haul sacks of late harvest olives to the press, and that before heading to town for his afternoon shift at Dirty Dick's, he would be off to yet more work, this time at his Aunt Sophia's house.

For forty years Sophia's magic fingers had spun yarn, woven fabric and made clothes for all and sundry. But despite a legendary reputation, over recent years she had been steadily losing customers to a flood of ready-made, mostly imported clothing. Since these store-bought clothes were both more expensive and of inferior material, the old woman was baffled. Eventually, however, she realized that the store clothes all had non-Greek writing on them. So, she began to slip a few of the Roman letters into some of her own fabrics. But her customers only puzzled at them and no one chose that cloth. Then she discovered that these were names on the clothes. So, she began asking her customers where they wanted her to put their names, but this tack met with no better response than had the random lettering.

When Nosey returned from working abroad, he explained to Sophia that these were not the names of the people who wore the shirt or dress, nor of the person who had made it, but rather the name of the company that had sold the thing. Well, this was beyond her. If people were buying expensive, poorly made clothes just to have the seller's name on them, then selling things had become much easier than it used to be and was certainly easier than making things. Sophia had never been off the island, had no idea what tourists wanted, and spoke only Greek. But in the face of this clothing craziness, she agreed to Nosey's proposal that they open a tourist shop where her loom had always been: the cottage was on a main road from Corfu Town, plenty of tourists would come by in summer, Nosey knew about foreigners, he'd take care of everything.

So, Nosey was now heading for Sophia's to continue getting things together for the coming influx of "grocks," as he called the tourists. "Them what has money and no brains is made for them what has brains and no money," he said, grinning. Considering importantly an oversized watch, he promised he'd be back later to save Jonas's aching back from another night at the bus driver's house, then coasted down the hill on his battered motor scooter.

True to his word, that evening Nosey led Jonas to an ancient, sagging stone house built into the mountainside, overlooking a fertile valley toward the distant rooftops of Corfu Town. The house belonged to Korina, a sturdy woman in black whom Jonas had seen in the *taverna* kitchen. Her face showed hard lines and hollows, but at the corners of her eyes and in the softness of her lips there resided a kindness which seemed to distinguish between a man and the madness of men.

An extra room had been added to the rear of the house as dowry for Korina's daughter, but shortly after her marriage the daughter and husband had moved to Athens to find work. Korina smiled warmly as Nosey explained this to Jonas and translated her wish that he should make himself at home in the room: "Have someone in 'em, that's what beds is for." Jonas thanked her and asked how much. Ten *drachmes*— about thirty cents—a day, Korina said after a long pause. Clearly, it was not a matter she had considered before Jonas asked.

The next few days Jonas spent exploring the quiet blue-black hills, the narrow furrowed valleys, the deep-shadowed olive groves that staggered down to the coves of the island's west coast. On the third day, from a goat path over the water, he saw the green blouse. An outcrop of rock jutted over the cobalt sea, patches of gorse, purple thyme and flowering capers breaking the barren gray of the stone, a lone cypress at the tip of the rock, its branches swept back by the wind. She was sitting against the trunk, staring not out to sea but away from it. Poised not at land's end but at its beginning.

Jonas tried to find a path down, a connecting ridge, but there seemed no way to get to her from where he was. He tried a ravine, got caught in some gorse, slipped on loose rocks, got nowhere. When he pulled himself back up, she was gone. He looked for her on the surrounding hills, in the canyons and valleys, but she was gone.

4

Nosey called them The Good, The Bad and The Ugly.

No one knew exactly how long The Good had been a *kafeneion*. The rough stone foundations of this nameless whitewashed cube were rooted centuries deep in the Corfu soil. Before Glaros ever amounted to a village it had been a crossroads for goods moving down the mountain: olive oil, feta cheese, hand-woven wool from ancient looms still worked in many hillside houses. The walls that eventually were to become The Good had begun merely as a shelter where people would build a fire and wait with their animals for traders from the port. Over the generations it became a local gathering spot—to sit when waiting to work, when work was done, when there was no work—and people began to store there an irregular supply of ouzo, local wine and coffee. Water was drawn from a well in back. After a time, two small tables appeared, and eventually an old man who could no longer work the mountain had become somewhat proprietary and began to put out *metzedes*—bits of bread, cheese, tomato, olives—and to oversee the boiling of coffee and the barter of local ouzo and wine with those who did not bring their own.

And that was how The Good had always remained: no cooking; nothing hot except coffee; no menus, prices or pretenses. In black jackets and rough white shirts, walking sticks resting between knees, the male village elders would sit outside The Good for hours on end, working their *komboloi* worry beads, playing an occasional fierce but unstudied game of *tavli*—backgammon—and watching. It was one of the original proprietor's descendants who now supervised the filling of glasses. "My *kafeneion* is older than your country," Nosey translated the old man's greeting to Jonas.

In 1950, the village got its second cafe. Korina—the woman who had given Jonas a room—had a brother, Leonides, who lost a leg fighting the Nazis. It turned out to have saved his life. And given birth to The Bad.

Leonides had been a *socialistis* in the 1930s, when that term in Greece had still referred more to the impulses of one's heart than to a party affiliation or to the foreign government from which one took aid. Early in the Second World War, *socialistes* had formed units of *andartes*—Partisans—to resist the German occupation. And almost immediately the Allies began working as hard for the defeat of these leftist Partisans as they did for that of the Nazi occupiers. To ensure a postwar Greece ruled by factions firmly in their grasp, the British and Americans handed official power to so-called Nationalists, ignoring that their councils were polluted with Nazi collaborators. The hard core of this ruling Nationalist bund had no interest in distinguishing among independent socialists, democrats or any other subversives: they were all "infidels" and "communists" ... or close enough. And in their ensuing lust to consolidate power, these Nationalists gave a nightmare literalness to "Better dead than Red." The land had been starved and brutalized by Nazi occupation, but the German retreat failed to loosen terror's grip: in a bloody, famine-maddened fratricide of civil war which began even before the Nazi withdrawal, the slaughter of Greek by Greek became epidemic.

Leonides fought the Nazis on the northern mainland, near the Yugoslav border, but his unit of Partisans spent almost as much time fighting right-wing Greek militias. Among the Partisans, too, there was deadly dissension: *kommandantes* supported by outside regimes eventually dominated the loose coalition of resistance fighters. Leonides and many like him wound up chafing and balking at what became a steady stream of party imperatives.

In 1944, on the eve of the German retreat, Leonides was hit by a shell. He was taken to Yugoslavia where his life was saved, if not his leg. By the time he recovered, full-scale civil war had erupted in Greece, then halted. When the second and third blood-soaked rounds were fought during the next several years, Leonides was back on Corfu, away from the fighting on the mainland, away from the blind sectarian subservience demanded by both sides, detached from the madness by the space of one missing leg.

Nosey's own family was not so lucky. His father, too, was a Partisan. While he was away fighting in the mountains, Nationalist troops swept through his home district on the mainland seizing, and worse, anyone with a hint of Partisan sympathies. As the wife of an *andarte*, Nosey's mother would be among the first taken. And toddler Nosey would likely be shipped to a Nationalist "reeducation center." Word of the impending pogrom, however, reached the village before the soldiers, and Nosey's mother managed to slip him to an uncle whose small fishing boat crossed to Corfu under cover of darkness. Nosey lived with his Aunt Sophia near Glaros while his mother languished on a barren prison island in the northern Aegean.

A Nationalist prison was a luxury Nosey's father was never given the chance to enjoy. The party-line leaders of his Partisan unit sent the disruptively independent thinker on a doomed foray behind Nationalist militia positions. He was wounded and captured; the Nationalists executed him on the spot. A year later Nosey's mother died in prison. Nosey had very little use for politics.

Korina's husband was another who never made it back. He had been the Glaros village baker; during the wars Korina kept the ovens going, though there was rarely any food in the village for baking. Since her brother Leonides's missing leg prevented his return to fishing, he and Korina decided after the wars to add onto the three-sided enclosure which held the village ovens. The Bad *kafeneion* had been born.

Though right next to each other, there was no rivalry between The Good and The Bad; they served different needs. The Good was the old men's roosting place. At The Bad the rest of the village would sit, and the women staked out one corner as their own, to rest and chat while their midday meals baked in the community ovens. In the evenings and on Sundays, when families made their *volta*—their stroll around the village—The Bad gave them a place to alight. Leonides and Korina made a bit of hot food at The Bad and, unlike The Good, could manage more than one coffee every twenty minutes (though not much more). Over the years a modicum of solvency returned to the hills and The Bad branched off its kitchen, opening Glaros's first and only *taverna* a little ways up the hill: Korina was the cook; Nosey assisted. With a second *kafeneion* and now even a *taverna*, Glaros had become a village of distinction, the little square no longer merely a crossroads but, at least in local eyes, a *platea*.

And the third cafe? The Ugly? The mere mention of the place on the opposite side of the square made Nosey look as if he'd sucked a lemon. The owner's name—Xhirakos, Jonas later learned—never passed Nosey's lips. "That One" was as close as Nosey would come.

The Ugly had opened in 1969. That One had been on Corfu for two years in the ESA—a military branch of security police. And rather than return to his hardscrabble native Sparta when he left the army, Xhirakos had decided to remain on the green and prospering island.

Because of his work for the security police, Xhirakos had immediately been granted the various permits required to open a *kafeneion* and bar. Securing such permits and obtaining equipment, liquor and anything else not made locally was an immensely convoluted affair. One had to overcome both a shortage of goods and an arcane communication and transportation system which had changed little since Miltiades sent a runner from Marathon to report the defeat of the Persians. It had always required ingenuity, loose *drachmes* and a positive balance of favors to get things done in Greece, Nosey said. But under "the Colonels"—the ruling military junta, since 1967, he explained—the traditional ways had been supplanted by a new set of methods that layered ideology over, under and in between massive bureaucratic inefficiency. And the ability to negotiate this new labyrinth was directly proportional to one's standing with the military.

Two years before, for example, Leonides had applied for permission—one constantly needed permission—to buy a small generator for the *taverna*. After months of entreaty and the payment of exorbitant "permit fees," he had been allowed to prepay an order to Athens. Eight more months and more fees finally got him the reply that he needed a special army clearance. Leonides braved an inquiry to the military, who told him they had to have proof the equipment could not be used for subversive purposes.

Leonides leaned heavily on his crutch: how could he demonstrate, he asked the army officer, that a generator capable of powering no more than a cooler and a few lights was not a threat to national security? Of course this problem could be avoided, the officer replied, if Leonides would simply obtain from the security police a Certificate of Civic Responsibility. And the officer grinned: they both knew that the infamous certificates were never issued to former Partisans.

Though under the Colonels such treatment was in general to be expected, the details were a continual surprise. For those suspected of even faint democratic yearnings, Nosey explained, daily life could be a nightmarish combination of *ad hoc* and *ad hominem*: government actions were haphazard, unpredictable, often incomprehensible. The military machine not only spread terror, it leaked it. Random absurdity demoralized as effectively as did brutality.

A few days after his interview with the army, Leonides heard on the quiet from a Port Authority clerk that his generator had actually arrived two months earlier. Leonides returned to the military police, who readily admitted they had the generator but said they couldn't release it because they were investigating whether the equipment had been used without a permit. "But how could anyone use it if you still have it?" Leonides protested. "Yes," the officer replied, "so you can see how difficult that makes it for us to investigate." It was now two years since Leonides had begun what seemed an endless series of payments for the little generator. He was still waiting.

For Xhirakos and The Ugly, however, there had been no such difficulties. That One was able to order on credit and have readily delivered a modern restaurant-size stove, refrigerator, freezer, extra-large generator and twelve sets of chairs and tables, even though as yet he had no place to outfit as his cafe. And thanks to an invidious twist to an old Greek tradition, Xhirakos also had that problem quickly solved.

It was long an accepted rule in this small country with limited arable land that untended trees, vines, soil and associated structures may be forfeit to anyone who makes productive use of them. In Glaros, a house on the village square had been owned by the district doctor, a respected man of moderate views. Soon after the Colonels' coup, however, he had been arrested "on suspicion." When released after a month in custody, the doctor reported to their families about several local people who were being held incommunicado on charges of having "dangerous ideas." The military found out about the doctor's conversations, vouched that no people were held merely for what they thought or said, declared the doctor a danger to the State, arrested him, and exiled him to a distant island prison. When his wife and children were finally informed of his whereabouts, they went to stay nearby in order to visit him the once per month they were permitted.

After a year, the doctor was released and allowed to return to Corfu. But he was not given the Certificate of Civic Responsibility required for him to resume his medical practice. And his "abandoned" house was gone. Xhirakos had taken care of that: Glaros had its third cafe.

Despite its large collection of "international" foods and imported drink, plus the only television in the village, The Ugly was usually conspicuously empty. A handful of the regime's local claque patronized the place, but most locals regarded Xhirakos an interloper and stayed away regardless of their political sympathies. That One made money in the summer, though, when tour buses came to the mountain for the sunset view and for dinner at what Xhirakos arranged for government tourist pamphlets to highlight as the "authentic village cafe" Poseidon—as The Ugly was officially named, despite being two miles from the sea. A few other tourists also made their way to the cafe because The Ugly was the only foreign exchange office in the district, its government emblem—soldier superimposed over phoenix rising from flames—prominently displayed outside. When business waned at the end of summer, That One would close the cafe and head for Athens. The Ugly remained shuttered until spring.

"But what about the doctor?" Jonas asked. "I mean, the tradition . . . Why doesn't he just move back in when That One abandons the place?"

Nosey just stared, the rage of an unspoken reply moving his enormous moustache back and forth.

It was quite a power, Jonas's second sight. The ability instantly to test his intellectual and emotional registers against hyperaesthetic evidence. Indeed, a way to connect emotion with intellect through a process which combined the best of both: an immediate preconscious response free from the whipsaws of cogitation yet based on physical data. An added way of checking that one's view of the truth is true.

A power, yes. But also a burden. On one hand, simply too much information. Merely sorting through the incessant shifts in human hues and intensities could be overwhelming. Moreover, Jonas knew that his talent was not magical but empirical and, as he matured, he understood that visual evidence, like all other kinds, is partial, provisional and subject to conflicting and misleading interpretations. All in all, then, he had to be careful with those eyes. But being careful could be a lot of work. So, most of the time he just tried to govern the talent. Make use of it only when it mattered.

It mattered, of course, in affairs of the heart. But when exercising close attention here, Jonas was forced repeatedly to see the hesitations and slippery states of emotion that ripple through most anyone who considers embracing another's life. Unfortunately, the result of this barrage of others' doubts was a deeply fearful heart of his own: such a clear view of other people's reticence and emotional confusions translated for Jonas into a constant caution against falling in love.

In vocation, too, the vision mattered. With a well-placed uncle's assistance, Jonas took up the trade-union-organizing mantle his father had left upon his death in Jonas's childhood. But by the time of his accession to the organizing ranks, old-line unions were showing serious sclerosis. And among the entrenched New York cadres, Jonas's eyes couldn't help but see clearly the evidence of chronic disease. So, although his commitment to unionism remained fundamentally unshaken, after a couple of years' work in a central council office Jonas hungered for a field of images beyond the narrow strictures of internal union politics and wage-labor bargaining.

Once again his eyes led the way. His early forays into Manhattan museums had eventually sent him to the galleries, too. Contacts he'd made in that scene later put him in touch with a variety of emerging Manhattan avant-gardes and countercultures. And from there it was but a short plunge into the social and political tumults—it was now the 1960s—beginning to churn in the streets, studios and academies of New York.

Jonas threw himself into these new frays with the passion his union work had not called for and his too-close reading of hearts had not allowed. His involvement was initially undiscriminating, relishing mostly for their sheer exuberance several large, university-centered antiwar groups: after the rigid hierarchy of entrenched unionism, Jonas found liberating these groups' unkempt youthful pushing at limits. But soon he tired of their endless meetings and their utter lack of awareness, let alone inclusion, of laboring men and women. So, he began to gravitate instead to smaller, more marginal avant-gardes whose political thinking went beyond specific antiwar or civil rights battles and whose willingness to be outrageous in the service of radical ideas Jonas found intoxicating.

For their part, these smaller groups found Jonas a refreshing addition to their ranks: savvy, articulate and politically literate, he was also an actual member of the working class, and avant-garde politics just didn't see too many of those. Unlike the larger political shoals, these smaller groups tended not merely to tolerate Jonas's rash, impassioned, sometimes truculent reactions but actually to appreciate them. And once they discovered Jonas's Brooklyn basketball credentials, his status rose even more: in New York, most militants, and even more than a few intellectuals, had respect for someone who could really play.

⚶

While Nosey was in the courthouse on the Old Port, Jonas nursed an ouzo at Dirty Dick's. But he couldn't sit still, couldn't find a comfortable position, as if his pants were too tight and an invisible twig was scraping the back of his neck. Nosey had reassured Jonas that he would be back—Nosey studied his oversized watch—soon. But Kalliope had also said "soon" when she and Alekos had entered the customs shed. And Jonas had never seen them again. After an hour, though, Nosey reappeared, muttering but apparently unscathed.

They left town on Nosey's scooter and headed for a shepherd's hut where Nosey was to pick out a Paschal lamb. Easter was just a week away and while waiting at the port for Nosey, Jonas had watched numerous Corfiotes arriving from Athens and abroad for this most important holiday of the Greek year, some of them leading hand-picked lambs off the boats, festive ribbons around the animals' necks.

The straining scooter slowly made its way up winding mountain paths. From the heights, Jonas looked down at a solitary almond tree in a narrow valley, a stout woman sitting against it, black sweater, gray smock, white head cloth. Steadily she worked some wool in her lap while a few feet away a single goat was grazing. On a nearby hillside thick with green from winter rains sparkled a tiny white shrine with room perhaps for one icon and one lamp, one shepherd or olive-tender. Jonas was struck by how life in these hills presented itself in units of one. And by how clearly he could see each individual piece. After so long a time in which his otherwise preternatural sight had been unfocused and flat, he marveled at the three-dimensional.

At the top of a large hill, Nosey stopped the scooter for a moment. Small plots of planted ground, separated by boundaries of twisted olive branches, quilted the next valley floor. Bushes of flowering lilac dotted the ground with pink. A goat or sheep path running the length of the valley was framed by two low, rough stone walls: not monuments or even truly structures, Jonas mused, just somewhere to pile all the stones. Didn't matter how they'd been built, these walls, or how well, but simply that they'd been built at all.

Jonas and Nosey coasted into the valley. As they neared the bottom, they could see a large old car—Jonas was startled when he noticed that it was a Chevrolet—bumping toward them, spilling over the path like a fat man on a hobby horse.

"'El-lo, 'ello," Nosey said, and Jonas felt him stiffen.

Clearly there was not enough room between the stone walls for scooter and car to pass each other, but neither slowed until, at the last possible moment, both slammed on the brakes. Jonas had to leap off the scooter in order to stay upright.

The driver stuck his head out: Xhirakos, proprietor of The Ugly. That One flicked the fingers of one hand at Nosey and grunted "Nya!" followed by a brief but obviously unpleasant burst of words.

Nosey waited for Xhirakos to finish, then returned the flicking gesture with both hands, plus a foot. He ended with a vituperation slightly longer and more impassioned than Xhirakos's, then crossed his arms over his chest and waited.

The car door opened; two young goats bleated from the back seat.

"Better give him some room, mate." Xhirakos was not exactly a figure to strike fear in the heart, but to stay out of a fight that was not his own, Jonas gladly moved aside.

Xhirakos got out of the car. A short, heavy man, he was wearing a brown business suit that was rumpled and dusty. His stiff black hair was trying in vain to stay plastered to his scalp. His jowls quivered and Jonas could see heavy perspiration glistening on his forehead as he picked up a stone. Five yards away, Nosey didn't blink. Xhirakos gathered several more stones and ominously tested their weight, but then flipped them harmlessly to the side. Now he climbed onto one of the walls, all the while glaring at Nosey, teetered over the spot he had cleared of stones, then leaped into the air while flicking and kicking both hands and feet and roaring a venomous "Nyaaaaa!" An awkward crash landing unleashed from him a final string of invective longer and obviously more complex than Nosey's in the previous round. The goats now bounced wildly around the back seat of the Chevrolet, frantically squeaking and bleating.

Having shown no emotion during Xhirakos's performance, Nosey now pursed his lips and nodded slightly in apparent judgment on the quality and import of Xhirakos's gestures and curses. Nosey climbed off the scooter and with elaborate ceremony sat down, swept away the stones around him, removed his shoes and socks, and lay on his back. He gathered strength and resolve, then thrust his hands and bare feet into the air and began a frantic cycle of flicks and kicks accompanied by a volley of "Nyaas!" that rang through the valley. After a minute he rested his limbs, though marking the space with curses called down on Xhirakos with crackling urgency. Then the arms and legs shot up again, followed by another curse, and so on.

This was impressive. And Xhirakos knew it. So, instead of waiting for Nosey to finish, he hauled himself up to the roof of his car, lay on his stomach and began a frenzied four-limbed gesturing reminiscent of someone on psychoactive drugs trying desperately to swim his way out of a watery hallucination.

From the edge of the path, Jonas looked around at deep green hills flecked with the colors of Greek spring and set off by a luminous sky, at olive trees and grape vines flowing down to a verdant valley where here and there a few sheep grazed contentedly. And immediately in front of him . . . two complete lunatics. He might have laughed but for the men's intense gravity and the irritating possibility that somehow he'd get himself mixed up in this madness.

The men were getting tired. The elaborate sets of curses were mutually abandoned, then the "Nyaas!" grew weaker and the gestures smaller until both men lay faintly wheezing. The goats in the back seat of the

Chevrolet had also exhausted themselves and were still. Xhirakos slid to the ground and got into the car. Jonas moved over near Nosey, squatted, and waited for Nosey to speak. The only sound now was the cicadas scraping their song in the bushes.

"Bleedin' black stain on humanity, That One is."

"What, ah, was all that?"

"Well, he calls me a bleedin' Bulgarian and says to make way for a Christian Greek. Coo, with Christians like him, I'm gonna get m'self a new Savior. . . . No offense."

Jonas absolved Nosey with a solemn nod. Xhirakos and the goats stared out at them from behind the dusty windshield.

"So, I calls him a fascist goat ridin' round with his relatives, stinkin' up Corfu like his Sparta village where they shag their own sisters." Nosey permitted himself a little smile. "Not bad, ay?"

Jonas nodded but didn't know if he should smile himself.

"Then after that pitiful wall jumpin' thing, he calls me a sheep-wankin' pervert . . . infectin' the body of the fatherland. Says if he has his gun, he shoots me down like a dog."

Jonas winced.

"Ahh, all mouth and trousers, That One. So I tells him he ain't worth wastin' a bullet on, that I'll just beat him with a stick, like a snake . . . then send cockroaches up his nose to feast off that dung heap he uses for brains. . . . Rough translation, mind ya." Nosey took a breath. "After that, he's on with some rubbish 'bout the phoenix of the fatherland peckin' out me eyes, but I ain't payin' much attention. I mean, he got no imagination, That One."

They were quiet. It was hot on the dusty path. Jonas squinted at the sun. "Damn sight hotter in that bleedin' car," Nosey reminded him. "And think what them goats is smellin' like."

The glare off the dirty windshield said Nosey was undoubtedly right, but it gave Jonas little comfort. He had never found much solace in the logic of comparative misery.

"Not the first time, doncha know. That One's the reason I got to call 'round the courthouse all the bleedin' time."

There was a history to this siege. Two years before, Nosey had been coming down this same path when Xhirakos was driving up. There was a wide spot just behind where Xhirakos stopped, and if That One had merely rolled his car back a few feet, Nosey could have slid by. But neither man had budged and they had sat on the path for hours until Nosey hopped over the wall for a piss. Xhirakos had taken quick advantage, starting the car, smashing the scooter and driving off.

But there had been witnesses: a family from their hillside cottage, and two shepherds. So, Nosey availed himself of a Greek tradition almost as venerable as revenge itself: he took That One to court. The family witnesses were cowed by Xhirakos's political connections and failed to show up. But the shepherds appeared and backed Nosey in his ridicule of Xhirakos's contention that it had been the scooter that had run down the car. Nosey beamed with the memory: "Coo, did That One ever look like dead meat!"

But Nosey's victory had been short-lived. Although he knew well that, under the Colonels' regime, the courts made rulings with a constant look over their shoulders, Nosey had assumed that in this simple case they could not possibly fail to render the obvious verdict.

Nosey now shook his head: "Musta had me loaf up me arsehole."

The three judges had not taken long to decide. After a moment's consultation under the watchful eye of the phoenix on the wall behind them, they ruled that the shepherds' testimony had to be discounted since they lived in the same district as Nosey and were thus "his people."

So it came back to Nosey's word against Xhirakos's. But according to a new junta law, Nosey's testimony was to be afforded less weight since he was named on a Certificate of Social Beliefs (a notorious government list—the obverse of the Certificate of Civic Responsibility—which branded whole families *personae non gratae* for crimes of political belief "committed" perhaps generations before). Thus the case would be declared an accident, each man to pay for his own damages. Xhirakos's car, of course, had only a scratch while it took Nosey six months to get parts to fix his scooter. There would also be court costs of ten thousand *drachmes*, the court ruled, divided equally between the two.

But even that had not ended it. In Nosey's argument, he had cast aspersions on the honor of a former member—Xhirakos—of Army Intelligence, and thus had sullied the military itself. Which was contempt against the State . . . and thirty days in jail. They had hauled Nosey out of

court and into a basement cell "wid'out so much as an 'ow-do-you-do."
And the court costs? Paying the last of Nosey's half was the reason he
and Jonas had gone into town that very morning, the reason Nosey was
on this path again. Nosey's face was grim; there was no room on the
path for irony.

The chirping of cicadas and an occasional bleat from the back seat of
the car were the only sounds now. Jonas sensed that his presence might
be complicating things, but he couldn't tell if he was making it more
awkward for Nosey or for That One.

"I could walk up to the village ... if you want."

"What for?" Nosey responded brusquely, as if Jonas were suggesting
that Nosey might need help from there.

"Nothing. I just thought, you know, maybe I'm in your way."

"*You* ain't in my way. *That* One's in my way."

"Yeah, it's just ... I mean, I don't want to cause any problems."

Nosey raised his eyebrows. "Well, I don't neither, you know. And
that's a privilege they still leave us here these days: not wantin' to do
things; you don't have to *wanta* do nothin' ..."

Along the path came a tiny, bony, bowlegged old woman in black
leading a donkey and three goats tied to the donkey's tail; bundles of
gnarled branches stuck out several feet on either side of the donkey. The
woman assessed the situation, then dropped the donkey's tether and
without a word walked past Nosey and Jonas to the car.

"She can't get by That One neither," Nosey said.

Xhirakos tried to dismiss the woman but she was undeterred, her
voice, head and arm movements becoming insistent. The commotion
woke Xhirakos's goats, who bleated and bounced around, setting off the
woman's goats, which raised her ire that much higher.

Xhirakos got out of the car in order to speak — which is to say,
gesture—more effectively. He growled and waggled his arms toward
Nosey and Jonas, at the walls, at his car. When he stepped away from the
car for extra emphasis, though, the now-frantic goats banged their way
over the front seat and out the open door. Xhirakos made a dive for the
first one but succeeded only in smacking his head on the door while the
second goat used his back as a running board to freedom. The animals
bounded over the wall and into the fields.

Xhirakos clambered after them, howling in turn at the goats, the woman, and Nosey. While Jonas and Nosey were watching Xhirakos's pursuit, the woman got into the car and fiddled with everything she could push, pull or turn. In a moment the hand brake popped and the car slowly started to roll. Although almost certainly she had never been behind the wheel before, the woman turned the car to miss Nosey's scooter and hit the wall with a satisfying crunch.

There was now just enough room for her little entourage to get by and she collected her animals without showing the least curiosity about Xhirakos or damage to the car. Glancing at a reverently silent Jonas and Nosey, she said, "*Ela, martirakes mou*," then moved up the hill without looking back.

"What was that?" Jonas asked.

"She said, 'Come on, my little martyrs.'" Nosey watched her for a moment. "Course, *martirakes* also means 'the ones who just sit and watch.'"

Nosey and Jonas pushed the scooter past the car and rode up the hill. At the top they looked back: Xhirakos was still scrambling after his goats, his Chevrolet a beached whale expiring in the sun.

⚮

The flirtation between Jonas and the political avant-garde didn't survive the stresses of heavy petting. The most avant of the gardes seemed to Jonas more interested in rooting out each other's "errors" and trashing each other's "positions" than in ever leaving their smoke-filled rooms. They were constantly splitting into factions of factions, which Jonas— his visual scopes registering all the personal jealousies and animosities behind each realignment—found extremely difficult to keep track of. They also showed a combination of paper bravado and corporeal timorousness, these post-modern pols, which first frustrated Jonas and ultimately led to his literal downfall.

It happened like this. There was to be a Vietnam antiwar demonstration outside an army recruiting office in lower Manhattan. Seize the Daze—the Surrealist-inspired group of which Jonas was a member at the time—had noticed that the corporate headquarters of one of the chemical companies which made huge profits off the war was right next to the recruiting office. So the group printed a leaflet exposing the connection and urging the expected large crowd to "let the war profiteers feel what you think." At the demonstration, Jonas and other Daze members—there were, in fact, only ten altogether—distributed the leaflets outside the recruiting office and led scores of cheering demonstrators into the high-rise next door, past the overwhelmed security guards and up the elevators toward the corporate headquarters.

By the time they reached the thirtieth floor, the company had locked its doors. So the demonstrators sat in the hallways, banged on the walls, chanted antiwar slogans and generally disrupted the building's business. The police would certainly arrive soon, and the question was, "Now what?" This question often arose in such moments and so the Daze had anticipated it, agreeing that when this point was reached, the next course of action should be left up to the demonstrators themselves—"the masses," in Daze-speak—and to any accordance they might reach. What they had failed to discuss, however, at least in Jonas's presence, was what Daze members themselves would do. When the moment arrived, Jonas found himself following one of the other, more veteran members of the group into a stairwell. Jonas stopped at the landing and asked where they were going. The other Daze said, "Out of here," and Jonas replied, "But it's not over." As two more Daze members fled past him and down the stairs, Jonas realized that none of the group had any intention of sticking around for the next, undoubtedly riskier, round of action.

It was not that a decision to leave was anathema to Jonas: he didn't feel that to make your point it was always necessary to let the cops exercise their batons on your skull. But the unspoken agreement among all the other Dazes that they would make a painless escape here was too sheer for Jonas, too obviously premeditated, and instinctively he was repelled by it. So without actually answering "Now what?" for himself, he turned to go back through the door. Unfortunately, two more Dazes were just then rushing out and slammed into Jonas, sending him crashing onto and down the stairs, where his fall was abruptly halted by the solid meeting of an iron railing and the side of his head.

The doctors said that, for the most part, he would recover. And, for the most part, he did. The dizziness and nausea were gone in a couple of weeks, the headaches not long after. His swollen-shut left eye gradually opened; the bloodied pupil cleared in a month, his blurred vision back to normal in two. Normal, that is, according to the charts. But not for Jonas. Something strange had happened to his remarkable eyes. When the red finally disappeared from his left eyeball, he noticed that the iris had become slightly etiolated, the vivid preternatural green faded to a lackluster greenish blue. Nor was the change merely cosmetic: the left eye not only *had* less color now but also *saw* less color. Although the eye still retained most of its former formidable optic strength, the blow had dulled its deep sensitivity to saturation and hue.

As for the right eye, the doctors initially thought it unaffected by the injury. But over time it, too, registered a change. The right eye maintained the color acumen the left had given up but, seemingly in sympathy with the left, its telescopic power was reduced. None of these changes was consistent, however, and Jonas found that at different times and places, with different light or different moods, the right eye would register the world more clearly through its colors than the left eye with its outlines . . . and vice versa. The whole thing was very troubling. Not so much the loss of some of his second sight as the unreliability of what remained: sometimes now he would see things clearly out of one eye, only to have them the next hour or day seem clearer—but somehow different—out of the other eye. The doctors had no answers. Except, perhaps, for time. The eyes might finally adjust to each other, they said. With time.

The doctors warned in the strongest terms, however, that another blow might cause severe damage. How bad, they did not know, but the next time Jonas could lose his second sight entirely. Or worse. So, although he made no fully conscious decision, after his recovery Jonas found himself resolving to keep a cooler head. And as he had with love, soon found that maintaining a distance was, whatever else, something of a relief. Still, he knew that fires still smoldered in the tinder of his personality: keeping out of harm's way would not be easy. How to avoid caring too much about things such that their miscarriage would not loose his emotions from their new restraints? He disconnected from the Daze group and sought out no others on the cutting edge, so the odds of political collisions, at least, seemed greatly diminished. He had returned to labor organizing but this time in the field, keeping away from the union's clotted bureaucracy and its squabbles over the perquisites of power. And though it hurt to let go, he gave up basketball altogether. He also grew a moustache: long and thick and a shade lighter than his curly chocolate hair. In the past few months, three strands of gray had appeared.

5

Despite his considerable resolve, Jonas's effort at self-restraint was a constant, often losing, struggle. He knew that the hyperclarity of his vision was no longer as reliable as it had been before his head's collision with the stair railing, but the habit of its certainty remained deeply ingrained. As his wife described it, Jonas needed a muffler of doubt on the engine of his judgments. And he did truly wish he were more chary with his critical salvos. But often he was simply unable to stop himself. It was a pathology, he explained: he would be overcome by a kind of momentary derangement and just could not keep his mouth shut, any more than someone with hay fever could keep from sneezing.

Since arriving on Corfu, however, Jonas had noticed how soothing it was not merely holding his tongue but shutting down the critical engine altogether. To his increasing relief, he was able to leave behind the ultimate and universal for the immediate and particular, which in the case of his island existence was simple, healthy and without neurosis: long, slow days without reacting precipitously to the modern world's random doses of madness. So, after returning to Glaros following the confrontation on the path between Nosey and Xhirakos, Jonas was looking to recapture his island equilibrium with a quiet ouzo at The Bad.

"I beg your pardon."

It took Jonas a moment to realize that the words were addressed to him. She was behind him, must have come up through the canyon since he had not seen her cross the square. A dusty duffel bag lay at her feet; on the table was a smaller, rough wool drawstring sack like those Jonas had seen the goatherds carry. She wore the same faded jeans, scuffed boots and green silken shirt, now well-soiled, as she had when he'd seen her on the ferry.

"I wonder would you know if there is a bus into Corfu Town?" She spoke with the eroded remnants of a well-brought-up Home Counties England accent, her voice deep and certain but as distant and without affect as had been her passing glance on the boat deck.

"Is . . . there something I can help you with?" He lit a cigarette although he had put one out only moments before.

"Thank you, no. Only a bus."

"Oh. Well, yes, there is one. In the morning, about seven. And back in the evening. Two on weekends."

"'Tisn't a weekend by chance, is it?"

"Ah, no. I think we just had one."

"Mm." She thought for a moment. "Thank you so much."

Her tone clearly signaled the close of the conversation, though instead of looking away or otherwise punctuating an ending, she continued to gaze out toward Jonas and the square. Jonas wanted to continue their talk, but almost any comment now would either mark him as needing company or would bind them together as outsiders in the village, as curiosities. Given how much pleasure he had found these last days in having reached this place where he knew no one and no one knew him, he was surprised by his urge to keep chatting. And a bit befuddled by it. To resist the urge, he turned away to face the square and sat quite still. Her presence was a heat on his back. After a few minutes, she spoke again.

"Do you stay here in the village?"

"The village? Glaros, yes," he replied with an air that suggested he might have been one of its original inhabitants.

"Would you know whom to ask about spending the night?"

"Ah, well. There's no hotel, I'm afraid. No *pensione*, either. Things are pretty basic around here." He spoke with a kind of pride in the village simplicity.

"Yes, well, I'm a basic sort."

"There are a couple of beds at Mikhalis's, the bus driver's."

"Mm."

"Bus pulls in right here. Shouldn't be long now. I'll point him out if you like."

"Oh, I think I can manage to see who it is that's driving."

Jonas swallowed. "It's nothing special, Mikhalis's," he ventured again. "But I did survive one night there." He hoped she might pick up what he intended as a pregnant remark but she simply nodded.

Leonides's ten-year-old daughter, Elektra, came out of The Bad with a glass of ouzo, a tumbler of water and a plate of *metzedes*. After setting the things down in front of the woman, the little girl stepped back and gaped. The woman smiled, opening her faraway face. At the turn of her head, Jonas could see with his blue eye a delicate vein pulsing on her throat.

"Thank you," said the woman; the little girl beamed. The woman poured some water into her glass, turning the ouzo to its characteristic milky color.

"Elektra," Jonas addressed the little girl, "*pou einai o* Spiros?" Jonas struggled to trot out a bit of the Greek he had managed to cobble from his phrase book and from Nosey—Where is Spiros?

"*Pio* Spiros?" Elektra asked, her eyes staying fixed on the woman. Which Spiros? Jonas translated to himself. Ugh—Elektra's question had already reached a blank page in his repertoire. "You know: Spiraki," Jonas made the name a diminutive and held out his hand at the height of the bus driver's son.

"*Dthen xero*," the girl shrugged—she didn't know. Leonides's voice now called her back into the cafe.

"I thought maybe the bus driver's son was around," Jonas explained. He had already rejected the idea of escorting the woman himself to the bus driver's house: having fled their lumpy hospitality after only one night, Jonas didn't relish trying to explain his abrupt departure to Mikhalis's wife.

"No matter," the woman said. "I can wait."

They waited together. Jonas found himself drawn to the woman, in particular to her solo self-assurance: her ability to go it alone seemingly without needing to know exactly where she was or would wind up. An ease, a contentment even, in her solitude. Of course, to be attracted to someone else's solitude presents something of a conflict: if you succeed in breaching it, you will have diluted the very thing you admired. You may even have proved that your assessment was wrong, that the person's solitude was not as successful as you had imagined it. But if so, and if your own strive for distance has been proving less than fully satisfying, there might be some comfort in knowing that the same is true for someone else: a sort of "solitude loves company." And so Jonas talked on, albeit casually, staying at his one-table remove from hers. As he babbled, he found himself giving the impression that he'd been in the village longer than he had, knew the area more thoroughly than he did, and had some explicable though unstated reason for being there, which he didn't.

Her name was Liana. He reckoned that she was somewhere in her early thirties, with wide, angular cheeks and shoulders, a tapered jaw, and a long, slender neck framed by a fall of thick chestnut hair of almost the same hue, Jonas noticed, as her eyes. In contrast to Jonas's sudden volubility, Liana yielded information more than offered it. Yes, it was she whom Jonas had seen on the ferry; she said nothing of having seen him. She volunteered neither where she had come from nor where she was going, though she did describe briefly her time since arriving on Corfu, most of it spent sleeping out on a cove south of Glaros. An old couple in a stone cottage there had given her fruit and bread, and water from their well, and had visited with her each evening; as she spoke of the old couple, Jonas could see her eyes brighten. That morning, though, the police had rousted her from the cove and she had climbed to the nearest village, Glaros: "So here I am."

The bus pulled into the square and Spiros, the driver's son, appeared. Jonas explained that Liana needed a bed, and Spiros went over to ask his father. He returned and said, "*Endaxi*"—Okay—then slid off to join some other boys in the square. Liana was already moving. She put a coin on the table and picked up her bag. "Thank you again," she said and stepped through the tables and chairs.

Her peremptory departure caught Jonas by surprise. "Maybe we'll see you later?" he said offhandedly.

She turned and smiled—not the expansive smile she had given little Elektra but a genuine smile nonetheless—and seemed to rest her gaze for a moment on Jonas's moustache. Then, without another word, she moved into the square and walked off with little Spiros. Jonas's willing it notwithstanding, she did not turn back to look.

The moustache had outlasted a number of other attitudinal convolutions. The question of a watch, for example. As an adolescent, Jonas had regarded watches, and those who wore them, with disdain. Father gone since Jonas was a child, mother's long work hours leaving her neither energy nor capacity to control him, Jonas went home when he wanted, stayed out if he chose. Who needed to know what time it was? Besides, a watch was something someone would try to take off you: Jonas didn't like carrying things around, nothing you had to look out for. And a watch would break when you got into a fight. Anyway, he didn't like the way a watch felt. And it looked funny on his skinny wrist, never fit right over the protruding bone. The first watch he had ever owned, the one an uncle gave him, had a metal expando-band that went cockeyed and pinched his skin. And it was too big, the band. The whole thing was too big. Made his wrist look even skinnier. Then the spring, or something, broke. And he didn't want to ask his mother to spend the money to fix it.

It wasn't until many years later, until the pressures of his early days in union work, that wearing a watch made sense to him. Still, he hadn't actually done it: a watch was okay for others now, but it wasn't something Jonas wanted. One of those small ways to be different. Stubborn. Jonas, being Jonas.

Then he had read an interview with one of the obscurely legendary textile mill labor organizers. Always had a watch, the man said in passing: much to be done, never enough time to do it. During his activist days, this old organizer had often been jailed, and he had died of pneumonia contracted behind bars. If you are imprisoned for your principles, Jonas's feeling had been back then at age twenty-three, the principles themselves somehow go up in value. And if you die for them . . . So, for a couple of years Jonas wore a watch. Sort of. He had a habit of taking it off when he sat down, often forgot it, resented the inevitable tendency to peek at the time. He would take it off as soon as he got home and several times spent months between losing one watch and buying another.

Still, a watch was useful. By the end of his third year of union work, Jonas was as disoriented as he was frustrated. More and more hours, less and less purpose: up before dawn to talk with a graveyard shift; into the office of a local consumed by petty power intrigues; out to another site for the afternoon shift change; then to a workers' bar to hear management and the union bureaucracy pilloried with equal vehemence before finally heading to his room at seven or eight, where he would take off his shoes, drop the watch into one of them, and flop onto the bed. After a short nap he would check the time, get up, open a can of dinner, and do his paperwork or head out to a work site for the late shift change. Then four or five hours sleep, sometimes still in his clothes, get up, do it again.

One miserable, sleeting January evening, he came back to his room, dropped on the bed, and woke up feeling like shit. He glanced at the watch in his shoe and saw to his disgust that he had slept through the night. He stumbled into the bathroom, stood shivering until the water got lukewarm, peeled off his sticky clothes, showered, shaved. Then repacked himself: long johns, thermal undershirt, two pairs of socks, thick wool overshirt, double-layer work pants. The room was so cold and damp that he pulled on his snow boots before going into the alcove which the landlord unflinchingly referred to as the kitchen. As he put the coffee on, he glanced at the clock over the stove: two a.m. Shut his eyes, looked again: still two a.m. Christ! The watch must have stopped before he fell asleep, and so here he is, standing at the stove, showered, shaved, dressed to climb Everest, watching the water boil... and it's fucking two o'clock in the morning.

At eight o'clock he quit his job. He put the watch in a drawer as soon as he got home.

<hr>

Returning to Glaros from a walk the day after meeting Liana, Jonas was unexpectedly joined on the main road by entire families in their Sunday best. Although Easter was imminent, Jonas had been told that the celebrations began on Good Friday, still several days away. And these pilgrims had no sign of a holiday air about them. They were silent, grim, eyes staring straight ahead but darting sideways glances, as if reproach might be lurking in the shadows and trees.

Other families were gathered in the glades by their low stone cottages, looking out at the road, holding their children still. Their work clothes contrasted with the outfits of those who passed. No greetings were exchanged between houses and road.

Jonas had come to relish the moments of exuberant hospitality to which he was daily treated during his walks around the island: "*Yia sou!*"—Here's to you!—called from a man working his field; a smile and backhand wave from a woman tending goats or sheep or gathering olives, fingers wagging as if beckoning rather than merely greeting. In fact, the first time Jonas saw this local gesture he mistook it for an invitation; the old woman who'd waved had responded to his blunder by insisting that Jonas share bread and goat cheese laid out on a tree stump, an hour's conversation in sign language and broken Italian ultimately satisfying her that Jonas did indeed have a mother somewhere. Now Jonas thought over the day he'd just spent: such greetings and encounters had been conspicuously absent.

At the edge of the village square, he stopped. The Ugly—Xhirakos's cafe—was festooned with blue and white ribbons, an oversized Greek flag posted above the doorway. Extra chairs had been added out front and were filling up with people coming in from the road. The cafe's television had been moved outside to a pedestal placed directly under a large emblem of the phoenix; all the chairs were turned to face it. Two military jeeps were parked next to the cafe, protruding well out into the square.

Across at The Bad, Nosey and Leonides sat out front with a dozen or so men whom Jonas recognized from the *taverna*—shepherds, farmers, fishermen; Leonides's wife and several other women were gathered near the doorway. Outside at The Good sat a larger than normal contingent of its old-men clientele, perhaps fifteen in all. And under the square's massive plane tree, sitting silent witness, was Korina.

Jonas had established a routine of heading for a beer or an ouzo at The Bad when back from a walk, but now he hesitated at the palpable tension in the square. He tried to get a read from Nosey, but Nosey's stare was fixed on The Ugly. Then Jonas noticed that Leonides was watching him. There was no particular information in Leonides's expression; simply one man looking another in the eye. After a moment, Jonas felt himself edging toward The Bad.

Leonides held out a chair, put a hand on Jonas's shoulder.

"21 April," Nosey said, his eyes never leaving The Ugly.

Jonas drew a blank.

"21 April 1967. Day the Colonels put the boot down. . . . Six bleedin' years today."

"Two thousands, one hundred, thirty and eight days," Leonides pronounced slowly, tapping the ground with his crutch. They were the first English words Jonas had heard him speak.

Xhirakos came out of The Ugly and turned on the television. He fiddled with knobs, moved wires and wiggled the antenna but got only shadows and fuzz. He cursed and banged the set, argued with those who gave him advice, fiddled some more. At each failed effort, he turned up the volume, as if to compensate for the lack of a picture. But the sound reception was off, too, and so he succeeded only in steadily increasing the level of static.

"I mean, it's in the hills, innit? Two years now he's had that thing and he ain't once got his self a decent picture. Course, that don't stop him watchin' the bleedin' thing."

The village church bells rang and the people at The Ugly all dutifully stilled themselves. The bells stopped, the square became quiet. Then martial music blared through the static and Xhirakos and the others at The Ugly rose to their feet; four soldiers saluted the TV screen. The people at The Good and The Bad all stayed in their chairs.

The music ended; the people at The Ugly sat down. A few glanced uncomfortably across the square but most remained fixed on the television. Two soldiers glared at the men sitting at The Bad.

A voice now pierced the static and at The Ugly all murmurs and movement stopped, as if the shadowy head on the screen could tell who was paying attention and who was not. The men at The Bad reacted by turning their chairs around, backs to The Ugly. The old men at The Good moved in unison to the far side of the cafe.

Jonas peeked over at the TV, but because he could neither make out the face nor understand the language—the only words he was able to catch were *Xhristianos* and *Kommounismos*, repeated over and again—he focused on the quality of the voice: it didn't so much speak as it did squawk, screech and whine. On and on it went. For half an hour, the people at The Ugly stared silently at the glowing shadow and submitted to the acrid voice.

When the voice finally finished, music blared again and the people at Xhirakos's staggered to their feet. Then the music ended and once more static filled the square. After a minute someone turned off the set, and only then did the people at The Ugly begin to move, as if suddenly released from a spell. Without lingering, without talk, they slid away from the cafe. Those who lived in the village slipped behind closed doors; those from outside quickly melted into the hills. Within five minutes, Xhirakos and the soldiers were the only ones left. Not until everyone from Xhirakos's had gone did those at The Good and at The Bad begin to drift away. Little was said. Leonides and Nosey went inside the cafe. Under the plane tree, Korina was the last to move.

For a couple of years, Jonas didn't need a watch; he worked as a substitute teacher, and schoolrooms have clocks. But also, after the injury which had dimmed his second sight, none of the old organizer's political dicta—including the one about needing a watch—seemed to Jonas terribly persuasive anymore. At every turn, now, he could see only reasons why this or that act was not worth the cost, this or that effect illusory: demonstrations which led to endless debates about tactics; strikes which led to one more buck for the same miserable work; organizing which led to ... organizations.

But there was a salutary side to his retreat. Jonas's visceral responses to the world had always smoldered and burned, eating at his insides until at seemingly random moments they burst out in furies beyond his control or understanding. His temper was notorious, and even though rarely directed at anyone, the sheer heat of its explosions often seared those who stood too close. Pulling back from organized engagement now permitted these passions a much looser, less agitated flow. The random, the unmediated and the gratuitously contrary, exercised more freely but without an accompanying fury, became balm for his unrequited ideals. Passions may cloud the mind, he now concluded, but they also free it from the narrow corridors of reason. His pantheon of patron anti-saints grew wider, wilder: not just Karl now, but Groucho; Buñuel and Blake up with Blanqui; and newfound room for Nietzsche: "Objections, digressions, gay mistrust, the delight in mockery are signs of health: everything unconditional belongs in pathology." Loosed passions plus the power of negative thinking: the combination began to draw from Jonas moments of subversion that were spontaneous, exhilarating and—for the first time since leaving the basketball courts—even joyous.

The problem of a life lived in such moments, though, is that there are all those other moments, the ones before, after and between. Example: the morning he got a call to substitute-teach at a high school in the South Bronx. A class in something called Values Clarification. Six a.m., the phone rings, and you're supposed to prepare Values Clarification for kids in the South Bronx. Jonas premeditated nothing particular in bringing his tape recorder and soul tapes, but he knew he had done the right thing when his students danced out into the hallways, pulling other kids out of their classes, singing at the top of their voices to Sly and the Family Stone: "Thank ya . . . fa lettin' me . . . be mahh-self . . . agaiiin!" The moment, however, defined perfectly the expression "hard act to follow"; Jonas got no more calls to teach in that school district.

Eventually he found a job at the J.F.K. Academy, official euphemism: Continuation School. It was a makeshift operation to keep teenage boys off the street after they had been "exempted" from public schools for "habitual behavioral dysfunction"—a condition not unlike Jonas's own. The job seemed made for him: few rules; no truancy chastisements (What were you going to do if a kid didn't show up, "exempt" him?); the content of any given class created in the moment by the teacher and whatever boys happened to be there. Jonas and the three other teachers taught some basic math, worked with the more than a few boys who could barely read, and tried to introduce them to a few ideas beyond those of the streets to which they were confined. But the primary daily struggle was just to keep the boys out of deeper trouble (probation officers were frequent visitors) and to keep alive in them some flicker of hope—though for what, exactly, Jonas didn't really know—while they waited out their "exemptions."

The school was located in an industrial section of Queens, in an empty shipping company warehouse. No desks, no supplies. No clocks: among other things, Jonas could have used a watch. And after school one day a student offered him a selection of new watches at, well, greatly reduced prices. Jonas bought one and slipped it into his pocket to cool off. At home he cut off the hideous fake skin band, intending to buy a replacement. A year later—a month ago, now—when he and his wife had left to visit her relatives in Italy, the same bandless watch was in his pocket.

6

Jonas was sitting outside The Bad with Nosey and the second of his morning's grainy Greek coffees when Liana walked across the square. Jonas had assumed she'd left on the early morning bus, was surprised at how pleased he was that she hadn't. In sandals, white cotton smock and comparably casual face, she sat at the next table and gave Jonas a nod.

"So, you got settled at Mikhalis's all right," Jonas said after deciding whether to say anything at all.

"Yes, thank you."

"Mikhalis's?" Nosey put in. "Oh, *po-po*."

Jonas introduced them. "Nosey here thinks Mikhalis's beds are a little questionable."

"*Nosey* thinks? Cooo, didn't take *you* long to come lookin' for another kip, did it?" He turned to Liana. "Sleep there, you'll have dreams that's downright diabolical."

"So I found out last night," Liana said. "Though I'm not certain the bed holds full responsibility."

"Yeah"—Nosey's giant moustache twitched—"there's somethin' real dicey goin' about round here. Had me a bleedin' nightmare of me own last night." He pulled his chair closer. "I'm sittin' out on the water, see—in me nightmare—but I dunno if I'm meant to stay out there or not. So I'm tryin' to suss it out, and I'm gettin' all nervy-like, when all of a sudden, floatin' 'round in front me eyes is this here Uncle Ned—this head—all by its lonesome, and it's *Aghios Yiannis O Prodhromos*—Saint John the, ah . . . the first, you know . . ."

"The Baptist?" Liana put in.

"Yeah, himself. And he says to me, he says, 'All right?' And I says, 'All right.' And he says, 'Yiorgo'—Yiorgos, that's me real moniker—'Yiorgo,' he says, 'all your troubles is over, me lad. From now on, no more worryin' about nothin', cause I'll be takin' care of the whole lot. No more decidin' what all you got to do, what you ain't, just leave it all to me . . . and relax.'"

"I thought you said it was a nightmare," Jonas said.

"*Course* it's a nightmare! Some dodgy saint runnin' me life! What the bleedin' hell'd be the point of livin'?'"

"Sounds like 'The Grand Inquisitor,'" Jonas said.

"Who's that?"

"Well, it's a story . . . a high priest, sort of," Jonas groped.

"Bah! Priests," Nosey barked. "That's somethin' I liked 'bout Australia: not so many priests messin' about with people. I hear you ain't got so many in the States neither, eh?"

"Oh, we have plenty. Just most of them go by different names."

"Really?" Liana asked with a hint of challenge. "And what are those?"

"Well, it goes in cycles, you know. Like clothes fashion. But I'd say the clerics of feelings are doing real well for themselves these days. You know, 'The world's not the problem, it's you. And making yourself feel better is your duty.' Sort of a Church of Holy Therapeutics."

"Therapeutics, eh?" Nosey said. "Me cousin had some of that in Melbourne after a smash-up with a lorry. Some lady jiggled his neck about for nigh onto three months. Didn't do his neck much good but he was dead chuffed 'bout havin' this nice lady give him a rub twice a week. . . . Course, it cost a bleedin' fortune. And funny thing was, soon's he moves back to Corfu, his neck's all jake again."

"Yeah, well, the people I'm talking about do pretty much the same thing. Around and around, only heads instead of necks."

Liana stared intently at Jonas, as if trying to choose between two widely disparate impressions.

"Hm." Nosey turned to Liana. "That goin' on where you're from, luv? You sound sorta like a Brit."

"Yes, well, I am sort of like a Brit. My mother was English. But I've lived in Toronto the past ten years."

"Canada, eh? Pretty much like the States anyways, innit?"

"Well, most Canadians don't think so. But yes, I suppose they're more alike than not. Canada just isn't quite . . . as far along."

She looked at Jonas and, to his relief, offered them both a small smile.

For Jonas, pleasure had always been a predominantly solitary experience; it built no bridges. Anger, outrage, criticality, on the other hand, were the stuff out of which bonds could be forged. So although there was certainly pleasure in his morning wander with Liana—lush green hills, warm sun through the trees, cicadas and goat bells—it was their tentative references to the demons each had left behind which for Jonas truly seeded their connection.

They spoke only occasionally and briefly, the quiet hills an accompaniment to their joint circumspection. But the two came at restraint from decidedly different angles. Jonas probed and parried, drew her out while revealing little himself. Liana, on the other hand, would neither draw nor be drawn. Rather, she became engaged barometrically: when Jonas was forthcoming, she opened up; when he played cool, she was gone.

They were walking now along a dirt road and below could see the corner of a sheltered white pebble cove. Silently they agreed to head down.

When they reached the shore, Jonas looked back: there were no houses or other structures in sight, and the trees and cliffs secluded them from the road, seemingly from the world. He turned again to the water. Liana was unbuttoning her smock. It slipped off her shoulders and into a pile on the pebbles; she wore nothing underneath. Unselfconsciously she walked across the stones and dove into the chill springtime sea; as she surfaced, a groan escaped her. Jonas shed his own clothes and went in, too. He came up near her, but left some distance between himself and her sorrel skin. After a few minutes he got out of the water and lay face down on the warm, flat stones.

He heard the crunch of footsteps but kept his eyes closed, didn't move. She stood over him for a long moment, then lay down, the cool water off her body dappling his. After a minute he slowly turned his head and squinted. She was on her stomach, facing him, eyes closed. Water beaded in the hollow of her back; fine golden hairs lay over forearms and flanks, flecked with water drying in the sun. Her hands and feet were large and square, as if belonging to another body. Her head, too, was square, her cheekbones broad and pronounced, her mouth a size too big for her face. It was an odd face, its disparate features pulled together by a visible strength of character. At least, visible to Jonas. Through his green eye.

"How do you make a mule?" Liana asked suddenly, her eyes still shut.

"What?"

"The animal up by the road. That was a mule, wasn't it?"

"Lady, I'm from Brooklyn."

"Well, that was a mule."

"And . . . ?"

"And a mule is a cross between an ass and a horse."

"Okay by me."

"So how do they go about making a mule? That is, who does what"—she opened her eyes and looked at him—"to whom?"

"Wait a minute. You mean, does a male donkey, ah, get up on a female horse . . . or vice versa?"

"Well, that's one way of putting it."

"Hm. Can't say I ever considered it before. . . . But when you think about it, 'vice versa' might be kind of tough on a little female donkey, don't you think? . . . Anyway, I'm sure the horses and donkeys got it figured out."

"Yes," she said in surprising earnest, "but do the mules?"

"Well, by that time it wouldn't exactly matter, would it?"

"Not to know whether your mother is a donkey and your father a horse, or the other way around? Imagine"—she raised herself onto an elbow; Jonas had difficulty not staring—"if you are a mule, you are a completely different being from either of your parents. If you are a mule, you are . . . a genetic orphan."

"I doubt they think about it all that much."

"No, but don't you imagine they feel it?" She shook her head. "Such an overwhelming confusion. Perhaps that's why they look so sad all the time."

"You think they'd look happier if they knew how their parents had . . . gotten together? And mules are neuters, aren't they? No wonder they got sad faces." He squinted each eye at her for a moment, trying to read in her face the depth of her reflections. "Isn't the thing about mules that they don't *need* to understand? They just know what they have to do.

I mean, you can always worry about not understanding. Hell, half the people I know try so hard to understand, they never *do* anything. They're never quite … ready."

She searched his eyes, one and the other, then for a brief moment rested her gaze on his mouth … or moustache. They were sitting up now, facing each other, their bodies only inches apart.

"And some people rush to the doing," Liana said evenly, "so they won't have to face what they've already done."

The only sounds were their breathing and the ripple of sea on stones. She reached out and brushed away a pebble that had clung to his stomach, then got up, walked into the water and swam in a straight line away from the beach. Jonas's stomach muscles twitched from the memory of her fingers.

"Jesus fuck," he said softly.

✦

Jonas's moustache had survived more than the dialectics of watches. Toward the end of his union days, he was considered for an organizing job in New Jersey. A union official asked if Jonas was willing to shave it off and get a crew cut if sent to an area which might not be ready for so much hair.

"What's a moustache in the face of a need to organize?" Jonas's pun was unintentional but he couldn't help grinning. The official didn't get it. Jonas didn't get the job.

There had been other moments for the moustache as well. After several months together, his wife-to-be said: "How can I tell what I'm getting?"

"Would you really know just by seeing my lip?" Jonas answered with the bottom half of his mouth.

A year later they won three hundred dollars at a Reno craps table on a drive to the West Coast for a friend's wedding. Drunkenly, they decided to get married themselves, another tack at staying together. Outside the instant-wedding chapel, she asked: "Should I marry someone whose upper lip I've never seen?"

"Only if you want to," was the best Jonas could come up with by way of reply.

And just weeks ago now, as he'd staggered away from the apartment his wife's relatives had lent them for their stay in Bologna, Jonas had caught a glimpse of himself in the foyer mirror. Seeing yourself cry is a sorrow all its own; the moustache had kept him from the full depth of the sadness.

✿

Jonas and Liana spoke cautiously the rest of the day at the cove and the day after, watching each other's gestures and listening in the shadows and spaces alongside words, seeking their echoes more than their immediate clatter. But by the time they walked back to Glaros late the second afternoon, the space between them had halved; occasionally their bare arms brushed.

She had been on the move for a year, she told him. Stopped here and there to make a bit of money. Moved on. Most recently she had been an attendant in a home for the elderly outside Rome. It was her voice that told just how tired she was. At one point she mentioned "the man I was living with" in Toronto but offered no details. Jonas didn't ask. Nor did he mention his wife: their attenuation had been long and slow, the end a foregone conclusion, yet thoughts of the final demise just weeks ago were still too raw. In truth, he would not have known what to say.

In Canada, Liana had worked for several years with teenagers: runaways, pregnant girls, "troubled" adolescents of all varieties. She was quiet for a moment, then looked directly at Jonas: "I was trained in public health. But I wound up working with girls one to one. What, I suppose, you'd call 'therapeutics.'"

Jonas gulped, recalling his flip remarks of the day before. But there was no reproval in Liana's face. And on seeing Jonas's reaction, she gave a brief laugh—though it was only her voice that laughed.

"Listen," he said. "I'm sorry about yesterday. What I said."

"Why? Didn't you mean it?"

"Oh, I meant it. It's just... I didn't mean that for some people, you know, getting help can't be, well, helpful sometimes."

"That's generous of you."

"What I'm trying to say is, why don't you tell me I'm wrong? At least about you?"

"I suppose because I'm not certain you are wrong," she said after a moment. "At least about me. Since I left my work, left Canada, I've been living with these questions every day. You're talking about what to make of the last ten years of my life. And perhaps I could talk to you about things that matter to me . . . if I had an idea what mattered to you." She stared at him, then shook her head as if rejecting the beginnings of a thought. "But I don't, do I."

Jonas had often been told, and had come to believe, that he so frequently and painfully collided with the world because too many things mattered too much to him. But a few months ago his wife had charged that his caring so hard about so many things was also a way of not truly having to care about any one thing in particular. At the time, Jonas had deflected the accusation with some facile retort, and though he believed that he didn't believe her charge, it had stuck in him and festered. And Liana's remark now pained him again.

At the edge of the village, they stopped, both of them exhausted from two long days of sun, walking and the weight of each other's company. It was time for an *ipnos*, the Greek siesta, a retreat to cool shadows and the solace of silence. "So . . . see you later?" Jonas tried not to sound like he needed an answer. Liana blinked, then turned away to Mikhalis's.

Jonas ate alone that evening. Nosey joined him for moments here and there, chattering about the Good Friday festivities the following day, the Saturday midnight mass in Corfu Town and the two feast days after that. Jonas drank a little more than usual of the local wine, then still more at The Bad. Before Nosey could finish his tasks at the *taverna* and join Jonas at the cafe, Jonas was overcome by the impulse to know where Liana was, what she was doing. He headed for Mikhalis's on unsteady legs.

A faint light came from the attic where Mikhalis had the beds for hire. Jonas went quietly up the outside stairs, past the family's quarters. He tapped softly but got no response and edged open the door. She was asleep on a cot; a single candle flickered by her head. Jonas slid in, sat on the other cot and waited, wanting her to wake but not wanting to wake her. A half-eaten cucumber was on the floor next to a ragged paperback copy of *Alice's Adventures in Wonderland*. Jonas sat very still, watching her sleep, willing her awake. But after a few minutes it occurred to him that she might not be asleep, that she might only be feigning. He got up quietly and left.

7

The cobbled lanes of Old Corfu Town overflowed with celebrants Good Friday afternoon. Families had come into the main town from every corner of the island, their ranks swelled by boatloads of relatives who had returned from Athens or abroad for the festivities and by people who had come over from the northern mainland, each village distinguished by its indigenous holiday vests, sashes and head cloths. The town's major passageways were dotted with vendors hawking candles, nutmeats and an impressive variety of religious trinkets. Soldiers with field weapons leaned against building walls, watching intently.

By the time Jonas and Liana reached town, the afternoon processions had already begun, a delegation from each local church making an even dozen circuits of the Old Town's twisting lanes. Priests in ecclesiastic finery, surrounded by robed acolytes swinging Byzantine censers, were followed in loose formation by church elders carrying candles and singing hymns of the day. The makeup and bearing of each procession were remarked by the crowds, the fervor and quality of the singing judged. Since the Old Town's few wide lanes crossed at several points, these processions inevitably ran into one another. When two groups came within hearing, each redoubled its vocal effort, not only to evince the greater piety but also somehow to establish secular preeminence, for it was the winners—how this was determined or communicated utterly escaped Jonas—of each spontaneous choral contest who maintained their course while the losers waited for them to pass.

Jonas and Liana had been given a ride to town in the open back of a three-wheeled mini-truck which Nosey, who rode in the front with his friend who was driving, called a tricycle. The bumpy road and noisy engine had severely limited Jonas and Liana's ability to converse, but they had been alone with, and virtually on top of, each other for nearly an hour.

Nosey had family visits to make. Before he set off, Liana asked him about ferries to Italy. None until next Tuesday, he told her. But from the Old Port, he added, near the ancient sea baths, a small boat crossed the straits to the northern Greek mainland most evenings, and from there a train went to Italy every day.

As Jonas and Liana strolled among the crowds, he resisted asking her about heading for Italy, not quite consciously deciding that what isn't mentioned doesn't exist—a seductive notion not only because it suppresses the anxiety of anticipation but also because its truth is continuously affirmed until specifically refuted. That is, as long as Liana was still there, Jonas need not accept that at some point she might not be. Or to think about whether that mattered.

The afternoon processions ended and the crowds scattered through the town, making visits and see-and-be-seen *voltes*—destinationless perambulations—around the lanes and the broad main esplanade. Jonas and Liana strolled, too, Jonas distracting them both with impromptu imaginary biographies of selected passersby; inventing other lives made it easier not to think about his own. When they came to the port, he steered her toward Dirty Dick's.

"The old sea baths are just around there, aren't they?" Liana asked as they sat outside Dick's. Jonas realized she was thinking of the boat to the mainland.

"You seem like you . . . might want to be someplace else."

"No, not really. I mean, part of me does. But . . . I guess you could say that my other self wants to be here. Well, in Greece. If you were one to say things like 'other self.' I'm Greek, you see. Though not exactly. Conceived in Greece but . . . executed elsewhere. My mother was English. But I'm not. Not truly. Not according to the English, at any rate. If one's father is English, well and good. But if only your mother is English, then you are all your father's . . . even if he's not all yours. 'Left home early and arrived nowhere'—Edmund Jabes. Do you know Jabes? A mystic. You're not the type, are you? I'm not either, really. We're alike, you know. Not Jabes. You and I."

The holiday crowds surging past them seemed to provide Liana with a current of resolve, a boost over Jonas's parallel walls of reticence and blather. She began to speak as if she had been holding her breath for days.

Her mother had been called Fiona, she said, daughter of a frightfully proper family from Kent. In 1938, Fiona had gone to Greece to study antiquities and to paint. The recklessness of such a trip—"Greece? But my dear, it's so . . . foreign"—was confirmed for the family when, after a month, Fiona's older travel companion returned alone to England. And what at first had been seen as merely folly soon degenerated into scandal: Fiona was not returning, she wrote; she had met a most wondrous man, an artist and a scholar. And—her family read in horror the name Aphinotis—a Greek.

Liana spoke of her mother, Fiona, with a love and admiration deeply shadowed in sadness. When she spoke of the man who was her father, her tone vacillated. At times it reflected her mother's unextinguished love. At others it carried her mother's insuperable loss. And behind both lay a confusion that was Liana's own.

Aphinotis, as Liana called him as if speaking of a stranger, came from the mountains of northern Greece. A painter and a teacher at the university in Thessaloniki, to Fiona he was a man of vision, passionate, extreme. And to Aphinotis, Fiona was worldly and free, unfettered by traditional Greek mores, which allowed women of the time so little room to breathe. Together they roamed the mountains and sailed the waters, sought the magic light of the islands and eventually landed in a cave at the western tip of Crete. They also conceived a child.

Her family's nightmare had come true: Fiona returned to England pregnant and alone. That she'd returned only to escape the Axis invasion of Greece mattered not at all to the family, nor that Aphinotis had failed to join her only because the British authorities in Crete refused him papers to enter England. The family was equally unimpressed that the couple was married: "In a tavern? By a monk?"

Aphinotis did not manage to get to England before the war made it impossible. "We don't know how hard he tried," Liana said with an edge to her voice. Instead, he joined the resistance fighting in the mountains of Crete. Liana's mother received one message during the war that Aphinotis was alive. And that was it: five years, one message. In 1946, though, Fiona got a letter, a scratching really, smuggled out of the prison where Aphinotis had been incarcerated since the outbreak of civil war. "Greek politics," Liana said by way of explanation but not, apparently, excuse. Over the next several years, Fiona got a few more letters, from a different prison and from an island exile. Liana did not say whether her mother wrote back.

Meanwhile, Liana was growing up in various English boarding schools, recognized by but never fully a part of her mother's family. She and Fiona were not so much ostracized as merely held apart. Turned into distant relations. Distant from a family and a class that had no terms by which to acknowledge the existence of a man in Greece whom they—and Liana—had never met.

In 1950, Fiona got another letter. Aphinotis was out of prison, heading for his home village, looking for a way to resurrect a life. He was also looking for his wife and child.

"After all those years not knowing him, not having him in her life. Or in my life." Liana shook her head. "Ah, but my mother. My delirious, unquenchable Fiona..."

Despite glaciers of family disapproval, Fiona packed up nine-year-old Liana and headed for Greece.

"I remember the moustache," Liana said of her first meeting with her father, "that enormous moustache. He was a tall man, Aphinotis. But everything else in the village seemed so small, after London. We went to his village in the north, you see. Aghios Stephanos." Liana nodded toward the mainland across the straits from Corfu Town. "Where he was born."

Aphinotis, however, found himself an outsider in Aghios Stephanos: he hadn't lived in the village for some twenty years; had barely been heard from during the long years of wandering, war, prison and exile; had no house, no land, no work. Aphinotis, Fiona and Liana lived with his aunt and uncle, around whom Liana was far more at ease than she was with Aphinotis. It wasn't that Aphinotis was not good to her, Liana said; he doted on her, in fact adored her. But the strain between him and Fiona doomed any bridge over the enormous gap of time and cultures which separated father and child. "Who is this man?" Liana recalled the child Liana wondering to herself. She had known Aphinotis was her father, known it like she'd known God lived somewhere in the sky, but to *feel* him as her father she was just never able to do.

Liana stopped speaking and looked off, somewhere else. Their ouzos arrived and for a time they sipped in silence.

"It's the *idea* of a father," Jonas said after a while. "You can't embrace a man as your father if you don't really know what a father is. That's just the way the world shaped itself around you. And maybe that shape makes as much sense as any other. I mean, what are the rules, anyway?"

It was several moments before Liana spoke. "You mean, the pain from losing something important can be erased . . . by simply deciding it was unimportant?"

Jonas held down a swell of defensiveness. "Okay, you feel bad that you don't have certain feelings you think you're supposed to have. But what the hell does 'supposed to' mean?"

Liana stared at him, then drained her glass and looked away. Jonas got up, went inside the cafe and returned with two more ouzos, which they drank without speaking. Finally they managed to release each other by getting up and heading, a bit unsteadily, for the sea wall. They sucked in salt air and sea smell, let themselves be lulled by the lapping water on the stones below; the blue-black sky and breeze off the water were soothing after the heat and noise of the holiday crowds. As they shared a cigarette, Jonas looked down at the ancient sea baths. A small tug-like vessel waited at a nearby landing: the boat to the mainland. Liana saw it, too.

Moving around the promontory, they passed the former royal palace and came out onto one end of the long main esplanade and its brightly lit arcade. As they faced the crowds again, Liana took his arm. It was not something she had done before.

They crossed into town but soon were overwhelmed by the human tide roiling between the esplanade and the port. Ducking into a quiet alleyway, they found a *taverna* with two small tables outside. But just as they sat down, a crowd of people came out of the *taverna*, a man closing the shutters and door behind them. Jonas took out his watch and realized that it was time for the evening *Epitaphios*. He and Liana went back into the crowds and found themselves an observation spot.

The *Epitaphios* was a much larger, more organized and solemn procession than those of the individual churches in the afternoon. Bearers of ten-foot candles, flames encased in gilded cages, were at the point, more candle bearers stretching far back along both sides. Immediately behind came the bishop in golden robe and miter, flanked by high clergy in multi-color vestments and by a like number of high-ranking military and police. The bishop blessed the faithful as he passed; many older women in the crowd crossed themselves repeatedly, appearing at once reverent and ecstatic. Following the bishop and the officers came more clergy and local dignitaries, then the *Epitaphios* itself, a bier representing the body of Christ, wreathed in spring flowers and sheltered by an ornate fringed canopy. And on a tall stanchion immediately behind the *Epitaphios* was the ubiquitous emblem: the bayonet-wielding shadow-soldier superimposed over the phoenix rising from flames. Bier, canopy and surrounding candles all were carried by quite real soldiers; their heavily armed brethren lined the route.

When the procession had passed, the crowd spread out through the lanes, some heading for church, some to homes or cafes, some for one more *volta* around the town. Jonas and Liana retreated to the *taverna* in the quiet passageway which they had spotted just before the *Epitaphios*. The door and shutters were open again and Jonas went in.

The low-ceilinged room pulsed with the heat and smoke of an olive wood fire and Greek cigarettes, with the gabble and barks of drinkers and eaters and cooks. As in many a *kafeneion* and *taverna*, it was difficult to distinguish patron from *padrone*, but a sloe-eyed man with a growth of beard finally spoke from a table: "*Oriste?* You pleasure?" Jonas asked for a bottle of retsina and a dish of tzatziki, the yoghurt with cucumber and garlic that cools the mouth and lines the stomach. Outside he found Liana sitting, looking up through the dark. He settled himself, took a mouthful of bread and tzatziki and washed it down with a gulp of the resinated wine.

"Listen to that," Liana said, cocking her head.

Indecipherable band music not exactly Greek, not exactly anything—drifted down from the night sky. Peering along the Venetian buildings which formed the narrow lane, they tracked the sounds past peeling paint and whitewash, green and blue shutters opened to the evening air, iron grillwork balconies dotted with geraniums. Finally they located it coming from third-floor windows almost directly above them.

"A phonograph?" Liana puzzled.

"Well, if it is, that record is warped to shit."

They listened for a moment.

"Nah," Jonas decided. "Even warped, no one would have made a record that sounded like that."

The two of them listened as the mystery music stopped, started, repeated itself over and again. Jonas stretched his legs, filled their glasses and drank, gazed up at the balconies, watched several families stroll by. When he turned back to Liana, she had slipped into a distant silence. He'd seen it several times over the previous couple of days but knew neither where it came from nor what to do about it. It disturbed him, but he wouldn't ask: he'd never attended the "You have to talk about it" school; things come out when they're ready, he would say. And more, he still smarted from the curious sparring with her earlier in the evening at Dirty Dick's. So he left her alone now, wherever it was she had gone. Besides, he sensed that the silence might have little to do with him. Which disturbed him, too.

He went inside to fetch another bottle of retsina, and when he got back Liana had returned from her private world as mysteriously as she had entered it. She smiled, but Jonas looked severe, trying silently to chastise her for her withdrawal. As he refilled their glasses, the phantom band struck up a new tune, and after a few particularly discordant bars, Jonas looked up and grimaced: "Why do they bother?"

"Does one have to play well in order to play?"

"Depends . . . on what they want to play for."

"Mm. . . . I've played since I was a little girl—piano. Not particularly well, mind you." Liana looked up toward the mystery band. "But it's the playing, you see."

Jonas took a long drink of the wine. "You sound . . . like someone I used to know." He thought about his wife, about her separate studio apartment. "She always kept a place to play. Piano, I mean. Well, not just for the piano. Tried to teach me to play once, too. Didn't last, though."

"Oh?"

"Me and piano, I mean. Well . . . anyway, I knew it was too late. If it wasn't going to go anywhere . . ."

"Where did it have to go?"

"No, it didn't, but . . . when I'd play, see, I'd be hearing in my head what the music was supposed to sound like. Actually heard it. And . . . I'd have to stop playing."

The band above them stopped.

"Knowing before doing," Liana said. "How do you learn to unknow?"

The top of Jonas's head was burning: from having spoken about his wife; from having spoken about himself; from not having spoken enough about either. Not to mention all the wine. He gulped another glass.

"Perhaps we should see about the bus," Liana said.

Jonas rose slowly under the weight of retsina and memories; he went into the *taverna* to pay. Forty *drachmes*—a buck and a quarter—for two bottles of wine plus tzatziki and fresh bread. And this was in the "big town," expensive compared to Glaros. As they weaved toward the square where the buses departed for the hill villages, Jonas began to think about how long, how very long he could stay in Greece with the money he had brought for the aborted visit to his wife's relatives in Italy. True, it was all the money he had in the world, but what would there be for him to spend it on . . . if he went back?

Three buses were waiting to leave the square, each filled to overflowing. Jonas and Liana found the bus for Glaros, Mikhalis at the wheel, and joined eight or ten people crowding outside the front door, a similar group pushing at the rear. No more could possibly fit, yet somehow one then another managed to edge their way on, accompanied by much loud complaining both from those on the bus and from those yet to make it on. Mikhalis repeatedly called out that the bus could hold no more, that it was leaving, but he didn't close the doors.

Jonas, Liana and a couple in rough-hewn black clothes were the only ones left outside the front when Mikhalis started the engine. The packed step up was a problem for the very short woman, though she might have managed it better were one hand not fervently clutching an icon. Mikhalis again called out imminent departure and the woman redoubled her efforts to get on while her husband, Jonas and Liana tried to help her from behind. Suddenly, a young soldier with bulging bags of holiday sweets shoved his way past them and began roughly to push those already on the steps in order to make room for himself. The short woman lost her balance and almost fell.

"Hey, man!" Jonas said with enough vehemence to get over linguistic barriers. But the soldier gave him only a cursory glance before pushing himself up and onto the bottom step. When the man in black had steadied his wife, he said something gruff to the soldier and began to try again to help his wife onto the bus. The soldier, obviously in his cups, was leaning heavily against the door frame and made no effort to leave room for the four still outside. The tiny woman stepped back, shaking her head and mumbling, and tugged her husband's sleeve away from the bus.

"Soldiers have priority," Liana explained quietly to Jonas.

"Priority? What the fuck is that?" But as soon as the words were out of his mouth, Jonas could see himself in some ridiculous escalating hassle over a place on a bus he didn't even really care about getting on. And although the soldier's aggressive stupidity cried out to be deflated, Jonas knew that whatever he would let loose toward the soldier might not easily be contained and could irrevocably rend what he and Liana had managed to weave together on this long and churning day. However much it would grate him to let it pass, in this brief moment of decision, let it pass he did.

The man in black, however, said one thing more, something which caused the soldier to turn and face him. Despite his uniform and his youth, the soldier was uncertain: the man was twice the soldier's age, but a man from the hills who looked earthen solid under his awkward holiday suit. The soldier hesitated, then from the relative safety of his perch on the step sneered words of bravado which caused the tiny woman to cross herself repeatedly.

People on the bus were leaning out the windows, wide-eyed; a small crowd was gathering to watch. The man in black put a foot up on the bus step and jabbed a finger at the soldier's chest, growling "*Malaka!*" at him, and "*Kerata!*" People on the bus gasped at the curses which Jonas had learned in far more playful contexts from Nosey—Jerk-off! Cuckold!

Mikhalis waved at Jonas and Liana to back away from the trouble. But having resolved that this mess wasn't worth getting into, the idea of anyone else wading in further now seemed to Jonas equally foolish. So he stepped forward to edge the man in black away from the soldier. Just as Jonas moved close, however, four men in uniform burst through the crowd, grabbed Jonas and the man in black and slammed them against the side of the bus. Jonas just managed to turn the blue-eye side of his head away. His nose took the brunt of the blow and he slumped to the ground; two of the men pulled him up by the arms and held him.

Vaguely he heard Liana's desperate voice: "*Parakalo, parakalo. Dthen katalavenei. Dthen xeirei.*" One of the men answered in rapid Greek and Liana immediately switched to English, repeating her plea: "He doesn't know; he doesn't understand. Please. He doesn't understand."

Blood streaming from his nose, they turned Jonas around, twisted his arms behind him, and pulled him and the man in black away from the crowd. Mikhalis quickly closed the doors and drove the bus out of the square. Off to the side, the small woman in black stood weeping.

Two of the uniformed men dragged the man in black toward the far side of the square, out of Jonas's view; the other two hauled Jonas to a wall and propped him up. Liana followed close behind, speaking to them rapidly, without a breath, her hands moving at the speed of her words: "Please. He doesn't know. He doesn't understand."

The men in uniform were unmoved and kept Jonas's arms pinned behind him. He felt the blood streaming over his lips, tasted it in his mouth, sensed it at the back of his throat. From across the square, a man in a suit now appeared and the men in uniform turned Jonas toward him.

"I assure you he meant no harm," Liana raced on, now addressing the man in civilian clothes. "He thought the soldier pushed me, an insult, you see.... A mistake, of course.... A Greek soldier wouldn't push a woman, and a visitor..." She became self-deprecating: "My husband... our honeymoon, our marriage holiday... just married, you see. Just now. And we've come to Corfu... the beauty of Greece..." She clasped her hands and rocked them against her breast. "Just married and an insult, you see.... What would you have done, Greek men, an insult to your wife, your new wife?... I can tell you are men, you would have done the same." Her voice rose with emotion. "A matter of honor, you'd have made him apologize... just as my poor husband tried to do." She softened. "Of course, he was wrong, my husband.... We don't understand about Greece's soldiers.... We are just tourists. We don't understand these things.... Stupid tourists.... My husband..."

Liana fluttered her hands in a gesture which at once implied despair, frustration, a plea for compassion and a conspiracy of understanding with the men. Jonas's pounding head removed things to a great distance, but even through fear and pain and rage he could tell that Liana's performance was a work of art.

The man bought it. At his signal, the two uniforms relaxed their grip. The man put his scowling face close to Jonas's but addressed his words to Liana. "Yes, there are things you do not know. This is . . . a new Greece. Here you must understand what is right and what is not right. A soldier keeps Greece free. And so a soldier must always go first. This is the law. And what is right." His voice became unctuous: "Of course, you are strangers here. Our guests. But you must have good manners, eh? You make a mistake; you learn by it. This is how life is. You are tourists? Visit Greece like tourists. Understand?"

The man pulled up Jonas's shirttail and used it to wipe some of the blood from Jonas's face.

"There. Now he is nice again. Go on. Go and be tourists." The others released Jonas's arms. The man looked Liana up and down, then for the first time spoke directly to Jonas: "Go and buy something for your wife."

Liana helped Jonas out of the square. He leaned against an alley wall and swiped feebly at the blood on his face. Liana wet her fingers and cleaned him up a bit. He winced with pain.

"Thanks." They both knew he meant her act with the police more than the cleanup of his face.

He felt his nose: "Not broken, anyway." Liana looked doubtful. "Well, not really. Believe me, I'm an expert."

Liana clucked and lit a cigarette for him. He took a drag, blew it out slowly and slid down the wall to the ground. Liana slid down next to him. They smoked and were quiet. The adrenaline slowed. Imagining now where all this might have led was enough to chill Jonas's anger and to crack Liana's composure. They both shivered.

"Now what?" she finally said.

"A recurring question, it seems." A new stream of blood came from his nose.

"What a mess. Look at you."

"You know, it might not seem like it to most people," Jonas said, "but a nose can be a dangerous thing."

With the only bus now gone, they headed for the Old Port to find a room for the night. The Brooklys was full: "*To Pascha*"—Easter—shrugged the proprietor. Same story at the other port hotels.

It was very late and Dirty Dick's was closed but the night barman was still cleaning up inside. Happy to see Jonas again, he pulled out a bottle of local brandy. Jonas's head was pounding from his collision with the bus, and from all the ouzo and retsina he had poured down during the evening, but if he was to ask for help finding a room, he couldn't refuse a drink first.

They sipped the rough brandy and Jonas told the barman briefly of his move to Glaros; he volunteered nothing of his relationship with Liana—he would have been hard-pressed to describe it in any event—or about his battered face. The barman eyed them with ill-concealed curiosity, but it was no challenge—impolite, in fact—to ask directly. You ferret, you wheedle, you trick into revelation. But you do not flat-out ask. And so the barman settled in for the long, slow process of drinking and probing.

Jonas cut things short by explaining their predicament. Furrowing his brow, the barman waved an arm: "No problem." They finished their brandies and the barman walked the weaving couple into the *platea*, where a half-dozen people remained under the trees. It was now so late that along the road lights were still on in only one cafe. The barman sat Jonas and Liana at a table and with twinkling eyes that belied his straight face asked how many beds they needed. Jonas's mouth opened but nothing came out; he didn't look at Liana. She blurted, "Ah, two," though more in reaction than decision, it seemed. The barman permitted himself a little smile at having elicited such a telling piece of information. "*Dthio Metaxes*, Costa," he said to someone at the next table, ordering yet another round of brandies, then left on his errand of mercy.

Jonas and Liana sat without talking: the soldier and his priority; Jonas's misunderstood intervention; the security police, or whatever they were—it was too soon to speak of these things . . . or of the pulse-quickening question of beds.

A man came up and set two large glasses of brandy in front of Jonas and Liana. Jonas stared at the liquor: another hill to climb. The fumes seeped through his swollen nose and reflexively he picked up the glass and took a sip. His stomach turned a flip but after a moment of doubt landed right side up. The alcohol already in him was serving to numb not only his battered face but also myriad other discomforts which at the moment he did not even want to identify. He drank again.

Costas, the man from the next table who'd brought their latest round of brandies, called to them: "Is coming for you something very special."

"*Epharisto*," Jonas and Liana thanked him in advance, though for what they didn't know.

Someone carrying a tray now emerged from the lighted cafe, came over and set down a basket of bread and a plate of unidentifiable food. "*Oriste*," the man said, beaming at the anonymous plate. "Very special." He noticed Jonas's puzzled expression. "*Chtapodthi*," he said, as if stating the obvious. "*Kali orexi*—good eating."

"*Chtapodthi?*" Jonas echoed when the man had moved off.

"Octopus," Liana said. "Very special."

Jonas could now make out two tentacles, each about ten inches long. With throbbing, swimming head and churning stomach Jonas now faced the brandy and a purple-gray octopus. He recalled the old childhood query "Would you rather be deaf or blind?" then cut into one of the tentacles. He held up the piece—white inside gray—as if it were an experimental drug he'd been told would either cure him or kill him, closed his eyes and took a bite. The texture surprised him: firm, almost crunchy. And the taste quite mild. When the olive oil, lemon and herbs kicked in, Jonas's mouth brought in a verdict of delicious. He had several more bites and followed them with a careful sip of brandy.

"*Endaxi*"—Okay—the barman said upon his return. "Everything fixed up.... Ah, *chtapodthi*. Very special."

At the barman's urging, Jonas and Liana reluctantly finished their brandies. Then, by some mutual assent that Jonas noticed only after the fact, he, Liana and the barman got up: no easy task. As Jonas fumbled for money, the barman spoke to the man who had brought the octopus; the man gave a brief reply. "Costas say they are finished... closed," the barman translated. "You can't pay to somebody if they are closed, eh? ... *Pamay*—we are going."

The barman led Jonas and Liana off through dark twisting lanes, the couple stumbling behind like addled lemmings. At a vaulted doorway, he told them to wait, disappeared inside, and in a moment returned, accompanied by a woman.

"Katia," he said. "She takes you a room. Students' room, but they go for *Pascha*. She is my cousin. *Endaxi?*—Okay?"

Jonas and Liana heard only part of what he said but got the gist and were too far gone to respond with anything more than a grunt.

"*Endaxi*," the barman answered his own question. "*Kali nichta*—good night." He gave Jonas a pat on the back.

The woman led them to a room on the second floor, opened the door and said simply, "*Oriste*"—Here it is.

A bed and a small cot. Jonas looked at Liana but he had no time to negotiate. Ouzo and retsina; his nose; brandy and octopus. He had to lie down—right now—and toppled onto the cot.

The room was spinning. He was vaguely aware of Liana on the bed a few feet away. He managed to pull off his clothes and heard Liana turn the covers on the bed. Moving his head, he saw her long body unfolding on the white sheet. But instead of letting the covers drop over herself, she held them up. "Sleep over here?" she slurred.

Jonas's head pounded doubly hard. Gathering his strength, he willed himself over to the bed and crawled in next to her. Her arm slipped over his shoulder and he drew in his breath at the touch of her thighs, the warmth of her skin against his. Her other arm curled across his back, hand resting on his hip, and they were an immediate fit, locked into place by the tremendous weight of their limbs.

It was very still. Liana breathed deeply and steadily. Her face was turned; Jonas could see the tiny vein quivering in her neck. From a great distance, he heard a low groan and somewhere below his pounding, spinning head he felt a growing heat. But it was so far away. Liana moved slightly and nestled her head into the crook of his arm. He looked down at her . . . and she was out. He closed his eyes to feel her skin against his . . . and they were both out.

8

Liana stood by the partially opened shutters looking out at the morning. She saw Jonas awake now and moved over to him, reached down to place healing fingertips on the swelling of his face, then picked up her sandals, said "Coffee" and went out.

A less sympathetic greeting awaited Jonas when a minute later he tried to sit up. Headache is a pitifully pale term to describe the steel talons sunk deep into his skull. His nose and cheek were swollen and burning and his green eye partially shut, but the eye was seeing all right and nothing seemed to have been permanently rearranged by his collision with the side of the bus. Eventually he stood up and creaked to the window where Liana had been standing: framed by the washed-out pastel buildings was the cheering blue of the sea. But the sea suddenly reminded him of Liana's thoughts about a boat to the mainland, and as hurriedly as his head would allow, he dressed and went down the stairs.

As he emerged from the hotel onto the Old Port, he stopped to scan the *platea*. Liana and the barman were just coming out of Dirty Dick's next door. But instead of sitting, they pressed themselves against the cafe wall. Then Jonas noticed that people all around him were also flattening themselves against building walls.

Church bells rang the hour. The barman and Liana spotted Jonas and waved their arms frantically. Too late: without warning there was an explosion on the ground nearby, then another and another. With shards flying past his legs, he dove for a wall and covered his head in panic. After a moment, though, he realized the explosions were not terribly loud. Then noticed people watching him and chuckling. He looked up to find heads in all the upper windows, arms flinging things out and down to the streets, people along the walls cheering what Jonas now recognized was a hail of crockery.

In a minute the bombardment stopped and people threaded their way through the ceramic wreckage, talking animatedly. Jonas picked his way over to Dick's, where Liana and the barman were waiting for him, barely able to conceal their glee.

"No, not funny.... Okay. So, what the hell was all that?"

The barman grinned. "To scare away the evil eye. But the priests, they don't like talk about the evil eye, so they say it's to be angry at Judas. And also it's the time the *Pascha* lambs are..." The barman dragged his thumb across his neck.

Jonas scowled at Liana: "What are you smiling at?"

She let out the laugh she had been holding. "There's a bus to Glaros at noon."

"Well," Jonas looked around at the wreckage, "don't tell them in New York... but you know, some time out in the boondocks doesn't sound too bad right now."

Back in Glaros, Jonas shrugged off Nosey's distress at his swollen face: "Little bus accident. No big deal." Still, Nosey was contrite, as if it were somehow his fault Jonas looked like that, and promised to squire them more carefully at the midnight mass celebration in town that night.

Despite his dismissive reply to Nosey, Jonas's head was killing him and so, awkwardly, he took his leave of Liana. Heading for his room, he felt like a schoolboy after a first kiss: he shared with Liana the knowledge of their long evening together, and their night even closer together, without understanding what it meant or might become. He lay down and tried a spell of Nosey's not-thinking, but Liana... his wife... the police... Kalliope and Alekos the fiddler... all insisted on whirling by until finally he was rescued by his body's exhaustion and fell deeply asleep until evening.

When Jonas awoke, Korina's *taverna* was bustling with preparations for the end-of-Lent meal which was to follow midnight mass.

"Oh, lovely," Liana admired the ugly bruise which had spread across Jonas's face.

"Easter bonnet," he replied.

"Are you certain you're ready for more of Corfu Town?"

"Hey, come on. In New York, this is how you look when you had a good time the night before."

Nosey came out of the *taverna* along with wonderful smells from the kitchen and Jonas realized he hadn't eaten anything since the few snippets of octopus the night before. "Say, Nosey, there time for a bite of something before we head into town?"

"Ooiy, it's still *Nisteia*—Lent—'til midnight," Nosey reprimanded. "You'll be gettin' plenty of snap when we get back."

Korina emerged from the *taverna* drying her hands on her apron; she frowned at Jonas's swollen face.

"*Kanai kala*, Jonaki?" Making an endearing diminutive of his name, she asked if he was all right.

"*Kala kala*"—Fine, fine—he reassured her. Korina was too tired to press the matter and dropped onto a chair next to Liana. She studied the younger woman, then touched a hand to Liana's cheek.

"Since when do you believe in Lent, Nosey?" Jonas asked.

"You what? Just 'cause I ain't gone to no church?" He paused and looked at Korina. "She don't go to church, neither, and she been on Lent now six years runnin'. Every bleedin' day."

"Lent for six years?"

"Yeah. Some people gives up meat—she gives up church. Ever since them army mugs says it's a Greece for Christian Greeks, she says must be she's a different kind of Christian. So, church is right out. . . . Ain't easy for her, neither."

Korina listened intently, although she spoke no English. Then she said something quietly in Greek.

"'Life is now Lent,'" Nosey translated.

"It'll be worth the wait," Liana assured Jonas. "The *magheiritsa*, they've been making it all day. Korina even got me into the act."

"That's the special lamb soup to wind up the Lent with," Nosey explained. "Hearts, brains, gizzards . . . all the inside bits."

"Terrific," Jonas said, his bruise turning slightly green.

Once again Jonas and Liana rode into town in the back of the tricycle. The last mile took longer than the first ten: cars, trucks, motor scooters, bicycles, donkey carts and foot traffic packed the roads. The jam was so thick that many people simply abandoned their vehicles around the outskirts of town and walked in; Nosey's friend managed to get their tricycle as far as the Old Port *platea*.

The numbers seemed to have doubled since the night before. Each worshipper now carried a beribboned candle; Jonas, Liana and Nosey bought theirs from a street vendor and joined thousands of celebrants who pressed their way toward the great esplanade. As the hour passed eleven, Nosey led Jonas and Liana to an alleyway just off the covered arcade that ran the esplanade's entire length.

"Special accommodations," Nosey said. "Very posh."

They went through a wide, high-arched doorway into a marble foyer and climbed four flights past large polished double doors on each landing. In a cul-de-sac on the top floor was a window with an outside ladder. They climbed out and up to a roof with a panoramic view of the entire esplanade—three hundred meters by a hundred—and of the massive Venetian fortress behind it. A large open gazebo in the center had been wreathed with flowers and lit by candelabra. People completely blanketed the esplanade now, some angling for a view of the procession to come, some to get close to the gazebo, some for the best look at the crowd: greetings were exchanged, children admired, friends and family saluted. Flapping above the crowd from a long pole on the gazebo's peak was a giant banner of the phoenix.

As midnight approached, the sea of celebrants on the esplanade reached many thousands strong. The holy procession now came into view and the crowd's collective excitement billowed up to the roof where Jonas's trio was perched. Flanked by soldiers bearing enormous candles, the bishop and high clergy in magnificent vesture led military officers, monks and political notables through the crowd. When the procession neared the gazebo, all lights on the esplanade were extinguished, evoking an excited gasp from the throng. The crowd hushed as bishop and retinue climbed into the circular enclosure and arranged themselves for the mass. The candle bearers ringed the gazebo and torches on each pillar were lit; in the suddenly dark and silent night, the gazebo became a blaze of holy light.

The bishop began the mass by leading the clergy in a series of haunting, dolorous chants and the huge crowd swayed with the rhythms of the liturgy. A long spoken prayer, then an uplifting chant, were followed by another hush. With a flame from the altar, the bishop lit a candle held by a monk, who in turn lit candles held by priests on the gazebo steps, the flame then passing down and multiplying through the crowd. From high on the roof, Jonas, Liana and Nosey watched the light spread out in all directions, sweet candle scents wafting up to mix with the caresses of night-blooming jasmine and blossoming *kika* trees. As the esplanade continued to brighten with spreading candle flames, a buoyant chant and the crowd's anticipation rose on the soft night air, tingling Jonas's skin. Nosey lit their candles. Liana's face was radiant, her eyes glittering with the reflected light.

The chanting stopped and the multitudes drew a collective breath. The lone voice of the bishop intoned an impassioned prayer, then in an exquisite, expectant silence the cathedral bells rang midnight and the bishop called out with unrestrained emotion: *"Christos anesti! Christos anesti!"* Cannons fired from the fort while over and again the bishop cried, *"Christos anesti!"*—Christ is risen!—and the thousands thundered in response, *"Alithos anesti!"*—He is risen indeed!

When the antiphony and cannonade finally finished, people hugged all around in joyous release. Somewhere a band struck up a rousing if not entirely melodious song. Jonas and Liana smiled; they recognized that it was the ragged music they'd heard being practiced the night before. Slowly the exultant, babbling crowd began to filter out of the esplanade. "Bleedin' good show, eh?" Nosey grinned.

By the time Jonas, Liana and Nosey made their way through the crowds to the parked tricycle, the port was clogged by a traffic mash of monumental proportions, everyone champing to return to their Lent-ending feasts. The hive of vehicles struggled in all directions at once, cars and tricycles and small farm trucks, of every vintage and level of engine noise and exhaust fumes, vying with carts drawn by increasingly distressed animals while scooters and bicycles squeezed into every remaining crevice. The only tactic amid the crush seemed to be to establish and hold an angle over the closest other vehicles, so that while there was sporadic minimal movement, actual progress in any given direction was regularly lost to the imperatives of each local battle.

Frustrations were mounting. Arms waved with greater frequency and vehemence; cart drivers rose higher and higher off their seats. And the noise steadily grew, a combination of increasingly complex cursing, desperate animal braying, and the furious revving of engines and banging on vehicle hoods and doors. Inevitable bumped fenders and cart wheels created several special knots of turmoil.

Into the mess stepped a tall, imperious policeman. Jonas watched him make his way to the approximate middle of the Old Port road—since the entire *platea* was completely covered, the road itself was purely a matter of conjecture. The policeman surveyed the scene, directed an officious finger at the nearest car and blew his whistle. Given a total inability to move, however, the driver could not possibly have known what the whistle meant him to do. The cop blew in another direction with the same utter lack of effect. Soon he was turning this way and that, blowing, gesturing and staggering among cars and carts trying to get a response. The exasperated drivers soon invented one: when the policeman blew, drivers behind would honk, spinning the infuriated cop round and round, trying in vain to catch someone in the mocking act.

Jonas and Liana enjoyed the comic opera from the open back of the tricycle. Nosey and the driver, though, were anxious to get back to Glaros; Nosey leaned out the window and said they would try for a narrow strip of wharf beyond an abutment. With Nosey navigating and shouting, the tricycle made daring if incremental maneuvers, Nosey and friend taking pleasure in the struggle as if it were a good sporting event: when the tricycle managed to cut off a neighboring vehicle, Nosey would grin and give thumbs up to Jonas and Liana.

Amidst all the angling and shouting and lack of progress, the game of blind cop's bluff helped to keep up the crowd's mood. But soon other police, led by a severe thin man in plain clothes, picked their way through the jam and huddled around the embattled whistle blower. Jonas could see the original cop's rage as he reported what had been happening. The plainclothesman gave orders and with ready batons the police began to roam through the crowd. Now when a more or less legitimate horn sounded or someone failed to move when whistled, a cop would bang his truncheon on the car or cart or poke it at the driver. A car near Jonas and Liana briefly tooted at an impinging truck and immediately a cop came up, shouting; the cop moved away only after giving the driver a nasty baton blow on the shoulder.

The police went on harrying the crowd while ignoring the traffic jam itself, but the tricycle made it to and across a berm that protected the wharf's edge and then rolled alongside the water toward the far end of the port. Jonas looked back to see the plainclothes cop now standing on the hood of a motionless car, pointing out drivers on whom the other cops were to mete out justice. Finally the tricycle reached the road that led away from the port. The last thing Jonas saw behind him was two policemen dragging a man off his cart, their truncheons going up and down, up and down.

Glaros was bubbling with life when the tricycle finally pulled in around three in the morning. All the village lights were on and spirited voices could be heard celebrating the end of the Lenten fast. Korina's and Leonides's extended family was gathered at a long table outside the *taverna*. Nosey, Jonas and Liana were greeted with salutes of "*Kalo Pascha!*"—Happy Easter! Jonas and Liana were welcomed to the family table without hesitation or formality.

The wine and laughter flowed freely as about twenty adults and children ate steaming bowls of *magheiritsa* soup and picked favorite pieces from platters of grilled lamb and goat innards. Korina hovered around the table directing the movement of food and drink while Jonas and Liana sat among a chattering of children, their almost total lack of shared language somehow failing to dampen conversation. When the meal slowed after an hour, Korina said something to Leonides, who raised himself on his crutch. The table quieted. Leonides looked around solemnly and lifted his glass: "*Ston ghio.*"

"To the son," Nosey translated quietly. "Korina's son. Me best mate, since we was little. Been out the country, see. Ain't no one seen him since ... all the villainy."

The families drank a salute and after a moment's quiet reflection resumed the meal. Liana helped Korina bring more food and wine. Then the instruments came out. Leonides played slow, quiet tunes on a fiddle, accompanied by his brother-in-law on a *bouzouki* and a cousin on an *aulos* pipe. Children dropped off to sleep and were carried home, and as night became morning the revelers all headed for a few hours' sleep before rising again for Easter. Jonas was among the last, mesmerized by the wine, the music and the familial warmth. He watched Korina speak quietly to Liana, touching her cheek. The next thing he knew, Liana's mouth was next to his ear.

"*Kali nichta, Jonaki mou*"—Good night, my little Jonas—she breathed. "Sleep well."

Before Jonas could respond, she was threading her way through the chairs toward her cot at Mikhalis's.

⭐

By the time Jonas awoke and got to the *taverna*, Nosey, Korina, Leonides and his wife were preparing for the afternoon's feast. Leonides's daughter Elektra was weaving flowers into the trellised grape vines; a wreath of spring blossoms with a center of garlic hung above the *taverna* door. Movements were slow. Talk was quiet. Energy was conserved for the Easter meal to come. Jonas said his *kalimeras*—good mornings—and joined Elektra decking the trellis.

After a thick Greek coffee, Jonas asked what he could do to help and Leonides indicated the roasting pit, which had been dug in a small level area down a slope behind the *taverna*. A lamb and a young goat were roasting there on parallel spits over a fire of almond and olive wood. Leonides's brother-in-law sat with a large thatch of wild thyme and oregano tied to the end of a grape stake, which he would dip into a bowl of lemon juice and olive oil to desultorily baste the animals before they were turned. A cousin sat nearby with head in hands, occasionally feeding and poking the fire which had been going since the night before.

The men clearly had had little sleep and were glad for Jonas's arrival but neither was ready to admit that he was the one who needed relief or that his specific task—basting or fire-tending—could be handled equally well by someone else, particularly a foreigner. Jonas squatted between them while each gave him pantomime instruction in the secrets of his art. As one demonstrated the movements and timing of his job, the other would cluck softly or raise his eyes to the heavens. The men also had to instruct Jonas in turning the animals, which, since it required two people, was the subject of considerable dispute. The lesson soon degenerated into full-fledged argument, the gestures of which left no hands free for the tasks of roasting, and the moment, perhaps the entire Easter meal, was only saved when Leonides called his brother-in-law up to the *taverna*. So, Jonas assumed the basting mantle. At first, the remaining cousin smiled: it was the brother-in-law, and not he, who had abandoned the argument. Then the cousin frowned: it was the brother-in-law, and not he, who'd been relieved of his tiresome duty.

Jonas, on the other hand, literally warmed to his task. The morning sun loosened his joints and the heat from the fire drifted out of the pit to stroke his swollen face. The sounds and scents of crackling wood, of lemon, herbs and roasting meat were at once soothing and exhilarating. Gazing over the green hills and valleys to the blue Ionian Sea, Jonas felt the quiet thrill of taking true part in a world one has never before imagined.

Liana came down the path with an old shepherd who made his way with the aid of a polished wood staff. The old man took the cousin's fire-tending place and Liana sat down next to Jonas. Her sudden presence flustered him: her arrival yanked him out of his reverie but did not land him anywhere else. She had been so protean in their time together that he still did not know how to approach her. Yet here she was again, approaching him.

"How are you?" she asked.

He eyed her warily, trying without being too obvious to look at her alternately through the green eye, then the blue. For a few minutes he responded in monosyllables to her small talk, watching carefully for one of those sharp turns in her emotional road. But none was forthcoming; she chatted amiably about the morning air, the lamb and goat, the Easter festivities to come.

"You know," Jonas finally said, "one minute you're... I don't know... you're here. And the next minute..."

"Yes," she smiled, "I'm not certain if it's part of the disease or of the cure."

"Ah, what disease, exactly, are we talking here?"

"Exactly? I'm afraid I couldn't say exactly—there's no name for it. At least, not an accepted one."

"Therapeutically speaking," Jonas said.

She smiled, then gazed toward the sea. She was silent for so long that Jonas thought she must have left the conversation entirely, but then she turned and faced him.

"For the longest time I struggled to find the name for it . . . for what was missing for me." She chose her words carefully. "Naming things can be useful."

"Unless it's the wrong name," Jonas put in.

"True. And not committing to a name avoided that. Although merely avoiding what's wrong . . . But without naming it, defining it, I couldn't get a grip on it. Of course, the more human the problem, the tougher to define. People are just too complicated."

"Are they? I don't know." Jonas thought for a moment. "Maybe just specific to their own histories. Which is why naming is always off the mark. I mean, any term you use is just a name someone else used"—his voice was rising—"to summarize other people's separate pieces of life. And no way that can tell you what you need to know about yourself."

Jonas found his hands waving in the air. He grabbed the stake and basted the animals to close a soliloquy he had not intended. Liana stared at him with her head tilted, as if trying to see him from a different angle.

"You're right, you know," she finally said.

Jonas almost dropped the stick into the fire. Right? He wasn't even sure what he'd said.

"You see, I thought I understood enough to be helpful, at least to some people," she continued. "But nothing I knew seemed to fit myself. So I tried to hide from the not understanding. And that's not easy—you can't tell where to set up your defenses." She took a deep breath and looked around. "Somehow, though, these past weeks . . . things have just felt, I don't know . . . true. Not big Truth. But true. A sort of feeling . . . I don't want to define it; I just know when it's there. And when it isn't." She stopped and studied Jonas. "I call it . . . 'Alice.'"

"Alice? You mean, like . . . Alice?"

"The name, yes. It's just a name. But you see, it's *my* name for it, a name that *I've* given it. Alice."

Jonas couldn't hide his incomprehension.

"Because, you see, as soon as you say something like 'true' . . . or 'honest' . . . or 'natural,' you've got all kinds of problems. And you're bound to be wrong. I don't want to name the feeling and sell it to anyone. . . . I simply want to hang on to it."

"The feeling. . . . You mean, 'Alice.'"

She shrugged: "What do you think I should call it, 'Bob'?"

Sitting in the Greek sun on Easter morning, Jonas had to smile: he was so far from what he'd ever known that even understanding Liana somehow didn't seem impossible.

"And in my work, too," she went on, "something crucial was missing. Here were young people in periods of great doubt in their lives, and all I seemed to do was help them go a bit more capably back into the mire. But if I was helping fit them back into worlds they were right to be resisting . . . ?" She leaned forward on her haunches and spoke as if confessing a sin. "It always seemed there was something in the next room I pretended not to hear." She sat up straight again. "Maybe at some point I'll go back to it, the work. If I can stay a bit closer . . . to what's in the next room."

"Alice?"

Liana smiled: "I guess you could call it that."

Korina, Nosey and several others came down the hill to check on the roasting. The animals were undoubtedly close to ready but whether the exact moment had arrived was the subject of debate for another twenty minutes. Aunts and uncles and cousins gathered round and with huge knives sliced off tasting bits. Out of numerous opinions finally emerged a majority verdict, not necessarily that the animals were now cooked just right—there were still grumbling outlier opinions—but that now was the moment to eat. So, the animals came off the fire and onto wooden slabs the size of doors. Then came the traditional allotment of delicacies, with special honors for guests. Popping a whole testicle into the mouth was the greatest treat, Nosey said, a combination of good luck and epicurean delight. Fortunately, Jonas got a piece of tongue before the greater honor could be bestowed on him.

Whooping and shouting, the family carried the lamb and goat up the path, and despite occasional attempts to preserve order until the table was reached, hands repeatedly snatched pieces of crisp, herb-coated skin. The procession ended at the *taverna*, where the long outside table overflowed with spring bounty: bowls of tzatziki and pink *taramosalata*, a salty fish-roe salad; platters piled high with golden *tiropites* and *spanakopites*, cheese- and spinach-filled pockets of fillo dough; pyramids of deep green *aginares*, the wild artichokes Jonas had seen on his walks through the hills, with bowls of egg-and-lemon *avgolemono* mix in which to dip the leaves;

steaming bowls of *koukia*, emerald beans cooked with vermillion sweet peppers and masses of garlic; billowy clouds of freshly pressed *kaseri* and feta cheeses; mounds of deep purple olives; loaf upon braided loaf of *tsoureki tou Pascha*, the special glazed Easter bread with red-dyed eggs pressed into the braid; and endless bottles of local retsina and a garnet wine that Leonides himself had aged a full seven months for the occasion.

The eating and drinking was seamless, beginning before people sat down and proceeding without reference to courses or servings. Nosey sat between Jonas and Liana and gave a running translation of the table's boasts and banter, though this did nothing to slow his own contributions to the verbal fray nor to distract him from ingesting remarkable quantities of food. In fact, about the only time during the long afternoon that Nosey did not have something going in or coming out of his mouth was when the old shepherd stood and performed an exaggerated impersonation, his wooden staff a mock microphone. The old man's facial contortions, squeaks and squeals while stroking his naked scalp at first brought an eerie silence to the table, then produced a moment of raucous laughter. It took Jonas longer than the others but finally he, too, recognized the bald head and screeching voice from Xhirakos's television, the blustering speechmaker from the military coup anniversary broadcast.

Eventually people slowed under the weight of the food and wine. It was time for a long Easter *ipnos*. Nosey and Leonides stretched out under the trees; others were yawning and gathering children. Jonas also was sleepy but for the moment too comfortable to move, and so he simply leaned his chair back against the *taverna* wall.

He was jolted awake by the bang of his chair legs hitting the ground. Children were shouting in the village square below; the grown-ups were rousing themselves to see what the commotion was. Several older children came running up from the square, their faces wild with excitement. Leading the way was Elektra, Leonides's ten-year-old. Tears of joy streamed down her flushed face as she shouted, "Alekos! *Erchetai*! Alekos! Alekos *erchetai*!" All the other children were shouting now, too: "Alekos! *Erchetai*! Alekos! Alekos!"

Two people were painfully struggling up the lane toward the *taverna*: a long, thin figure draped over the shoulder of a shorter, stocky one who shambled as if trying as much as possible to avoid the shock of feet meeting ground. The tall one's legs dragged helplessly behind on the cobbles.

Leonides's wife cried out and rushed down the lane. Nosey stood transfixed, rubbing his eyes as if wondering whether he had yet wakened from his nap. Leonides pulled himself up on his crutch and balanced against the trellis, his mouth opening and closing. Near him stood Korina, rocking back and forth on her heels and nodding, nodding, her mouth set against her tears.

As the family reached and embraced the tall figure, Jonas could make out his face: Alekos the fiddler. The stocky one who'd been supporting Alekos now stepped back: it was Kalliope.

9

Jonas and Kalliope sat alone under the trellis in the early evening. Alekos—Korina's son, Nosey's boyhood friend—had been taken behind closed doors by his family, to be nursed and to begin bridging the six years he had been away. Kalliope, though, was from Crete; she knew no one here and was glad to have found her lanky American friend from the train and ferry.

Initially Kalliope was reluctant to speak of her and Alekos's treatment the past weeks in the hands of the authorities: she knew nothing, really, about Jonas, and conversations could be dangerous. But the fact that Jonas wasn't Greek made it easier: he had no scores to settle, no official favor to curry, was involved in no intrigues. And Kalliope needed to trust Jonas. She needed to talk.

"For me, was nothing," she said of her ordeal in the dungeon cells, though her drawn face and quivering voice betrayed a different truth. "But Alekos . . ."

Kalliope had at first been isolated in a dark cell, more a cement box than a room: no bed, no blanket, sewage seeping in from the corridor, where a hole supposed to serve as a toilet remained beyond reach. Out of the cell only once every few days, for interrogation, she was forced to live with her own excreta, with that of whoever had been in the cell before her, with the vermin it attracted.

And the interrogations. The security police knew little about her. The only apparent reasons for her detention were what seemed some kind of association with Alekos and a passport which showed that, like Alekos, she had left Greece shortly after the military junta's coup and had remained away the entire six years of its rule. Kalliope told them her home was a certain village in Crete where, in actual fact, a namesake cousin had lived an innocuous life before she, too, had left the country. So if the authorities checked, they would find nothing untoward in Kalliope's—that is, the cousin's—background. Though Kalliope did not say so to Jonas, he assumed she'd used this false identity because her own background was not so free from blemish.

Her interrogations had focused on Alekos and other Greeks whom Kalliope was suspected of having known in Germany. But more often than actual questions, Kalliope was simply tormented and abused, terrorized against opposition to the regime: she and her family were repeatedly vilified and threatened; she was humiliated by groping hands and batons and by lurid promises of what the soldiers of Greece would enjoy doing to her should the army finally be permitted to "fully operate" on "diseased" Greeks; and finally—here Kalliope's voice caught—they had given her "some small *phistikia*." Jonas didn't know the term, but Kalliope's words were tumbling out now and he didn't want to interrupt by asking for an explanation. Her body rocked back and forth and her head tilted to the side while she spoke, as if she couldn't quite bring herself to believe what she was describing.

Eventually Kalliope had been thrown into a larger cell with five other women who had also been detained upon reentering the country. None knew exactly why she was being held nor what might prompt her release. Two had been confined for months. None had been allowed contact with the outside. All had been abused and beaten.

There were four pallets and blankets in the cell; the women shared them in shifts. Their food consisted of one communal pot a day of watery gruel and a few chunks of stale bread. Normally, Kalliope explained, run-of-the-mill jail prisoners are fed by money or food packages from relatives, but since these five were all held incommunicado... A hole in the floor for waste was hopelessly clogged so that fetid water and feces formed a swamp in the middle of the cell. The women were all dehydrated, believing their small ration of drinking water came from the building's waste pipes. They had no water for washing, no ventilation, and no light but a single bulb which shined day and night. The only reason any of the women ever left the cell was to be interrogated.

Jonas listened incredulously. It wasn't that he was unable to imagine such official malevolence: he'd seen heads split open on picket lines and demonstrations, had friends maltreated in jails and was well aware that nightmare political prisons existed round the world. But he wasn't able to imagine it here, on this exquisite, quiet island. Or rather, he refused to imagine it here: if this, finally, might be a place where the world would not press *him* from all sides, how could it exact such a horrific price from anyone else? Until Kalliope's release, Jonas's belief that he had found safe ground and solitude had been so tenacious that he had ignored not only the chilling customs police, not only Nosey's and Leonides's battle-scarred histories, not only Xhirakos and the malignant television screen, but even the very nose, the battered and swollen nose, on his own face. Now his Eden was undeniably gone and, to his dismay and confusion, he felt a twinge of resentment at Kalliope and Alekos as bearers of the poisoned fruit.

Kalliope took a deep breath. But it was Alekos, she continued, with whom the security police had been most persistent. Alekos was first of all his father's son, Kalliope explained, and though the leftist Partisan had been dead for thirty years, his ghost remained an insult to the new Greece. Also, Alekos was a shame to the nation for having left after the coup and remaining away. And worse, the security police had reports that he frequented known hangouts for treasonous Greeks in Frankfurt. Alekos tried to explain that he was a musician, that these were merely the cafes where he could play his music, his Greek music. Oh yes, they knew the type of songs he played. And who, they wanted to know, played with him? What else went on there? What leaflets? Journals? Who wrote them? Where did they meet? Where did they work? . . .

The questions had been asked over and over, day after day, sometimes two or three times a day. Yet the questions themselves were a blessing; the periods in between were the curse. Unlike the sporadic brutality intended merely to intimidate Kalliope, Alekos's tortures were frequent, relentless and purposeful. His head was beaten repeatedly with a rubber truncheon, excrement-covered towels wrapped around his face to avoid telltale wounds. He was stripped and held naked for hours, his torturers—the special interrogator from Athens left the room during the more prolonged sessions—beating his genitals and prodding his anus, calling him names and threatening to emasculate him. And between these formal sessions, the torment continued: Alekos was not allowed to sleep, the guards frequently—but irregularly, so he never knew when to expect it—shining a bright light in his face, screaming insults at him or banging on his isolation-cell door.

Worst of all was the *phistikia*. Kalliope looked down as she again spoke the word, then saw that Jonas did not understand. "*Phistikia*," she repeated. "The *phalanga*, the beatings on the feets." Still Jonas did not understand. Kalliope took another painful breath. They hang you upside down, she explained, or with your legs over the end of a table. Then slowly, steadily, they lightly swat—not much more than a tap—the soles of your feet with a baton or braided cord. They swat and swat and your feet swell until they are no longer recognizable, until the pain is no longer in your feet but merely begins a journey there which reaches and wrenches every fiber of your body. Eventually your legs go numb; then they drop you onto the floor, drop you again and again onto the cement until the blood rushes back into your feet and the feeling there—the searing pain—returns. Then they hang you up again and the slightest tap is now excruciating. On and on they go, tapping, tapping, and finally stopping just before your swollen feet split open like overripe melons . . . or like *phistikia*—pistachios. That is, they are meant to stop just before.

Kalliope collected herself. She and Alekos had been released early that morning, she said. At the Hotel Brooklys they'd cleaned themselves as best they could; Alekos didn't want to go home, for the first time in six years, looking the way the junta's torturers had left him.

Kalliope fell silent and after a moment staggered away from Jonas like a sleeper who turns on the light and walks around the room to get distance from a nightmare. In a minute or so she returned; she wasn't yet ready to be alone.

Jonas hesitated to ask why it was they'd been let out. Afraid that their release might imply some capitulation he shouldn't address, Jonas stumbled around the edges of the matter. But Kalliope quickly understood, and explained. Early on, Alekos had tried to make a point with his interrogators by reporting that in Germany he had worked as a maintenance man at the communications center of a US Army base. He certainly could not be a subversive, he told the security police, if the US Army trusted him there.

Alekos's story had not impressed the security police and the beatings went on unabated. Several days later, however, a senior interrogator from Athens arrived. And when Alekos mentioned the names of several US officers he claimed to have worked for, the interrogator became interested. As it happened, this man as well as other Greek security officers had received advanced interrogation training at this same US Army center. A phone call to Germany now confirmed that Alekos had indeed worked at the base. So, in honor of the interrogator's halcyon days there, he decided to release Alekos and Kalliope. After all, it was Easter. Their release would be a gesture, the interrogator said while Alekos hung on the wall awaiting his next round of *phistikia*, in the spirit of the Resurrection.

⸎

There was no formal celebration that night. Just the family gathering again under the trellis to share in Alekos's return. Nosey was at Alekos's side the whole evening; Jonas would never have believed that Nosey could go so long without talking. Korina watched with pride, anguish and relief as her son Alekos received well-wishers. "Yes, *stin Kriti*," Kalliope said quietly to Jonas as Alekos was embraced by family and friends. "I must be to Crete, to my own home, very soon."

The night air cooled and the family moved inside the *taverna*. Though this was a more intimate gathering than the afternoon feast, Kalliope, Liana and Jonas were all made to feel welcome. Kalliope had shared pain with Alekos, so for her there was a place of honor, though she was teased good-naturedly as one of those "crazies" from Crete. Liana was given a special invitation by Korina—"*Ela*, Lianaki"—who led her by the hand into the *taverna*. And Jonas was connected as both Nosey's friend and Korina's boarder. Alekos seemed inordinately pleased, relieved even, that Jonas was in Glaros, a reaction that seemed odd to Jonas: their meeting on the ferry had been brief, and certainly Alekos had far more important things on his mind. Besides, it had been Kalliope rather than Alekos who had kindled a friendship on the train and ferry.

Leonides whispered to his daughter Elektra, who scurried off and returned with a fiddle. "*Opaah!*" several relatives exulted as the little girl handed it to Alekos. And when he touched bow to string there was a collective sigh, as if only now were they certain he had come home.

Alekos had difficulty with swollen hands but when Kalliope joined him with voice and *aulos* pipe they managed some simple, plaintive *kantades*, Alekos leading, Kalliope counterpoint.

Leonides brought out his own fiddle, the brother-in-law his *bouzouki*, and the music heated up. Tables and chairs were pushed aside to make room and several people linked arms and began to dance in an arcing line. To Jonas's surprise, Nosey was among the first onto the floor, his exuberant steps fueled not as much by wine as by the day's emotion. Soon Nosey brought Korina to the floor, then others joined the dipping, kicking line, all connected by arms draped over the neighboring dancers' shoulders. Even a game but gawky Jonas was eventually pulled into the line.

After a while Alekos said something and Kalliope, Leonides and the brother-in-law stopped playing. Alekos drew out several long, sweet notes, then almost imperceptibly increased the tempo until a lively melody was revealed and "Aaah" and "Bravo, Aleko" came from around the room. The new song revived flagging energies, the other musicians joined in, and everyone began dancing a lively *syrtos*. Leonides motioned to Elektra, who jumped to close the door and windows. Jonas found this curious since they often played music well into the night without such concern. He looked at Nosey, who said simply, "Panastakis." Jonas didn't know what he meant.

"Bloke who wrote the tune. Panastakis. Everybody knows his songs. But we ain't allowed to play 'em, see? Serious nick if the goons get wind of it."

"Why? What are they about?"

"About? Not a bleedin' thing. Just music. It ain't the songs, see. It's himself, Panastakis. Livin' off in Europe and tryin' these six years to get people interested in what all's been goin' on 'round here. So, the army lot, they up and put out a law on him: 'No more Panastakis.' Boof. Just like that—he don't exist. Banned his songs, smashed up all his vinyls, torched all the music. But... they ain't torched ol' Uncle Ned"—Nosey tapped his head—"least ways, not yet."

A new song began and a cousin stepped a lively solo. Korina tossed a plate in front of the dancer, shattering it on the floor as the others yelled, "*Opaah!*" Elektra quickly went out and closed the shutters over the windows that faced the village.

"*Spasimata*," Nosey said. "Not allowed to do that, neither. Too much fun, see. B'sides, plates is property. And destroyin' property is near a mortal sin here these days."

"Even if it's your own?"

"Sets a bad example, know what I mean?"

"But what about yesterday? In town?" Jonas wondered. "All those people throwing stuff out the windows?"

"Yeah, but that's for Easter, innit? Goons won't have a go at Easter. But this here, this is just people doin' things on their own, like. See, nowdays, well, there's plates . . . and then there's plates. Know what I mean?"

✳

The morning of St. George's day, last day of Easter festivities. Leonides didn't open The Bad, so Jonas joined the old men at The Good. He had just settled into a sunny seat when Liana approached and immediately began recruiting him to her purpose. It was the holiday still, she reminded, but there were no celebrations, just family visits. No place for them, so they should head off on their own, didn't Jonas think so?

He could only blink, no coffee having yet come out of The Good.

She told him of a beautiful cove she'd seen while hiking one day. A boat was the only way to get there, but she'd been up very early and had visited the old couple near whose cottage she'd slept her first week on Corfu; the couple had offered their dinghy.

Jonas squinted and tried to process the hues of her invitation.

"Good, that's settled," she said before he could say anything, and she showed him the picnic she'd gathered from the *taverna*: olives, feta, tomatoes, oregano, two bottles of retsina, and a bottle of newly pressed olive oil nearly the color of Jonas's green eye.

The old couple were waiting for them at the cottage. They showed how to operate the dinghy's ancient motor, gave a bottle of homemade wine, then headed up the hill to begin their holiday visits.

As the dinghy moved along the rocky coast, it was difficult for Jonas and Liana to speak over the motor and the slapping sea. Neither of them minded, though, the pleasure of sun and salt air sufficient by itself on this warm-breeze day stolen out of time. In a while they reached a cove tucked between two steep rock cliffs. Behind the white pebble beach not a cottage, shepherd or goat could be seen. Liana cut the motor, letting the dinghy glide to shore over a palette of pale blues and greens. In the shallows she jumped out and, cotton smock billowing around her waist, guided the prow of the dinghy onto the beach. They put the food in the shade, set the wine and retsina among sea-cooled stones at the water's edge.

"You know," Liana said, "once when Lord Byron was on a Greek beach, some cohorts suggested they hike up a hill to look for Homeric ruins. Know what he said? 'Antiquarian twaddle! Let's have a swim!'"

They stripped off their clothes and dove naked into the water. Jonas was floating languidly, wondering which of the several Lianas he might have on his hands this day, recalling Byron's club foot—no wonder he preferred a swim to a climb—when Liana surfaced next to him. "How about some of that lovely wine?" she said.

Liana snatched a bottle and they dropped themselves onto the pebble beach. As Liana took a drink, the sun turned the vermillion liquid to a golden rose; Jonas watched a stream of wine slip out the side of her mouth and join beads of water on her thigh. He took a long drink, too, the wine sweet and cool with a touch of salt from his lips, then stretched out on the warm white stones.

They were silent for a time. Liana sat up and took another drink. "I suppose this was the sort of thing Fiona and Aphinotis did once upon a time. . . . All I ever saw them do was argue."

Jonas could see muscles tightening in her arms and neck. She drank again, trying to loosen the knot between heart and head.

"Fiona and Aphinotis . . . ," she began once more.

During the war years and after, Liana related, Fiona had pulled together for herself something of a life apart from her adamantine family. Curiously, the mantle of sin she was forced to wear freed her from a measure of constraint: her unfathomable—to the family—and unrepentant love for the mysterious absent Greek, plus the undeniable existence of their child, brought to Fiona a universal censure which, since she could not overcome, she chose finally to disregard. She led what the family described as a "rather bohemian" existence in Soho, comporting herself as an independent—which at the time was enough to be deemed disreputable—woman. Fiona did, however, maintain a veneer of civility with the family: when invited on formal occasions, she and Liana heeded the call; she gratefully if painfully accepted tuition for Liana's boarding school; and she tried to refrain from conduct by which the family might be too broadly scandalized. After all, Liana said, Fiona was still English of a certain class.

When Aphinotis surfaced in 1949, however, Fiona's fragile balance was upended. She had forged a survivor's state of heart and mind without him. And though her life was still shaped by his existence, on most levels she had ceased to imagine him. Now, to find a place for him, she would have to create a new place for herself.

As soon as she, Aphinotis and Liana arrived in Aghios Stephanos, though, Fiona knew the mountain village would not be that place. She could not be a Greek village woman, yet there was no room there to be herself. Aphinotis fared little better. His years in larger worlds had rendered him unfit for Aghios Stephanos. The village knew it, too: his reputation as a free thinker and political agitator did not endear him to war-ravaged villagers who now only wanted bread and peace. So there they were, Aphinotis and Fiona, a man whose dreams had been shattered and a woman who no longer had any dreams, apart for ten years and now together in a place where neither could be at home. And there, too, was a nine-year old English boarding-school girl with the Greek name Liliana.

Within a short time Fiona began trying to convince Aphinotis to go with her to England but he argued that he had no place there. He had no place in Greece, either, Fiona retorted, and besides, she was an outsider in England, too. But no, Aphinotis replied, there was a difference: in England, Fiona would always be an outsider because she had no wish to get back in. But in Greece, Aphinotis was not so much an outsider as an outcast. He was outside because of what he believed in, Aphinotis said; Fiona was outside because she no longer believed at all.

Outcast, not outsider. Through the years Fiona had repeated the phrase many times to Liana, as if by saying it enough her daughter might comprehend a distinction she herself had never come fully to understand.

After two years in Aghios Stephanos, Liana and her mother returned to England without Aphinotis—Liana to boarding school, Fiona once again to Soho. But Fiona had lost her resilience. No longer impervious to backdoor treatment by the family, less willing to accept her lot quietly, she became both obstreperous and morose.

Aphinotis came to England, once. He spent a tumultuous few days with Fiona in London, then traveled to Kent to see Liana at school. It was all terribly stiff and confusing, Liana recalled, the boarding-school girl wrenched out of her rigidly structured life to meet again the tall, moustached Greek... in a tidy English tea room. Aphinotis stayed a night, had two brief, fraught visits with Liana, and was gone. Liana was twelve years old. She never saw him again.

Liana and her mother carried on, but Fiona grew increasingly disheartened. A year later Fiona announced they were moving to Canada. Liana had only the vaguest notion of Canada and was upset to leave the life she knew at school, but even at age thirteen she could sense her mother's desperation. Within weeks they were off to Toronto, where Fiona was to work in the art gallery of an old school friend who had married a wealthy Canadian businessman.

Liana adjusted well to life in Canada, particularly to the freedoms she discovered living at home and attending a municipal high school. She stayed in Canada for university but returned to England for advanced study. Over the years in Canada she received an occasional brief note from Aphinotis—whose English was fluent but whose ability to communicate meaningfully with his faraway daughter much less so—but he seemed to have no fixed abode and they fell out of touch after Liana returned to England.

Fiona was in failing health when Liana moved back to Toronto. There seemed to be no particular disease, just a "withering away of all the important parts," as Liana put it. And Fiona seemed resigned, showing neither fight nor grief. "She had nothing left of either," Liana said.

When her mother died, six years ago now, Liana sent a note to the aunt and uncle in Aghios Stephanos asking whether they were in contact with Aphinotis. Months later a cousin wrote in reply that the old aunt and uncle had both died and that the family had had no word of Aphinotis since Easter, shortly after the military junta took power. They had heard only that men had come to Aphinotis's room in Athens and taken him away. No one knew where.

Liana became quiet. Only when she went into the water again and he sat up to watch her was Jonas aware of the insistent beating sun and the equally insistent wine in his head. He followed her into the water and when they came out together he said, "I think I'd better eat something." He retrieved the food and the olive oil, which the shadows had by now abandoned to the sun. Liana pulled one of the retsina bottles from the water.

They laid out their feast on the pebbles, both of them happy for relief from the emotional weight of Liana's saga. Jonas ripped off hunks of bread; Liana cut into a ripe tomato. Bites of cucumber, onion and tomato alternated with olives and feta, sun-warmed olive oil poured over each bit of food just before it went into their mouths, coating their lips and fingers, dripping onto their legs. As they washed down the food with large swigs of retsina, the alcohol made it increasingly difficult to negotiate with oil-covered hands the crumbling feta, bursting tomatoes and slippery bottles. They laughed as a surge of oil missed some bread almost entirely and wound up on Liana's chest. She closed her eyes and rubbed the oil into her breasts. Watching her, Jonas finished off the bottle of retsina.

Liana brought the third bottle from the water and sat down facing Jonas, closer now, her legs under and grazing his. She wiped the oil from her fingers onto her calves and shins; the back of her hands brushed the underside of Jonas's legs. As she opened the wine, Jonas wiped his hands on his own legs, then lightly massaged his fingers' remaining oil into her calves. She looked at him evenly. Jonas reached for a cigarette; the movement brought them inches closer.

They shared the cigarette and several more sips of wine, not talking now, just occasional small noises in their throats. Liana bit into a tomato. juice and seeds streamed onto her shoulder. She laughed, legs moving under Jonas's, her heat, sweat and oil nudging his thighs. Slowly she turned her head and licked off the juice and seed. A little liquid still on her shoulder, Jonas reached up and worked it into her glistening skin. Liana exhaled slowly. Jonas caressed a bit of warm olive oil into her other shoulder, his hand gently exploring the textures of oil, salt and skin. Liana trembled and Jonas held his breath.

She settled again, then poured a bit of oil on her fingertips and began lightly to knead the flesh on his forearm, moving gradually up to his biceps, his shoulders. At some moments Jonas felt that she was drawing him to her, at others that she was carefully holding him away. He let his hands slide down her arms and along her ribs, her muscles quivering slightly as his fingers trailed to her hips. Barely touching her, he traced across the weightless golden down on her flanks, but as his hands neared the shadows of her thighs he saw the light in her eyes darken ever so slightly. He stopped. The delicate vein pulsed on her throat.

Liana reached for a piece of feta, squeezed the moist cheese between her fingers, covered it with oil and placed it on Jonas's lips. They laughed when bits of cheese and oil slipped from her fingers; Jonas breathed deeply as she spread the oil across his chest. He reached for several oil-soaked olives and fed them to her one at a time, his elbow resting on her knee, his hand close to her mouth while she sucked and chewed the fruit, warm oil dripping onto her legs. When she had taken the last olive between her lips, Jonas stroked the remaining oil on his fingers up and down her arms.

She closed her eyes, opened them, took a drink of retsina, then another, Jonas watching the spasms of her throat as it pulled the liquid down. Then she reached for a sprig of oregano, crushed the herb under Jonas's nose and rubbed it into the oil on his chest.

They were sitting closer now. Jonas poured a stream of oil over a slice of cool white cucumber, then slipped it between Liana's lips; the oil dripped down her chin, between her breasts and over her stomach. Jonas traced the track of oil with his fingers, rubbing gently between her breasts and along her belly. Jonas's aching was urgent, terrible, wonderful, but he watched the light in her eyes and waited. Liana closed her eyes for a moment, now; she breathed through an open mouth. "Go on," Jonas wanted to tell her, and as he leaned forward to brush his lips lightly across her mouth, her hands crawled up his shoulders, around his neck. "Go on, go on," he wanted to say, and she opened her eyes, searched his face . . . "Go on" . . . clung to his neck, hovering, moving neither toward him nor away. He brushed her lips again and felt her let out a breath. She tilted back her head, Jonas slid his mouth to her neck, and she pulled herself closer, against him, their legs sliding together.

She pulled herself closer still, pressed her belly against his. Olive oil mixed with sea salt and sweat as she rubbed up and around and down, balancing on his thighs, holding herself up with hands locked around his neck, rocking back and forth. His mouth wandered hungrily over her neck, her shoulders, her arms; deep rumbling sounds came from the bottom of her throat. Jonas pulled back and watched her head move from side to side, watched her tongue slide over her lips. "Go on," he told her silently, "go on," and she began to rock again, drew back her lips and put her teeth onto his shoulder, slid her arms up his back, lifted herself and held there, poised, hovering... "Go on, go on!"... rocking, quivering, until with a shudder she lowered herself and he felt her heat and wetness sink onto him.

They were still. Jonas waited, burning. He listened to her ragged breathing, watched the sweat on her neck, and waited. Then slowly she was moving... "Go on"... rubbing against him, rocking. Salt, oil, her skin, her sweat. She rocked and rubbed, back and forth, until he no longer watched, no longer waited. The wetness, the slippery rubbing of his skin against her breasts, against her belly... the heat, her haunches in his hands, holding her while she rocked, back and forth... "Go on, go on"... The stones were moving beneath them, then damp cool pebbles, the sea lapping his legs. His hands ran through her hair, brought her face up, his mouth against hers, her mouth chewing his lips, raising herself, higher, then sinking down on him, deeper still, closer, rubbing, rocking... "Go on, go on"... oil, skin, rubbing, rocking... "Go on, go on!" but this wasn't the voice inside him now... "Go on, go on!" she groaned, rocking, rocking. "Go on!" she cried, "go on, go on, go on!"

10

It was the sense of abandon that confused him. Liana was the first woman in a long time other than his wife with whom Jonas had made love—a long time, that is, considering the terms he and his wife had acceded to. His last extramural encounter had been at a cousin's wedding that his then not-yet wife had begged off attending. A bridesmaid had stalked him around the reception, made him stupidly high on marijuana much stronger than his judgment, and dragged him out to the garden. He had spent the entire scrimmage on his back, his attention alternating between whether a red-winged sparrow above understood what they were doing below, and how he would manage to rejoin the reception since the drug had clamped his tongue firmly to the roof of his mouth. Although memory gave the episode a comically pleasant enough cast, it was not an experience he sought to repeat. That had been three years ago.

In their earlier days together, before their impulse marriage, both Jonas and his wife had, albeit infrequently, indulged in the liberties not merely sanctioned but almost insisted upon by the antimonogamous tide of their generation. And though Jonas was drawn to the novelty of these secondary adventures, he was never really comfortable in them. It was not exactly that he believed such encounters wrong, but he could never escape the feeling that somehow *he* was doing wrong. There were no repercussions from his wife-to-be: she neither chastised nor drew back from him, being as mildly active on this front as he was; nor was there reproval from their friends, many of whom were similarly peripatetic— this was, after all, New York City in the latter days of the Sixties. Yet an encounter with another woman invariably made Jonas feel, in a word, bad. Bad that he could give so little to this other, the "lover." And bad because he knew that each occurrence diminished for him what he had managed to forge with his wife. Even after six years together, the feelings he had become capable of sharing with his wife were still so constricted that to worry them unnecessarily seemed to Jonas unconscionable. So, over the years Jonas had only rarely gone through the motions of a fling. And despite marriage having left their fluid arrangement technically intact, affairs he had avoided altogether.

Yet it was not really the long time between lovers which confused Jonas now. Rather, it was the way he had let go so completely with Liana. His habits of romantic restraint had become so congealed that his momentary feeling of freedom with her both surprised and distressed him. Liana seemed at first not to sense Jonas's consternation: she was relaxed, playful even, which confounded Jonas even more. From the beginning he had found her vital introspection extraordinary. But from where this sudden passion? And if he was uncertain about Liana, he was still more unsure of himself. Why was he letting himself be buffeted so convulsively by her strange oscillations? Wherever it was she was going, where was it taking him? Just what did he think he was doing?

They swam again and lay in the sun until shadows covered the cove. Jonas wanted to reach out to her, touch her, but his hands kept fluttering helplessly at his side. By the time they put their things in the dinghy, conversation had all but disappeared. Liana had retreated into one of her distant corners. And for the first time Jonas knew that he was part of the reason. Which made him feel even worse than when he had known that he wasn't. On the way back, neither tried to speak over the grind of the motor.

They said little as they climbed the hill toward Glaros. Jonas had become almost cranky with indecision. He was unsure of how to raise the curtain that had dropped between them, unable to tell himself what he wanted. He thought he wanted her to come stay with him at Korina's. But what did that mean?

They stopped at the edge of the village: Mikhalis's in one direction, Korina's the other. Liana hesitated, and when Jonas said nothing, she started off.

"You know," Jonas blurted, "those beds..."

She stopped and turned to face him.

"I just thought... if it's a problem..." His words trailed off. "I mean, it's your back.... Whatever."

"'Whatever,'" she repeated, measuring the word. And when Jonas said nothing more, she turned toward Mikhalis's. As Jonas watched her go, his hand came up and pressed hard on the damaged side of his nose. The pain made him drop to one knee.

Kalliope and Alekos were hauling themselves up the path from Jonas's room. "Tzones!" Kalliope pronounced his name with surprise. "But... it is not yet the bus."

"I wasn't on the bus. I didn't go to town."

Kalliope and Alekos glanced quickly at each other.

"Oh. Well. Yes. Well, we, ah, are seeing the new room. Alekos, he is never seeing it before. Now your room, eh?"

While Kalliope babbled, Alekos looked steadily at Jonas: "How's your face, man?"

"My face? Oh, fine. It's nothing. Little accident."

Alekos smiled oddly, then put his hand on Kalliope's shoulder, and together they continued painfully up the path.

Jonas ducked through the low doorway and into the cool of his room. Strange, he thought, Alekos and Kalliope struggling down here on their battered feet; the room wasn't going anywhere...

He went to check the time. When it wasn't in his pocket, Jonas stowed his watch in a top corner of his bag. But now it wasn't there. He thought about the last time he'd had the watch and remembered putting it in the bag that morning. His hands became damp at the idea that someone from the village would have taken it, and he became nauseated when, despite himself, he thought of Alekos and a distracted Kalliope just having left the room. He searched again and was relieved, and ashamed, to find the watch near the bottom of the bag. He took off his shoes, revived the old habit of putting the watch in one of them, then stretched out on the bed.

It was after midnight when he woke. He wanted to wash off the sea salt but didn't relish the cold outside shower in the dark, and it was too late to risk waking Korina by going up and turning on the little hot water pump inside the house. Instead, he put on some clothes and went down to the *taverna*; from the door he could see Alekos and Nosey talking quietly inside. He decided not to disturb them. And anyway, he didn't want to talk to Alekos and Nosey. Or anyone else. He wanted to see Liana. But Liana as she was right after they had made love, as she was before he had wedged his reluctance and confusion between them. He went back to his room and climbed into bed again, the salt still on his body.

So, things were complicated. Already. The next morning Jonas rose early, slipped out of the village and went alone for a confusedly preoccupied walk in the hills. Without the distractions of daily life that normally can be counted on to step between troublesome thoughts and disquieting emotions, it was a very long day.

When he returned to Glaros in the late afternoon, he headed for a coffee at The Bad. A black car pulled into the square; two severe men wearing city suits got out and went into The Ugly. The car seemed a sore thumb on the square, so Jonas skipped the coffee and headed for his room. Passing the *taverna*, his ear was unexpectedly brushed by a faint fiddle sound; the *taverna* was normally empty at this hour, except perhaps for Korina preparing the evening food. The door was closed, windows shuttered. Jonas tried the latch, found it locked; as he did so, the music stopped abruptly. He went around to the back where Korina often sat cutting broad beans or peeling garlic, found the door ajar and quietly went in.

From the kitchen he could see Korina, Alekos, Nosey and Kalliope looking anxiously toward the front door. A strikingly beautiful man with immense bronze cheekbones, blue-black hair to his shoulders and a distinctive Romani vest was holding a *bouzouki*-like instrument, a large red rose fastened above the pegs. Poised like an animal that has scented a predator, the Roma man spotted Jonas and gave a start.

"*Endaxi, endaxi*"—It's okay, it's okay—Alekos calmed the Roma. "Come in, man," he said to Jonas. "Was that you on the door?"

When Jonas nodded yes, the others relaxed.

"We are having some . . . special music, eh?" Kalliope said.

Alekos spoke in Greek to the Roma musician, who eyed Jonas cautiously, then nodded. Alekos resumed playing softly, Kalliope whisper-singing the words. The Roma man listened carefully, Alekos and Kalliope repeating the phrases several times, then the man played and sang with them. When they reached the chorus and sang together, "*Axion esti to timima, axion esti to timima,*" the Roma man smiled with satisfaction. After several rounds, the players took a break and Korina brought out beers. Through it all, Nosey sat silently to the side, a chafing restraint barely holding back his irritation.

"Some songs we bring home with us," Kalliope told Jonas.

"That repeating part, the last bit, what was that?"

"The *Axion esti*? Yes, very special. It says, 'Worth it is the price we pay.'"

"Huh. What's it supposed to mean, 'the price we pay'?"

Kalliope thought for a moment: "It supposes to mean what people will make it to mean."

Jonas glanced at Nosey. Behind his moustache was a sour expression he usually reserved for Xhirakos.

The players worked on some new phrases, Alekos and Kalliope teaching, the Roma man learning, and at the chorus again they all sang softly, "*Axion esti to timima.*" All except Nosey.

"Panastakis," Nosey grunted derisively the name of the exiled composer of whom he had spoken to Jonas with seeming respect the night before. "Oh, yeah, it'd all be lovey-dovey with his lot runnin' the show. Share and share alike, eh? No one out for hisself, right? I mean, cradle of civilization, ain't we."

Alekos gave Nosey a dirty look and Nosey glared back. "Well, there it is," Nosey concluded. "Rest my case."

The players worked a bit more, then put down their instruments and began earnest conversation. Unable to understand, and not truly a part of their concerns in any case, Jonas felt superfluous, isolated. He decided to head for his room. But outside he realized he didn't want to sit there, alone. He wanted to be with someone. He wanted to be with Liana. He hadn't seen her all day, hadn't heard her name. And soon there would be the evening bus. He hurried up the hill to Mikhalis's, stopping along the way at the house whose small front room served as the village store. He bought a handful of dried peaches. By the door he saw a box of miniature wooden animals, children's toys; he picked one out.

"May I come in?" Jonas entered and sat on the foot of her cot. "I slept on the one by the door." He felt her thin, lumpy mattress. "Hobson's choice, eh?"

Liana's mouth nudged toward a smile but didn't quite make it. Jonas held out the little wooden animal. "A present."

She cocked her head to that different angle she sometimes chose to view him, then accepted the toy. "A mule?"

"No, this one's a donkey." Jonas smiled. "And knows it." He spread out the dried fruit. "So, what, ah, were you up to today?"

"Cheese. Making cheese. Well, helping. With the old couple. You know, by the cottage . . . just a quiet day."

"An 'Alice' day?"

"Yes," she softened. "It was at that."

"Me, I took a long walk . . ." He hesitated, unable to find the words to describe his convolutions since their afternoon at the cove. And it all seemed so far away now. He got up and went to a window under the eaves. The sun's last rays were slanting across the valley. Over the village roofs Jonas picked out Korina's house, the *taverna*, the square and its three cafes. Beyond the village, the road to Corfu Town curved back before dropping out of the hills. On the bend, Jonas could make out a parked black car and two men. One of them stood on the car roof, watching the village through binoculars.

Jonas turned around: "Why not come to Korina's?"

He looked closely for a change in the tone of her cheeks or the light in her eyes but he wasn't able to decipher the hues of her reaction.

Liana stared down at the wooden donkey in her hand. "I was in the sea today," she finally said. "After the cheese making. All it truly did was exchange sea salt for sweat salt."

Jonas couldn't tell whether she was deflecting his offer or merely giving him an opportunity to restate it more forthrightly. He recalled that at Mikhalis's what they called a shower was little more than a trickle, and a cold one at that.

"The water's warm at Korina's," Jonas exaggerated.

"Do you suppose she'd mind me coming round? I'm sure she wouldn't," Liana answered her own question. She opened her duffel bag and Jonas, with racing pulse, went back to the window. He could see the Roma musician slip out the rear of the *taverna* and weave his way up the hill, avoiding the main village paths. Nosey followed a moment later, heading in a different direction. When Nosey had disappeared from view,

Jonas's eyes were drawn across the valley: the man with the binoculars and his partner jumped into the black car and sped off.

"Ready." Liana held a towel and some clothes, but her bag was still on the floor. Jonas tried to hide his disappointment.

In Jonas's room, he said he would go up to the house to start the small water heater. When he came back down, Liana was sitting on the edge of the bed with only her towel around her. "I know: the water will take ages to get warm, won't it? Sometimes I forget where I am. No, actually it did occur to me how long it would take, but I carried on anyway. Odd how sometimes you just keep going…"

"Wait. You're not going to analyze wanting a shower, are you?"

"No," she laughed. "I think I'll spare us both…. Have you looked at these?"

Jonas peered past Liana to the wall: a color picture of the Virgin; a rendition of the Prophet Elias in his chariot of fire; a plastic place mat reading "Ritz Cafe—Greek Food—Steinway Ave., Queens"; formal family photo portraits covering several generations; a large group photo labeled in English "12th Annual Sunday School Teachers' Convention, Greek Orthodox Cathedral, Melbourne, Australia, 5–6 March 1952"; a small Mona Lisa in a gilt-edge frame; and, next to the bed, a four-inch icon of the celestial John the Baptist holding the mortal John's head.

"A far-flung bunch," Jonas said of the photos.

"Mm. But a bunch nonetheless."

She leaned back against the wall. Jonas sat down and lit a cigarette. Passing it to her, he touched the back of her hand. She looked at him and waited, but he didn't know what to say, what she wanted him to say. They sat with legs against one another, Liana looking at Jonas, Jonas looking over her shoulder. She leaned over to put out the cigarette and her hair brushed his face. She made no sound as his mouth moved to her neck. They made love without speaking, Jonas avoiding her search for his eyes.

When Jonas roused himself, it was dark; he lit a candle. Liana was staring at the icon.

"An extreme fellow, the Baptist," Jonas said quietly. "Of course, it cost him big."

"Yes, but worth the price. At least, to him."

Liana's words vibrated in Jonas, gave off an eerie echo. Of his wife? His mother's Polish priest? He tried to locate it in memory but was taken too many places at once. "Water's probably ready," he said. Liana got up and gathered her towel and clothes. "Here," Jonas offered, "you'll need the candle."

He followed her out and when she got into the shower stall he continued up the path and through a rear shed into the house. Voices and a strange glow were coming from the back room. The Roma musician squatted by a chair on which he balanced a flashlight and a thick lens with a tiny strip of film stretched between them. The light projected through film and lens onto the rough whitewashed wall, from which Kalliope was haltingly deciphering the blurred markings. Alekos sat on the floor putting to paper Kalliope's dictation.

The Roma noticed Jonas and leaped up, sending the light careening crazily around the room.

"Fuckin' A, man!" Alekos shouted. "What are you doin'?"

Jonas froze.

"*Sigha, sigha*"—Easy, easy—Kalliope calmed. "May it always be him at the door. . . . Sorry," she said to Jonas. "But this"—she gestured vaguely toward the wall—"is not for everyones."

"Okay, no problem, I just . . ." Jonas pointed toward the tiny water heater in the corner behind them. ". . . the water."

"Oh, your shower," Alekos said testily. "That . . . that's important, too, ain't it."

"Yeah, well, Korina told me to make sure and turn it off."

"He's right." It was Nosey, standing in the doorway. "Generator can burn out fast. And in case you ain't heard, Aleko, they ain't so easy to get around here these days . . . unless you think someone'll trade one for one of your songs."

"Some people'd think they're worth it," Alekos snapped.

"Oh, course," Nosey shot back. "How'd I forget? '*Axion* bleedin' *esti*,' right?"

Nosey and Alekos switched to Greek and snarled at each other until Kalliope intervened. Alekos and Nosey backed off, and they all moved into the front room. Alekos sat scowling, the Roma man behind him. Nosey stood apart, arms folded.

"Look, there's some dangerous shit here," Alekos said. "So, you gotta stay all the way buttoned up. Anything slips your lip, our business'll be all over the street, you get what I'm sayin'?"

"No, as a matter of fact I don't."

"Like your face. You figure you don't tell nobody how the Man fucked you up the other night, but your girlfriend got talkin' to Nosey, and Nosey got talkin' to us, and now your business ain't just your own no more."

"Hey, you're the one doing all the talking. And I got no idea what about."

"This," Alekos barked, holding up the tiny strip of film. "I say we don't tell you nothin', but Kalliope says since we run the game on you, you oughta get told."

"Game? What game? What the fuck is going on?"

"You see, my friend," Kalliope explained, "Alekos and me, we are having all this in our heads—by memories. But what good is knowing it if the police are putting us . . . away? So, when Alekos is working in the Army base, he has some GI friends and they are putting it on the small film for us. To be bringing it quiet back into Greece. But still, even so small, they will look very close in all our things. . . . And then, on the boat, we meet a tourist, who is stopping in Corfu . . ."

"My bag!" Images rolled back to Jonas: Kalliope holding him out on deck while Alekos was inside with Jonas's bag; Alekos and a nervous Kalliope coming out of his room; his watch dislodged from its usual resting place at the top of his duffel. "You fucking used my bag!" Jonas snatched the film out of Alekos's hand and waved it in their faces. The Roma man leaped and grabbed Jonas by the shirt.

"Wait, wait!" Kalliope said, separating them with Nosey's help. She spoke rapidly in Greek, then finished, for Jonas's sake, in English: "He is right for being angry. We tricked him dangerous."

"Sheeit," Alekos spat. "An American? Big danger. They'd just cut him loose and send him home. So, he'd miss his Greek holiday. *Po, po, po.*"

"Hey, I'm not here on a goddamn holiday."

"No?" Alekos stared defiantly. "Then why *are* you here?"

Jonas's neck went hot. "Well, if they won't mess with an American," he finally spluttered and pointed to his still-discolored face, "what the hell am I doing with this?"

"Hey, if you weren't a Yank, you wouldn't be here to show it."

Jonas looked at Kalliope, who looked away; using Jonas's bag obviously had not been her idea. "Okay, so would someone mind telling me just what I've been carrying around?" He held up the film.

"Wait 'til you hear this one," Nosey put in scornfully.

"Well...," Kalliope finally said, "poems."

"Poems! Poems?" Jonas looked at the film, incredulous.

"Ain't just poems," Alekos objected. "They got music now. Greek poets and musicians, man, some heavy exiles. And me and Kalliope, we been a long time gettin' all this together, see..."

"Fiddlin' while Athens burns, eh?" Nosey put in.

Alekos glared: "Yeah, well maybe you'd think different if you'd come with me six years ago."

"Maybe you'd think different if you'd stayed." Nosey barely held off the quiver in his throat. Alekos responded in Greek and he and Nosey again exchanged bitter remarks.

"Christ," Jonas waved a hand. "Fools for fucking poems."

"Gonna be a fool, might at least be for a reason," Alekos said, turning from Nosey and staring evenly at Jonas.

Nosey got up: "Listen, I'm sure this'd be right educational and all, but I got things to get on with." He moved toward the door.

"Yeah, 'Them's what has money and no brains,' eh?" Alekos mocked one of Nosey's favorite phrases. Jonas could see the hurt on Nosey's face. Nosey started to speak but looked as if his voice would fail if he made any sound at all; he turned and walked out. Alekos raised his hand to call him back, but dropped it and let him go. Kalliope looked sadly at Alekos, then went after Nosey out the door.

"Poems?" Jonas shook his head. "Come on..."

"Songs, man. Mouth to mouth. See, in Greece, songs, they go straight back to Homer. Everyone in Greece gets taught his Homer...and taught it as a song. So, they hear some of the same words...in a new song..." Alekos stared hard at Jonas. "How old are you, man?" he asked after a moment.

"How old?" Jonas had to think. "Thirty-one."

"Mm. And in the States—TV your whole life."

Jonas made a feeble gesture of dismissal and out of the corner of his eye saw Liana standing in the back doorway, listening to his disparagements. Shaking her head, she retreated out the door; Jonas caught up with her on the path. She looked down at his clenched fist and he realized he was still holding the piece of film.

"What do they think they're going to do with a few lousy songs?" His tone was softer than his words.

"Why is it so important to you that they do nothing?"

He started to speak, but she stopped him. "Whatever it is, first say it to yourself. Later you can decide whether you want to say it again . . ." And she went down the path toward Jonas's room.

Alekos and the Roma man up in the house. Liana down in the room. Jonas on the path, staring blankly at the ground, grinding his teeth.

A loud crash came from the house, then shouting, another crash. As Jonas rushed to the door, he sensed people behind him in the dark. He ducked inside and from the front room heard the angry noises of a melee and howls of pain from Alekos. Then he realized the strip of film was still in his hand and, with the instincts of someone who had ridden the New York subways on his own since childhood, stuck it in his shoe.

Seven or eight men, in uniform and not, were grappling with Alekos and the Roma musician. Three of them had the Roma man on the ground and another was hitting him with the butt of his rifle. Two police held Alekos down while a man in a suit kicked him on the feet, Alekos screaming in pain. Jonas charged the man in the suit, but as he reached him, a uniform turned from the Roma man and swung his submachine gun. Jonas saw it coming but could only manage to get his arm up and turn his head before the metal reached his jaw. He could do nothing about the gun butt that slammed his head from behind.

II

He can't get comfortable in his mother's arms. No, it's his mother who can't get a grip on him. She can't hold him, he's slipping out of her arms, his little body bouncing down hers, bouncing onto her knees, hurting him. Her hands can't hold him, they hurt him when she tries to grab on, fingers poking him, pinching him, hurting him, but it isn't his mother, it's Father Janusz the priest, his mother's priest, poking him in the arm, in the cheek, Father Janusz's thick stubby finger poking him, the big square face coming closer and closer, "You don't try, you don't care," the priest is saying, "You don't try, you don't want to know." And Father Janusz is poking and poking, his face coming closer, cabbage and pork, the smell of rotting pork, the flesh of his face, his rotting face ... "You don't care . . . you'll end up ... you'll end up ... ," but Jonas can't hear and the priest's face is closer, a head, a head without a body, and the finger poking, the twisted rotting face shouting, the mouth moving, twisting, turning. . . . But he can't hear the face, the noise is too loud, the machines, the grinding, whining, roaring machines on the floor of the factory and Jonas is on the floor, flat on the floor, and the noise is too loud, he can't hear what the foreman is saying and it's Father Janusz but it's the foreman, his tie clipped to his shirt, clipped to the priest's collar, and the knot and clips are bobbing up and down as he yells, he snarls, his face so close, the smell, the noise so loud it hurts Jonas's head. And the foreman is poking Jonas's cheek, poking the back of his head, his hips, his back, and the foreman's head is so large and it's howling, it's floating around Jonas and over him, John's head, John the Baptist, calling out to Jonas, floating, a twisted face of pain, crying out to Jonas, a head alone on the floor, close to him, calling, but the machines are so loud and Jonas wants to answer, tries to answer, but can't move his mouth. And John's head is so close, rocking back and forth on the floor and Jonas tries to call John's name but he can't move his mouth and he tries and tries and the horrible pain but no sound comes out, the pain a finger poking deep in his face, a knife in his face, and he wants to call out to John but no sound comes out. And John's head is screaming but Jonas can't hear him, the machines, the machines, and John's eyes are closed, and he has no eyes, can't see Jonas so close, Jonas reaching out to touch him, John's face so close, rocking on the floor, calling, crying out but no sound from his mouth, the roaring machines too loud. And Jonas's hand is moving to John's head, to stroke the head, his hand moving closer and so much pain, John's head, so much pain, rocking on the floor and Jonas reaches out to touch it, his fingers reach the head and touch the face and the knives go deep into the face, it's Jonas's head, Jonas's face, he screams with the pain, and the scream stretches his broken mouth and his eyes open, his hand is on his own face and he feels it, enormous, swollen, matted with blood, and then he's vomiting with the pain, vomiting blood onto the floor of the cell, onto the rough cement of the tiny cell the walls of which he cannot see because there is no light.

Jonas opened his eyes but saw nothing. He considered moving but was cautioned by manifold pains: his back was raw, his shirt stuck to torn flesh; his knees and hips were battered, wrists swollen stiff; his shoulders throbbed so intensely that they must have been disjointed. When finally he tried to shift his weight, the pain at the back of his head made him gasp, and the escaping breath told him how bloodied and torn his mouth was. He moved a hand to his face: his jaw was enormous, swollen shut. Blood caked his lips and a monstrous tongue pressed against the jagged edge of a broken tooth. He moved the hand to his nose, so recently swollen and bruised; it now felt small and cool compared to the lower part of his face.

He tried to focus on the surfaces around him. Rough cement, one shoulder pressed to a wall, the undamaged side of his face against the floor. A faint ghost of light seeped under what must have been a door and just in front of him it reflected off something he realized must be his own blood and bile.

Suddenly the floor began to vibrate. A roar, a malevolent roar, forced its way up through the cement, under the door, along the walls. Soon it filled the tiny cell, filled Jonas's head, his body, until there was nothing else, only the noise, the terrible roar. Jonas lifted his head off the floor but was stopped by a crush of pain at the back of his skull. He hung suspended until the pain subsided a bit, then let himself down with excruciating care. In the moments of blinding pain, he realized, he'd been oblivious to the horrible roar. Now it was back. Pain or noise, noise or pain.

The roaring stopped. A black, evil silence. Then a low moan seeped into the emptiness, starting deep in the walls and spreading like a stain in every direction, a moan that grew to a wail and to a howl, the sound of an animal crushed in a trap, calling for death. Jonas felt as much as heard the cry, felt it moving through the floor directly into his bones. Somewhere outside his cell, a door opened and the cry became louder, then a thud and a piercing scream so sudden and terrible that Jonas also screamed and the wrenching of his head and mouth sent shocks of pain through his body and again he passed out.

Glaring white and two shadows. A growl, rapid Greek. They grabbed him by the arms and he knew why his shoulders hurt so bad, yanked him to his knees and dragged him out of the cell. The light from a single corridor bulb was blinding as they pulled him along, knees banging, legs dragging in the fetid water on the floor. Every few steps they would lose their grip and drop him, each cement collision sending bolts of pain that left him gasping and gagging in the foul swamp of the floor. When he fell they cursed him and kicked him, but more than the blows it was his revulsion at the floor that made him raise his head. As they hauled him along, he could make out other doors, small metal doors like those to the cages of maddened animals. He thought of Kalliope and Alekos, expected to hear them call his name. But there were no sounds except his own labored breathing, the scrape of his legs on the cement, the grunts and boots of the guards.

They pulled him down a flight of stairs, steps gouging his hips and back, dragged him to an open door at the end of another corridor, and slung him through. He bounced once and came to rest against metal legs bolted to the cement. It was dark again and silent. On the floor inches from his face Jonas could make out a pool of blood and a piece of what could only be human flesh. He retched, then cried out from the pain.

Voices reviled him; arms pulled him onto a table. The door closed—total darkness. Silence. A penlight snapped on and shined into Jonas's

eyes; arms jerked him upright. For several moments there was no movement, no sound, the arms and silent voices hovering somewhere nearby.
The penlight fixed the blue eye, then the green, and suddenly there was
a rush and a blow to his stomach. He doubled over, gasping in terror as
much as pain. The penlight went out. Again no sounds, no movement,
no sense of how close were the voices and arms. He sat on the table and
trembled.

A single voice addressed him in Greek. Jonas tried to reply, to say he
didn't understand, but his mouth was so swollen and painful, so caked
with blood, that he could make no intelligible sounds. At his mumbling,
the penlight came on and searched his face. There was laughter, the
voices spoke to each other, then noises to the side. A hand came out of
the darkness and pawed his face with something wet. In a moment Jonas
screamed at the rub on his broken mouth of a cloth soaked in chlorine,
his head exploding with pain from the bleach and from his own scream.
There was more laughter.

Voices, and the penlight came to rest on Jonas's feet. Arms pushed
him onto his stomach, his feet hanging over the table. Something hard
tapped the sole of his shoe and a voice asked in Greek if he would like
some *phistikia*—pistachios; the other voices laughed.

Feet split open like pistachios.

The arms strapped Jonas down. Another tap on his sole, a light tap,
to increase the terror of anticipation, a tap which landed directly over
the tiny strip of film he had shoved into the shoe as he stood on the path
behind Korina's house.

Jonas squirmed and tried to shout something to stop the impending
assault on his feet, but he could form no words. Rough hands tore open
his mouth and stuffed in a rag stiff with urine. Jonas gagged, choked;
his head banged onto the table. Then tapping, lightly, first one foot and
the other. The penlight shone on something large and metal, a shadow
moved, then the room exploded with the roar of a terrible machine. The
noise drove into Jonas's body and filled it with a pain that was the noise's
own, until there was no more machine, no more body, only the roar and
the pain...

And then it was over. Jonas did not hear the machine stop but he
realized it was over. The door was open and the room was coming back

to him, the table, his body, its myriad pains. There was a single voice, an authoritative voice Jonas had not heard before. Light in the room, and Jonas glimpsed the horrible machine against a wall: nothing more than a car engine without muffler or cover. The new voice gave orders. Hands untied Jonas and took the putrid rag from his mouth. The voice stopped. The door opened wider, then closed.

*

"Hard work is the way for people to be heard."

The voice was deadened, as if coming through gauze, speaking English with a clipped Anglo-Greek accent. Another voice followed in a high-pitched, squeaking Greek, then the first voice spoke again: "The colonel says: 'Work is our democratic institution.'"

"And we read you loud and clear," responded a sharp American twang.

Jonas's eyes opened at hearing the anomalous accent. He found himself on a cot in a different, larger cell with a window slit high on one wall. He was covered with a blanket.

The squeaking voice spoke again in Greek, and the original voice translated: "The colonel says that Greece, like all nations, is a living body. And that we must doctor to the body of our nation. Cut out infected cells so the healthy ones can live full Christian lives."

The squeaking voice then ranted at length, rising in urgency and pitch to an almost porcine squeal. When finally it ended, the original voice translated: "The colonel wishes to say to the American people that we are, after all, the cradle of civilization, a Greece of Christian Greeks... and, of course, a longtime ally. But bacteria have slipped inside the bloodstream of our nation, microbes and poisons that are not truly Greek. When the body of a nation has been contaminated by disease, that nation forms antibodies... which must be allowed to do their work. And antibodies cannot be judged by the terms set for normal cells."

"Amen to that," the twang said.

"Greece and America," the squealing voice itself now pronounced gingerly in English, "together again."

There was static, then a Greek announcer, followed by music unaccountably familiar to Jonas. He was struggling to place it when the cell door opened and a pale, fleshy man in a suit came in, flanked by two guards.

"I am a doctor. I will examine you."

The man's tone was hardly soothing but neither was it threatening. He examined Jonas's head and face, cleaning his mouth thoroughly if not gently and rinsing it with a solution that gave Jonas insight into just how jagged and torn it was. The doctor applied salve to Jonas's raw back and checked his shoulders, arms and legs. "Bones are okay."

As Jonas was thinking to test the possibility of speech, the music came on again, more clearly now through the open cell door.

"Bo...nan...za," Jonas mumbled.

"What do you say?"

"Bonanza," Jonas struggled to repeat the first word he'd spoken since he'd been taken during the raid at Korina's house. "Theme...from Bonanza."

The doctor listened to the music: "Ah, yes, television. American, eh?" He took a step back from the cot: "Feet?"

It was the first time since he'd regained consciousness that Jonas had thought about his feet. Immediately he recalled the introductory baton taps on his soles...and nothing else. He closed his eyes and concentrated: shoes still on; no pain.

"Fine, *endaxi*," Jonas urged, moving his mouth as little as possible. The doctor shrugged his assent.

The quality of the air changed suddenly, became thicker, heavier; the throbbing at the back of Jonas's head became more insistent. The doctor glanced at the guards and then Jonas knew: the noise. Somewhere below, in the dark room at the end of the corridor, next to the table bolted to the floor, the engine had been started.

"This is to sleep." The doctor gave Jonas an injection, said he would be back, and left with the guards. The cell door slammed shut.

Jonas tried to sort his thoughts. Why hadn't they gone ahead with the *phistikia* on his feet? What about Kalliope and Alekos? And where was Liana? But the noise, the engine's roar, kept dragging him back to that room at the end of the corridor. And soon the drug put him out.

The cell door opened. It was night: he could tell from the darkened window slit. A guard wordlessly set a cup of broth on the floor and left. Jonas took a few sips but his stomach quickly sent it back up. When the convulsions stopped and the pain eased a bit, he put a finger in the broth and anointed his parched, cracked lips. The effort exhausted him and again he was out.

Sometime in the night he woke with terrible cramping in his gut. After several minutes of agony, his insides exploded: he vomited and, as he did, his bowels let go. The attack was so sudden and violent that he could not get to the hole in the floor: the waste rushed into his pants. Jonas lay on the cement, could not get up. The pain and humiliation which was his body overwhelmed him. Then the noise began again, that sound to cover the sounds of torture, that sound which itself was a torture to those who knew. Jonas looked at his feet, his untouched feet, and thought of whoever was down there, thought of Kalliope, Alekos, Nosey. And he wept.

After a time he gathered himself, took off his pants and cleaned himself as best he could. He sipped some broth and kept it down. Twice more during the night he was wrenched by cramping and sudden rushes from his bowels but at least made it to the hole in the floor. Because the back of his head ached terribly, he could not sit up for long; because of its ragged flesh, he could not lie on his back; because of his mouth and jaw, he could not put down one side of his face. He moved very little. It was a very long night.

In the morning a tall, silver-haired man in suit and tie entered the cell with two guards who, unlike when they accompanied the doctor, stood stiffly at attention. The man looked without expression at the prostrate Jonas and at the mess on the floor. He spoke to the guards, one of whom left the cell.

"Jonas Korda. American." The man held Jonas's passport. "Why didn't you say this?"

Jonas considered the man and struggled onto one elbow.

"Ah, yes, I can see," the man said evenly, gazing at Jonas's mouth. "So, you have been on Corfu some weeks now."

"Who . . . says?" Jonas mumbled.

"Who do you think?"

"I . . . don't know." Jonas had no strength to form words, let alone to parry with the man, and sank back on the cot.

"Your passport tells me that. Most of the time you are in Glaros, eh? . . . Your girlfriend tells me that."

Jonas was stunned by the mention of Liana.

"She says you hire a room in a house. This is true?"

Jonas nodded.

"A most unfortunate house. And it seems you came to Corfu the same day as someone else from that house. Curious, no?"

"Met . . . on the boat."

"Yes, your passport tells me you have been in Italy, but not Germany. Why were you in Italy?"

Jonas saw his wife's face: "Family."

"Ah. A pity to be so far now from family."

The guard returned with a basin of water and set it down.

"The doctor says soon you will have not too much problems. When you leave here you will be told where you must go. Please do what you are told."

The man turned to leave.

"What . . . about . . . ," Jonas struggled.

The man came back to the cot and bent his head close to Jonas's, in order to hear.

". . . the others?"

The man studied Jonas's face for a moment, then slowly pressed a finger into Jonas's swollen jaw. Jonas shrank in pain.

"Is this your concern? I think not."

The doctor visited once a day. He showed no interest in Jonas's wild onslaughts of cramping and diarrhea. Rather, he would check Jonas's face, apply salve to his wounds, give him an injection for sleep, and leave without speaking. The second day, Jonas asked where he was and when he would be released but the doctor did not respond. Guards brought Jonas broth, then rice. In the evenings, an old man perfunctorily swabbed the floor. No one else came to the cell. No one spoke.

On what Jonas thought was the sixth or seventh day, the doctor gave him no injection. Soon after he had gone, two guards took Jonas to an office where a man gave him a slip of paper with a name and address: Jonas was to report there in three days. Jonas tried to ask what this meant but at a signal to the guards he was pulled out of the office, down some stairs, and unceremoniously pushed out a door.

The daylight was blinding. Jonas groped along a wall until he reached some shade, then slid to the ground. When his eyes adjusted somewhat, he realized he was on the square from which the buses departed. He got to his feet and struggled the few yards over to the Old Port. The sun hit him again and made him dizzier still. He wobbled to the road that marked the edge of the *platea* but a motorcycle almost ran him down, then from the other direction a donkey cart forced him back. Finally he lurched across and collapsed under a tree. The pain at the back of his head was ferocious; he reached back to get his hands on it, to tear it out of his flesh and throttle it. He pressed his fingers harder and harder into the base of his skull, felt he was going to be sick, then cool hands were on his neck, gently stroking his head, his face, and he leaned back and allowed himself to fall.

✦

Jonas spent the next two days in and out of a delirium of fever and dysentery in a room Liana had taken at the Hotel Brooklys. She brought him lemon rice and tea and told him what little she knew, most of which she had learned from Mikhalis the bus driver. Kalliope, Alekos, Nosey and the Roma musician had not been seen or heard from since the night of the raid. Leonides had been taken away the next day. Korina, too, had been questioned—and threatened—but released; they gave her no information on her son Alekos.

When Liana left Jonas on the path that night, she told him, she went down to his room; she heard the commotion upstairs but was stopped at the door by security police. They questioned her, looked around the room, and told her to stay inside. The next day she took Jonas's passport to the police in Corfu Town and asked about the arrested American. Surprised, the police made a call and after a time someone in civilian clothes appeared. He became agitated by Liana's information and took Jonas's passport but would not say where Jonas might be. Liana returned every day to the police but they told her they knew nothing. On the eighth day, Jonas had been released.

Other than a brief, halting report of his ordeal, Jonas said very little. He was febrile; his frequent, sudden rushes to the toilet sapped him of what little strength a bit of food could build; and his torn and swollen mouth made speaking difficult. But these were only the physical imped-iments. More important, he could not settle on which of his fevered responses to all that had happened was the true one. He was angry and resentful at having suffered so hyperbolically from the credulous folly of poem smuggling. Yet the price he had paid could also be said to prove how much the songs were worth. And if his cost was high, how much more had been exacted from Alekos and Kalliope? And from Nosey, who had wanted no more part of it than Jonas had? And even from Leonides . . . yet again?

Poems, for chrissake . . . or songs . . . whatever they were. And Jonas thought of his shoe, of the strip of film in his shoe. By ridiculous fortune he still had the tiny piece of celluloid . . . though what the hell would he do with it now? He asked Liana for his shoes.

They had been so badly torn and caked with filth, she said. She had his other pair and his travel bag. So, along with his ruined clothes, she had thrown the shoes away.

Staggering away from his meeting with the lawyer Skilopsos—the meet-ing at which he'd been given his passport and an unofficial if blunt enough instruction to leave the country when he was fit to travel—Jonas found himself on the esplanade arcade. Blinking repeatedly, he was startled to see people sitting in cafes, going in and out of shops, talking casu-ally: the simple doings of quotidian existence. He leaned against a pillar, then spotted Liana waiting for him at a table and shambled over to her. When he'd steadied a bit, he repeated for her Skilopsos's remarks, the encounter seeming to him more and more spectral as he described it. When he finished his description of the meeting, the two sat silent, struck dumb by the weight of what had befallen them, all of it so far from their intendments or control.

A waiter appeared from behind and Jonas flinched. Liana ordered two teas and the waiter moved off. Jonas was relieved by the banality of the exchange and now looked around him, trying to pull himself out of the dense and shredding thicket in which he'd been lost. He followed the comings and goings of waiters and customers among the row of cafes, the flow of people along the esplanade. The more he watched, the calmer he became. Alekos's conspiracies of song, the security police madness, the farce that had been Skilopsos's performance. Aberrations, mere spectacles, he began arguing to himself. Histrionics. Of real consequence only to those who chose to play in the petty if gruesome dramas. Not the stuff of wider life, anyway. Not the stuff of the long run . . .

"Starting to feel human again," he finally spoke. "You wait: I'll dry so fast you won't even know I got wet."

"Yes, somehow I think you might." Her voice was flat.

Jonas took one of her cigarettes, his first since he'd been taken. The smoke hurt his mouth and made him dizzy but the tobacco smell reminded him of Kalliope and he would not put it out. Their tea arrived.

"To mules," Liana toasted with a tight mouth and held his gaze until he looked down at his cup and took a sip.

Jonas wanted no part of Liana's solemnity. "You know," he said, cranky, "this could have turned out a whole lot worse."

"Why is it that doesn't seem to me the measure?"

The cigarette smoke reached Jonas's stomach. In a few moments the cramps hit again and he doubled over. Later, he could remember nothing of his trip back to the Brooklys on Liana's arm, nor of the Dirty Dick's barman helping her get him up to bed.

Evening. Liana sat on the room's single, slat-wood chair, under the open window. Jonas was in bed; he woke but didn't stir. They watched each other for a time across the darkening room.

"The 'Now what?'" she finally said.

"That recurring question."

"How are you feeling?" she asked in another while.

"Better. I think. Maybe . . . we can get moving soon."

"Where is it you're thinking of going?"

"Don't know. Just out of here, I guess. . . . Does it matter?"

"Only if you think so. . . . I thought perhaps you'd be ready to give it a go again. New York, I mean."

Since he'd left Bologna, Jonas had thought as little as possible in the future tense. And New York? He had barely begun *not* thinking of New York. He shook his head. "I'm in no hurry." He couldn't make out Liana's expression across the room. "I was thinking maybe down to Crete," he invented after a moment. "I hear it's beautiful. And peaceful . . . for a change."

"An island," Liana thought out loud in a tired voice. "I don't know that an island is what I need."

"Well, maybe Yugoslavia. It's quiet over there, I've heard. I'm sure we could catch a boat from here."

"Just move on," she said. Jonas could not tell if she was asking him or describing to herself.

"Well, for a while. I don't know. I just got started."

"Did you? I was gone long before I went anywhere."

It was deeply dark now; he could barely see her face.

"You know, maybe I could do with a stroll," Jonas said. "That'd be . . . a start."

They walked along the cobbled street above the ancient sea baths and came upon the small boat for the mainland, casting off. Liana leaned on the seawall and watched it move into the channel, then took Jonas's arm and walked him into town. It was a short walk—Jonas was still so weak—and they soon returned to Dirty Dick's, where the barman made Jonas tea. When the inevitable attack was finally upon him, Jonas went directly from toilet to bed and passed out.

In the few moments of predawn awareness before his guts once more drove him down the hall, Jonas caught a glimpse of Liana sitting on the chair again, looking out the window. A candle flickered by her feet. When he got back to the room, shaking with fever, Liana came to the bed and silently took him in her arms. She held him until his shaking stopped and they both fell asleep.

Late that morning they found a shipping agent for Yugoslavia. The next boat left in three days. When Jonas turned to ask Liana what she thought, he found her standing by the door to the street, staring out.

Jonas barely made it back to the hotel, where he fell into a fevered sleep. He woke at dusk to an empty room, dressed hurriedly and went downstairs. Liana was sitting quietly outside Dick's, staring across the water. An empty wine bottle and a full ashtray said she had been there awhile. She was wearing the thin white dress she had worn their day at the cove.

"Did you ever have the dream?" she said, still looking across the channel toward the mainland. "You think you're watching a play, and then you turn around ... and realize you're in it?" She turned to face Jonas. "Have you read Wells's *The Research Magnificent*? No? He is terribly English, Wells, I know. It's about fear. But everything, really. You see, to deny one emotion is to deny them all."

Jonas shifted uncomfortably in his chair. Liana spoke with more unabashed emotion than he had ever heard from her but, as so often before, he was far from certain what she was trying to say.

"But, if you're fortunate, one day you wake up and understand that you are precisely who you've always feared you were. And, for good or ill, it's over. . . . But if it's all been just a terribly long and arduous performance ... been that play you've dreamed. . . . Well, how difficult for any actor when a play is over. . . . Shall we walk? I've been sitting such a long time."

Jonas was silenced by the force that had emerged from her disjointed ramble and by the utter confusion it had engendered in him. She helped him up and they walked across the cobbles to the water, then along the rampart until the small mainland ferry came into view. The crew was loading cargo for the evening departure.

"My father," Liana said after staring a moment at the ferry. At first Jonas didn't understand that she meant Aphinotis; he had never heard her say "my father."

"Aghios Stephanos." She looked across the water. "The village, where we lived." With effort she shook her head. "Just foolishness, I'm sure. But perhaps someone has a name ... who might know a name..." Her voice trailed off. She took Jonas's arm again and they walked along the water. Across the channel, the mainland mountains loomed larger in the fading light.

"Maybe," Jonas groped for words that might somehow slow her down, "you just need to let things be for a while."

They walked to the end of the *platea* and sat on a bench, away from the lights.

"I've finally been able to think, you see. . . . No, that's not exactly right. I'm always thinking. One of my problems. Yours, too. No, my thinking has been as muddled as ever. But, well, I've been getting to something ... something I can live with. Shall we give it a name? No, I don't think so. It's just a small light so far, but comforting ... like a match in a cavern. Of course, I'm still burning my fingers just at the point of seeing ..."

The back of Jonas's skull throbbed wickedly. He couldn't clear his head enough to speak.

"This time here. All this ... it's been a stone through my window," Liana went on. "The shards are out there now. And some of them are lenses. All sharp, though; wounding. Have to watch where I step. But bloody feet, I suppose, is the price of the journey." Liana moved her hands to his cheeks. "You're trying so hard not to inhabit yourself," she said. "Still too painful a house, I imagine."

The Church of Saint Spiridion, Corfu's patron saint, rang the hour. When the bells finished, Liana helped Jonas up and led him back toward the Brooklys. Past the base of the Venetian fortress, they neared the security police building; they crossed the road, walking instead through the middle of the *platea*.

"Did you know"—she stopped and faced him—"that astronauts now have to look out for space rubbish?"

Jonas was exhausted. At the passageway that led to the Brooklys, he gestured vaguely toward the town center and said, "I think I'll keep going. For a while."

"Okay," she said and smiled faintly. "I'll see you when you're ... back." She reached up to him and softly kissed first one eye, then the other, lingering for an instant on each, then held herself against him for a long moment. She broke away and went up the passage to the hotel entrance. Jonas watched her until the final swirl of the white dress disappeared in the doorway.

For a minute Jonas stood quite still. Then he headed toward the water to retrace the steps they had taken their first night together in town. He walked along the wall by the sea baths, turning his head away from the mainland boat making ready to depart, then continued on to the palace and through the arches onto the esplanade. He stopped and had a glass of tea at a cafe, then wandered through the lanes of the Old Town. He sat to have a smoke outside the *taverna* where he and Liana had heard the woeful band, then walked some more. At a little outdoor restaurant, he sat over a plate of lemon rice long after it had gone cold. Eventually he came out again on the Old Port. As he crossed the *platea*, he could see the small ferry out in the channel, framed against the mountains, on its way to the northern mainland. He watched it for a long time, then finally went up to the room. On the floor next to the window was her candle.

PART TWO

Belly of the Beast

*He enters into a labyrinth, he multiplies a
thousandfold the dangers which life brings with it in
any case, not the least of which is that no one can see
how and where he loses his way, becomes lonely, and is
torn piecemeal by some minotaur of conscience.*

—F. Nietzsche, *Beyond Good and Evil*

12

Lost in translation. A sign over the counter for long-distance calls at the port of Athens telephone office read: *It Is Probably Sometime Having Outer Interruptions On Service Correspondence In Metaphoric Media*. Fair enough. Besides, whom would Jonas call? And what would he say?

If at times two languages became ridiculous—soon after his arrival on Corfu he had tried to say "Good morning" in a *taverna* and discovered that instead he had ordered a plate of squid—what about throwing in a third? Jonas struggled mightily to render the Greek government tourist brochure *La Belle Athènes* into English via the tattered remains of his high school French. *Transductio ad absurdum*. Nonetheless, he felt he had the gist of the wrinkled brochure that he'd found at The Nike—or The Nice, as it was rendered in English, beneath the Greek version, on a sign by the front door. The brochure, which as far as Jonas could tell was the rooming house's only amenity, seemed to make a particular point of the pride Athenians took in the city's antiquities. To illustrate, it recounted in glowing prose—or so it seemed to Jonas—a tale from the nineteenth century War of Independence. It seemed the Greeks had trapped an Ottoman garrison on the Acropolis, and when the Ottomans began to tear down the Parthenon's columns to make shot from the metal rods inside, the Greeks sent a message: "We would rather die by our own bullets than live to see the Parthenon destroyed." Or words to that effect. And actually sent ammunition to the enemy. The siege lasted for weeks; many Greeks died by Greek bullets shot from Ottoman guns, but the Parthenon stood.

Such grandiloquent portrayals of Athens's transcendent spirit, however, bore little resemblance to the mottled flesh Jonas saw. Hundreds of thousands of Greeks from the islands and mainland countryside had been drawn into Athens—and away from traditional worlds that had at least made sense—by a Good Life very few seemed able to find. Once they reached the city, they were beaten down and driven behind walls by the noise and the fumes and the sheer unremitting ugliness. Lost in translation were trellis, courtyard, *platea* and pace of life. Jonas's bus into the city had passed through vast urban barracks, endless sprawling piles of right-angle concrete, block upon block of gray, seemingly half-finished buildings, the rubble of decaying cement merging with chaotic heaps of material for new structures never quite completed. Much of the city looked like a war had just passed through.

Getting off the bus near the city center, Jonas found himself in a sallow jumble of cracking plaster soiled and battered by the rattle and exhaust of a million motors and the exhalations of eight million lungs. The air was thick with fumes, soot and midday heat. His eyes soon ached from the smoke and the relentless concrete glare; within a few blocks of walking, his body was layered with grime and sweat. And the Parthenon? Jonas never quite got there, stopped short of the Acropolis by the collar of commercial raff around its neck: curio shops; plastic cafes; neon *tavernas* complete with barkers shouting multilingual solicitations for an authentic Greek experience—"guaranteed."

Later, Jonas took the funicular car up Lycavettus hill, only to be disheartened there by the *nefos*, the pestilent cloud of smog that hung over the city and corroded the very pillars that Greeks of a different time had given their lives to save. The view disinterred from Jonas the horrible refrain of a television detergent commercial: "Ring around the collar, ring around the collar . . ." Concentric rings of tawdry shops choked the Acropolis, modern cement tombs for the living encircled the old central city, and the *nefos* enshrouded it all. Even in the bay beyond the port, a ring of warships had the city surrounded. "Six Fleet," said the funicular car conductor. "America."

Then there was The Nice. Oh, wicked Nice, high priestess to sleepless nights, slattern lover to taxis, trucks, three-wheelers, motorbikes and other fume-spewing marauders of the dark. The barman at Corfu's Dirty Dick's had recommended it: "Cheap. You go see there my cousin Dodo." Cheap it certainly was. And during the day a relatively tranquil if somewhat seedy four-story rooming house near bustling Omonia Square. When night fell in earnest, though, The Nice became a pylon around which every vehicle in Athens made a roaring, screeching, honking turn. Since speed was impossible on the narrow, congested streets, a certain vehicular status seemed to be evinced by the noise one's motor could make. And never had so much been achieved with so little: Jonas was convinced that the internal combustion engine had become the national folk instrument of Greece. Still vigorous, too, were the more traditional musical forms of cross-street dialogue and point-of-honor argument, so that the symphonic sum easily overwhelmed Jonas's nearly desperate need to sleep. And when he did finally manage to doze off during a brief interval of relative silence, he was immediately wakened by what, in the middle of the city, he could not quite believe was a crowing rooster.

Not being able to sleep gave Jonas plenty of time to think. More than he wanted. Forced to leave Corfu, he had wired an old New York friend for a loan, knowing it would come no questions asked. But that had meant waiting for the money in Athens. Anyway, with his insides still a mess he didn't relish trying to go anywhere just yet.

Four a.m. his second sleepless night and for a moment it was quiet. He finally drifted off... and the rooster again.

"I'll kill him!" Jonas fumbled in the dark for his knife. "So help me God I'll cut his skinny goddamn rooster throat!"

There was no light in the hall but Jonas knew the way along the passage and down: he had already managed the dark voyage several times under urgent compulsion to the closest toilet, on the floor below. He felt his way along now but just before the landing he stumbled against an unexpected obstacle. Reaching out as he fell, his arms wrapped around something firm but pliant, something human, and female, which collapsed on top of him. In the brief moments before untangling, Jonas formed two distinct impressions: first, that despite the sudden collision, the other falling body had remained loose and relaxed; second, that it seemed to have been leaning against the wall... upside down. Jonas extricated himself and got to his feet; the other body didn't move.

"Sorry. You... all right?"

No response. And too dark to make out a face. At least she was breathing: slow, even, shallow breathing.

"I'm really sorry. It's just… I didn't…"

Jonas sputtered on for a moment, but when the only answer was what seemed a calm sigh, he stepped around and went downstairs. By the time he reached the next floor, he had forgotten where he'd been headed. Only when he was sitting on the toilet did he remember the rooster. But now he was wide awake. And what did he really think he would do with the stupid bird if he found it? He went back upstairs. The woman was gone. Just before daylight, Jonas fell asleep.

He thought he might ask The Nice's reception guy, though he wasn't quite sure what: "Say, Dodo, know anyone who sleeps in the hallway? Upside down?" When Jonas came down to the main floor, though, Dodo was fast asleep in the cubbyhole which served as The Nice's office, so Jonas headed out for a coffee.

Three of The Nice's North African student residents were standing just inside the front door, talking quietly and looking out at the street like mountain men at the sea. Things were strangely quiet outside. On his way to a *kafeneion*, Jonas passed the Polytechnic University, where students were gathered in small knots, talking with great energy but without laughter or the usual extravagant gestures. Along the streets, people stood in pairs and spoke in low voices, watching for the approach of unwanted ears. Soldiers were conspicuous at all intersections; Jonas couldn't tell whether there were many more of them than usual or only that many fewer civilians.

The *kafeneion* owner and another man were deep in discussion and ignored Jonas. The two previous mornings there had been a half dozen or so men there in desultory conversation, drinking coffee and worrying their *komboloi* beads, but today Jonas was alone. When finally he tried to order a coffee, the man waved him away.

Back at The Nice, Dodo told Jonas that sailors rebelling against the government had tried to take over a ship; the mutiny had been crushed, the sailors imprisoned. There had been no official announcement but word was spreading anyway. Jonas tried to ask questions but Dodo would say no more and retreated into the cubbyhole.

A young woman came down the stairs: small, lean, moving lightly. Despite a bright patterned sub-Saharan wraparound dress and heavily hennaed hair, her pale skin, blue eyes and narrow features told Jonas she was definitely not African and probably not Greek. Jonas stared for a moment, then started up to his room.

"*Pardon.*"

Jonas didn't realize that she was addressing him.

"*Excusez-moi.*"

He turned to see her looking at him. He came back down.

"*Excusez-moi, mais . . . vous parlez français?*" she asked.

"*Pas* much," Jonas answered truthfully: roughly translating the little *Belle Athènes* tourist brochure had taken him most of an afternoon.

The woman said she'd been trying to find out from Dodo what was happening in the streets. She spoke a contorted and thickly accented English, so in pidgin Franglais Jonas explained what Dodo had told him and what Jonas had seen outside. The woman, Marielle, took the information without comment, then stood awkwardly for a moment, leaning toward the door but not quite moving. She ran fingers back through her short hair, causing a bit to stand up innocently on top.

"*Alors.* I think this is maybe yours." She pulled Jonas's knife out of a little woven bag. "You talked English last night," she explained. "Dodo say there is only one here. . . . You must be it."

Jonas took the knife and coughed a thank-you.

"I was making yoga; there is more emptiness in the passageway."

"Yoga," Jonas repeated.

Marielle looked at the knife, then back at Jonas: "What was it *you* were doing?"

Jonas stared at the knife. Good question. He looked at Marielle's open, disarming face, her lips slightly parted, querying eyes crinkled at the corners. His abortive assault on the rooster now seemed craven and stupid, made him uncomfortable, then suddenly he realized it was not only chagrin that was disturbing him.

"Ah, listen. You'll have to excuse me. *Je vous en prie.*" He backed toward the stairs and gestured for forbearance but only succeeded in waving the knife in her face. "I gotta go. I've just . . . gotta go." He turned and bolted up the stairs.

"This shit has got to stop."

Jonas often spoke out loud to himself. "Hungry for intelligent conversation," he would say if caught in the act. In truth, though, he spoke to himself as one speaks to a nervous animal, not to instruct it but to calm it and make it manageable.

"This shit has got to stop." Jonas heard his pun but refused to be amused. He would need the energy of his anger: it would be no easy task in a strange city, in a strange language, to find a remedy for this unyielding dysentery.

Following the afternoon *ipnos*, during which almost all commerce shut down, he headed for nearby Omonia Square, the usually bustling crossroads. Today, though, the streets lay still, as if stunned from the heat. But the silence was more ominous than merely somnolent: there was almost no traffic, and tension strained the faces of the few people who ventured out.

Jonas found two large pharmacies near Omonia but, like almost everything else, without apparent reason they were closed. Passing the Polytechnic, he saw scores of students in the courtyard, others scurrying up and down a large building's outside stairs. Two blocks away, Jonas saw squads of soldiers mustered in an otherwise empty street. He decided to circle back toward Omonia. As he entered the huge but now almost deserted square, amplified music suddenly blared from a parked car. The few people nearby leaped away as if to avoid being touched by the song.

Jonas recognized the music: Panastakis, the banned composer, one of the songs Kalliope and Alekos had played behind closed doors at the *taverna* in Glaros. The music stopped and a passionate, exhorting voice boomed from the car. Without the normal din of traffic, the amplified voice filled the square: faces appeared at windows and doors opened tentatively but no one came out for a better look.

Two policemen appeared and approached the car drawing their guns, threatening, shouting over the amplified voice until they realized the car was empty. They moved closer but were reluctant to touch it. The voice continued to echo through the square. The cops conferred, then one left on the run, the other training his gun on the car as if it might animate and try to escape.

Soon a squad of soldiers rushed into the square: faces moved away from windows and back through doorways; the few people outside on the square dove into buildings or down side streets. Half the soldiers encircled the car while the rest formed an outer ring facing away from the car and toward the buildings. After much confused shouting and positioning, an officer fired his pistol into the car. When it failed to explode, he ordered two soldiers to break in. They flopped around inside but could not stop the defiant voice. In a rage, the officer ordered the two soldiers out, then signaled the squad to open fire on the car. At the first burst, Jonas backed out of the square; from the next block, he could hear the voice still calling out over the sound of the automatic weapons.

Jonas decided to forego his search for medicine and retreat to The Nice. But in an empty side street he came across a storefront with ancient sun-bleached medicine boxes in the window and *Pharmakeion* in faded Greek script on the wall. The door was open.

An old man in a coat that had not been white for many years sat reading a newspaper by the dusty light of the window. The room was small and cramped, with jumbled boxes and bottles which looked like they had long retired from commerce littering the shelves, the counter and much of the floor. The old man lowered his paper and looked at Jonas but otherwise made no shopkeeperly moves.

"Ah, *parakalo*. Do you have—*Exete . . .*? Ah, shit." Jonas struggled for a word to describe his problem. "Shit," he repeated to himself. "Oh, yeah, 'shit,' there we go."

"*Skata*," he pronounced one of Nosey's valuable contributions to his vocabulary and gestured vaguely. "*Skata, skata.*"

The old man squinted for a moment, then nodded and shrugged: "*Ti nea?*"

Jonas knew that expression, too—"So, what's new?"

He decided on another tack. Parts of the body. Stomach. "*Iy stoma mou*," Jonas said, and made a face of pain. "*Katastrophe.*"

The old man studied him for a moment, then stood and turned Jonas toward the window, tilted back Jonas's head, opened his mouth, and peered in. Gently he probed Jonas's teeth. "America, eh?" he said appreciatively of the dental work.

This seemed to Jonas a strange approach to his problem. "A moment. I'll be…a moment."

Jonas backed out the door and pulled out his Greek phrase book: Stomach—*stomachi*. Well, *stoma* had been pretty close. But then he noticed up the list: mouth—*stoma*. Oh. So he scanned for a word to locate his trouble more precisely. Bowels—*entera*." Jonas stuffed the phrase book in his pocket and went back inside.

"*Iy etera mou then einai kala.*" Jonas accompanied his carefully composed sentence—"My bowels are not good"—by pressing his legs together and grimacing.

The old man puzzled for a moment, then held up his hands to make curling and uncurling finger movements while repeating Jonas's grimace. A rather abstract representation of his problem, Jonas thought, but the emotion seemed right enough.

"*Neh neh*"—Yes, yes—Jonas said.

The old man crossed himself, knocked on wood, and mimed a spit over his shoulder, then led Jonas behind the counter. "Jeans." He indicated Jonas's pants. Jonas did as he was told. The old man brought out a small flashlight, shined it around Jonas's groin and searched there with a tongue depressor.

"Ah, excuse me…*Doctore*. Excuse me."

The old man's head popped up: "*Then einai iy pseires*," he said and turned off the flashlight. Jonas understood "*then einai*"—there isn't. But what were *pseires*? There isn't…what?

Frightened shouts and running in the street made Jonas quickly pull up his pants. The old man went to the door and returned shaking his head and muttering. Jonas decided to forget body parts and go for the cure. Throughout his childhood he had been given one medicine for any problem remotely related to his bowels: paregoric.

"*Paregorica.*" Jonas gave it a pronunciation he thought made it sound Greek. "*Tha ithela iy paregorica*"—I would like paregoric. He rubbed his belly and sighed deeply to indicate the medicine's desired relief.

"*Parigoria, neh,*" the old man seemed to agree.

More shouts and frantic footsteps outside. The old man listened, then sighed as Jonas had sighed. "*Tzk,*" he sounded with tongue and teeth, meaning "No" in the Greek way that adds disappointment to the simple negative. "*Simera, then einai iy parigoria stin Athina*," he said.

Today there's no paregoric in Athens? Jonas translated to himself.

A man swathed in sweat and distress darted into the shop. He stopped short and looked with suspicion at Jonas. The old man spoke briefly and the newcomer slumped in a chair.

"Consolations?" the younger man said in a weary voice. "My father is right. There are no consolations to find in this Athens."

"Consolations?" Jonas wondered.

"Is that the word? *Parigoria*. My father says you come inside from the troubles and ask for *parigoria*."

Jonas explained that it was his physical condition that needed attention. The son translated the problem and while the father mixed some medicine, Jonas asked about the strange examination the old man had given him. Among the three of them they pieced it together: Jonas had said *etera*—kept woman—instead of *entera*—bowels. Added to Jonas's pantomime, the old man had thought he was complaining of *pseires*—crab lice. They shared a laugh, but frightened shouts in the street quickly dampened their amusement.

"I am sorry not to offer wine in the *taverna*," the old man spoke gravely, the son translating. "But this is not a day for *taverna*. This is a day not to be out at all."

＊

If nothing else, the medicine helped Jonas sleep. And, too, the night was strangely silent: hardly a car or motorcycle; no singing or arguing in the streets; even The Nice's normally nocturnal residents stayed quietly in their rooms. Faint crowd noise and bullhorns did trickle down an air shaft, but they were no match for Jonas's exhaustion.

Next morning he made a foray to the telegraph office on Constitution Square to see if his money had arrived. Soldiers patrolled the streets with automatic weapons. Shops were shuttered, cafes closed, the ubiquitous taxis conspicuously absent. In Constitution Square, the royal palace was surrounded not by tourists but by troops, two tanks facing the square. Jonas slipped into the telegraph office but nothing had come. He would check again when the office reopened in the late afternoon.

Athens weighed on him. A blanket of early summer heat covered the city and pressed it down. And everywhere the soldiers. Jonas decided to get out as soon as his money arrived. Maybe Yugoslavia after all. Why not? On Corfu he had almost sold himself on the place even though he knew nothing at all about it. Or maybe that was its attraction.

None of the travel offices between Constitution Square and The Nice was open; the entire city had moved behind closed doors. At the Polytechnic, windows were broken, benches and tables piled outside the doors. The students had retrenched inside, the large main courtyard now an empty no-man's-land framed by hand-lettered banners. The detritus of their demonstrations littered the road by the main gates. On side streets, scores of helmeted soldiers waited beyond the students' view.

The telegraph office was closing early when Jonas returned, the whole building shutting down. But his money had arrived. And on a silent street near Omonia, Jonas spotted a ticket agent in his office. After persistent knocking, the man let Jonas in. Yes, an express for Yugoslavia left at midnight . . . if any trains at all were running that night, the man added. Jonas bought a ticket. On his return to The Nice, the streets were even more deserted than they had been in the morning. Four million people holding their breath.

Back at The Nice, Dodo was listening with knitted brow to a radio broadcast—Jonas recognized the screeching colonel's voice. When the speech ended, Dodo tried to explain, though he was not certain himself what it all meant. The government was blaming the sailors' rebellion on the king, though he had been in exile and barely heard from for years. The military was therefore abolishing the monarchy and declaring a new Greek Republic, the president of which—the *permanent* president of which—was to be the screeching colonel. Jonas went upstairs to pack for his midnight departure and, recalling his train ride in Italy, decided to first get some sleep.

The Nice was vibrating when he woke, shouts and sirens down the air shaft and a deep rumble up from the streets. Jonas was surprised to find Dodo still downstairs: the night man should have been on duty long ago. Knots of lodgers were peering out the door and windows into the darkness. Dodo's radio was on, an excited young voice crackling through static.

"Not possible," Dodo said when Jonas wanted to pay his bill and head for his train. "There is no going out from here tonight."

Demonstrations had broken out again at the Polytechnic. Troops were massed to keep the protesters from making contact with people outside and to protect a large security police building—a notorious interrogation center—near The Nice. The surrounding area had been sealed off: no one in, no one out, no one on the streets.

An urgent young voice again came on the radio: an illegal broadcast from the Polytechnic, Dodo explained. Shouting and running in the street pushed the lodgers back from the door, then a siren screamed nearby. Jonas headed back upstairs. Halfway up, the power went off. He groped to his room and dropped on the bed.

Street battle sounds floated down the air shaft, a battle Jonas could not see from a window to nowhere in a room without light. He took a swig of medicine. Rustling sounds in the halls, then nothing. For a long time he lay still, listening to shouts, sirens, bullhorns. From time to time, gunshots. It was miserably hot and airless. He got up again. At the far end of the hall a light flickered through an open doorway. Jonas moved quietly toward the door and peeked into what was little more than a closet with a long, narrow window opened over the street; Marielle stood on a tiny balcony.

The entire street was dark and empty; the power had been cut all over the area. Crowd sounds and the penumbra of bright lights seeped over blocks of darkened buildings. From the balcony, Jonas and Marielle stared as if watching a sunset behind a mountain. Behind them, what was left of a small candle in her room sputtered its last and went out.

"Politics," Jonas finally said.

She looked up at him blankly, then turned back to the night.

"*Comme mai, soixante-huit.*" He assumed a reference to the Paris street revolts of May 1968 would get a rise of some sort out of any French person.

"I am from Belgium," she said flatly.

Two young men fled down the block, chased by several soldiers. One soldier spotted Jonas and Marielle on the balcony, stopped, shouted, raised his rifle. They dove back into the room and lay flat on the floor, hearts pumping hard. There was a burst of shouting, then popping sounds and flares that lit the night sky. Jonas's eyes began to water and burn. He closed the window, but too late: they choked and coughed in the tear gas.

Jonas's room was in the back; they closed his door behind them. The gas was much less there, and though sounds still reached them down the air shaft, the fact they could no longer see or be seen was calming.

"Dinner time, no?" Marielle said after a minute. Given the level of alarm in the streets, Jonas was amazed but quickly pleased by her cheery change of subject.

"How 'bout we call out for pizza. Pepperoni? Sausage?"

"I eat no meat," she said seriously. "But wait."

She went down the hall and returned with bread, cheese and a bottle of water. Sitting cross-legged on the bed, she put the food between them. Jonas dug the candle from his bag.

"And you have a knife, I think," Marielle said.

The air shaft continued to bring messages of the city's convolutions: Jonas's ears were pricked by occasional ominous popping sounds but Marielle enjoyed her bedtop meal seemingly unmindful of the chaos outside.

"Politics. Makes strange bedfellows, huh?"

"Bedfellows?"

"Bedfellows, yuh. People who share the same bed."

"Hm. . . . In these days, it is more easy than to share the same thoughts." She looked at his packed bag. "You are leaving?"

"Yeah, I'm not so crazy about it here anymore."

"Yes, my crazy here is finished, too. Where do you go?"

"Well, doesn't look like I'll be getting anywhere for a while. But I was thinking Yugoslavia."

"Yugoslavia." She considered the notion. "Why Yugoslavia?"

Jonas's mouth was suddenly dry. "No particular reason."

"Ah, the best reason," she replied brightly. "People who need big reasons always are left behind. The good moments have no reasons. . . . *Alors*," —she got up— "these noises, and *le gaz*—so upstressing. I make some yoga to release me. *Bonne nuit*, Jonas."

There was nothing to do but wait. The medicine had made him drowsy but his eyes and nose were smarting from the gas. Recalling a remedy from his student demonstration days, he fished out a T-shirt from his bag and wet it in the sink. He blew out the candle, lay down and put the shirt over his eyes. Within moments the shirt was warm, and he fell asleep thinking of the compresses they had made him keep on his eyes for days after he had realized that his left eye was turning blue.

"*Phíle mou.*"—My friend. A hand nudged his shoulder.

Jonas took the shirt off his face and opened his eyes. It was Dodo, hovering over him. "Now is the time. A friend just comes here," Dodo whispered. "And he tells me a way to go out."

The air shaft was quiet. The watch in Jonas's shoe read 4:30 a.m. There was no sound in the corridors as he headed down the stairs with his bag.

"My crazy here is finished, too," Marielle had said. He stopped. "No reason—the best reason." He went back up.

Sitting cross-legged on the floor of her dark room, she faced the open door as if waiting for someone to come through it. Jonas leaned in and whispered what Dodo had told him about a way to get past the curfew. Marielle asked nothing, said nothing, but immediately got up and quickly packed her duffel bag.

Dodo was waiting by the front door. He stepped into the street with them, pointed out an alley halfway down the block, and gave instructions on where to go from there. The power was still off, the street empty, dark and littered with burnt-out flares and tear gas canisters. Jonas and Marielle hugged the walls and turned into the narrow alley, then zigzagged between buildings until they came out to a wide street, the ends of which were blocked by army jeeps. They darted across to the mouth of a different alley and scurried along its twisted course. Finally they reached some lights and emerged onto Omonia Square, near the bullet-riddled corpse of the loudspeaker car.

"Maybe *le métro*," Marielle said. "If it runs, the first train is five o'clock." They moved to the subway entrance, a huge sign over the stairs proclaiming "A Greece of Christian Greeks."

"*Le métro*, it goes to the port. The boats, eh?"

Jonas had the train ticket in his pocket, but he didn't hesitate before starting down the hole.

It was still dark when they reached Piraeus, the port. A dozen ferries were tied up along several passenger piers but there was no activity on any of them; army patrols were the only people in sight. The dockside shipping agents were all shuttered and there was light at only one pier cafe. They drank a coffee there, then Marielle walked along the piers checking each gangway board announcing destinations and departure time. But Jonas had already noticed that all the boards were either empty or had their information crossed out. There was one large ferry loading cargo, and Marielle called to some dockers behind the gate. One of them turned and waved his arms: "Nobody nowheres," Jonas heard him say. "Nobody nowheres."

Behind one of the other large ships, Jonas noticed a small ferry hugging the tip of a pier. And several people gathered near its entry plank. Jonas went over to it and saw a chalkboard with the mostly indecipherable names of several island ports of call and a departure time of 6:00 a.m. Jonas called to Marielle.

"Where does it go?" she asked. Jonas shrugged.

She looked at the board and the ferry, ran her fingers back through her spiky hair, said nothing. Jonas waited. It was getting light. He picked up his bag, waited another moment, and turned for the ferry. She caught up with him at the foot of the gangway.

"You have the candle," she said.

13

"I was *malade*, in my bed, so much time. But it was reliving to be sick."

Time is not a problem when you are vaguely ill, Jonas was thinking as Marielle talked, except to the extent that there is too much of it—sort of like a voyage at sea. Marielle was stretched out on the deck, rambling about the years leading up to her departure from Belgium. More to hear it all herself, it seemed, than to enlighten Jonas. But he didn't mind. There was something relaxing in her weightless volubility, particularly so after the specific gravity of all Liana's carefully considered words.

Marielle was a painter who had fought numerous battles to support herself and her artistic production. At several jobs she'd been told she'd get to make Art for her living: doing drawings for an Antwerp tattoo parlor; painting Waterloo historical markers; taking psychedelics in Amsterdam to come up with designs for shower curtains. The jobs without such illusions had been many, including chimney sweep; packer of what Jonas realized must be Brussels sprouts; even "escort" (which did not, she offhandedly mentioned, include actual sex acts but which provided a number of enlightening moments, such as riding around in the back of a Rolls Royce wiggling her bare feet on the bald scalp of a German industrialist).

Her avocations had likewise been many and varied, including Talmudic studies, tae kwon do, and something she called nephrologism (the belief, Jonas thought he'd decoded from her description, that the kidneys are the locus of God). She'd been both an apprentice acupressurist and a novice tightrope walker, and for a while ran her life by the tarot until someone slipped a trick card into the deck and she spent three weeks in bed eating nothing but prunes. These seeming solipsisms notwithstanding, she had also worked for years on antiwar, antinuclear and anti-highrise causes. But always being *against* things, she said, had finally made her very tired.

Throughout these peregrinations, Marielle had steadfastly refused to be either a wife or a mistress, or to live "up with expectations." She had wanted to be both unpredictable and dependable; to be an artist but remain a member of the working class; to forgive human folly but to cut from her life the vain, the venal and the crude; to be spiritual yet irreligious; to be a "free lover" and to love one person so totally that neither would need anyone else; to support herself but not give up living for laboring; to be political but above politics; to have her art appreciated but to paint in blissful obscurity; to taste the fruits of faraway vines yet to plant herself deeply in a place and people that were her community, her home.

Her last job before leaving Belgium, she told Jonas, had been as an *artificière de publicité* for an advertising agency.

"Commercial art?"

"They say so," Marielle replied. "Not me."

The job had been to create visuals for slogans like "*La Reine*, a soap you can be loyal to" and "Security begins with the shoes you wear." Working on the ads while trying not to think about them had made her ill: she would carry around an unnamed anxiety like a time-release poison until finally it would force her to bed. A few days alone would bring relief, but as soon as she returned to work her throat would tighten and she would teeter on the edge of collapse until her body "relived" her with another bout of illness.

The final straw, she said, had been the ad for birth-control dog food—"You will be happy, so your dog will be happy"—at the same time she was herself practicing herbal contraception. The combined result had been first a case of hives, then a false pregnancy. That was when she quit her job. And, she said after a moment, stopped painting.

Jonas watched her dig a piece of bread from her bag and chew in silence. In someone else Jonas would have found spoony the peripatetics she described, dismissed the person as a flake. But Marielle spoke with such self-effacing perspective on her own follies—"*Un buffon* can be your teacher as much as *un philosophe*," she said at one point—that the whole of her floundering seemed greater than the sum of its sometimes silly parts. The multiplicity of her experiments, Jonas realized, resulted neither from an overabundant naivete nor a truncated attention span but from her ability quickly to penetrate and be nourished by whatever small kernel of truth lay buried in each of these worlds. Yet just as quickly as she entered it, she would sense that too strong and insular a connection to any particular world was a threat to her fragile self-definition. And so she'd move on. It was a tumultuous life, without standards or guides or the slightest simulacra of security. And finally, always driven from inside in several directions at once, it seemed she had become slightly but irretrievably mad from the constant strain of it all.

Two men approached, collecting tickets. Jonas asked what the destinations were and one man ticked off a list of islands. In reply, Jonas just smiled at Marielle and shrugged. She seemed to accept with mild amusement, even pleasure, that he didn't know where he was going.

"How much for the whole way?" Jonas asked. Two hundred *drachmes*—six bucks. They each bought a ticket to the end.

After two hours at sea, the ferry slid into an island harbor crowded with yachts and cruisers. Eight or ten cafes ringed the waterfront, each with matched umbrellas and chairs. A score of well-dressed Athenians emerged from the ferry's first-class lounge and went ashore; local retainers fetched luggage from the ferry and piled it into small motor carts while the new arrivals themselves were immediately whisked away by waiting taxis toward a row of large villas perched above the harbor. Jonas looked at Marielle; in unison they shook their heads no and settled back on the deck.

In midafternoon the ferry glided for a while parallel to a long, brown, mountainous island. When the ferry reached the island's port, Marielle translated for Jonas from her *Guide Rouge et Noir*, and the place sounded convivial enough: quiet, visited mainly by former inhabitants living in Athens, known for apricots and sulfur springs. But just as Jonas and Marielle were gathering their things to disembark, out of the ferry's lounges shuffled a congeries of the halt, the afflicted and the shame-faced—all women. Jonas and Marielle could now make out on shore a procession of black-clad candle bearers crawling on hands and knees up a stony hillside path toward a chapel. At the bottom of the hill, families were gathered, praying for the climbers.

Marielle opened her *Rouge et Noir* again: two hundred years ago, she read, a long-childless woman on this island had followed a vision and under a bush found a stone in the shape of female genitalia. Nine months later, she was a mother, and the Church covered the spot with a shrine. The stone was believed to be invested with gyniatric healing powers, particularly fertility to the barren; women came from all over Greece to crawl up the hill for its blessing.

Abruptly Marielle snapped the book shut and shoved it in her duffel. Without giving the island another glance, she pulled out her sleeping bag and lay back on the deck.

The boat pushed gently through calm seas, into the dark. Night air and moonless sky were soothing after a long siege of *meltemi*—the dry, insistent afternoon wind—and a relentless sun from which shade provided only token relief. Jonas and Marielle fell asleep on deck.

Deep in the night, Jonas was wakened by the sound of the engines reversing. The ferry's lights made the darkness impenetrable: black sky, black land, black sea, impossible to separate one from the other. As the boat turned, though, Jonas could make out several whitewashed Aegean structures around a small harbor, three or four people in one lighted cafe. A three-wheeler, a small open-back truck, and two donkeys were on the pier with a handful of people next to a pile of full vegetable crates. A family also waited there for the ferry, two small children holding bouquets. On the boat, a half dozen people rubbing sleep from their eyes gathered by the gangway entrance.

Marielle woke as the ferry made a final slow turn. High above there came into view a series of lighted dots arrayed just above and below an invisible line: Morse code from the heavens. A debarking passenger noticed the two foreigners staring up at the lights.

"Cas-tle," the man said, smiling, "in the sky."

They turned toward a low cackling sound. It came from Appollonia, who was leaning against a wall, tattered sailor's cap atop thick black hair reined into a ponytail, willful swirls proclaiming their freedom around her ears. Deep lines at the corners of her eyes evinced the late nights of forty or so years, but her cheeks were smooth as ripe olives. Outsized paint-stained khaki trousers, flapping Polynesian shirt, and plimsoll shoes with more holes than canvas gave a greater impression of Caribbean layabout than of Greek village woman. A cigarette dangled from full, cracked lips. Had she been a man, she would have had several days' growth of beard.

The village of Kastelo was perched on a cliff atop the ruins of a fortress built by the crusading Knights Hospitalers. Bisecting the village was a flagstone walkway partially roofed by enormous tree-trunk beams anchored in ragged stone-and-plaster walls on either side. Cut into the walls were the closed doors and shuttered windows behind which crouched the village houses.

After hiking up to the village, Jonas and Marielle had searched for a little hotel or pension, a room-to-let sign, even a cafe or shop in which to make inquiries, but had found nothing, seen or heard no one. Several side paths only took them to dead ends on the cliff. Finally, they had just dropped their bags and waited. After a while a large flounder-faced woman came out of a door and with minimal interest tried to find out what the strangers wanted. The three had spoken past each other in several languages until Appollonia made her presence known.

For several minutes Appollonia had just leaned against a wall and watched. But when matters failed to move along, she began to interject bits of translation. She took Jonas's and Marielle's part in negotiations for a room, but casually, without apparent interest in the outcome, seeming to enter the process only to make it more interesting to herself and supplementing her translations with side remarks to the two foreigners regarding the locals' habit of intransigence. The large woman listened to Appollonia's translations but neither looked at her nor spoke to her directly, and when the woman did speak, said everything twice. Appollonia explained that the villagers always repeated things to her since they refused to believe she really was a Greek. This remark prompted a sudden, self-deprecating cackle—the laugh of a not-too-wicked witch who also happens to be your favorite aunt—which quickly degenerated into a hacking cough.

The large woman stepped inside for a moment. Appollonia said there were a number of empty houses but virtually no visitors to the village. The large woman reemerged and motioned for Jonas and Marielle to follow. Appollonia tagged along at a distance.

Curtains stirred as the little troupe moved along the walkway, but no one showed a face. In several windows Jonas noticed identical small boxes with the name *PROKI* and a flexing biceps superimposed over a rising phoenix; strangely, all the boxes sat outside the curtains and were faded with age. The large woman led them around to the rear of the houses, whose tiers were built against the hillside, hidden from the walkway above by its solid walls. Past a scatter of scrawny chickens scratching among the stones and a laconic donkey seemingly abandoned on the hillside, the group reached the base of a house which descended several levels down from the walkway. Appollonia cackled quietly as the large woman battled with a key the size of a pipe wrench. Finally the heavy door creaked open and Jonas and Marielle entered cool quiet rooms set into the cliff.

They stepped back outside to negotiate. The woman gave an opening bid and from several yards away Appollonia made disparaging noises and said, "Robbery, robbery," although as to one hundred *drachmes* a day—about three dollars—Jonas thought "robbery" was a bit strong. Following Appollonia's lead, he and Marielle merely shrugged at the large woman's impassioned, if to them unintelligible, defense of the price, and eventually they settled—the woman's expression suddenly transforming from aggrieved to victorious—on fifty *drachmes*. Jonas and Marielle put their bags inside but when Jonas came out again to thank Appollonia, she was gone.

The large main room and two bed chambers were still appointed with the furnishings of the family who no longer lived there: brightly striped handmade rugs; hand-loomed pillows and tapestries on a low bench around the main room walls; embroidered white cotton coverlets on the two beds and the wooden settee; and a yellowed photo of a tall bearded man and a little boy standing proudly in front of a fishing *caique*. Marielle chose the small curtained recess with the single bed and immediately collapsed onto it, leaving the larger chamber with the old four-poster bed to Jonas. From the front doorway, he looked out over a small inlet below; three fishing boats were moored, their nets drying on the single dock. Alone on a rocky point beyond was a small blue and white chapel. And in a clearing between hillside and chapel were three whitewashed buildings, a cross atop each of their connecting and enclosing walls.

Jonas and Marielle both slept until evening. They woke up famished but had no luck finding either *taverna* or village shop. A few villagers scuttled in and out of nondescript doors along the main walkway; Jonas tried to ask about getting food but people either mumbled and gestured vaguely or simply turned away. Then they heard the cackle again.

"We have not yet settled the question of free will . . . and you want to eat?" Appollonia stood a few feet behind them. "Ah, well. If you must." And without looking back, Appollonia went down a side path and ducked through a low doorway. Jonas and Marielle followed and found themselves in a tiny kitchen redolent of fish, garlic and olive oil. Mostly fish. A woman and a young teenage girl were standing over some pots. There was no sign of Appollonia but the girl motioned to another doorway: rough stone steps dropped through the branches of an acacia tree to a small terrace overlooking the island's port far below. Appollonia was settling herself at a table.

"*Ola*," the girl said to Jonas and Marielle. "*Ti theletai?*"—What would you like?

"*Ti einai?*"—What is there?

"*I marides.*"

"*Kai?*"—And? Jonas asked, not relishing the greasy sardine-like *marides* as his first meal in a day and a half.

"*Kai akoma marides*," the girl replied—And more *marides*.

"'Oh, but to rid myself of hunger as easily as desire,'" Appollonia recited as Jonas and Marielle joined her at the table. "Diogenes," she identified the source of the quote, then studied the two of them for a moment: "Of course, I do not suggest we have *all* rid ourselves of desire."

Desire for what? Jonas thought as he looked around.

"'Rid'? What is 'rid'?" Marielle asked.

"Rid. Get rid of. To give up, give away . . ."

"Give away desire? I don't know," Marielle said seriously. "You think it is more difficult than to keep it?"

Appollonia's mouth did not change expression, but with his blue eye Jonas thought he saw the rest of her face smile.

Down through the branches came a basket on a rope. The girl lowering it gestured for Jonas to collect its contents: two knives and forks, bread, two glasses, a bottle of wine.

Appollonia watched Jonas tear into the bread. "'Beauty may reign but hunger rules,'" she declared.

"Diogenes?" Jonas guessed.

"No. Appollonia Kinatis.... That's me." A cackle worked its way up from her chest, followed shortly by the hacking cough.

Jonas and Marielle introduced themselves.

"What about you, aren't you eating?" Jonas asked.

"Ah, no. Eating here too often leaves ... an impression. No, I come here ... for the company." The clandestine smile Jonas had seen a few moments before crept again into the muscles of her face. Jonas looked around the terrace at her "company." Several empty tables separated Appollonia from the decidedly cold glances of the four other patrons.

The last slivers of sun were disappearing behind the hills, leaving sheets of gold leaf shimmering on the silver-blue bay.

"I love the sundowns," Marielle said. "They relive me."

"Ah, yes, I remember," Appollonia sighed. "But for me here, the coming of night is different." Her secret smile was gone. "Excuse me for taking your leave, but ... *Kalispera*—Good evening to you." She stood abruptly, walked through the tables and up the stairs. The other patrons stonily watched her go.

The fish finally came down through the branches; Jonas and Marielle sat in the close evening air and ate greedily. No one looked their way. Only when he and Marielle dragged themselves up the stairs did Jonas realize how tired he was. His dysentery-weakened body was giving out, but there was yet another exhaustion. Though speaking over a language barrier often simplified conversation, with Appollonia Jonas found it made for an extra kind of work. The facile habits of everyday speech that serve as a buffer against meaning were not there: despite her comedic quotes and cackling, everything this strange woman said seemed to drag something unspoken behind it.

Not so with Marielle, however. She spoke directly. Plainly. Asked for nothing. When they got to their rooms, she said goodnight and went immediately to her bed behind the curtain.

Jonas pulled from his bag the copy of *Alice in Wonderland*. Liana's copy. He wondered where she was, then shook himself to stop wondering, got onto the bed and opened the book.

> Alice was beginning to get very tired of sitting by her sister
> on the bank, and of having nothing to do ...

Marielle tapped on the alcove wall and came in. She held up her own small paperback: "You have the candle."

Sitting cross-legged at the bottom of the bed, she saw the cover of *Alice*. "Ah, yes." She smiled. "I remember it from when I am a child."

"Would you like to borrow it?"

"No, no. If I take from you, you are giving up to me."

Jonas tried to sort out the verbs and prepositions.

"But . . . when we are childs, my sister reads me to it, and I read her. Maybe you and I, we could do like this . . . ?"

Jonas thought of the early days with his wife, when they had read to each other in bed. Over the years, though, reading had become again a purely private domain, an easily accepted way for each of them to be alone when physically they were together.

"But no," Marielle said when Jonas didn't answer right away. "That gives away your own pleasure."

"Might not be a bad idea once in a while," Jonas heard himself say. "Still a pleasure," he added, "just different."

Marielle gave a Gallic toss of the head: "Yes, this is possible. If it's your choosing, for real."

Jonas opened the *Alice*. Choosing a different pleasure. He tested the thought to himself, then read aloud:

> In another moment down went Alice after it, never once considering how in the world she was to get out again.
>
> The rabbit-hole went straight on like a tunnel for some way, and then dipped suddenly down, so suddenly that Alice had not a moment to think about stopping herself falling down what seemed to be a very deep well.
>
> Either the well was very deep, or she fell very slowly, for she had plenty of time as she went down to look about her, and to wonder what was going to happen next.

"That's the thing, *n'est-ce pas?*" Marielle wondered out loud. She had curled up on the foot of the bed. "If you think ahead of time about the hole, you never . . ." She blinked several times.

> And here Alice began to get rather sleepy, and went on saying

to herself, in a dreamy sort of way, "Do cats eat bats? Do cats eat bats?" and sometimes "Do bats eat cats?" for, you see, as she couldn't answer either question, it didn't much matter which way she put it.

"*Je m'excuse, mais* . . . 'bats'?"

"Bats. You know . . . in caves. Like rats, but with wings."

Marielle smiled and leaned on her elbow: "Rats?"

"Yeah, rats. You know, like mice."

"Mice. Mice?" She ran her fingers back through her hair.

Jonas squeaked and fluttered his hands over the sheets. "Mice." He thought for a moment. "Mouse. Mickey Mouse."

"Ahh, Mickey Mouse." She shook her head and grinned. "I am something confused."

"Well, if we're not both confused," Jonas laughed, "how'd we wind up here?"

"It's right," she said, suddenly serious. "All things funny are the truth." She got off the bed. "I'll try for sleeping now. *Bonne nuit*, Jonas."

"*Fledermaus!*" Jonas blurted.

"*Fledermaus?* . . . Ah, *fledermaus—chauve-souris!*" She smiled again. "The 'bat.'"

After she'd gone, Jonas read to himself.

> Alice opened the door and found that it led into a small passage, not much larger than a rat-hole.

Rat-hole. Jonas smiled. That'll be easier than *bat.*

> She knelt down and looked along the passage into the loveliest garden you ever saw. How she longed to get out of that dark hall, and wander about among those beds of bright flowers and those cool fountains, but she could not even get her head through the doorway; "and even if my head would go through," thought poor Alice, "it would be of very little use without my shoulders. Oh, how I wish I could shut up like a telescope! I think I could, if only I knew how to begin."

14

Early the next morning, Jonas and Marielle had coffee on the *taratsa*—the *taverna* terrace—where they had eaten the night before, then finally managed to find the walkway window behind which crouched the little village store—the repurposed front room of a home—where they bought bread and fruit while resisting the pyramid of *PROKI* boxes piled next to the door. Without discussion, they found themselves agreeing easily on things: plums among the other fruit; the direction of their walk down to and along the shoreline; the mere fact of spending the day together . . . a choice sanctioned by what seemed to Jonas an unspoken understanding, almost a contract, that it didn't matter to either of them whether they were together or not.

They walked in silence for a time, then Jonas asked how Marielle had wound up in Athens. He thought he was merely making conversation, but in truth he asked so that when she had answered she would ask him the same, would for the first time, in fact, ask him anything at all about himself.

"*Alors*, just before I give up my job, they send me to Paris. The first night I stay in the hotel with the others from the job, but the work and people was making me to be *malade*—bumps on my skins. So the next day I take a room in Belleville." She paused and took a deep breath. "That's where I meet Kabo."

Kabo was from Côte d'Ivoire, sent to France by his government for advanced study in economics, the first lesson in the discipline being to live in Paris on the same stipend given for Abidjan or Yamoussoukro. But despite their poverty and their cramped, multibed lodging house rooms, Kabo and his compatriot students—Ivorians, Malians, Guineans—managed to thrive: sharing everything, they not only acceded to a chaotically communal life but were enriched by it. Marielle, on the other hand, was by then living at another extreme, burrowed deep in a hole of passivity and isolation.

"There were no friends, no painters, no one," she said without affect, as if describing someone else. "My clothes all black. Cut off my hair. Most times I stay in my bed, like I say before."

The West African students in the lodging house were a revelation to her. They included her in what they did, in where they went, in all of what little they had. When her work in Paris was done, Marielle told her employers she was ill and would stay on there another few days. When the few days were up, she didn't even bother to call, just sent a message to send her final pay to her at the lodging house.

She spent time with all the West Africans of the group, but with Kabo there was something special. They would argue—he would chide her for her bourgeois Western habits; she would hold him responsible for his male-dominated culture and chastise him for excluding her from his all-night excursions on the Left Bank. It had been years since she had bothered to argue with anyone, she said. Living in the cold cramped lodging house without enough food or sleep, however, eventually had made Marielle truly ill and she returned to Brussels for care. The night before she left, she and Kabo became lovers.

Marielle spent weeks in Brussels gathering her health. Kabo phoned to ask urgently that she return. Marielle said she first had to make money to live on in Paris. Kabo told her he would share his money and to come quickly if at all. But Marielle would not budge until she had money of her own. "You cannot depend on anyone to give you what you need," she told Jonas firmly.

Jonas nodded, but as they settled themselves in a quiet cove, he thought it over. Her imprecise English made the emphasis difficult to decipher. Was it on the "one"—"cannot count on any*one*," as for years Jonas might have meant it? Or was it on "depend," the point being always to keep a backup? Or perhaps on the "give" of "give you what you need," implying that whatever you truly need, you have to get for yourself? With any of these notions Jonas could be reasonably comfortable. But what if her real emphasis was on "any"—"You cannot depend on *any*one to give you what you need." Replayed that way, it seemed to Jonas so bleak, and even if part of him couldn't help but agree, he didn't *want* to feel that way, didn't *want* to agree.

After three months in Brussels, Marielle returned to Paris. But Kabo and several of the other Ivorians had gone, ordered home by their government: apparently agents of the state had discovered that Kabo had been working with a clandestine restive political group during those unaccounted-for Paris late nights, rather than merely seeing other women, as Marielle had always assumed.

Marielle remained at the lodging house but things weren't the same and she was about to return to Brussels when someone quietly told her that Kabo had not, in fact, returned to Africa, that she might find him through certain people in Rome. When Marielle got to Rome, though, Kabo was gone: it had become unsafe for him there, too, and he had moved on, though to where the people there could not, or would not, say. So, Marielle had also decided to move on. She continued south, wound up in Athens. But it didn't matter where, she told Jonas, running her fingers back through her spiky hair. What mattered was not going back.

Marielle stopped speaking, as if there were nothing more to be said. Without looking at Jonas, she lay back on the sand and closed her eyes. He wasn't even sure whether she knew, or cared, that he'd been listening.

A fishing boat came partway across the mouth of the cove, then veered in sharply. Behind the deck housing, Jonas could see a tall, bearded man in shorts and T-shirt. Twenty meters out, the man cut the engine, climbed barefoot onto the tip of the bow and stood with outspread arms. As the boat ran onto the beach, the man leaped forward off the prow, gliding onto the sand in a dramatic swan dive. He lay motionless a few feet from Jonas and Marielle, looking up at them.

"Bravo," Jonas finally said. "Bravo."

The man snapped to a crouch, then exploded in a back flip, straightened up and stood quite still. He was about Jonas's age, with iron-cord arms and legs, thick russet skin lacquered by salt and wind, a bushy beard flecked with red and gold, and deep-set cobalt eyes. His visage was fierce, the forward lean of his body imposing. After a moment the man tied a line to a shrub, returned to the boat, pulled out a bottle and something wrapped in paper, leaped over the side and knelt in the sand. He offered the wine and when Jonas and Marielle had drunk, a big smile parted his beard. In the wrapped paper were thick white fillets of salted raw fish which he cut up for Jonas and Marielle. It was exquisitely fresh and flavorful; the man indicated by gestures that it was his own catch. After another exchange of the bottle, the fisherman retrieved a portable radio and tuned in traditional Greek music. Slowly he began to dance, arms high, head back, face to the searing sun, moving lightly over the sand, suddenly twisting, leaping, slapping his heels, then slowing again to the dance.

"Aaawwhh!" came a crow's cry from behind them. It was Appollonia, heading for the beach. "I see you have met."

"Sort of," Jonas said.

"Yiannis," Appollonia named the fisherman in a protective tone that somehow set him apart from the three of them.

Yiannis took a drink of wine. He did not exactly ignore Appollonia but neither did he respond to her. She was again wearing the billowing Polynesian shirt; the inevitable cigarette dangled from her mouth. "I was up there." She nodded toward a cliff. "Beautiful spot, eh? 'The sky is the daily bread of the eyes,'" she recited.

"Let me guess," said Jonas. "Appollonia Kinatis?"

"*Tzk*," she clucked. "Emerson—Ralph Waldo."

"What is it you draw?" Marielle indicated the paper Appollonia carried and the colored pencils peeking from her pocket.

"But the Aegean, of course. That wine-drunk sea. And little chapels. Flowers. The donkey. All the reasons to be on an island." Jonas noticed the shadow of a pacing animal darken her eyes. "As they say, Greece is to die for." She began to cough, and by the time she had stopped, Yiannis was stretched out in a patch of shade, asleep.

"They fish at night, the fishermen. The fish don't come up in the midday heat." She squinted at the sun. "At least *they* know better.... You aren't English, are you?"

"No, why?"

"Oh"—she glanced again toward the sun—"I just thought..."

Jonas looked across the cove: even the sea was slack and weary from the heat. Marielle nodded and they got up.

"What about Yiannis? I mean, shouldn't we say something?"

"You know something to say he'd like better than his sleep?"

Jonas, Marielle and Appollonia trod the goat paths back to the village. Yiannis's bits of fish had awakened Jonas's hunger; he suggested the *taratsa* for a meal. Fighting off whatever expression tried to take over her face, Appollonia trailed along. In the hot, greasy kitchen they found the cook sitting at her work table, head on arms, nearly asleep.

"*Yia sas,*" Jonas greeted her formally.

"*Yia,*" she grunted without raising her head.

"*Parakalo. Ti exhete simera?*"—What do you have today? Jonas glanced at Appollonia leaning in the terrace doorway, straight-faced, cigarette dangling.

"*Mousakas,*" the woman said and indicated with her eyes a large pan on the table. Swimming in a flood of scorched olive oil was an amorphous blob of burnt-brown eggplant, soggy tomato and recoagulated cheese. Only the heat of the room kept the pan vaguely warm.

"Ah, *mousakas!*" Appollonia moved to the table. "Spirit of the nation...in a pot. You know, to the whole world Greece means sun, water"—she peeked in the pan—"and *mousakas*. Oh, yes, the willing *melitzana*—the aubergine—so ready to give itself up to stronger flavors. And cheese of our goats, our national symbol, the goat—so quaint, don't you think? And of course, the olive: fruit of life, oil of life." Appollonia stuck in a finger and brought it out dripping. "Mm, and all prepared with such care and pride by the happy Greek, laughing, singing, dancing..." She glanced at the woman whose head remained on the table, then stepped to the doorway; Jonas followed and looked down onto the *taratsa*: three men, slumped in their chairs. "Such an authentic experience, this *mousakas*: two days to digest, a week trying to forget. Come on. Today I spare you such memories."

She led Jonas and Marielle to a rundown stone cottage which sat alone a hundred yards outside the village. A line was strung from the corner of the cottage to a scrawny tree; on the line hung a sheet, a sailor's cap and an octopus.

"Yiannis."

Jonas wasn't sure which item referred to the fisherman. Or all of them. Appollonia whirled suddenly and gestured back toward the village.

"Yes, my sweet neighbors," she called. "Put your eyes back in your heads before they roll away!...They want to know what we do," she said to Jonas and Marielle. "The sheet, you see. This evil woman from Athens, why is she always washing her sheet? But I don't really wash it. I just put it out here to make them crazy." She cackled, then went over to the line. "But this"—she took the octopus off the line—"is no trick. This, as you say, is good eats."

"Excuse," Marielle said, "*mais* . . . did it have a face?"

"A face?"

"Yes. I eat no things that had a face."

"Ach." Appollonia looked away for a moment, away to somewhere else. "Well, in my experience," she continued, speaking slowly in a lower register, "it's the things that eat you that have faces." She looked at the octopus. "But *chtapodthi*? Mm, a mouth, yes, it has. But, you know, it does not smile." Appollonia looked at Marielle. "And if it never smiles, well, can it really be a face?"

Appollonia cooked the octopus over a small wood fire; they ate in the partial shade of a trellis and its bedraggled vine. She told them that she had been an actor and theater director in Athens "before," and that now she was living a lifelong dream of lazy days on a beautiful Aegean island. She had been on the island a year; life was easy here, she said.

When Jonas sought details of Appollonia's life "before," she deftly deflected him and with great appetite asked instead about their wide urban worlds. Marielle disappointed, quickly dismissing Brussels, Paris and Rome: what was happening there was no longer of interest to Marielle and she could summon no energy to describe it. Jonas, on the other hand, enjoyed loosening his tongue for the first time in a while to someone who could follow most of his English. Appollonia was delighted by his flood of words: whenever his energy flagged, she spurred him on with wine and laughter. She asked about the New York stage and Jonas obliged with an inchoate rant about avant-garde pretensions, though in truth he knew little about the theater. Appollonia seemed to sense that his dissertation was mostly imagined, but this did nothing to diminish her pleasure: she reveled in his tirade which moved from performance art to the retreat from meaning, from structuralism and post- to what he called attempted murder on the life of language. From there he turned to the cultural imperialism of Hollywood and of commercial fashion, what he called junk food clothing and which, he noted, had penetrated to Athens, although at least most attempts there at the latest fads were refreshingly misappropriated. And mentioning Athens, Jonas was moved to describe the state of siege there that he and Marielle had fled.

The grin dropped from Appollonia's face. She had heard nothing of the military suppression of the Polytechnic demonstrations or of the sailors' rebellion: she had no radio, and the villagers discussed no politics with her, when they spoke to her at all. Jonas told her of the Colonels' "republic" and of its permanent president. Appollonia's hands skittered off the table but she did not speak.

Jonas, too, stopped speaking. The talk, wine and relentless heat had finally drained him. Appollonia's chin was on her chest when Jonas and Marielle got up; their thank-you was brief. Appollonia smiled wanly, and as Jonas and Marielle headed to the village she disappeared into the darkness of her cottage.

⚶

Marielle was out when Jonas woke from the afternoon *ipnos*. He wondered where she was but stopped himself from the impulse to look for her. She had neither waited for him nor let him know where she was going. And that's good, he reminded himself, the way he wanted it, too.

He sat on the bed and tried to identify the feeling he had wakened with. His ravings to Appollonia about New York had left him with a twinge of… what? Longing? Regret? He realized that he had just been dreaming his wife's voice, coming from the other room. He decided to write to her but when he sat down to it, he couldn't begin. For a long time he tried to conjure up her face. Then he tried the letter again, but couldn't find the right sentence in which to wrap the words "still love."

The sun was going down. From the doorway, Jonas watched the last rays silhouette the surrounding hills. A solitary figure made its way down a path toward the whitewashed structures on the far side of the inlet. Appollonia. Jonas was about to call down to her but the calm, quiet evening made a shout seem out of place. She disappeared behind one of the cross-topped walls.

Jonas considered going to the *taratsa*, but Marielle was probably there. She might find his arrival there cloying, a violation of their being together without having to be together. So, he got back on his bed, began to read some *Alice*. Later he heard Marielle come in; she went directly to her bed behind the curtain. That evening, he ate alone on the *taratsa*.

At dawn Jonas slipped out quietly. Four fishermen were tending their nets below in a steady rhythmic flow: examine, repair, fold, one man feeding, another laying the coils. They moved slowly, weary from a night on the sea, but steadily, to finish before the sun gained its strength. One of the men did all the talking, as if telling a story; the others occasionally nodded, remarked or laughed. Alone to the side sat Yiannis, one long shoeless leg outstretched, a net hooked to the big toe. Marielle sat midway between him and the others.

Appollonia was lurking in the walkway, seemingly waiting for Jonas to appear. She was heading out to do some drawing and invited him along. After considering and rejecting the idea of letting Marielle know, Jonas trundled off with Appollonia.

They walked for about an hour, climbing with the sun into patchy brown hills spotted with the greens and purples and heady scents of heather, wild thyme and marjoram. The stony middle hillsides were thatched with summer grasses that the village goats did not reach and mountain goats had not come down for. Floating on the grasses were daisies, blood red poppies and anemones the colors of dawning skies. Here and there between the rocks, yellow and orange jonquils marked their summer transfiguration with riotous wakes of color.

Jonas and Appollonia reached a crest above a series of narrow inland valleys patched with variously shaped and shaded plantings. One small village clung to a hillside, one chapel alone on a ridge, on one valley floor a solitary white stone dovecote. A sliver of sea peeked between two ridges, salt air freshening the scent of herbs baking in the sun. And in the bushes the cicadas were sawing their scratchy song. The rising heat softened the dry primal colors of hill and ravine. Outlines were blurred, yet with either eye Jonas could see each piece of the whole stand out clearly: chapel and dovecote; a single bush of flowering capers; exactly three goats next to the last hillside village house. And what brought it all to life was the remarkable transforming light: physical, palpable, engaging all his senses, flowing in his bloodstream and suffusing him with well-being. Heat, smells, sounds amid stillness, each was a part not of mere light but of a lambent phenomenon of light which transmuted everything he saw to an island Greekness: warm, beckoning, slightly askew, complete.

Appollonia settled herself under a small tree and began to sketch. Jonas watched her make seemingly abstract patches of shade with the flat of a pencil. "Negative space," she explained. "The things that are *not* there tell you what is. Emptiness gives perspective, you see. And since I have only pencils..."

Jonas looked at her paint-covered trousers.

"Well, yes, I have paints, but no spirit."

"Spirit?... Oh, you mean to clean up. Turpentine or something."

"Yes, right.... Bombs, they say."

Jonas didn't know who "they" were, wasn't sure he should ask. Appollonia continued to sketch.

"So whenever I go off like this, I wear these trousers. Then back at my house I put a bit of fresh paint on them and go into the village. So they think I must be painting someplace." She grinned. "They used to follow me in the hills, or search my house for spirit, but they can't find what I don't have. They don't bother anymore, but I still wear the trousers, just to make them a little crazy." She cackled.

"It was difficult at first, being here, after Athens. Then later I understood that Athens is for taking things in. But for putting things out again, for the imagination to do its work, a quiet island is the place. And there is enough for me here. Enough wherever you are. It's only a matter of creative attention. For what do I need cars and trolley lines, eh? For what do I need the theater each day and all its crazies? I have all this." She looked over the valleys. "The city is for angers; but here, beauty catches up and leaves anger behind. And that's the truth"—she scanned the hills—"or..."—she returned to her drawing—"...it isn't."

"Awk!" she cried a moment later and leapt to her feet. "*Karpouzi! Karpouzi!* Over there!" With a child's beam of pleasure, she pointed into a valley where a man and a donkey pulled a sled made of long woven vines. "The first of summer. Oh, *Panaghia!* Come on." She grabbed up her pencils and paper. "If you learn only one word of Greek, make it this one: *karpouzi!*"

Jonas scrambled after her. "*Karpouzi*. Okay. What is it?"

"What is it? It's summer! It's happiness and love! It's...watermelon!" she cried. "*Kar-pou-zi!*"

They hurried toward the hillside village where the melon man was headed, but when still a ways off, Appollonia stopped.

"Ach," she said. "We don't catch him."

"Won't he stop in the village?"

"Sure." She plopped down. "The problem is the village. I am not permitted. Kastelo only—no other village." Jonas was puzzled. "Never mind," she waved away his befuddlement. "Say to me the word."

"What word? *Karpouzi?*"

"Excellent. Anyways, you don't need language when things are for sale."

In the hillside village square, Jonas quickly negotiated for a huge melon and lugged it through the skin-crackling heat back to Appollonia. They set it in a small spot of shade and for several minutes buried their faces in the cool pink flesh, annihilating half the melon before stopping for breath.

"Ah, *karpouzi* in the hills," Appollonia said, leaning back against the tree. "A beautiful island, nothing to do but some drawings, perhaps a swim in the gentle sea when the day is closing. You know, this was my dream when I lived in Athens." She looked over the hills and valleys. "Yes, be careful what you dream..."

"The other village. Why is it you can't...?"

"Well, when they take me out of prison"—Jonas blinked at the word—"and bring me here, they put on me a Limited Movement Order: only in Kastelo I am allowed, and the land around it. There are many others like me, kept in small villages, away from... everything. You see, this way they can announce that they have let people out from prison. Anyway, I am lucky: I am not in one of the camps, and friends in Athens send a little money, so I am not hungry—at least, not for food."

"What was it? I mean, were you political?"

"Political? No. At least, I didn't think so. *Should* have been, but... No, I was being director in the theater. Of course, just to be a woman directing was bad enough for them. But for a while they did not disturb me... until the *Lysistrata*. Aristophanes. You know it?"

Jonas nodded.

"You can understand, then, that soldiers are anyway not so happy about this play. But I wasn't trying to say things about the army. I wanted the play because it's strong for women, eh? Then, an actor friend, he has no work. A homosexual, and not quiet about it like they want. So, ever since the Colonels come in, the theaters give him no work. Then we think, him and me, of a part for him in *Lysistrata*. As a woman. And then I think to have all men play the women parts. Just like when Aristophanes himself was director, eh? And women to play all the men." Appollonia was cheered by the memory of it.

"So, you ask, was it 'political'? I didn't mean for it to be. But all that, to the army...? *Po-po*. One performance...and whoosh!" The pleasure of her recollection abruptly ended.

"They wanted to know whose idea is it. Who is 'really' the director." Her voice began to scrape, as if stones were being ground by the tendons of her throat. "They would not believe there was no man behind me. So, they kept after me, to tell them of the man...who did not exist. Kept after me, and after me..." Her hand trembled as she lit a cigarette. "Finally, one day I say to them, well, the idea, it comes from Aristophanes." She smiled weakly. "So, then they want to know where he lives..."

She coughed and saw Jonas watching her. She looked at him carefully, taking in both color eyes.

"'Until forty you have the face you are born with. After forty, the face you have made.' Abraham Lincoln." She coughed again. "You know, I didn't smoke before prison." She tapped her chest. "Memories hide in strange places."

⸙

Yiannis was standing in the front room. He tugged Jonas to the larger bed chamber, pulled aside the curtain and pointed to Jonas, who nodded. Then he moved to the small alcove.

"Maria?"

"Marielle, yes."

Yiannis smiled and moved toward the door. "*Yia xhara*"—Your good health—he called back cheerfully. Jonas lay down, but in a moment a deep and sonorous sound like a French horn filled the house: Yiannis in the doorway, blowing on an enormous conch shell. After three prodigious fanfares, he smiled again at Jonas and left.

Unable to decipher Yiannis's curious visit, Jonas went to the *taratsa*, expecting to see Marielle. Not finding her, he took a wine and sat down.

The four fishermen he had seen working their nets that morning invited him to join them. There followed a profusion of cigarettes, polylingual and pantomime questions and answers—they already knew Jonas had arrived with the short-haired woman—and toasts to America, to Greece and to things Jonas didn't understand but drank to anyhow. Jonas would have enjoyed it all were he not so distracted by Appollonia's disturbing tale, by Yiannis's strange performance and by Marielle, or the lack of her. Where was she, anyway?

The setting sun signaled the start of the fishermen's workday. Jonas's slurred reply to their parting salutations hinted to him that he had gotten drunk; his stagger up the stairs confirmed it. As he rested for a moment against a wall on the main walkway, Appollonia shuffled up. Jonas was relieved that she had recovered her ironic smile. They were standing next to one of the many windows that sported a faded *PROKI* box.

"So, what is this stuff, anyway?"

"Ah, the village icon. *Proki*, it means 'proclamation'—you know, like government makes. But since the Colonels have been the government, the word becomes much smaller. Now it means only the proclamation that stops things: You know, 'It is forbidden to...'"

"But this *PROKI* here? These boxes?"

"Yes, forbidden to perspire. How do you call...? De-odor."

"Deodorant? Here?" He looked along the rough-hewn island walkway.

"Oh, no, people don't use it. Only buy it. For the window."

The many glasses of wine were not helping Jonas sort this out.

"What...like, some kind of superstition?"

"Superstition? No. No, Greeks are most practical. You see, the owner to the *PROKI* company is very rich, in Athens. With powerful friends. And his summer house is on the island, a few kilometers from here, up on the mountain. So, some people think, if maybe he comes by our village, it has the nearest shop and baking to him, it's good if have *PROKI* in my window. Because who knows...?

"Also, Pavlatos, of the shop, he delivers food and things to the important man's house. So, who can be sure if Pavlatos does not speak to the man himself? And what if the man wants to know who buys *PROKI*...and who does not? In these days, this is truly how some people have come to think." Appollonia shook her head. "Well, it gets dark now. I must go down the hill."

Jonas walked with her and as they headed toward the promontory below Jonas's rooms, he told Appollonia of Yiannis's strange visit.

"Well, it is his house. His grandfather builds it. And his father builds the low part, where you stay. Yiannis was born there."

"How come he doesn't live in it?"

Appollonia shrugged. "This is not something he talks about. But the village knows, and over the time I hear little pieces.... When Yiannis is a small boy, his father fights in the war, with the Partisans. He comes home, but then the civil war comes a second time, and straight away soldiers go to the house. Arrest him. And just... shoot him. I don't know for certain, but I think Yiannis sees them do it. Then Yiannis stays in the house with his mother, but she dies very soon and he goes away, to some relations. When he is older, he comes back, a fisherman like his father. But not to the house. He stays on the boat, or the beach. Most anyplace. But not the house."

Jonas and Appollonia reached the bottom of the hill. She stopped outside the whitewashed walls topped with crosses.

"I must go in here. Maybe tomorrow we go for another nitpic."

"Picnic. What is this place, anyway?"

"Monastery. Used to be. The Church gives it to the army, during the civil war, I think. I must come here every day, when the sun goes down. To make sure I have not run away."

Jonas's hand came up reflexively and rubbed his blue eye. "Look, I'll wait," he slurred. "We'll go back to the *taratsa*."

"Ah, no. You see, after dark I must be in my house."

Jonas's mouth opened and closed.

"You are in Transylvania, Mr. Renfield," Appollonia said in a strange new accent, "and Transylvania is not England."

"New York." Jonas was confused. "I'm from New York."

Appollonia laughed. "Dracula. You don't know Dracula?"

"Yeah, but..." He rocked unsteadily on his heels.

"Maybe you wait for me," she said. "I think the hill might be some trouble for you."

Jonas looked back up the steep stony path. It was getting dark, his legs wobbly. "Yeah, okay..."

"I will be only one minute."

Appollonia went behind the walls and Jonas slumped down to wait. Many minutes passed but Jonas was content listening to the sea gently lapping the rocks. Eventually the wine forced him up to relieve himself; behind the monastery he found some bushes next to a clearing.

The sun was now well below the hills but a few thin rays squeezed through an odd cleft in the ridge and streaked the monastery wall directly beneath a cross. Jonas was drawn to a pattern produced by a combination of wall contours, streaks of sun and evening shadows. He stepped closer. As the sun's rays shifted, the shape of what might have been a cloaked figure emerged from the layers of whitewash. Jonas stumbled up and put his hands on the wall; the surface was uneven, pitted. He stepped back again, squinting through the green eye, and the figure stood out: head floating to the side, feet off the ground, body unbound from the earth.

"John the fucking Baptist," he said out loud.

Appollonia called to him from around the corner. As he lurched back toward the front, he tripped, put out his arms to break the fall and gouged his hand on a rock. Numbed by alcohol and intoxicated by the vision on the wall, however, he felt little pain and got right up.

"You're not gonna believe this." He failed to notice Appollonia's dazed expression and pulled her around to the back. "You gotta see this. You're not gonna believe this."

The last streaks of sun now barely sifted through to the wall. The shape was visible but less distinct.

"See him? Can you see him? Look." Jonas ran his fingers over the wall. "John the Baptist."

"*Yiannis O Prodromos*, yes. That's the monastery name."

"Name? Hell, I just saw him. Right there on the wall."

Appollonia stepped up to the wall, then back. "If you say so."

The sun's last rays had moved up the wall now and John the Baptist was no more than a rough patch in the plaster.

"I'm telling you, the dude was there. His head off to the side, like. And by now I know him, believe me. It was him."

Appollonia sighed: "First, these people inside here tell me things exist, when I know they don't. And now you. It makes me think I am lucky to stay in my house at night."

Appollonia moved toward the path. Jonas looked once more for the saint on the wall, then decided not to lose sight of Appollonia.

"Wait a second. Did you see something on the wall or not?"

"Sure I see something. Just maybe not the same as you. It's not the first time *taratsa* wine helps someone to see a *thavma*."

"*Thavma?*"

"Yes. *Thavma* is . . . a wonder . . . a vision. Like a miracle kind of thing. Some people have . . . different kinds of seeing. Specially with this wine. But I warn you, the hungover last longer than the miracle. Tomorrow you are lucky if you can open your eyes." They reached the top of the hill. "I must go to my house now. *Kali nichta*—good night."

Jonas tottered over to the *taverna*; Marielle was there on the *taratsa*. "Man, am I glad to see you," Jonas said, plopping into a chair. "Fuckin' John the Baptist, again."

Marielle looked at him blankly.

"You know, like my dream . . . in jail. And that little icon, back in the room . . ."

Then he remembered: the icon had been in the room at Korina's, on Corfu; it had been Liana, not Marielle, to whom he had recounted his dream.

"Shit."

"Jonas, *calmes-toi*. What is it?"

Jonas took a deep breath. "Okay. Down on the rocks. The walled place, that monastery? Only now it's the army's? Anyway, the place with the walls and crosses. I'm down there, see, waiting for Appollonia, around the back, taking a leak . . . and there he is on the wall, right under this cross. John the Baptist. Like a vision, see? Right on the fucking wall. Some kind of . . . *thavma*."

For the first time, Jonas noticed Pavlatos sitting at the next table; the shopkeeper's eyes widened at the word *thavma*. Jonas turned back to Marielle, who was looking extremely skeptical.

"Hey, don't get me wrong. I'm not the miracle type. Yeah, okay, I was brought up Catholic, but it's curable, you know? I been over it a long time. It's just this damn Yiannis been following me around for months and I'm gettin' a little weird behind it."

"Yiannis?"

"No, not that Yiannis. *Yiannis Prodromos*. Something like that. Yiannis the Baptist. *Jean le baptiste*. Man, I don't know."

"He follows you?"

"Well, not exactly. But he keeps showing up. And now on the wall of that monastery thing, or whatever it is, down by the water. A *thavma*. *Yiannis Prodromos*."

Jonas peeked at Pavlatos, who was listening intently.

"That is where I am walking," Marielle said. "You want to show me this?"

"No, no. It's gone now. Tomorrow, though. We can see it tomorrow. I guess. Jesus, what do I know?... What do you mean, that's where you're walking?"

"To go with the fishing boat. Yiannis ask me."

"Yiannis? Oh, that Yiannis. Asked you, eh? So all of a sudden he knows how to talk?"

Marielle frowned and Jonas realized that he had broken their unspoken rules of nonengagement; he sought quickly to make it up.

"Look, here's what we do. We'll call them Yiannis One and Yiannis Two, okay? Keep 'em straight, that way."

Marielle's face still showed her displeasure.

"All right." Jonas's face and voice became serious. "While you're out there tonight, I'd appreciate it if you'd ask them something for me."

"If I can do. Languages is difficult..."

"Ain't that the truth. But it's really important. So give it a try, will you? Something I've just got to find out. So, ask them, will you?—'Do cats eat bats?... Or do bats eat cats?'"

Marielle gave in and smiled. "Yes, this we all like to know." She got up, gave Jonas a conciliatory peck on the brow and went up the stairs. Jonas waved goodbye and noticed that his palm was bleeding where he had gouged it on the rock following his monastery vision. Mouth open, Pavlatos gawked at the bloody palm. Jonas pulled it down quickly and pressed it under his other arm.

15

He heard voices. At first the murmuring merged with his morning dreams; he had slept little during the night but near dawn had fallen into a heavy swollen second sleep. Then the murmurs turned querulous, became bellows and barks. Leaning out of his bed alcove, Jonas was startled and not a little frightened to see three soldiers and a robed, high-hatted priest arguing in the main room. When they spotted Jonas, they rushed him; he flattened himself against the wall. Crowding the bed, the soldiers and priest began jabbering in staccato Greek—solicitously at Jonas, peevishly at one another. As they reached what seemed the verge of blows, the priest spread his robes and drew himself to his full height (made fuller by the cylindrical hat of his office). This assertion of ecclesiastic primacy momentarily silenced the debate, but before the priest could solidify his position, a soldier with epaulets spoke up in his best baritone and angled to the front. When the other soldiers responded by coming to a sort of attention, the priest gave in with an expression that attempted to maintain clerical dignity by way of a poorly feigned lack of concern. The ranking soldier enjoyed a moment of command, then turned to Jonas. It was immediately clear, however, that although this soldier had won the right to communicate with Jonas, he had no idea how to do so. Finally he burst forth with a fusillade of phrases Jonas was certain were not intended to convey information, threw Jonas's pants at him, and pushed the others back into the main room.

The procession snaked its way single-file down the hill. The soldiers were polite to Jonas, even deferential. Jonas felt the honored if not entirely voluntary guest. But he was also acutely mindful that in his first encounter with the Greek military his face had been battered against a bus and that, in the second, rifle butts had slammed his head and he had woken up in a prison cell.

Jonas and the soldiers crowded into a small office in the former monastery. Jonas was surprised to see Pavlatos the grocer, hemmed into a corner chair by two flanking soldiers and looking even more blanched and costive than usual. The ranking soldier sat down behind a desk; the priest stood at his shoulder; Jonas sat facing the desk. For a long minute no one spoke. Then the soldier produced a pack of cigarettes, a familiar American brand. He and Jonas smoked in silence, Pavlatos squirming in his chair. Finally the top soldier began to speak amiably to Jonas, smiling and making sweeping gestures beyond the walls, concluding with an interrogatory *"Endaxi?"*—Okay?

Jonas understood none of it, except the *Endaxi*. He cleared his throat and answered politely that he was sorry he did not speak Greek. The soldier became flustered and his layer of cordiality peeled away. He glared at a shriveling Pavlatos, then spoke again to Jonas, slowly, distinctly, loudly. But Jonas still didn't speak Greek. He did manage to pick up a word, though, that began to explain the whole thing: *thavma*—a vision.

Meekly, Pavlatos tried to speak. The soldier growled him into silence, then thought about it for a moment and relented.

"The Yiannis," Pavlatos said to Jonas. *"O Prodromos.* Yesterday night, yes? Please show to him. Yes?"

Things were becoming a bit clearer: Pavlatos, eavesdropping on Jonas and Marielle at the *taratsa*, must have gone straight to the army with a report of Jonas's drunken vision.

"Sighnomi"—I am sorry—Jonas said to the soldier, "but I don't think I can do that."

The soldier didn't seem to appreciate the difference between *can* do and *will* do but understood Jonas's shake of the head. He scowled, berated Pavlatos and slammed his hand on the table for effect. It had an effect. Pavlatos implored Jonas, and though it seemed the grocer was in hotter water than he was, Jonas, too, would have liked to make this soldier happy and get the hell out of there.

The expression "voice of an angel" normally conjures smooth and caressing tones, and Appollonia's rasp would not normally be thought to qualify. But so elated was Jonas to hear her "Caw!" out in the courtyard that he might have convinced the Inquisition itself of her celestial qualities. She stepped into the doorway, sailor's cap on head and cigarette between teeth, and spoke to the top soldier in tones which slid easily among cajolery, counsel and rebuke.

"Only when the sun goes down, I tell them," she translated for Jonas. "Everyone knows no miracles happen in daytime."

She spoke again to the soldier, but despite her blandishments he seemed unconvinced of the incompatibility of miracles and daylight. He turned to grill Pavlatos; Appollonia moved over next to Jonas.

"My brave captain would be very happy for a small miracle on his wall," she whispered to Jonas. "Good advertisement for the army, eh? Maybe it makes him big in Athens. But if he tells about this to Athens and then it turns out to be only a dentist in a teapot, well..."

Turning disgustedly from the grocer, the captain now fumed at Jonas and Appollonia. She remained calm, patiently answering him and translating for Jonas.

"Our shop-man Pavlatos ran to him about your *thavma* last night and they looked all over the walls but cannot find it. Still, my captain does not want to miss his big chance. And so, now he does not know what to do. This is not a happy soldier. Also not a very smart soldier. But for sure not a happy one."

The captain snarled an order and the soldiers flanking Pavlatos grabbed him roughly under the arms and yanked him out of the room. Then the captain rose menacingly and two other soldiers edged closer. Jonas instinctively raised his hands to parry any sudden moves heading his way, and as he did, the priest let out a gasp. Crossing himself repeatedly, the wide-eyed priest pointed at Jonas's hand; in the center of his palm was the bloody mark from his fall the night before. The soldiers backed away slightly as the priest continued rapidly crossing himself. Though the captain still seethed, he could hardly ignore such impressive evidence of the miraculous. Mumbling to himself, he stormed out the door.

❧

Appollonia set bread and cheese on her table under the vine.

"Why they cannot leave people alone?" Marielle spoke with as much pique as concern. "It is so far away here."

"Far away?" Appollonia said. "At the South Pole they find birds with the rings of drink tins in their throats."

"I just don't get it why that slime Pavlatos cares if I get drunk and start having visions? I mean, what's it to him?"

"*Philotimo*—honor."

"What the hell does honor have to do with it? Whose honor, for chrissake?"

"Mm. Yes, it is not so simple. You see, each one must keep home, work, thoughts to himself... to protect them. Because to know someone else's business can put his honor down, and yours up. In the villages it has always been like this. But in these last years, *philotimo* has become a twisted thing. Used to be, a person finds out something, he uses it some way by being clever. But now, a person can just run to the soldiers. And to make someone look bad to the army doesn't take much being clever, eh? Doesn't matter even if he knows what he talks about. Just, can he tell the soldiers something they want to hear. And become a big man. Like Pavlatos, that shop-man. *Philotimo*"—she turned her head and spat—"our honor has become our shame.... But not to worry about tonight."

"I don't know, that captain what's-his-name won't be too pleased if John the Baptist decides to take the night off."

"Ah, Stromos." Appollonia chuckled. "He is no captain, really. I just call him that. Stromos, he tries to be bigger than his trousers. So, yes, maybe tonight he makes a noise when there is no *thavma*. But after, he won't know what to do. So he will do nothing. Like always. You remember last night, when you are seeing your *thavma*, how long Stromos keeps me inside? No, the wine... you don't remember too much. No matter. But, the reason was a paper for me to sign. I tell you, you will laugh. Before, you see, for theater people there was a group in Athens, like a council. And just before the Colonels come in, the last person to be head of council was me. So now, after six years, the junta makes a paper for the head of council to sign—a paper for renouncing... denouncing?... against a director who lives exile in Italy, a director who does theater there against our junta situation. So last night, Stromos puts the paper in front of me, and does like this..." Appollonia hunkered herself into a Stromos imitation, then whirled around and slammed her hand on the table: "'You will sign or I cannot be responsible for what happens!'... Hah. Just like in the movies.

"So I say to him, 'My captain, my brave one, I would sign because if not, I cannot stand to think how well you will do to me what you must do to me. But my captain,' I say, 'I cannot sign because when they send me to prison those years ago, they also close and forbid the council. *Proki*, the council. Finished. So, what trouble would there be—what trouble for you—if you make me sign for the council... when the government has said the council no longer exists?'"

Appollonia pressed her hands together to reenact her votive pose of the night before, then broke into a grin. "He bangs around the room, but doesn't know what to do. And so, he does nothing. He lets me go last night, eh?"

Jonas laughed with relief but Marielle showed no pleasure at all. She had said almost nothing all day and now she chafed under Jonas's gaze.

"I am tired, I think," Marielle said to the ground. "The boat all night. Maybe I will take some sleep."

For the first time since his vision on the wall, Jonas thought of Marielle having spent the night on Yiannis's boat. He felt himself flush, wanted to know what was going on with her. "I think I'll go, too," he said. Immediately he looked for reproach in Marielle's face and was surprised to find none.

"Yes, for tonight we need rest," Appollonia added. "Specially me. I don't stay out late so much anymore." She laughed heartily, then waved them away as the cough racked her chest.

The village was a blinding sun-white maze. Jonas and Marielle were the only people out. The only sound was the brush and clip of their shoes on the central flagstone walkway. As they reached the top of the path down to their rooms, Jonas stared over the connected roofs which draped the hillside. He grinned and made a sound in his throat like a child first learning how to gargle. He hushed Marielle with a finger to his lips and fetched some donkey straw from near the path. Hopping onto a wall and then a flat roof, he indicated to Marielle a smooth plaster channel, about three feet wide. It sloped in a steep straight line down two successive hillside roofs and ended in a large communal trough into which rainwater ran and was stored.

"I can make it," he whispered to her.

He went below and very quietly removed the trough's wooden cover, then came back up, climbed on the roof and piled the straw at his feet. To Jonas's surprise, Marielle hopped onto the roof with him, pulling her skirt up between her legs. Jonas sat on the straw behind her, his legs outside hers, and pushed off. Within a few feet, they were flying down the channel, straw spewing, arms and legs waving, Jonas unable to suppress a cry of delight. They splashed into the cool water and came up laughing, but nearby voices sent them clambering out. Quickly heaving the cover back on the trough, they scurried to their rooms.

"For me, this was excellent." Marielle stood in the middle of the room running a hand back through her glistening hennaed hair. "I was having so much . . . congesting."

Jonas, too, was invigorated by the caper. He had always relished the impropriety of such spontaneous foolishness. "Silliness and love," he used to say to his wife, "are moments of freedom." And this was a moment he wanted to last. But here was Marielle heading into her bed alcove. He wanted to follow her past her curtain, not merely to keep their escapade alive, not only for the pleasure of continuing their laughter together, but for these things and more, to add to the many moments over their long days together that had steadily and without warning accrued into some sort of intimacy. Something between them that had thickened his blood. What, exactly, he didn't know: not romantic, exactly; nor lustful; not even comradely, at least not as he'd known that feeling. But . . . something. And in this place, this moment, something that mattered. But there were the rules they'd set. There were curtains. Jonas went to his bed, changed out of his wet clothes and picked up *Alice*:

> "Dear, dear! How queer everything is to-day! And yesterday
> things went on just as usual. I wonder if I've been changed
> in the night? Let me think: was I the same when I got up
> this morning?"

Jonas heard the familiar cough and stuck his head out: Appollonia, in the front room, motioning to him.

She pulled him outside and up to the main walkway. "Tell me, what kind of people see *thavma*? People with faith, that's who. Now, our captain Stromos, he very much wants to see *thavma*, but he has no helping faith. So, we help him. With the same faith that helped you, eh? Come on."

They reached Pavlatos's shop. It was closed.

"Give a knock. When Pavlatos will see it's you, he will open up. Then ask him for a bottle of *raki*. You know what is *raki*?"

Jonas nodded, recalling his first fiery sip from Kalliope's bottle on the train in Italy.

"Good. But nothing with printing on it; he will try to sell you that, because he makes more money. No, you want only the local-made *raki*, because you drink enough of that"—her hand twirled to the sky—"you see whatever you want. And maybe some things you don't want." She suppressed a cackle and stepped aside. Jonas knocked. Pavlatos's wife appeared at a window; when she saw Jonas she went wide-eyed and opened the door. "And some bread!" Appollonia whispered.

Pavlatos's wife was extremely nervous and responded to Jonas's request by immediately scuttling behind the counter. She brought out two bottles of *raki* and two loaves of bread, pressing them on Jonas and adamantly refusing his money. She seemed relieved, grateful even, when Jonas accepted. Outside, Jonas described the exchange to Appollonia, who guessed that the shopkeeper was now in deep water with the army and that his wife hoped the *raki* might somehow help him out.

"Maybe she is right. But not two bottles—only one."

"What if the first one doesn't do the trick?"

"Ah, not so simple. To bring *raki* is a proper thing; Stromos will open your bottle and bring out one of his own. But to bring two bottles? *Tzk.* Does Stromos not have enough *raki* of his own? Is his hospitality so poor? *Po-po. Philotimo*, my friend. And even if two bottles does not insult him, he must bring out two bottles of his own. Do you know what we will be like after four bottles *raki*? Dead, we will be like. No, we bring one bottle only."

After gorging bread as prophylaxis, they headed down to the erstwhile monastery. In the little office they found a stern but jumpy Stromos, several soldiers and a decidedly anxious Pavlatos.

Jonas offered the *raki*. Stromos accepted with formality and ordered glasses but poured only for Jonas and himself. Jonas was not surprised that Appollonia was left out, but the exclusion of the other soldiers was a bit distressing: not from a surge of egalitarian spirit but at the thought of any Greek soldiers connecting him with an affront to their dignity.

Stromos began the toasts—to Jonas; Jonas—to Greece; Stromos—America; Jonas—*Yiannis O Prodromos*; Stromos—the army; Jonas—the island beauty. By now they had almost finished the first bottle and if Stromos felt at all like Jonas, he was well on his way to seeing any vision he wanted.

A second bottle was brought in along with plates of *metzedes*. An expansive Stromos now filled glasses for Pavlatos and for the other soldiers, and soon they were all smoking, toasting, munching, talking. Appollonia grinned, her coup a success. But suddenly Stromos's face tightened. In the doorway stood a small, handsome man in his fifties dressed in an impeccable white linen suit. He looked on the room with no overt disapprobation but the tilt of his body indicated that he would not enter until a greater measure of decorum was restored. Behind him stood the priest who'd accompanied the soldiers when they'd first brought Jonas here.

The soldiers hastily straightened up. Stromos rose and introduced the man to Jonas as Mr. Idronis, who greeted Jonas politely, if distantly, in perfect English. He ignored Appollonia. Jonas took a peek; her expression of triumph had vanished.

Stromos gave his chair to Idronis, who took it as if it were his due. The priest stood by Idronis's shoulder as he had by Stromos's that morning. Stromos poured more *raki* and Idronis offered a toast, translating for Jonas: "To this holy place." Then he recounted how, as a young officer during the civil war, he had been posted on this island and that part of this same monastery had served as his bivouac; he had spent many happy months within these walls, he said. Years later he built a summer home here and constructed a chapel of St. John the Baptist on the rocks nearby. When the military again came to "deserved prominence" several years ago, at his urging the Church gave over the entire monastery to the army, as a gesture toward their common goals.

"This is a special, holy place," Idronis repeated to the assembly, none of whom appeared to understand the English but who listened raptly nonetheless, "where God's favors can be seen." Idronis turned to Jonas: "And now the sun is almost down, which, I have been told, allows another of God's favors to be seen."

Idronis said something in Greek, and Stromos brusquely ordered the food and *raki* taken away, as if suddenly they offended. Idronis got to his feet, smoothed his suit and led the group outside. Appollonia trailed behind with Jonas. "Idronis," she whispered, and made a muscle with her arm like that on the *PROKI* boxes, "the de-odor man."

It was a solemn if not entirely sober procession which weaved its way toward the rear wall. Waiting there were two well-groomed, muscular young men in suits who nodded to Idronis. Jonas glanced up at the village: he could see no one but noticed movements at windows and sensed many eyes watching. Idronis now looked to Jonas, who checked the sinking sun, the shadows, the wall: "Another few minutes, I guess." Idronis nodded patiently and the entire group stared with reverence at the empty white wall. The scene reminded Jonas of the emperor's new clothes fable and he smiled to himself. Until he realized that maybe he was the emperor.

The sun dipped lower. The rays that squeezed through the cleft in the ridge threw odd patterns onto the wall but as yet described nothing saintly. Village lights came on, combining with the last darts of sun to speckle a rough spot on the wall. But still no figure appeared. Idronis remained impassive but Stromos was growing increasingly restive. Jonas's bloodied palm was beginning to sweat. He could now make out shadows which the night before might have formed part of the image, but if one had not previously seen the whole, it would be impossible—*raki* or not—to extrapolate from this fragment to a John the Baptist, head or no head.

The refracted light was moving inexorably along the wall, soon to leave the crucial spot altogether. And still the image had not materialized. A shadow suddenly darkened part of the crucial section of the wall. Jonas looked up to see a human silhouette in the branches of a dead tree high up on the hill in the opening of the crevice, blocking a portion of the rays that filtered through.

"The sun," Jonas said, and gestured toward the tree.

Stromos moved to the base of the hill, waved his arms and yelled at the man in the tree. Nothing. He cursed and ordered a couple of his men up the hill, but it was a futile gesture: the sun would be gone before they could reach him.

Stromos now took hold of a soldier's rifle, calmly raised it and fired. A puff of dirt kicked up near the tree. The figure didn't move. Stromos fired again, hitting just in front of the tree. Still the person didn't move. Stromos paused, then raised the gun once more, aiming carefully.

"Jesus Christ," Jonas blurted, and turned to Idronis.

The *PROKI* man merely stared back coldly, and when Stromos saw Idronis's tacit approval, he poised again over the rifle.

"*Panaghia!*"—Holy Virgin!—the priest bellowed, a sudden exclamation occasioned not by Stromos's gun but by what now appeared on the wall. There, among the shadows, rough spots and last glints of sun, was Jonas's John the Baptist. At least for those who had faith.

Stromos rushed the wall, casting his own shadow over the image. The priest screeched and Stromos jumped back, but now it was the priest who, crossing himself repeatedly, moved closer and cast a shadow. Stromos snapped at the priest and the two cursed and bumped shoulders, completely blocking the image until a sharp word from Idronis parted them. By now the image had deteriorated and in another moment was no more than amorphous textures and shadows. The show was over.

"I have always said this is a most holy place," Idronis declared. Jonas tried to read his face, to see what else might be lurking there, but there was not enough light. Without further ado, Idronis went up the path. The two young men in suits trailed behind him.

For the next several days, Jonas and Marielle disappeared under a thick cover of Aegean heat. They would leave the village in the early morning, succumb gratefully to the lassitude demanded by midsummer days, and not appear again for a meal on the *taratsa* until well after dark. Jonas sought no village life, kept a distance from Stromos, soldiers, priest and Pavlatos. And while he would not have admitted avoiding Appollonia, in truth her mere presence would have felt too injunctive, too much a reminder of the larger world.

Without saying as much, Jonas and Marielle chose to spend whole days together. Each was by the other's company simultaneously protected against both solitude and human complications. There were many hours hardly speaking. Relievedly so. At times Jonas thought of Liana and how different, how apostrophic and weighted, her silences had been.

The fourth day after the confrontation at the wall, summer turned itself up another notch. The island lay passive and helpless in the heat. Jonas and Marielle spent the day moving between shade and water at a cove several miles from the village. In late afternoon, when the sun and searing *meltemi* wind combined to scald the very stones, they headed back for the relative cool of their rooms. Coming around a bend, they stumbled onto Yiannis sitting by a bush. There was nothing around except baked rocks and barren ground, no reason for a fisherman to be there except for a view of the cove Jonas and Marielle had been on. With a morose, distant face, Yiannis barely looked at them. And so surprised were they to come upon him, so disconcerted by his failure to greet them, that they walked by without stopping.

Next morning at the *taratsa*, there was Yiannis again, heavy eyes struggling to stay open after his night on the sea, head nodding on his chest. Marielle chose a different table and sat staring down at the port. From time to time Yiannis would look at Marielle with a blank expression which could not entirely hide its yearning. He was asleep in the chair when they left.

Marielle was distressed by Yiannis's pitiful sleepwalking but refused to speak of it. She said she was going off by herself; Jonas was happy to let her brood alone. He wandered around the village, watched women washing clothes at a well, listened to their ritual exchange of raucous remarks. He returned to the *taratsa* at midday, an hour when it had become too hot to work but the afternoon meal was not yet ready at home, an hour when the men of Kastelo gathered for the tug and nudge of conversation over cups of grainy coffee. Jonas followed through tones and gestures the flow of argument, insult and exchange. These men saw each other every day, year after year, yet Jonas could see that their familiarity had bred a relation among them far richer than boredom or contempt.

In the early afternoon, the *taverna* closed for *ipnos* and the village retreated behind silent walls. Jonas was lost. He didn't want or need to rest. Rest from what? He didn't want another placid afternoon by the sea, didn't want to sit in his room and read a book, read about other people's lives. After several empty turns around the village, he headed for Appollonia's and was surprised to see Yiannis, shirt in hand, coming out the door. The fisherman went to a rusted barrel, dumped water from it over his head and chest, shook himself like a dog and walked away. Jonas waited until he had gone, then went up and knocked at the open door. From deep in the darkness, Appollonia said something which ended in "Yianni" and was followed by her inimitable cackle. Jonas called through the doorway; the cackle ended abruptly. There was movement inside, then Appollonia said to come in.

It took a few moments for Jonas's eyes to adjust but immediately his nose took in a powerful musk of bodies. A barefoot Appollonia stood by the bed in an old wrap.

"I've not seen you for some days. Come, sit down. Please excuse me, but for me here appearances are not much use." She wiped the sweat from her brow.

"Sort of like deodorant," Jonas said, wiping away his own sweat.

Appollonia laughed and lit a cigarette. "You've seen Yiannis?" she said after a moment. Jonas nodded. "We have an understanding, you see. Days are long; we are *parea*—company—to each other. That is worth sometimes a lot."

"Yeah, seems Yiannis likes company more than he first lets on."

Appollonia raised her eyebrows, then understood: "Ah, Marielle. Yes, he speaks of her." She shook her head. "But that, I think, is about more than just *parea*. You see, some of us can do perfectly well alone . . . but know that we do not want to. Yiannis knows. Then there are others of us who imagine we can go alone . . . but don't do it nearly so well."

Jonas and Appollonia spent the afternoon near her cottage making drawings, Appollonia patiently teaching, Jonas clumsily but happily—he surprised himself—following. She spoke to him of basic shapes, of light and shadow, movement and stasis. They finished by drawing noses, and finally Jonas understood what she meant by "negative space."

When later he turned down the path to his rooms, he saw Yiannis stationed on a rock below, standing watch on the door. Inside, Jonas found a drawn and tired Marielle.

"I try to explain him. . . . On the boat, he was so . . . *gentil*. He shows me all the fishing. And when I am sleeping he covers me with his coat. *Et c'est tout*—that was all. No . . . bothering to me. But now this, this following, this all the time looking on me." She shook her head. "He see me with you and I explain, I am with you, but we are not together. Then, after I am all night on the boat, he want to talk to me all the time, be with me, again and again." She clenched and unclenched her fists. "I say to him many times, a person can be with someone but not really *with* them, but..."

"But he doesn't understand," Jonas finished her sentence.

"No.... Always people want... more," she said plaintively.

Marielle went to her bed behind the curtain and did not come out again that night. Jonas had supper alone on the *taratsa*. In the morning he invited her to join him and Appollonia making sketches of the village but Marielle said she wanted to stay inside. Anyway, she said, she no longer cared about making pictures.

"Something is happening," Appollonia said when Jonas found her perched on a spot a hundred yards or so above her cottage, a spot over-looking the main harbor. She drew deeply on a cigarette. "This is Sunday; no boats come here Sunday."

Down at the harbor Jonas could see a different ferry from the one that made two regular weekly stops. Three jeeps rolled off the ferry followed by several men in uniform and a procession of priests. The new arrivals were greeted by a large black sedan; Jonas could make out Idronis's white linen suit. The soldiers and priests got into the car and jeeps, but instead of heading for the island's main town, they turned onto the dirt track leading up to Kastelo. They drove up and rolled into a field, the closest place to the village which could accommodate cars. Stromos and his soldiers were waiting; they led the newly arrived officers and priests down to the former monastery.

The central walkway was filled with people on their way to the village church. Jonas had witnessed the two previous village Sundays, and either the local population had grown significantly since then or, in this Greece of Christian Greeks, Kastelo had not until today been quite as Christian as the government would have wanted. It also seemed to Jonas that, like the faithful, the village *PROKI* boxes had suddenly gone forth and multiplied.

Appollonia and Jonas moved over to the other edge of the cliff to get a view of the officers and ecclesiastics as they gathered outside the former monastery. One military man was speaking with Stromos off to the side.

Appollonia drew in a breath and strained to see him, but the man and Stromos disappeared behind the walls. Appollonia stood quietly for a moment, lost in thought, then shook herself as if trying to dismiss the lingering image of a bad dream. She and Jonas went to the *taratsa* where she lit a cigarette and stared out toward the harbor. Jonas left her alone until finally she spoke.

"I thought . . . someone I used to know. Before. . . . But, probably I just imagine. Another *thavma*, eh?" She laughed weakly; there was no cackle.

Marielle came clattering down the stairs, agitated, frightened.

"Soldiers," she said out of breath to Jonas. "They come and ask where are you. And they ask my papers. I tell them you are with Appollonia. One soldier, I never see him before. . . . The others, they look through my bag, but this soldier, he stops them. . . . Him," she whispered, "that is him."

A slight, pale army officer stood at the top of the stairs. Appollonia's jaw tightened and she looked away. Followed by Stromos, the officer came down to the table. Stromos grunted Jonas's name and the officer—who disarmed Jonas with a soft voice and a face that held more sadness than menace—introduced himself in English as Captain Lakis Skoriasos. As Skoriasos's eyes darted back and forth toward Appollonia, Jonas gestured for them to sit.

"I hope we did not disturb you overly much," Skoriasos said to Marielle. "Soldiers are trained in certain ways."

Marielle merely stared; she wanted no part of a conversation.

"*Lipon, milate ellinika ligho*, eh?"—So, you speak a little Greek?—he turned to Jonas as if they had just settled in together for a long voyage. Jonas took in Skoriasos's once-handsome face, now sallow and creased beyond his forty or so years.

"No, not really. Hardly at all."

"Well, then, we will speak in English."

The English clearly made Stromos uncomfortable but Skoriasos proceeded as if the other soldier were not there.

"It is my understanding that you have experienced quite unusual things since you are in Greece."

Jonas blanched, uncertain how many parts of his unorthodox sojourn Skoriasos was aware of.

"You mean the wall. John the Baptist."

"The wall, yes. The...illusion." Skoriasos pronounced the word in a way that seemed to acknowledge its several shadings.

"Listen. People should understand. Just because I thought I saw something, doesn't mean it was really a *thavma*. I mean, all my life I've...seen things."

"Yes," Skoriasos said quietly, "not all our visions turn out to be miracles..."

Out of the corner of his blue eye, Jonas saw Appollonia shiver.

"...However, this vision now appears to have a life of its own."

Several churchgoers filtered onto the *taratsa* but kept a distance from this portentous group at the corner table.

"You see, a man of...considerable influence believes that what happened at the monastery may be of some importance."

"Idronis."

"*Kyrios* Idronis, yes."

Stromos sat up straight at the mention of the name.

"But let us not speak of questions too large," Skoriasos continued. "It can make one very tired. And one should not be tired for this evening's celebrations..." He glanced at Appollonia but she was holding tightly to a strained impassivity, staring at the sea. "...for which your presence, Mr. Korda, will be appreciated, at one hour before the sun is down."

Jonas swallowed and nodded.

"And when you return to Athens," Skoriasos continued, "the nation of Greece will be pleased to make you its honored guest."

The taste in Jonas's mouth turned rancid.

"That is, if all goes well," Skoriasos added.

The *taratsa* was now crowded. Stromos's exclusion from the conversation was obvious to the villagers and he was afflicted by it. He spoke to Skoriasos, who wearily closed his eyes. Stromos got up and growled something, clearly meant as show for the neighboring tables, then went up the stairs. Skoriasos fixed on Appollonia's profile.

"You are looking well, Ionia," he finally said, in English.

At first Appollonia did not move, then slowly she turned and examined his face: "You are not."

Their eyes locked on each other for a moment.

"Still a captain, I see."

"Yes," he smiled wanly, "I do not seem to be the kind of soldier the army puts ahead these years."

"Well, things could be worse. You could have spoken up in these years . . . and then you would not be with the army at all."

Skoriasos blinked several times; his tongue sought his lips.

"You could be on a small island," she continued, the corners of her mouth softening. "Or worse, on a small island with me."

Jonas nudged Marielle. "I think maybe we'll leave you now."

"I would appreciate it if you stay," Skoriasos said. "It gives us a reason not to speak Greek, you see. Us two . . . old friends."

Jonas glanced around at the villagers on the *taratsa*, whose eyes were averted but whose ears were anything but. Appollonia lit a cigarette.

"You never smoked before," Skoriasos said.

"I was never in prison before." She turned to Jonas and Marielle. "We were at university together, you see. And in theater. There were many beautiful times. Until Lakis had to leave us. We waited for him to return, but . . ."

"To become an officer was . . . different then." Something caught in his throat and stopped the words which tried to follow.

"It is no accident you are here, is it," Appollonia said after a moment. Skoriasos closed his eyes.

"Again you will take me to prison," she said quietly.

"I did not take you to prison, Lonia."

"No, no, that's right. They only sent you to warn me. To tell me to stop being . . . who I was. They got to punish us *both* that way, didn't they, Laki?"

Skoriasos looked down at the table.

"And this time?" Appollonia asked.

It was a long moment before he raised his head. "The theater council. A statement against the Kamanos plays. Stromos has already told you, I think."

Appollonia's body relaxed and she almost smiled.

"Ach. What can I do, Laki *mou*? The council was *proki*, remember? The Ministry of Culture forbid it six years ago. It no longer exists. So, no council, no one to sign any council paper, eh."

Skoriasos closed his eyes again briefly, then spoke slowly, as if to ensure that he would not have to pronounce the words more than once:

"A new rule has been made. For one day only, to make a statement against Kamanos. On this one day there is again a theater council... and a head of the council. For this one day, Lonia, they have declared that you exist."

His words fell on the table between them. Appollonia stared at him, then turned away.

"They have told me your name will not be used in any public announcements." He spoke quickly now and unfolded a paper on the table. "But you are to sign." His voice softened: "Just leave this for me by the morning. There is no need to see me again if you don't wish.... I hope we have not too much disturbed your holiday," he said to Jonas and Marielle as he got up.

When Skoriasos had gone, Jonas noticed tears in Appollonia's eyes. But her stoic countenance did not change, and the tears lasted only a few moments. "It was a long time ago," she said, and got to her feet. "I will see you later, when the sun is going down."

The paper from Skoriasos sat on the table like a sore.

"Miracles," she said, picked up the paper without looking at it, and walked through the silent gauntlet of tables. As soon as she had gone, the villagers filled the terrace with talk.

16

"But if I'm not the same, the next question is 'Who in the world am I?' Ah, *that's* the great puzzle!" And she began thinking over all the children she knew, that were of the same age as herself, to see if she could have been changed for any of them.

By midafternoon the heat that radiated up from the ground was as fierce as that from above: Marielle was sitting cross-legged on their flagstone floor; Jonas was stretched lengthwise as he read to her, trying to touch as much skin as possible to the cooling stones. Then he heard the wooden cover come off the water trough. Though reluctant to dip into the precious water supply on his own, whenever Jonas heard villagers there, he would join them to fill the tank which served his and Marielle's rooms. Now he put down the book and went outside.

Not until he brought back the first bucketful did Jonas notice Yiannis sitting against a wall a few feet from the door to their rooms, holding and stroking some sort of small furry animal. The fisherman didn't look up, so Jonas continued to the wall, climbed up the outside steps to the platform that supported the rooms' gravity-powered water tank, hoisted the bucket and poured it in. Six times Jonas repeated his trip from trough to tank without a flicker of recognition from Yiannis. Then Jonas noticed Marielle in the doorway, lines stretching from the corners of her eyes. Yiannis saw her, too, but did not stir; the possum-like fur-ball slept peacefully in his hands. Marielle went back inside. She was on the floor sitting against his bed when Jonas came in. Her jaw set, she held the copy of *Alice* out to him. Jonas sat next to her and read in a low voice.

"No, I've made up my mind about it: if I'm Mabel, I'll stay

down here! It'll be no use their putting their heads down and saying, 'Come up again, dear!'"

He could see Marielle struggling with something other than the words.

"I shall only look up and say 'Who am I, then? Tell me that first, and then, if I like being that person, I'll come up...'"

Marielle stared at her bare legs stretched in front of her. She began to rub them as if speaking with her hands, trying to awaken a response she knew they could give if only they would listen.

"'...if not, I'll stay down here till I'm somebody else'—but, oh dear!" cried Alice, with a sudden burst of tears, "I do wish they *would* put their heads down! I am so *very* tired of being all alone here!"

Jonas read on. Marielle didn't look at him as her hands continued to rub. She wet her lips, not in false display but as part of a larger effort to loosen herself. Her breathing became deeper. She rubbed an arm now, then the other, slowly lolled her head around, stretching her neck in all directions. Jonas watched her look up at the ceiling and beyond: the lines around her eyes were softening, her face becoming calm. She stretched forward now until her forehead touched her knees, then slowly she straightened herself, got up, and went across to her own bed, saying nothing. The curtain fell behind her.

"Don't worry 'bout my money, honey, just don't waste my time."

The line popped into Jonas's head and he tried to recall what it had meant. He couldn't remember where the line had originally come from. Or who had said it to whom...if it had ever really been said at all. He glanced toward Marielle's bed; the closed curtain gave him no help and he drifted off to sleep with the line repeating in his head: "Don't worry 'bout my money, honey..."

Papers!

Jonas sat up with a start. The soldiers had asked for Marielle's papers. Of course. They were always checking papers; in Athens he had seen them stop people randomly on the street. That had been one of the advantages of The Nice, one of the reasons the barman at Dirty Dick's had steered Jonas there: it was a place that did not bother too much with things like papers. Because when Jonas was released from jail, his passport had been stamped with an exclusion mark; the barman had showed it to him. And now, here, if the army saw it...

Jonas dug into his bag. The passport was still there. Of course it was still there; if it weren't, he wouldn't be either. Or would he? Maybe they'd already seen the passport and were just waiting for him to show them the *thavma* before hauling him off. Jesus fuck!

No, no, he calmed himself. They didn't need him for the *thavma*. Idronis had seen it. Stromos, too. No, if they'd found his passport, he'd be history by now. But wait. Appollonia's old flame Skoriasos, on the *taratsa*, what did he say? "The Greek nation will make you its guest." Whatever that meant! They were bound to see his passport, then. Shit!

Jonas hurried outside; below, he could see the soldiers moving around at the rear wall of the monastery.

Appollonia was squatting on a hillock behind her cottage, sketch pad and pencil in hand.

"Can I talk to you, Appollonia?"

Despite Jonas's obvious agitation, she barely acknowledged his presence. She tilted her head, first one way then the other, appraising the village. "It's a place, this place." Her eyes were glazed, as if she had taken a blow to the head. Jonas squatted beside her and offered a cigarette; she ignored it. He lit a match for his own cigarette and the flame jolted her; she backed away from it like an animal from a torch, then stared at the glowing tip. "I cannot go in again," she said in a rush, "I cannot, cannot..."

Jonas swallowed. His own panic paled. In her face he could see the fear of imprisonment itself. And of torture. But more, a terror for the death of her spirit: she had reached the very edge of her sanity and was facing the abyss.

"Because, you see, what good does it really do? The paper to sign is anyway stupid. No one pays attention." Her voice took on a strange, higher pitch. "If I don't sign, they just go to the next person of the council, then the next. What good would that do? Only put the others in trouble. But if I do sign, the worry stops. For everyone."

Jonas looked at her sketch pad; it was empty.

"I was not political," she continued, more firmly. "I have told you this."

Jonas nodded but knew nothing to say.

"I cannot remember when I slept all the way through the night," she finally said, then got up and walked off the hill. Jonas followed. "What was it?" she asked. "You came for something?"

Jonas had almost forgotten his own problem, was embarrassed by it now. They sat under her sagging trellis, and at Appollonia's urging he told her—in a truncated, round-cornered version—of the events on Corfu: visiting a house; some political people had been arrested; wrong place, wrong time for him.

And what had they done with him after the arrest? she asked.

Jonas told her he had spent a week in the cells.

But did they suspect him? she wanted to know. Did they . . . question him?

"No, no. They didn't really do anything. Just wanted to scare me, I think. And give me time to heal."

"Enough of negative space," she said. "Tell me."

And she pressed him until his anger and frustration came boiling back up. The whole thing a stupid waste, he raged: his face smashed and his guts turned inside out; Kalliope, Alekos, Nosey all in prison. Probably Leonides, too. And for what? A lousy bunch of poems?

"These were poets, these people?" Appollonia asked quietly.

"I guess. And musicians. I don't know. Some of them weren't anything." Jonas thought of Nosey's recalcitrance and resentment. "Just people trying to get over."

"Some of them were out of the country, you say . . . but they came back?"

Jonas nodded. Appollonia chewed her lip where there was usually a cigarette. "And you. Why are you still here?"

"Where am I supposed to be?" he said testily. "Anyway, I'm keeping my nose clean."

"And what could that mean here, 'keeping your nose clean'?"

Jonas couldn't tell if she was unfamiliar with the expression or too familiar with it. She squinted toward the village; three people were watching them from the shadows. Appollonia got up casually and went into the cottage, came out a moment later with a sheet. She stopped to caress Jonas's hair, then hung the dry sheet over the line. She returned to Jonas with her face set hard.

"'What good is a philosopher who makes no one angry?'" Appollonia recited, indicating the village busybodies. Jonas could see that the sheet plus Appollonia's caress had set them waggling their hands in excited conversation.

"Diogenes," Appollonia identified the author of the adage, and broke into the cackle Jonas had not heard for days.

In a clearing between Appollonia's cottage and the village, a farmer was winnowing grain with a wooden pitchfork, golden chaff floating away on the hot afternoon wind. Last day, Jonas thought: last day smelling thick Greek coffee on the *taratsa*; last day seeing the village children return from picking wild berries, their fingers and lips stained crimson; last day waiting for the heavy figs to burst their thick purple skins.

"Awwwk!" he heard Appollonia caw from the cottage. "Pavlatos!" she cried in the doorway, still holding the long handle of her coffee cooker. "Pavlatos. That's it!"

Back in her familiar cracked and rasping voice, she explained her idea. The Church and the army would make a fuss over Jonas—and thus see his passport—only if he were central to the official *thavma* ceremony and its aftermath in Athens. But what if Jonas had not been the first to see the vision? What if someone else had seen it first? Someone like Pavlatos? Appollonia was certain the authorities would prefer that a Greek rather than a foreigner had discovered the image. And after all, it was Pavlatos who first reported it to Stromos, wasn't it? If Pavlatos would now claim that he had seen it first, and if Jonas backed him up, well, the priests, soldiers and Idronis might be happy to forget all about this scruffy American.

Jonas and Appollonia rushed into the village and knocked on the closed shop door. When Pavlatos finally answered, Appollonia pushed her way in and pressed the idea on him without permitting him a word of protest. At crucial moments she would turn to Jonas and ask, "*Endaxi?*"— Okay?—to which Jonas would dutifully reply, "*Endaxi, endaxi,*" nod his reassurance, and look grave.

Appollonia soon changed tack, no longer talking at Pavlatos but asking him questions, to each of which he responded with a simple if uncertain Yes. After the third or fourth Yes, Pavlatos crossed himself and mumbled, "*Christos kai Panaghia*"—Christ and Holy Virgin. Within a few minutes he was nodding, babbling and crossing himself repeatedly, and when Appollonia finished with a peroration in a ringing voice about the honors to come his way, the shopkeeper was beaming.

"Jesus, he just about wet his pants," Jonas said outside.

"To see a vision? This is a very religious man."

Jonas looked doubting.

"Well, the Church can be very important to you when you believe in absolutely nothing."

They agreed to meet at Pavlatos's shop in a little while. The three of them would then go to the monastery and explain the "misunderstanding" about who had first seen the vision.

Back in his rooms, Jonas tiptoed around Marielle, who was doing yoga against a wall. He put on his cleanest clothes.

"Is it so late yet?" Marielle asked.

"No, I'm heading down a little early. We're going to tell them it was Pavlatos. Maybe then they'll leave us in peace."

"I would like that. I would like it very much if *everyone* leave me to be." She turned upside down, leaned against the wall and closed her eyes.

Jonas got to the shop before Appollonia. Pavlatos's wife was serving a crowd of villagers who were buying sweets and wine with which to celebrate the as-yet-mysterious event they had been notified to attend at the former monastery. Several of them also bought boxes of *PROKI*. Pavlatos appeared in a white shirt buttoned to the collar and a rough black suit that likely had fit considerably better on his wedding day. Sweating profusely, he almost smiled to see all the customers but on spotting Jonas became nervous. Jonas decided to wait outside.

The main walkway was throbbing in anticipation. People in doorways were jabbering about the hastily announced sundown ceremony; others carried extra water from the cisterns for unanticipated baths; children returned from the hills with wildflowers for garlands and bouquets. Appollonia soon flounced up in her Polynesian shirt and sailor's cap. Jonas squinted at the outfit.

"What can they do," she grinned, "arrest me?"

They retrieved Pavlatos and, each with private trepidations, the three went down the hill.

To their immense relief, Idronis immediately liked their suggestion that it was Pavlatos who had first seen the vision. Clearly did not believe it. But liked it. Skoriasos stared at Appollonia while Jonas and Pavlatos told their new version, but even if he sensed something amiss—Why hadn't Jonas told him all this on the *taratsa* that morning?—he said nothing. Stromos, on the other hand, tried to protest this revision of his official report, but Skoriasos cut him off. Idronis nodded at Skoriasos's prerogative but the officer did not bother to acknowledge his approval. The visiting high priests, meanwhile, remained impassive during Pavlatos's claim, deferring to secular powers on the question of who discovered the *thavma* but reserving judgment on whether there was truly a *thavma* at all. A disagreement broke out among the clerics and Idronis on some point of ceremonial procedure. Idronis held up the disputation to turn a cold stare on Jonas, Appollonia and Pavlatos, who all gladly left the room.

Soldiers were guarding the back wall of the monastery enclosure as if the vision might be spirited away by subversives before it could appear for the glory of the Nation. Laurel branches had been hung on the wall and ribbon draped on the bushes that Jonas had drunkenly sprayed the night of his epiphany. A few villagers tentatively made their way down the hill and were sternly directed by the soldiers to stay back at the edge of the clearing. There the villagers tried to arrange themselves so that later arrivals could not claim vantage points in front of them; as each family group arrived, there was new jockeying and rearranging of positions. People from other villages also began to appear and soon there were gestures, postures, arguments. The soldiers now warned the swelling, restive crowd and the crowd grumbled back, pushing closer and closer until the putative restraining line at the clearing's edge had all but disappeared. The soldiers began to shove people, the villagers nudged and shouldered each other, and in no time there were two or three shouting matches going on at once. Jonas, Appollonia and Pavlatos kept their distance and looked away.

As the sun dipped behind the hills, Idronis led Skoriasos and several other formal-dressed military officers into the clearing, followed by the coven of priests, now decked out in high raiment. Jonas and Appollonia moved away from the wall and over to the edge of the clearing, to blend in with the crowd of villagers, who quieted somewhat but not enough for Idronis's liking; he stopped, and only when the civilians moved back completely out of the clearing did he again lead the procession forward. Jonas looked up: Marielle stood in the doorway to their rooms, watching.

The priests arrayed themselves in a semicircle facing the wall and Pavlatos stepped forward. But after a moment it was obvious that he knew neither what to look for nor exactly where to look for it. While all eyes were on the grocer, Skoriasos was staring at Appollonia. She refused to meet his gaze.

Shadows deepened on the wall. A white-bearded monk began to chant, the other priests joining the refrain. Pavlatos turned with a pathetic expression, hoping for someone to direct him, but the priests only intoned louder and more fervently. The sun dipped lower; the crowd at the edge of the clearing was now completely in the dark.

When the sun's rays finally darted through the chasm in the ridge and struck the wall, the villagers drew in a collective breath. The sun slid farther along but its path to the crucial mid-wall was blocked by the ring of holy men. There were murmurs, then open cries of distress from villagers who had heard about the miracle and saw it slipping away on the backs of the priests. Idronis recognized the problem and with a dramatic sweep of his arms cleaved the row of clerics in two. The churchmen raised their prayers to a higher pitch and there were gasps and cries of *Panaghia!* as the diffused bits of sun joined reflected village lights on the rough and shadowed plaster. Villagers, soldiers and priests alike began to make signs of the cross: there, taking shape on the wall, was a figure—if one wanted—of John the Baptist, saintly head off slightly to the side.

Idronis took advantage of a general paralysis and stepped to the fore. He raised his arms for quiet, looked proprietarily over the crowd, and was just about to speak when a terrible piercing cry rent the clearing. Yiannis, arms high, chest bared, lurched down the hill, seeming at any moment as if he would lose his balance and fall headlong onto the rocks. Halfway down he stopped and howled again, then staggered to the clearing where, though his eyes never saw them, the villagers made room for him to pass. Mortified by this spectral figure, no one made a move;

only Idronis stepped up but Yiannis brushed him aside unaware. Past the priests, Yiannis stopped abruptly and stared at the figure on the wall.

"*Babaaa!*" he wailed and flattened himself against the outline on the wall. "*Babaaaaa!*"

"He says 'Father,'" Appollonia whispered to Jonas, her brows pinched in anguish.

Yiannis clawed at the wall, dug his fingers into the plaster. "*Baba!*" he cried. "*Babaaa! Baba! Baba! . . .*"

Each time he pronounced the word, he slammed his forehead against the wall. Then suddenly he whirled around, eyes wild, blood streaming down his face, and pressed himself back against the outline on the wall, head tilted to the side to match the shadows. "*O pateras mou!*" he wailed. "*O pateras mou!*"

"His father," Appollonia groaned to Jonas. "*Panaghia!* This must be where they shot him, when Yiannis was a boy . . . where Yiannis *watched* them shoot him."

"*Baba, babaaa!*" Yiannis bellowed, turning back to face the wall and dropping to his knees. The priests backed away and Idronis barked at the soldiers but they were unsure what to do. Skoriasos gave no order and before Stromos could decide whether to intervene despite his subordinate rank, two fishermen stepped out of the crowd and gently brought Yiannis to the edge of the clearing, where the villagers made a place for him. The whitewashed wall was now streaked with Yiannis's blood and showed the holes his fingers had gouged, the holes first made by a firing squad twenty-five years before. It was dark now, but in streaks of blood a remnant of the image remained.

The oldest monk led the priests out of the clearing, around the corner, and back within the enclosure; Idronis smoothed his suit and joined them. Stromos ordered the soldiers to attention and they followed the priests, Pavlatos scuttling after. The villagers, too, left the clearing en masse, climbing back up the hill.

Skoriasos remained in the clearing, staring across at Appollonia: "*Dthos mou to engrapho*, Lonia. *Parakalo.*"—Give me the document. Please.

"*Avrio*"—Tomorrow—she answered.

Skoriasos started to speak again but Appollonia turned away, and after a moment he dropped his head and disappeared into the monastery.

"I am very tired," Appollonia said to Jonas. "I still do not have that night of sleep." She gave him a hug. "*Kali nichta, phíle mou.* Good night, my friend." She moved to the path but stopped after a few steps. "*Andio,* Jonaki," she called. "*Perastiká.*" And went up the hill into the darkness.

All through the night, Jonas heard noises. Every twenty minutes or so there was a thud and the sound of breaking glass on the hillside. Jonas went to the door but could see nothing in the dark. He brought his Greek phrase book to the main room and read by the light of the candle: "*Perastiká*"—Get well soon.

He went back to bed and looked down at Marielle. She had asked nothing of what had happened and had silenced Jonas when he tried to tell her. Later she had come to his bed, slid in silent beside him, and gone to sleep.

At first light Jonas went to the doorway. On the hillside and in the clearing behind the former monastery were dozens of battered *PROKI* boxes and broken *PROKI* jars. Soldiers were beginning to clear them away as Skoriasos led Appollonia to a waiting jeep.

17

They had sensed Crete's raw-boned presence well before its shadow loomed on the midnight horizon. Warm breezes had carried out to sea the redolence of sun-baked herbs crushed by the hooves of mountain goats and by the high black boots of herdsmen. An island beyond islands, Greece beyond Greece, Marielle translated from her guidebook; a landscape and a people apart. "One century after the Ottoman has conquested Greece," Marielle read as they waited for a bus heading west, "Crete is not subjected."

"Not subjected?" Jonas said, half listening.

"Staying free? *Pas subjugué?* It's the same? My English . . ."

They had managed little sleep on the overnight ferry. And Jonas was feeling it now on the hard floor of the bus station waiting room. Marielle, however, prattled on proudly about the fiercely independent Cretans, as if merely by having reached their shores she had become anointed with a measure of what she imagined was their indigenous character.

"Seventy years more the Turks cannot conquest of Crete."

Jonas tried to pay attention, if not for information at least for distraction: it was six a.m. and if the handwritten schedule was right, the first bus west didn't leave until eight. Something other than lack of sleep, though, something beneath the sound of her voice, made listening to her difficult.

"Hussein Pasha, he is general here of the Ottomans. For eighteen years he tries to conquest the capital, Candia. . . . Candia—that must be Chania, where we are going, yes?"

Jonas struggled to loosen the knots in his neck.

"Think of that"—Marielle picked up her head—"eighteen years! This Crete can hold the world away."

There was a sharp edge not exactly *to* her voice but *behind* it. Jonas's hip throbbed against the cool stone floor; his head pounded where the rifle butt on Corfu had slammed it from behind.

"The sultan in Constantinople, he is so angry. He orders to Hussein Pasha to return and explain about this Crete."

Tight vibrations bore their way up through the floor and twisted around Jonas's spine; a high-pitched whine pressed his temples.

"The Hussein Pasha comes back to explain of Crete but the sultan will not listen and *Whttt!*, off is the head of Hussein."

The noise was coming from behind Marielle, outside the wall. Growing louder. Coming closer. The vibrations surged through the floor and Jonas winced with pain.

"Then the sultan orders that no one must ever speak to him again the name of Crete..."

The roar grew and grew and blotted out Marielle's words. Jonas watched her lips move; his green eye blurred with tears.

"*Alors*, for five years no one speaks the name. And so the sultan does not know what was happened at Candia..."

A door burst open and the roar slammed in, knocking Jonas back; he covered his head and cried out. The doorway was filled by a bellowing bright blue phoenix, chest displaying proudly the silhouette of the bayonet-wielding soldier. The creature lurched, then stopped abruptly as a wing crunched the door frame. Belching smoke, the roaring phoenix backed up, then squeezed into the room. Behind it came a close-cropped young man in a blue uniform who surveyed the machine's domain while holding its long, lawnmower handles as if they were the reins of a stallion, then with a nod to its rumbling power moved with the machine across the waiting room floor. Two large brushes churned under the machine, splattering out a mix of soapy water and oil. The brushes turned asymmetrically, one side grinding against the floor and lifting the machine such that the other side spun without touching the floor at all and liquid spewed in a wide and useless arc. Like a diseased animal, the machine left a zigzag trail of murky streaks and puddles.

Into the room, behind the first man, slouched another, older man with several days' grizzled beard, his baggy uniform pants held up with rope, carrying an armful of rough woolen rags. As the phoenix bumped and roared its way along, the older man followed and cleaned up as best he could the oily mess it left behind. The younger man did not look back.

Seeing that the noise came from nothing more sinister than a floor cleaner transmuted Jonas's panic but did not eliminate it. His terror lodged just under the surface, as if he had entered a room where a tiny wayward bird is flying around raggedly, trapped, shrieking and flapping while trying desperately to escape the walls.

"What? What were you saying? The sultan?"

Marielle studied him a moment, then let go of whatever she had considered asking him. "Yes, no one dares to speak the name of Crete, so, what is finally happened at Candia, the sultan does not know for five years more." She smiled.

"And? . . . I mean, so what did happen at Candia?"

Marielle's eyes narrowed. The machine turned and headed toward them. She read again from her guidebook and frowned.

"The Turks, at last they conquest the city," she said softly, as if hoping her words would be lost to the machine.

⁂

Marielle soon discovered that present-day Chania was not the brave old capital of Candia. Rather, old Candia had become Heraklion, the larger port city they had just left. Marielle sulked and seemed to hold her misapprehension against Chania itself. Jonas, however, was secretly pleased: he had no desire to hear Greek military heroism romanticized, even a version three hundred years old.

Jonas and Marielle spent most of the next few days apart. Jonas went each morning to Chania's large covered market, small trucks and three-wheelers squeezing through the lanes with rainbows of tomatoes and peppers, oranges and lemons, melons of every kind. From a little park behind the market, Jonas would watch the farmers unload, then rattle back toward the mountains before the sun got too high. Soon after, they'd be replaced by modern panel vans bearing names like Poseidon Palace and King Minos Hotel, loading up with produce and large quantities of meat.

Afternoons Jonas found himself enjoying solitary walks around Chania's narrow, flower-draped lanes. Its ancient harbor and old sandstone buildings were soothing despite a certain urban bustle. In fact, the bustle was part of what Jonas enjoyed: people propelled in specific directions, having work, performing tasks.

But if Jonas was pleased by the town's color and movement, Marielle's flare of Cretan delight quickly burned itself out. The active town was more than she wanted and after three days she declared she was leaving. When Jonas asked where to, she merely shrugged, "More away."

In the morning Jonas found her speaking fragments of Italian and English with the man who ran their rooming house. Jonas overheard something about a place called Xeros, somewhere east of Chania; the man's friend Manolis ran the *taverna* there.

Jonas and Marielle resumed their now well-practiced dance. Jonas had a coffee. Marielle left without a word, returned, stopped to tell Jonas only that she was leaving in an hour for Xeros, then went up to the room. Jonas waited. They passed each other on the stairs, Jonas going up, Marielle coming down. Jonas packed and came back out. She was gone. He hurried to the bus station, spotted her sitting calmly in the shade, slowed a casual stroll. She looked up at him without expression and asked him the time.

They were surprised at the wide new tarmac road because the map showed a nearly empty peninsula with no towns and few villages; Xeros itself was not even noted. The other bus riders were a dozen Greek women—four of them wearing identical orange dresses—and two local teenage boys in tight black pants and white shirts open to the middle of their hairless chests. The bus chugged through foothills, past a bright sign pointing the way to "Xeros Palace Hotel–Luxurious," and emerged above a stretch of coast along which Jonas counted eight large boxy cement buildings squatted a few hundred yards to a half mile apart. Between the buildings were flat expanses of dirt, weeds and rock. There were no villages, no houses, no other structures.

The bus stopped at the first cement box, a sign in English reading "King Minos Hotel." The morning was already hot and the motionless bus soon became stifling; an occasional deceitful breeze stirred through the windows, promising relief but bringing only dust and more heat. Finally someone waved from the hotel door. As the bus pulled away, Jonas saw two wide pink bodies waddling from the hotel toward the sea.

The bus passed another sign for the Xeros Palace, then two more new cement hotels standing on patches of empty ground; neither showed any life except for one straggling tourist on a footpath to the sea. Further on was a gray blob called Hotel Kromos, where a tour bus was disgorging its contents: thirty pasty people in the harsh sun grappling with luggage piled on the ground. Four fair-haired men and women in identical orange outfits with the word *Willkommen* across the back were circling and yelling in German at the men unloading the luggage, at the passengers, at each other. Gathered near the hotel door was a replica of the arriving group, this contingent distinguishable from the other group by their painfully red sunburnt skin and divided into two parts, the photographing and the photographed. On Jonas's bus, the four Greek women in orange got up to leave, the last woman pausing at the door and sighing deeply before plunging into the sun.

After two more seemingly identical cement-box hotels and another sign announcing the impending Xeros Palace, the bus pulled up to Your Pink Heaven, which differed from the other hotels only in its top-to-bottom coat of what appeared to be cheap fingernail polish. Lolling by the entrance to the Heaven was a cluster of blonde, tan young women, all of whom wore white tops and shorts and around whom a swarm of dark-haired young men appeared to be performing some sort of complex ritual. Each performance ended with either a blonde girl getting on a scooter behind a dark-haired boy, or two blonde girls going off together followed at a slight distance by two dark-haired boys, or two or three girls turning on their heels and ignoring the rude remarks made behind them by an equal or greater number of boys. The two teens on Jonas's bus smoothed their hair, rearranged their tight black pants, tamped down their grins into expressions of utter unconcern, and got off.

Jonas and Marielle were now alone on the bus as it turned slightly inland. There were no hotels now, no trees, no fields. Nothing but the flat new road. Brown nothing. The bus rounded a bend, the heat seemed to turn up several degrees, and there it was, the Xeros Palace: twice the size of the other hotels but just as gray and graceless. It sat alone on a parched plain, a good half mile from the sea and watched from above by a couple of dozen stone cottages that dotted a barren hill like goats that had scattered for meager forage among the bitter brown rocks.

"Xeros?" Marielle asked the driver.

"Xeros Palace, yes. Last stop."

Outside, the sun exploded in Jonas's eyes; he leaned against the bus to get his bearings but the searing metal sent him spinning away. On the hotel door was a polar bear and the words "Fully Air Cooled." And perhaps it was faintly cooler inside, but dashed expectation made it seem just as bad. There was no one in the large lobby, no one at the counter. A large phoenix stared down from the wall. They waited, walked around. Still no one. After several minutes a lobster-skinned woman spreading out of her bathing suit charged through a swinging door, followed by an equally pink and well-fed man wearing a T-shirt with "WATNEYS" on the front and "Farking Legless" on the back.

"You don't call that a proper cup of tea!"

"Yeah, but plenty of lager, Shirl," the man consoled.

The couple stepped into the elevator but in a moment came out, the woman pained with exasperation. They took the stairs, instead.

A man emerged from a room behind the counter and was startled to see Jonas and Marielle and their bags.

"*Oriste?* Yes?"

"Excuse me," Marielle asked, "but is this Xeros?"

"Xeros Palace, yes."

"But the village Xeros?"

"Village?"

"Village, yes. Itself. The ... village."

The man narrowed his eyes at what seemed a subtle notion.

"Do you know Manolis Kokonas?" Marielle asked about the man whose name she had been given by the Chania pension proprietor.

"Manolis? Of course."

"Is his *taverna* near to here?"

The man indicated the door through which the pink couple had come; a sign over the door read "Sugar & Spice—Very Nice."

"But is not open 'til now. Maybe one hour."

The man went back into the room behind the counter. Somewhere a phone rang. Rang and rang and rang. A minute later the man returned.

"Just out of curiosity," Jonas asked, "how much is a room for a night?"

"One night? Huh.... We never have peoples by one night. Package only. All package. But...might to be...two hundred *drachmes* the night."

"Maybe while we're waiting we could see a room?"

"For you? To stay now? *Tzk*. Sorry. Finished. No rooms."

Jonas looked around the large empty lobby.

"Sure, sure, there are rooms," the man corrected. "Plenty rooms. But...no water."

"Oh. The plumbing, huh?"

"Yes, yes, we have plumbings. But no water. It's never been water here." He pointed out the door to arid hills. "Near to here everything is *xeros*—dry."

"*Xeros*. You mean, like Xeros Palace."

"Mm. They are bringing us water by truck. But never enough. Tourists, they want to wash all the time."

Jonas looked behind the man at a wall full of room keys. "Well, if there isn't any water...?"

The man shrugged. "Package holiday. The tourist don't know before they come. And after they are here already..."

"Seems like the word might get around."

"Oh, there are many peoples in England. And not so much sun."

"On the hill there must be a room we could have. And quiet. None of these...people," Marielle insisted. Since there was no return bus for several hours, Jonas didn't bother to argue and they went into the restaurant.

Sugar & Spice—Very Nice was bright and clean and appointed in the latest pastel plastic. A large window overlooked an empty terrace and a dry swimming pool. There were wall posters for McVittey's Cider and English Pride Lager and a hand-lettered announcement of "Hi Tea—19:00." Three men sat near the kitchen; one of them said something in Greek and another nodded but the third disagreed and they argued, then the first got up and flipped a switch on the wall. A box set into a window started whirring; it sounded something like an air conditioner. One of the men came over. Manolis.

On the hill? A room? Yes, possible, Manolis admitted. But an empty place up there: no *taverna*, no sea, no nothing. Why there? But here, in the hotel... Well, okay, up the hill you go look. But first you eat something from Manolis, eh?

"*Voilà*," Marielle said when Manolis had gone to the kitchen. "If only you look far enough, you find the right place." Jonas held his tongue.

Manolis brought plastic menus that in sort-of-English gaudily described, under the heading "Continental Cuisine," a selection of British pub food. A separate handwritten paper listed pizzas with various toppings, each of which included pineapple. Jonas asked Manolis if he had *dolmades*.

"Grape leafs? Sure, sure. Very special. But... for today, finished. Pizza very good."

Jonas passed up the pizza and asked for a simple *souvlaki*.

"*Tzk.*" Manolis tilted his head in the way that means "Sorry, no." "But pizza very special. With pineapples. Very tropics. You try it."

Marielle asked if there was tzatziki, the ubiquitous Greek summer yoghurt dish.

"Sorry, finished."

As Marielle studied the menu again, Manolis said, "You have a beer, then you decide."

He brought them two large bottles of English Pride.

"Do you have any Greek beer?"

"Greek beer?" Manolis was a bit surprised. "Yah, okay."

The pink couple Jonas had seen in the lobby came in with another similarly tinted pair.

"Lagers, Manolis," one of the men called. "And some of that moussaka would do lovely, wouldn't it, Shirl?"

"Mm, would do, I s'pose," Shirley answered without conviction.

A couple in their sixties also came in. As one of the Sugar & Spice men came over to take the couple's order, four young tourist women on two motorbikes pulled up to the terrace outside; the Sugar & Spice man turned his head so fast he nearly banged his nose on the window. Manolis came from the kitchen with plates of moussaka but stopped short at the window and gaped out at the young women. Marielle watched him with the expression of a child who discovers that a grown-up has lied to her.

"Ooiy, Manolis," a pink man called, "our moussaka!"

Manolis turned briefly, looked at the plates, turned back to the window, then finally tore himself away and delivered the food.

Jonas went to the toilet. Passing the kitchen, stacked against the kitchen rear wall he saw case upon case of canned pineapple, the boxes stamped "US Army."

"Been here before?" Jonas asked the older couple when he returned to the eating room.

"No. Our first time," the woman said. "Saw it in a brochure, actually."

Jonas couldn't suppress a small smile.

"Yes," the woman said good-naturedly, "we did expect it to be . . . a bit different. But, then, it's only a holiday, isn't it?

⚘

Matters of choice. Jonas believed in positing extremes as a way to sort out his feelings—Would you rather suffer the contempt of the rich for the poor, or of the poor for the rich? Rather be overdressed, or under? For the larger extremes, though, the dialectic didn't always cooperate— Rather have everything work and nothing matter, or nothing work and everything matter? He was glad to be back in Chania after the Xeros Palace fiasco, but Marielle had announced that the next day she would head for the island's empty west coast.

Jonas walked the lanes behind the old port late that night, trying to sort out what to do. Marielle was company, even a bumpy sort of affection. She provided a sense of belonging. And however equivocal, in some way he mattered to her, while at the same time she left safely undisturbed the private corners of his heart and mind. And more, her doggedness, though peremptory and foolish at times, added mettle to his wandering. It was getting light when finally he realized that he would go with her. What surprised him was that it had taken all night to decide.

The first bus took them west along the north coast past more newly constructed tourist hotels: gray, elephantine, utterly out of sense and proportion to the landscape. A second bus took them to Kissamos, the island's northwestern port town, and the next day they rode an empty fruit truck down the west coast. Coffee in a village elicited not only the description of a still smaller village farther south but an offer of a donkey ride there for their bags. A withering three-hour walk behind the donkey brought them finally to a tranquil nest of whitewashed houses—village lanes lined with geraniums, sun-drenched walls draped with sashes of scarlet and burgundy bougainvillea—cradled in the gentle arc of a cove.

There were no rooms to rent—visitors, especially strangers, were extremely rare. But the *kafeneion* owner had his sons' room empty; they were away working in a big hotel. The house was at the back of the village, facing a wall of mountains that closed off the coast from the rest of the island. The room itself looked onto an orange and lemon grove and beyond it a wheat field necklaced by purple crocus and pink and white cyclamen. Jonas and Marielle sank gratefully into the cool of the room. The only sound through the open door was the lullaby of bees lazing round the field's vast banquet table of flowers.

18

August and its merciless sun finally exhausted itself and drifted away on welcome wisps of September. But slow village days left Jonas with the vague discomfort of a recent pensioner among still-working cronies: things were familiar, people friendly, but an invisible wall separated him from what was real. A walk in the fragrant hills, a swim in the tongue-warm Aegean, a kindred moment with an increasingly unfettered Marielle—she laughed, called him Jonaki, late one night told him tales of her youthful follies—were not enough. Tranquility and repose brought him no pleasure. Pleasure brought him no pleasure.

At least September brought motion. Early grains were reaped, threshed and stored. Wine barrels were scoured in the sea for the coming grapes. Itinerant peddlers and laborers appeared: coopers to repair the barrels; sellers of resin to turn wine into retsina; young shepherds and farmers to hire on for harvests more bountiful than their own. Bright woolen blankets were washed and aired in preparation for the winter, their colors rippling on lines like flags on the rigging of a victorious armada.

As for Marielle, it could not be said precisely that all this brought her happiness, but at least it blunted her desperate insistence on unhappiness. She scattered herself around the village: one morning at a loom with a young woman weaving for her dowry; an afternoon with girls gathering honey; an evening with two old sisters discussing in pantomime the mysteries of the silkworm. She often smiled, though her pleasure at village life seemed to Jonas more willful than heartfelt. Her francophone guidebook she left alone: she no longer had any interest in an outside view of Crete and no further use for history.

Jonas, meanwhile, waited impatiently for the grape picking to begin. He had been promised work in the vines, but the grapes were still not ready and each cloudless day passed as slowly as a rainy week. For hours Jonas would watch the grain fields being cut; watch the donkeys being loaded then goaded, slowly, slowly, toward the village; watch others of the sad-eyed animals on their endless rounds of the flagstone threshing circles, grain covering and uncovering the spiderwebs of mortar between the stones.

One morning Jonas picked up Marielle's guidebook, intent on the time-consuming task of translation. In it there was brief mention of a geologically notable cave on an islet somewhere farther down the coast. The villagers he asked had only vague notions of the cave, though, and arranging to get there took several days of doing. But it was the only doing Jonas had, and he was grateful for it.

Marielle was less than enthusiastic about the cave, seeming now to mistrust anything beyond the village, especially since word of it had come from the guidebook. Only Jonas's assurance that there were no people there persuaded her to go with him. An early morning garlic cart took them to the head of an isthmus, then a walk of several miles to a hamlet from which one could see the island.

It was a choppy half hour in a *caique* out to the island. The boatman pointed to an uphill winding mile of stony track, handed them a water jug and a bag of fruit and held up fingers to indicate when he would return. The boat ride had been rough and the rocky climb looked daunting, but there was no shade where they'd landed and the sun was brutally unforgiving, so they started up the hill. It was tough going: the earth was baked hard, their legs judged the incline even more harshly than had their eyes, and still there was no shade. A mile was a long way.

Halfway, they stopped to rest. Marielle took two oranges from the bag, and out with the fruit came frayed printed pages describing in English the geology and history of the cave. Jonas began to read but it was too hot to sit still. A leg-aching half hour later they rounded a switchback and there was the yawning thirty-foot mouth of the cave, guarded by two stalagmite incisors the height of several men. In a nearby stone enclosure, Jonas found the hemp torches the boatman had said would be there. They lit two and went in.

The entrance narrowed, darkened, and dropped precipitously. The air was damp and cool and smelled of the sea. They felt their way along a narrow ledge where pitons strung with rope had been driven into the rock. The ledge was wet and slippery, the wall and rope were wet, the smell of the torch smoke was wet. Jonas nudged around a corner and there, opening fifty sudden yards straight down, was an enormous cavern of flickering, dripping shadows. Tightly packed clusters of sharpened stalactites, pipe organs made from monsters' teeth, hung from the roof; massive rock headstones leaned out from the walls; and stalagmites like poison limestone mushrooms sprouted from a sloping floor that fell away to the center of the earth.

Jonas and Marielle inched their way down to a plateau and hoisted themselves onto a stone slab the shape of a refectory table. Looking up now, the depth and breadth of the cave was even more impressive. So, too, the treacherousness of the stone ledge. They breathed deeply in a combination of awe, fatigue and relieved acrophobia. Jonas pulled the printed pages from his pocket.

"Listen to this. Some French bishop came down here for a Christmas mass. 1673. Hey, three hundred years ago, exactly."

Jonas read and muttered in mounting amazement.

"Didn't have anything to hold on to back then. Had to tie a rope at the top and lower himself straight down, carrying a torch. Jesus. . . . Bishop Noindel, the guy's name. French ambassador to the sultan. . . . You remember the sultan."

Marielle was not amused.

"So, this bishop hears about the cave and decides he's going to cele-brate Christmas mass down here. . . . Dig it: high mass, full tilt boogie, you know, all the priests and outfits and shit? . . . With a choir. . . . And a fucking orchestra! Do you believe this?"

Jonas found himself delighted by the sheer outrageousness of this three-century-old piece of theater and barely noticed that Marielle's astonishment was of an entirely different sort. The more Jonas described, the more she shifted uncomfortably on the stone.

"And a feast, too, for all those people. My god, listen to what he dragged all the way from Constantinople . . . priests, altar boys, choir, orchestra, and all the people to put on the feast . . . two hundred and fifty people!" Jonas rocked back and forth. "Took him a year to get it all together . . . three ships full. And what is it, a thousand miles or something, down the Aegean, all the way around Crete?... And wait! Listen to this: then he has to float it all in here on rafts, because his ships can't get into the beach! I mean, two hundred and fifty people, and all that holy stuff, chasubles and miters and god knows what all. On rafts! And an orchestra, with all those instruments... and tables, dishes, Jesus Christ, all that food! Then up the mountain, and all the way down here, all the people... by torchlight... on a fucking rope!"

Jonas was standing and waving the pages like an evangelist just before he asks for money.

"And he does it. He makes it. Midnight, Christmas Eve, the guy stands right here, looks around, all this stuff and all the people, and the choir's singing, the orchestra's playing..." Jonas's voice echoed off the walls. "... I mean, this dude has got to be smiling!"

Marielle gaped at Jonas, then slid down and walked away.

"But for what?" she croaked from the other side of the cavern, the pained crack in her voice amplified by a granite echo. "All of this for what? A mass *catholique*?"

"No. No, that's not the point."

"No? Then for what the point?"

Jonas peered across at her. The lines creasing her face seemed to mesh with the cavern's water-gouged walls.

"It wasn't for any point," he barked, then tried to modulate his voice. "Hell, he knew a mass doesn't mean anything—he was a bishop, for godssake. But he *did* it, see. He actually *did* it."

"But for what difference to do it? What difference?"

"Difference? Christ, how should I know? How should anybody know?" Jonas moved toward her, his voice rising again. "Starting it. Finishing it. Think of what the guy pulled off!"

"But why? If you know it will just be the same? If already you know..." Marielle's voice collapsed in on itself.

"Why?" Jonas stopped. "Why? Because what if you don't?" he shouted. "What if you don't?"

As his voice careered around the cavern, Marielle put her arms over her head and curled up as if she were being pummeled in the dark. After a few moments she looked up at Jonas, who stood with fists clenched, eyes sparking.

"I am sorry to see you so angry," she finally said.

"I'm not angry." He took a deep breath, let it out slowly. "I don't really get angry anymore. . . . That's what I mean."

⚜

Village life separated men and women much of the time, so it wasn't difficult for Marielle to keep her distance from Jonas for most of the next few days. And since they'd made a point never to declare themselves together, Jonas was in no position to complain if Marielle was more apart than usual.

O trighos—the grape harvest—brought them together again. It brought everyone together. Brothers and sisters and cousins who had feuded for months over some subtle offense now joined forces in the vineyards. For days before the harvest began, the vineyards resounded with arguments about whether these or those grapes were ready, whether rain was on the way, which vines should be picked first, which grapes should go into which barrels. Then finally it was time. Jonas woke to the sounds of banter and laughter, the entire village heading for the vineyards with the donkeys, huge wicker baskets bobbing at the animals' sides. Jonas spotted Marielle already out and skipping along with the Mavrodakis family. He had himself been promised to the Kordakis clan, Grandpa Kordakis insisting that since all civilization had begun in Crete, the name Korda must originally have been Kordakis and that Jonas, therefore, was family.

The morning was spent picking, eating and occasionally throwing grapes. A long line of donkeys waddled back to the village, their baskets overflowing with clusters of ruby and amber. The work stopped in deference to the midday sun but resumed after a meal and an *ipnos* in the shade of the nearby orange grove. Well into the night the village bubbled with wine-making at various stations of the crush: piles of bountiful wicker baskets; stone troughs in which the grapes were first reduced by the barefoot dancing of those who thought they could stay upright and who were willing to take the consequences when they did not; ancient creaking wine presses in which the last juice was hugged out of the trampled fruit; and sea-scoured barrels into which the gurgling liquid was finally siphoned. When all his day's grapes had been pressed, Grandpa Kordakis doted over the scraping of the *tsikoudha*—the stems and skins—into two special barrels. Jonas wondered at this inordinate attention to what seemed mere sediment until old man Kordakis gave him a large toothless grin made up of pride, the pleasures of his many years and the single word *raki*.

Jonas rested against a wall. *Raki*. Kalliope's magic bottle of *raki*, on the flow of which Jonas had been floated from the cold cramped corner of a midnight Italian train all the way to this quiet Cretan coast. "Very beautiful, Kriti, very special," she'd said proudly. Kalliope...

Two Kordakis boys, pants rolled up their grape-stained legs, called to Jonas: "*Ela, ela*"—Come on, come on. The night was warm and all the unmarried young people were heading for the bay. Jonas and the Kordakis boys reached the pebble beach where thirty or so young villagers with crimson feet were laughing and calling to one another. The boys took off their shirts; the girls tied string around their cotton shifts to keep them from billowing away in the water. There was a pretense of males to one side of the beach and females to the other, but it was as much honored in the laughing, teasing, touching breach as in the observance. Within its night-deep blue, the sea offered up a warm green plankton phosphorescence, as if the harvest god had touched it with a fingertip and infused it with the sap of renewal.

Older voices came from the edge of the village; Jonas could make out the shadows of the elders, gesturing and hooting but keeping their distance. None of the young people paid any attention. House lamps next to the beach were extinguished and somewhere there began rhythmic drumming on a wine barrel. The young people's voices dropped to excited, expectant murmurs and after a minute the drumming stopped. A teeming silence, then a blast on a conch shell, at which the young people howled with delight. The boys dove headlong into the water, green and gold sparks streaming off their bodies. The older girls and young women were slightly more circumspect and waded in. Jonas realized that the only time he'd seen grown village women in the water was up to their knees on a Sunday afternoon or a particularly hot evening. Within moments, though, the young women also were plunging full in.

There was a tug at Jonas's arm and then he was running, too, grinning and diving. Underwater he felt wriggling bodies, then came up with liquid sparklers flaring from his head. Another head came up near him and sort of smiled. Marielle. He sort of smiled back. She dove under again and away.

Jonas stood chest-deep in the water. That half smile of hers. . . . But then, all her expressions were like that. And he was tired of it. But what of his own smile, his chameleon response? Had half measures become reflexive? He was tired of that, too. He looked around but could not find her in the dark.

The young men and women were moving into deeper water. Soon the noise level dropped. They still floundered and splashed as they sought each other, still laughed when they found one another, but movements were more languorous now, sounds more muted and round. Couples dipped and bobbed, moved closer, moved apart; arms reached over and under water; heads lowered and suddenly tossed back, giving off rumbles and prideful laughs. The longer they were in the sea, the greener it became and the brighter the sparks that shimmered off their bodies. It was the first time Jonas had seen young village men and women touch one another.

The elders began to call in the younger children. Jonas came out with them and sat on the stones. After a time the older girls and young women began to come out and move to the far side of the fishing boats, out of sight. Jonas decided to head for his room, to be there when Marielle got back, but Grandpa Kordakis spotted him and dragged him off to the *kafeneion* for several rounds of last year's wine. By the time Jonas got back, Marielle was asleep.

The next day, Jonas broke away from the Kordakis family—a language barrier can sometimes be useful—and went instead to the Mavrodakis vines. He had left the room before Marielle and without saying that he intended to join her: he knew she wouldn't explicitly object—it seemed that lately she didn't do anything explicitly—but he hadn't wanted to face even an ambiguous response. When he showed up, Marielle gave him a brief smile but otherwise ignored him, and they began work without talking.

To Jonas's great surprise, given how far off the beaten track they were, there was another foreigner, a voluble young Austrian, picking grapes. The past few months, Harald had been living in the mountains in his Volkswagen van. He had come down for the grape picking in order to be promised some of the wine: he planned still to be in the mountains next Easter when the vintage would be ready.

Jonas was immediately wary of Harald, of his stringy blond hair and paisley headband. But the Austrian's demeanor was so benign that by afternoon Jonas had let go his active dislike, if not all his distrust. When work stopped that evening, Harald sat with Jonas in that facile alliance that so often forms between even the most disparate of strangers in a strange land. Harald's presence also seemed to ease Marielle's discomfort with Jonas; she sat with them, though next to Harald.

Marielle urged Harald to speak about how he had been living "so much away" since he had come to Crete: away from the influences of his past and with only such contact even to village life as his own still simpler life required. It was obvious that Marielle had heard some of this from Harald the day before, but she wanted him to keep talking, both to convince Jonas about this life "away" and to continue to convince herself. Happy to comply, Harald spoke ingenuously and did not proselytize but invited them back that night to have a look at his hilltop site. When Jonas was unenthusiastic, Harald took no offense.

"But you could see what is possible," Marielle urged with an edge to her voice. Jonas looked away and waved her off.

"Don't you *want* to see?" she challenged. Jonas bristled.

As further inducement, Harald mentioned what he called *"Pflanze-Scheisse"*—plant-shit—and cajoled that it would be worth the walk: "With just a taste"—he made an inhaling sound—"you can see pretty far, man."

Jonas had little curiosity for Harald's van-life or his drugs. And he didn't like being goaded, didn't like Marielle's summoning of the hippie ethic "You'll never know if you don't try it," which had always seemed to Jonas just another version of parental coercion. But she had now made his decision a point of contention, and he was loathe to put more distance between them.

"Well, let's go then," he finally rasped.

They stumbled into the hills for more than an hour until they reached the rainbow-painted van. Harald showed them the plants and herbs he collected, the hatchet he used to cut wood, the crystals he looked through to get what he called "a different sight of the world." He would go into a mountain hamlet once a week, he told them, for extra vegetables and lamp oil; goatherds would occasionally stop to barter milk and cheese: "I ask nothing from them and them nothing from me. We get along good. They have never been defected." Jonas looked at Marielle: she was nodding, nodding.

Harald mentioned his *Pflanze-Scheisse* again. "Always I smoke after I have been in the village," he said, as if referring to Athens at rush hour. "It helps for leaving things behind."

Although Jonas had always abhorred the marijuana subculture, he didn't hold the drug itself fully responsible. He didn't like getting stupid too often, but on occasion... He was weary from grape picking. And weary, too, from trying to negotiate an entry into Marielle's shuttered spirit. This was an occasion.

They walked in bright moonlight over several hillocks and emerged on a bluff high over the sea. It was magnificent: a long series of bays stretching for miles in both directions, the moon unwrapping gentle waves onto wide-mouthed beaches, phosphorescent foam bursting silently on the stones. There were no structures, no boats, no signs of human presence. And the open sea stretched on forever. It was the farthest away Jonas had ever been.

Harald dug out from behind some rocks a gummy black ball of hashish. As they drew on the first pipe, Harald gestured toward a neighboring cliff: outlined against the night sky stood a wild *kri-kri*, the big-horned Cretan mountain goat.

The drug and the immense and spectacular silence blanketed the desire for speech. The impulse to follow thoughts withered: thinking was for the other world, and the other world was not here.

Not-thinking. Jonas had had no capacity for it when Nosey had introduced the notion back on Corfu. But over time Jonas had cultivated a passable talent for it and had clung to it through the folly and madness he had encountered since. Perhaps here he could truly refine it. Here, on an utterly peaceful hilltop at the end of the world. Jonas was euphoric... yet at the same time somehow utterly despairing. Something about picking grapes...

"You know, I had a garden once"—Jonas rolled thick, heavy words out to sea—"when I was living over in Jersey... on the roof... the garden, I mean. . . . We spent a lot of time there, nights like this. . . . Well, more humid there. . . . But I'm not complaining. . . . People make fun of Jersey. . . . But you know, on the pike, the turnpike, all these rest-stops. . . . 'Rest-stop'—funny word. . . . They got one named for Whitman, Emily Dickinson, ah . . . huh. Can't remember. . . . Guess that's why this stuff's illegal," Jonas chuckled. "You forget things . . . and don't care."

Harald cut another piece of hashish and they smoked again.

"A garden in the Garden State. Like on the license plates . . . All these baby vegetable seeds. . . . Guess that's what seeds are, huh? . . . But it takes time, you know? . . . Got to be patient. . . . I remember the waiting. That I remember."

The moon was setting and the stars took advantage by puffing out their chests.

"And you know what?" Jonas mused after a time. "They came up. These little plants. . . . Put things in, and they came up. . . . Really did. . . . You grow anything here?"

"Yes, it would be nice." Harald thought for a moment. "But, you must pay attention of so many things."

Marielle was staring at the sea as though it might disappear if for one moment she looked away. Jonas's own view of the sea was becoming marred by irritating spots before his eyes. They smoked again and stretched out under the weight of the drug. When Jonas looked up at the stars, the spots disappeared.

"Yeah, the pruning and stuff . . . ," Jonas continued as if he had only paused for breath. "Pulling off the suckers—the leaves that don't do anything. . . . 'Suckers.' I love that. Used to go pull them off and say, 'Take that, suckers!' . . . And you know what? These vegetables started to happen. . . . Took forever, but here they come, these little vegetables . . . tomatoes, beans. . . . Amazing."

Jonas smiled and was silent. The first pale whispers of dawn brushed the air and caressed the mountains behind them.

"Night is big," Harald said. And they knew what he meant.

"Of course, the mice got a lot of it," Jonas continued after a while. "Screened them off but the little fuckers always got in somehow. . . . Knew they would . . . but went ahead and planted just the same. . . . And anyway, even the things that made it, you weren't sure you wanted to eat, all that crap in the air, the chemicals.... I mean, it was Bayonne, you know?... I like Bayonne, though... Elizabeth, too... The town Elizabeth, I mean.... Used to live right by the Minuteman statue.... Cool statue, I liked it.... They musta been somethin', the Minutemen.... Got right down, no messin' around."

Jonas lost his thread and stopped. He sat up. The spots in front of his eyes had grown larger. And there were more of them. As the sky became lighter, the spots seemed to move closer. Jonas shook his head and looked away. "But that's what I mean," he began again. "I knew all that, but... I put stuff in the ground anyway.... Just a couple of plants. Didn't really feed anybody or anything. But they came up.... You know what I mean?"

Marielle hugged her knees to her chest; her face was pinched and drawn. Jonas wondered if it was his words, the dawn light on her tired eyes, or an entirely private knot of pain.

"I'd like to bake an apple pie," he said after a time. "You know, I've never baked an apple pie... and I'm an American."

The black spots were spreading like water bugs now, dozens of them, moving in jagged lines toward shore. They began to multiply and soon many more, smaller bugs covered the sea. Jonas looked at Marielle and Harald: they saw the bugs, too. It was getting lighter; a low growling sound filled a space behind the sky. The three smokers huddled together on the bluff as if suddenly it had become cold. They couldn't move, couldn't take their eyes off the swarm of insects closing in on them. Harald began to make noises, rocked back and forth, trembling. Jonas felt a pain in his mouth, then realized he was biting his own lip. Unconsciously, then almost frantically, Harald began to scrub himself, as if the insects had landed and were crawling over his skin. The growling sky became louder and they huddled closer still, hypnotized by the invasion of the invertebrate legions, prisoners in their own nightmare.

Marielle leaned forward: "Ships," she said. "Ships."

Jonas, too, could now make out the larger spots: warships, dozens of them, massive, gray and bristling with huge guns pointed directly at the cliffs. Then he recognized the smaller dots: landing craft, wave upon wave of them, spreading over the water like a poisonous spill. From the bluff he could see their exposed insides, rows of dark helmets like the carapaces of beetles. The growling noise grew louder and higher-pitched, louder and higher, until finally the beaks of screaming jets tore through the tissue-paper sky and screeched low over the cowering trio.

As the first soldiers poured onto the beaches below, Jonas, Marielle and Harald ran through the brush on drug-thickened legs. Marielle fell but got up immediately and ran on, her face wild with panic. Shrubs and stones battered their legs; the sun leered over the rim of a hill and hit them painfully in the eyes and they were lost, but ran on. Finally they reached Harald's van and dove in, slammed the doors and pulled a tarpaulin over their heads.

Covered with dirt and sweat, they trembled together for an eternity. Marielle's knee was streaming blood; the flesh on Harald's bare legs was torn. Slowly their breathing deepened and the shaking calmed. Still unable to speak, they heard a rustling outside and froze. Bam! Bam! The fist of God pounded on the van. Then silence. Bam! Bam! Silence. Suddenly the door was wrenched open and two enormous green faces thrust themselves in. Harald screamed.

"Hey, take it easy, boy," one of the faces drawled.

"We're just backing up these maneuvers," the other face said. "Saw y'all through the b'nocs. Thought you might have some good smoke. Or some acid, maybe? We got dollars. What d'ya say? . . . Any of you speak English?"

$\leftthreetimes$

Jonas's life might be described as an endless hand of Go Fish, a card game he had played as a child. Seeking a meld of four, one player would ask, "Got any fives?" "Got any queens?" If the other player had that card, it was forfeit to the asking player. But if the other player didn't have that card, the asking player had to "go fish" for it out of the deck, keeping all the unwanted cards until the right one appeared. Perhaps because he so rarely experienced such moments in the rest of his childhood, Jonas had always felt an extraordinary sense of well-being whenever he had quickly fished out the right card from the deck. "Got what I asked for!" had been his gleeful cry. The phrase still had the power to make his memory smile.

Much of his adult life had been spent in a search for something to stimulate again that dormant nerve, to resurrect that feeling . . . but without having to pick up unwanted cards from the deck. Like Kafka with his

Felice, Jonas strove to be completed from a distance. Marielle gave him the distance. She sensed that he was someone of value without particularly knowing what that value was. Or trying to find out. And the noises she made—the unwanted cards—she kept in the other room. Got what he asked for.

> The Caterpillar and Alice looked at each other for some time in silence; at last the Caterpillar took the hookah out of its mouth, and addressed her in a languid, sleepy voice.
>
> "Who are *you*?" said the Caterpillar.

Since arriving on Crete, Marielle had not asked Jonas to read from *Alice*, had shied away whenever Jonas brought it out. But now he insisted on reading aloud. He knew he was taking a chance. Insisting on anything is taking a chance.

> "Who are *you*?" said the Caterpillar.
>
> This was not an encouraging opening for a conversation. Alice replied, rather shyly, "I—I hardly know, Sir, just at present—at least I know who I *was* when I got up this morning, but I think I must have been changed several times since then."

Marielle leaned against the wall of their room, seeming to struggle against the impulse to grab her things and run out the door.

> "What do you mean by that?" said the Caterpillar sternly. "Explain yourself!"
>
> "I can't explain *myself*, I'm afraid, Sir," said Alice, "because I'm not myself, you see."
>
> "I don't see," said the Caterpillar.

It was now two days since their precipitous retreat to Chania from paradise lost on the west coast. Marielle had said little in those two days, had been alternately stern and lachrymose. But a few minutes ago she had burst into the room, flushed, eyes flashing. A freighter bound for Tunisia, she said in a rush. From Heraklion. Leaves in three days. Tunisia, and from there we could get to West Africa. To the people of West Africa, the people who had cared for her in Paris, people who knew a different way . . .

Marielle spoke not so much with conviction as with a tremulous resolve. And, for the first time since they had met, she said *nous*—we. Jonas merely opened *Alice* and read in a quiet voice.

> "I'm afraid I can't put it more clearly," Alice replied, very politely, "for I can't understand it myself, to begin with; and being so many different sizes in a day is very confusing."

Marielle stared out the window as if searching for her next place of safety. Her skin was stretched taut to hold back the accumulated force of her disappointments: all the things she had hoped for—but were not; all the things she had refused to admit—but were. As Jonas read, the life drained from her face until it seemed no more than ash, waiting for the slightest touch to collapse it completely.

> "...being so many different sizes in a day is very confusing."
> "It isn't," said the Caterpillar.
> "Well, perhaps you haven't found it so yet," said Alice; "but when you have to turn into a chrysalis—you will someday, you know—and then after that into a butterfly, I should think you'll feel it a little queer, won't you?"

There were tears on Marielle's face, despite the distance they had always measured between them.

> "Not a bit," said the Caterpillar.
> "Well, perhaps your feelings may be different," said Alice; "all I know is, it would feel very queer to *me*."
> "You!" said the Caterpillar contemptuously. "Who are *you*?"
> Which brought them back again to the beginning of the conversation.

She held Jonas close that night but spoke no more to him of Africa. In the morning as she packed for the boat, Jonas didn't need to tell her that he wasn't going with her.

PART THREE

A Gathering of Shades

sparse the earth beneath your feet
that you may have nowhere to spread root
and must reach for depth continually
and broad the sky above
that you must read the infinite on your own

—Odysseus Elytis, from *The Axion Esti*

19

The last mile or so Jonas had to walk. He was conscious of Marielle's absence but it was only in the conscious that his sense of loss resided. He thought he should have felt something more. "Should have felt?" he caught himself. "Why *should* have . . . ?" And just what was it he should have felt? Nonetheless, there had been feelings . . . which might have become . . . "Might have . . . ?" In truth, hadn't they been for each other no more than palliatives for their respective estrangements? Clutches at someone so as to approximate emotions they wished they had? Still, is an emotion less important, less worthy somehow, if one comes to know it only through the process of conjuring it? Well, maybe not. But which emotion, exactly? "Might have become . . . ?" Might have become *what*?

Stepping off the bus to Martissa, Jonas felt a temblor, composed equally of anxiety and belonging, in the spot Marielle's absence had not reached. The feeling quickly dissipated, though: this couldn't be sweet, ancient Martissa, the home village Kalliope had described so lovingly; not this motley plaster parish pressed tight against the road. "Motel *Zimmer Frei*" read a sign on the commercial strip's central edifice, a squat U-shaped structure that with a bit more weathering wouldn't have looked out of place in a forlorn West Texas town bypassed by the new interstate. Next door, four identical mini-cars gathered dust around a single gas pump; against the pump leaned a hand-lettered "Car Wash" sign pointing to what appeared to be an empty hill behind. Three expressionless restaurants lined up next to the gas pump, each exactly the same except that one had a blue awning and blue chairs; the second, red; the third, green. There were also two tourist shops which featured mass-produced ceramic mountain goats, ceramic minotaurs and ceramic replicas of ancient ceramic dishes. On opposite ends of the strip, identical two-story blockhouses proclaimed themselves "Tour Agent." Loudly proclaimed. Apparently each believed that the amount of business one could garner was directly proportional to the number and variety of transports described in bright paint on the outside walls: bus tickets, ferry tickets, car-to-hire, boat-to-hire, motorbike, scooter, trip-along-the-coast, fish trip, donkey-trip-to-valley-of-flowers, and at one place "Tour Special," at the other "Special Tour."

A lone structure—a blockhouse with two large front display windows—stood on the far side of the road. Above the door were painted the large words "Kwik" and "Stop." Brightly stacked in the windows was every conceivable amenity for the traveler, including an impressive number of canned goods. And on the roof, a monstrous maze of steel struts and neon tubing that rose twice as tall as the building itself.

Behind the commercial roadside row was a tightly packed grid of about eighty new, tiny, identical box-houses with corrugated tin roofs. The lower edge of this tract was bordered by a dirt road and flanked by a police station—really no more than a shed—and an electric power generator behind a chain-link fence. Two policemen were sitting in front of their shed, a sign over their heads informing Jonas that the tin-topped collection of boxes behind them was indeed not Martissa but something called Xhrimatos. Martissa, he learned, was behind a promontory, out of sight at the far end of the bay.

Jonas hoisted his bag and headed down the dirt road toward the promontory. Below the road were broad sand dunes and glimpses of sea; above it, stubbled fields and behind them what it took Jonas a few moments to recognize was a sizable stand of banana trees; and on the gentle slopes beyond, the soothing silver-greens of olive trees. A single line was strung from the power station through the banana grove; a gang of grinning crows lazed on the sagging wire.

Jonas rounded the promontory and there were the pastels and whites of Martissa, resting quietly in the gentle morning sun. From the dirt road the village appeared just as Kalliope had described it: a semicircle of very old, low, whitewashed traditional Aegean houses nestled in front of a set of hills; a ring of slightly larger pastel-painted nineteenth-century houses just behind and framing the original settlement; and on the first hilltop beyond the houses, commanding a view of the sea, the school where Kalliope's mother had taught several generations of the region's children.

It was preternaturally quiet as Jonas crossed the empty village square: the *kafeneion* was closed, its windows boarded, paint peeling; against the church wall, an escaped bell rope flapped in the breeze; a pile of cement blocks sat in front of a vacant pale blue house. Jonas put down his bag and went along a passageway off the square. The doors on all the houses were closed, the windows shuttered or boarded, a number of roofs collapsed and walls cracked open. Behind two houses, building materials were piled. There were no people. The only sound was a rattling hinge.

The hilltop school was also closed and derelict. Jonas peeked in: one large room, empty except for a battered old table. Around behind he found a packed-dirt basketball court with a single weather-beaten basket framed by olive trees and the Mediterranean beyond. Covering the court were a dozen rows of benches and old chairs facing the rear wall of the school.

The rest of the village was more of the same: houses empty and shuttered; walls cracked and crumbling; silence. But just before reaching the square again, Jonas heard someone humming. The tune was anomalous, and remotely familiar. A man appeared, roughly Jonas's age and almost as tall, cradling gently a battered clarinet. Though listing markedly to one side, the man bounced on the balls of his feet. He seemed mildly but pleasantly surprised to see Jonas, smiled and raised a hand: "*Guten Abend*," he greeted Jonas.

"Hello."

"Oh, Australia." There was a wiggle in the man's voice, as if his vocal cords had once been stretched beyond their limit and now permanently flopped about. It was a doubling sound, simultaneous echoes, comic and tragic.

"American."

"American!" The man grinned. "What town America?"

"New York."

"Ah! Bowery up, batteries down." The man became lost in thought for a moment. Jonas noted his incongruously pale skin and long black hair oiled into something vaguely resembling a pompadour. One side of his face drooped; pronounced ragged scars marked his temples.

"You seen before Ellas?" the man asked, brightening.

"No, I haven't." Jonas knew the Greek word for Greece—*Ellas*. "It's very beautiful."

"Yes, house of Apollo. I am seeing in pictures," the man said, added something which seemed to be about holes in the ground, then without a pause crooned: "How high the moooon . . . skooty-oo-bap-badaa!" He held out his hand: "Calling me Silly."

Jonas shook hands.

"What are you called?"

To avoid the "covered with garlic" confusion—Jonas Korda: *tsonas skorda*—in an already confusing conversation, Jonas said simply, "Jonaki."

Silly smiled and nodded as if this were a reasonable enough American name, then suddenly became solemn.

"I am sorry of President Kennedy."

Jonas nodded an equally solemn thanks.

"I was seeing him one time."

"Really. When was that?"

"Before he died."

They were silent. Silly eyed Jonas's feet: "No cuffs, eh?" He began to move his mouth and head as if he were humming again, but no sound came out. Jonas watched him stroll away, tilting to one side, bouncing to music only he could hear.

Jonas resumed his wander around the village: no shop; the bakery shuttered, its roof partially caved in; a *taverna* abandoned and desolate. Three or four houses appeared lived-in but Jonas saw no inhabitants. Eventually he heard scurrying, scraping and what sounded like snoring from a large Italianate house toward the rear of the village. Jonas went over to the wrought-iron gate. In the courtyard a trough had been dug, and partially filled with water, into an elaborate stone mosaic floor, right up to the house's large front double doors that were open onto a marble-floor interior. A score of small, almost pygmy pigs were wallowing in and out of the house.

Jonas headed back to collect his bag and almost tripped over a pair of high black boots sticking out into the walkway. Attached to the boots and the trousers above them was a woman with short, thick white hair who sat stringing tobacco leaves in the shade of the courtyard tree just behind her. Her large square head lifted unconcernedly; Jonas judged her to be late in her sixties.

"Sorry—Ah, *sighnomi*," Jonas apologized.

"It's quite all right," the woman said softly in well-articulated English, and went back to her tobacco leaves.

Jonas stood there feeling foolish. "Excuse me, but do you know of any empty rooms in the village?"

The woman looked up and considered Jonas for a moment.

"Empty rooms? Yes. Mostly empty rooms. But no place to stay, if that is what you mean. Did they promise you one of the villas? They have a way of promising things." The woman looked down the lane toward a pile of building materials. "I suppose next year they truly will be ready. Well, there are rooms back where you came from."

"You mean Xhrimatos?"

The woman did not respond, working again at her tobacco.

"I didn't come from Xhrimatos.... I just walked past it as fast as I could."

A brief chuckling breath escaped the woman.

"There is always a place to stay in Martissa," Jonas remembered Kalliope had said, "a stranger is a guest." He put his bag down and squatted in the shade. "I understood you could find a room here."

"Yes, most probably next year."

"No. I mean, always a place to stay here... in people's houses, I thought. I mean... before."

"Ah." The woman looked up from her work. "Before. Before the laws, yes."

"The laws... Which, ah, which laws are we talking about?"

"Yes, now only people from the family may stay in a house more than two hours—without an official lodging permission. So, forgive me for not offering, but in Martissa we do not get official permissions for too many things."

The woman went back to her tobacco. Jonas looked at the boarded-up homes all around them.

"Well, the houses... Why is it they're all...?"

The woman studied Jonas for a moment, then continued her work as she spoke. "*Seismos*— earthquake. At least, that was the beginning. Many houses were damaged. Also the water wells. But the government will not help to rebuild; or the banks. Our village is not to be trusted—it's too... odd. Of course, they build a new road back there and loan money to Athens men to build those ... house-cages, making that Xhrimatos. You see, there was no Xhrimatos, before. They put up those coffin-boxes in two minutes and say the people of Martissa can move there cheap, until they can fix up their Martissa houses. And for that, for moving into Xhrimatos, they'll lend money.

"The village council, we said we could put our money together and fix up our houses one at the time, if the government bank would give the council some loans. But the bank said no to that, too: our council could not make legal contract, they said, because ... we were all women. In Martissa, you see, our women decide for the village—it's very old tradition here. But not one they want in our new traditional Greece.... So, in the end, Martissa people don't want to move to that Xhrimatos, but without money to fix our houses ...

"So, that was four years ago. And people cannot even pay back the money for the Xhrimatos places, so they end up having to sell their Martissa houses to the bank, who starts fixing them up ... for holiday villas. We are close to the sea"—she looked around the dusty deserted square—"and we are quaint."

"You ... stayed, though?"

"A few of us, yes. The ones who still had good water wells. Not many. We could pump water from the hills for the rest, but there is not enough electricity. The power is run from Xhrimatos. Whenever they decide Martissa has had enough, off it goes. And they say 'enough' most of the time. They have all the electric they want in Xhrimatos, though. Pretty soon they'll be selling them televisions, machines to dry clothes ... and who will return to Martissa then?"

Under the direction of a uniformed foreman, three workmen were unloading equipment at the Xhrimatos power generator; another man in uniform was giving orders to several other workers who were assembling a prefabricated shack behind the fence. Jonas spotted the strange clarinet-toting Silly on the hill above, watching the work intently. Near Silly's chair leaning against a scraggly solo banana tree was a hand-lettered sign that read "Car Wash."

Jonas eschewed the motel and found a room instead above one of the tour agents, then went to the blue restaurant and into the kitchen to review the food on offer, as was custom. Greasy pork stew in one large pan, pork-stuffed tomatoes swimming in oil in another, or minced pork with some unidentifiable minced brown companion in a third. A sign on the window, however, advertised a bunch of dancing bananas. Jonas had seen the banana trees along the road, and he had never tasted the fruit fresh-picked, so he asked for yoghurt and a banana and went outside to sit down. The waiter brought him a packaged yoghurt and a tin of mashed banana. Jonas explained that he wanted an actual banana. The waiter said they were out of bananas.

Deciding instead to buy fruit that he would keep on hand in his room, Jonas went across to the Kwik Stop mini-market, which also displayed the dancing bananas sign. He found oranges and grapes but no bananas, so he waited until the proprietress and a male assistant had finished helping two German tourists. The shopkeeper was a large woman of about fifty, wearing an incongruous shiny electric blue pantsuit. Jonas asked if she had any local bananas. Introducing herself smilingly as Katsarida, she indicated a shelf of tinned mashed bananas. When Jonas picked up a couple of oranges instead, Katsarida looked at Jonas's bony frame and suggested that perhaps he could use some "real" food, in one of the restaurants. Which one? Jonas asked. Doesn't matter, Katsarida replied; the pork was especially good in all three. And, she said, it's local.

"Local?" Jonas thought of all the small pigs he'd seen running around the big house in Martissa.

"Oh yes." Katsarida gestured widely with outstretched arms. "Our local is very big."

It was getting dark as Jonas took a wander through the prefabricated Xhrimatos housing grid. There was no space between one identical cube and the next, the corrugated tin roofs forming continuous sheets over each parallel row like weighted lids that keep baby pets from crawling out of their boxes. Jonas noticed, though, that each household had added some small individual detail—a brightly painted door, an old knocker, a wreath—and that every otherwise identical front window showed a family portrait, special icon or picture of a favorite saint.

Jonas climbed a path behind the grid and through the dusk spotted Silly leaning in a chair against the solitary banana tree, dozing. Suddenly the hill was flooded by a monstrous green fluorescent glow: the glass tubing of Kwik Stop's metal rooftop sculpture lit up all the buildings along the main road, all the Xhrimatos box-houses and half the bay. Everything beyond the neon green became totally black; the stars disappeared. When Jonas turned back, Silly was in a low animal crouch, moving fearfully around the banana tree gathering his car wash gear into a sack. Jonas greeted him and Silly froze; Jonas came no closer: "It's just me. The American."

Silly glanced past Jonas toward the Kwik Stop, then without a word snapped up his clarinet and scurried down the hill toward the promontory, beyond which, Jonas could see, the green glow didn't reach. Jonas turned back and looked at the Kwik Stop sculpture: an enormous bird—a phoenix—with outstretched wings. Suddenly Jonas was very tired. He ate an orange then went to bed. During the night he was wakened by a distant howl coming from somewhere near Martissa.

From Silly's solo banana tree above Xhrimatos, Jonas could see down to a small pier where a row of matching numbered dinghies was tied. A group of eight tourists—Jonas spotted two Australian-flag T-shirts; he'd seen a group of Aussies coming in and out of the motel—was hopping into several dinghies. Jonas had thought he might find Silly at his tree this morning but the strange fellow had not appeared. Watching the tourists now, Jonas suddenly realized how starved he was for native-spoken English—even Australian—and he rushed down the hill. By the time he got to the pier, however, the tourists had already cast off. A boy watching over the dinghies made him understand that Jonas must go back to one of the tour agents to make arrangements if Jonas also wanted to rent one. Jonas looked to see if there was anyone else he might go out with, but there were no other tourists and all the fishing *caiques* were out of the water and up on blocks. There was only one other boat in the water; it had a police insignia on its side.

The tour agent said there was a small problem. Because Jonas was on his own, the agent said, he would need police clearance to take out a boat. The agent could not or would not say why this was so, but he assured Jonas that the permission would only take a minute.

A mother and young daughter were sitting stiff and still in the police shed. It was obvious they had been waiting a long time. Jonas sat next to them. On the facing wall was a sign with the ubiquitous phoenix-cum-shadow-soldier and a legend in Greek that by now Jonas could immediately translate: "A Greece of Christian Greeks."

Jonas peeked at the mother and child. Like the white-haired woman in Martissa, this woman wore not the shapeless cotton dress Jonas had been accustomed to seeing on most rural women but rather a rough shirt and work trousers tucked into well-worn high leather boots. Her willful, upright posture made obvious display of stubborn pride, but something in the cast of her eyes seemed to admit of a recognition that, in a dynamic she did not fully understand, she must somehow be in the wrong and that the phoenix chastising her from the wall must in some way be right. Jonas thought about the juxtaposition of the phoenix and the motto: moral imperative laid over martial authority. Opposition thus also becomes sacrilege: if you suffer, it's because only the righteous are chosen. He peeked again at the mother, saw her chafing at her own contrary inclinations.

After a few minutes one of the cops came up to the counter and beckoned. Jonas deferred to the mother and daughter but they looked at the cop and didn't budge. So Jonas got up and explained his quest. The cop pulled out a form: name; father's name; town; passengers; cargo; destiny. Here they hit a snag until Jonas realized that the cop meant destination.

"Well, I just want to putter around."

"No," the cop said. "No destiny, no boat."

"But what about those Australians this morning?"

"Tour group. Is different. So, destiny?"

"Well, how about along the coast."

"Mm, not good. Because who knows where along the coast you are going? Or what you are doing?"

"Okay, then. Fishing?"

"Ah, fishing—good. So, destiny?"

"Well, the sea. Fishing... in the sea."

"*Tzk*. The sea is not a destiny. For fishing, a village must can see the boat."

"You mean, I have to stay within sight of a village? But most of the fishermen are *lampari*, aren't they? At night, with lamps, out in deep water? A village can't see out that far."

"Ah, no, no, not here. *Lampari* must have special qualifyings—but no one here has the right ones." The cop glanced over at the woman and daughter waiting against the wall. "All people here must come back by night," he said. "Or we go out to find them, eh? And we are only two police here, so if we must go out, it's not good. You understand? So, destiny? Where you want to go?"

At the end of an hour's aimless strolling, Jonas walked to Martissa again and poked around the deserted houses. After a few minutes Silly came bouncing across the empty village square. He saw Jonas and smiled: "Goodday, mate," he attempted an Australian greeting.

"Hello, Silly."

Silly stopped, surprised: "You know I'm Silly?"

"Sure. You told me."

Silly was puzzled: "Australia?"

"America.... New York."

Silly's eyes widened: "Ah. New York." Silly smoothed his slicked-back hair. "You been before to the Apollo place?"

Silly's pleasure was so infectious that Jonas didn't mind repeating the previous day's litany.

"No, not before. It's very beautiful."

"Mm, Ellas place. The Queen.... And Silly is from Va-silly. It's meaning 'king.' What are you called, my friend?"

"Jonaki," Jonas told him again.

"Welcome to Martissa, Jonaki." He pumped Jonas's hand.

Silly's off-center artlessness released unexpectedly from Jonas the question he hadn't yet felt able to ask anyone else: "Do you happen to know Kalliope Savakis?"

"Kalliope?" The sagging side of Silly's face seemed to lift a bit. "Sure, sure. We are long, long friends. From little children. You come to see her?"

"Well, I didn't know if... I mean, is she...around."

Silly was lost for a moment: "Oh, a-tisket, a-tasket. She is gone a little time before." Silly tipped his head as if trying to get another view of his memory. "Some weeks, I think. For working in... England. Someplace like that." His eyes drifted as he struggled with a thought he could not quite grasp; the side of his face drooped more markedly.

Jonas felt a tremendous rush of relief to learn that Kalliope had escaped the security police on Corfu. He was a bit surprised, though, that after the Corfu incidents she could have returned so openly to Martissa, and that her movements would be so readily broadcast. But then, if she'd already managed to get herself out of Greece again, after only "some weeks"…

"Yes, she is always wanting to see other places…no matter I am here." Jonas squinted his green eye and could detect a faint blush under Silly's skin. "She is always talking, talking, but never going before now. This time really she is doing it."

Never going before now? But Kalliope had told Jonas that she'd spent six years away, working all over Europe. And it was already months ago that Jonas had met her on the train in Italy. Yet here was Silly saying that she went abroad for the first time only weeks ago…

"Well…do you know maybe where I could find Kalliope's mother?"

"*Theia* Nemosia? Sure. She teaches the school. You finding her…" Silly turned toward the hilltop school then turned back, disoriented. "But I don't think… Is it *Kiriaki* today? Sunday?" He looked at the neglected church, the wayward bell rope flapping in the breeze. "Because I don't see any little ones going up there today. So, maybe you see her…around." Silly tipped his head at the shuttered houses and a sad consternation slipped over his shoulders. His chin dropped; the side of his face sagged; a gurgle came from his open mouth. After a moment he stared at Jonas's feet; when he glanced up again the twinkle had returned to his eyes.

"No cuffs, eh?" Silly grinned and began to hum the same tune as the day before, ending with a "Scooty oo bap-ba-daa." He tucked his clarinet under his arm, nodded knowingly at the bottoms of Jonas's trousers, and headed off.

Jonas heard voices and found a young Scandinavian backpacker couple talking with the white-haired tobacco-stringing woman he'd met the day before.

"…someplace we could buy bread or cheese?"

"There is nothing for sale in this village." The woman glanced at Jonas. "Nothing…and everything. But you are welcome to drink from the well. And some of the fruit if you wish." She indicated the courtyard behind her: a fig and two orange trees, tobacco leaves strung between.

The woman got up and went into the courtyard to draw water from the well. As she passed, she looked again at Jonas and in her eyes he could see a rim of violet around the dark irises—Kalliope's eyes.

The couple picked two oranges, thanked the woman and left.

"You're the schoolteacher, aren't you?"

"There is no school here."

"Oh, well, I just ran into someone who said . . ."

"A tall boy?"

"Yes, Vasilly."

The woman considered Jonas over the water ladle.

"You are a tall one, too. Reach those figs, eh?"

Jonas pulled a few of the heavy purple fruit off a high branch, their sweet smell mingling with the scent of the oranges.

"I *was* the schoolteacher. Vasilly, he . . . forgets sometimes."

Jonas understood that this was kindness in the form of understatement. And realized, too, that Silly's sense of time—of when Kalliope had last been in the village—might be wildly unreliable. Jonas and Kalliope's mother sat on a low bench and ate the figs. Jonas's eyes were drawn to the open door, to the house in the rooms of which images of the long-absent daughter must linger for her mother. Six years she had been gone. Jonas didn't know how to begin speaking of Kalliope, how to tell the mother that her daughter was probably in the nightmare bowels of a dungeon in Corfu. Or incommunicado in some brutal political prison camp. Or banished to some barren stony island.

"You're Mrs. Savakis," Jonas finally blurted.

The woman raised an eyebrow. "Nemosia Savakis, yes."

"I, ah, I met your daughter Kalliope."

The schoolteacher clenched her jaw: "My daughter is in Germany."

"Yes, yes, I know. That's where I met her. In Italy, I mean. On a train."

Nemosia didn't try to hide her disquiet.

"She said I should visit Martissa."

"My daughter no longer knows Martissa. There is no reason to visit here."

"Well, I was . . . nearby."

"Nearby Martissa?" She scoffed, and with it an echo of distrust.

"I mean, I was already on Crete, so . . ."

Nemosia didn't respond, and after a moment got up and went to the doorway. Jonas heard clearly Nemosia's silence: he got up and thanked her for the fruit, calling her *Theia*—Aunt—as Silly had done. Jonas was almost out into the lane when Nemosia spoke again. "And what did my daughter say you would do in Martissa?"

For an instant Jonas pictured Kalliope standing next to her mother in the doorway. "Oh, maybe write a few poems." Jonas shrugged in the particular Greek way he had first seen from Kalliope on the train. "Sing a few songs. . . . And for sure drink some *raki*."

Nemosia stared, gave a little laugh, then turned and disappeared into the house. It was not an unfriendly laugh.

It was the afternoon *ipnos* time, but Jonas couldn't sleep. Why hadn't he asked Nemosia if she'd heard anything about her daughter? What the hell was he doing here if not to find out about Kalliope? And if Nemosia knew nothing at all, didn't he have to tell her what had happened on Corfu? He got off the bed and went out.

The red restaurant this time: pork chops, pork stew, pork *souvlaki*. No, sorry, no fish. . . . What was it that cop had said? "Special qualifyings" needed to do the normal night fishing, and no one has them around here. Jonas ordered a salad, ate quickly and left.

People in Xhrimatos were emerging from their *ipnos*. Three women stepped out through the open door of one of the identical tin-roofed boxes. Jonas looked in and found a *kafeneion*: four men at one table and several other tables of men and women together drinking coffee, talking animatedly and, the first time Jonas had seen women do so, playing *tavli*. They looked at Jonas with benign curiosity, but when he merely ordered a coffee and sat in a corner, they paid him no more heed.

A miniature sparrow-woman came in, ancient, hunched, covered from head to foot in black rags. She addressed no one, looked at no one. In fact, the tiny wizened creature didn't look at all but *felt* her way from table to table, sifting, by touch alone, through tin ashtrays and empty cigarette packets for usable bits of tobacco. Her twisted twig fingers raised the butts and loose tobacco for a sniff before she decided which to keep and which to reject. When she found a stub or tobacco to her liking, she dropped it into the folds of her apron. The patrons and counter man generally ignored her, though for moments one or another would watch with respect her sightless tenacity. One women rolled a new cigarette, and another broke in half a ready-made cigarette, and put them in empty ashtrays for the tiny old woman to find.

"*Ekato tria*"—A hundred and three—one woman said to Jonas. The tiny woman completed her silent round of the tables and left.

One of the power station foremen came in with another of the uniformed electrical men. Although no one made any obvious visible response, there was a palpable change in the room. The two newcomers were no louder than the other patrons, yet their voices stood out like metal buttons in a washing machine. A little boy came in and spoke to a woman near the door who made a show of complaint to her companions, then got up and left with the boy. This first defection seemed to loosen a hold on the tables and one by one all the other customers left. Jonas looked to see whether the foreman and his cohort registered a connection between their arrival and the other patrons' departure but they were busy talking and didn't seem to notice. Jonas got up and left, too.

"*Now*," Jonas told himself—he would talk to Kalliope's mother *now*. He hurried to Martissa as if his resolve might dissipate with the fading light. The door to Nemosia's house was open but there was no response to Jonas's call. He stood on the threshold trying to feel some sense of Kalliope in the shadows, then turned away abruptly from the temptation to go in. Instead, he moved around the deserted village, as much because he didn't want to return to Xhrimatos as in the hope that he'd find Nemosia. He passed the blue house with its wrought-iron gate; in the courtyard, a man Jonas recognized as a Xhrimatos restaurant waiter was trying to catch a piglet.

Jonas was near the road when he heard the familiar waggly voice call, "Americo!" Beat-up clarinet in hand, Silly filled the doorway of a crumbling hut; scratchy music was coming from the darkness behind him. Jonas bent through the door and could barely make out an old box radio on a small table, two frayed cane chairs, a cooking pot on an open hearth, and a sagging cot. On one dark wall was a framed Black Madonna that was unaccountably familiar to Jonas. At first, he didn't even see the ancient sparrow woman, so small, so black in the low-ceiling darkness. He only turned away from trying to make out the resonant Madonna face when the old woman moved her head and the fading light from the doorway caught the cigarette stub in her toothless mouth. She was grinning.

It was big band jazz coming from the radio, faint and full of static. Silly nudged Jonas into a chair and began to accompany the music on his clarinet. And at the sound of his playing, the tiny old woman began to dance. She and Silly bumped around the table, Silly tooting, the ancient woman humming, both of them giggling; Silly had to duck to avoid the jerry-rigged cord connecting the radio through a small window to a power line somewhere outside. The old woman felt for Jonas's arm and tugged at his sleeve. He needed no prodding, and the three of them pranced and hummed around the table. The song ended and a voice in German replaced the music. Silly struck up a new tune and played over the voice. After several bars he stopped and croaked the chorus, which, despite the strange pronunciation, Jonas understood as "Ain't nobody's business but my ooowwn..." It was obvious he had played and sung it for the old woman before: she clapped her hands and joined in to warble "...my oowwn" past the stub of her cigarette.

Another piece of 1950s jazz came on and Silly accompanied it again, but just as the three resumed their dance, the radio went off. Jonas looked out the door: the few dim lights around Martissa had also gone out.... "Off it goes," Nemosia had said of the electricity flow to Martissa, "whenever they decide we have had enough."

Silly was momentarily silent but recovered and began another tune, a delicate Greek vesper this time, quiet and pensive. Something about it made the old woman giggle. At first Silly seemed not to be in on the joke, but soon he, too, had a bashful grin. After the first melody he moved into another, more robust tune. And this one Jonas recognized: Panastakis, the forbidden music. Silly played it with rising energy and filled the dark little hut with life.

Through the doorway Jonas saw the sky above Xhrimatos suddenly fill with a ghoulish green glow: the Kwik Stop phoenix had been lit. Silly saw the light, too, and abruptly stopped playing. His tall figure slumped away from the doorway; the side of his face drooped; one arm went limp. The tiny woman moved her head from side to side.

"To phos?"— The light?—she whispered.

Silly didn't answer. He backed into the darkest corner of the hut, hugging his clarinet to his chest. The old woman went to him and soothed him. Neither one seemed aware any longer of Jonas, and quietly he left the hut.

Outside, he was surprised to see several groups of locals coming along the dirt road. They didn't enter Martissa—they even seemed to avoid looking at the village—but turned onto a path which paralleled a power line leading up the hill. Martissa was dark, but there were lights up behind the school: the outline of the basketball pole hovered over the schoolyard.

Jonas spotted one of the two men from the Xhrimatos tour agent shop where he had taken a room and asked where everyone was going. Cinema, the man said: cowboyindians, gangstermen, all kind of. Every *Savvato*—Saturday. People come out from the hills to see it, from other towns, from all over.

Jonas started for Xhrimatos, went partway, then turned around and followed the crowd up the hill. Outside the school, Katsarida the Kwik Stop woman loomed behind her assistant from the shop. The assistant said, "Movie?" then took Jonas's money and pointed to the rear of the school.

A film was already on, coming from a small hut at the far edge of the dirt basketball court onto the school's back wall. Sixty or seventy people filled most of the rows of benches. Everyone was standing at relative attention but few seemed to pay much heed to a grainy bald head projected on the wall. One old man held a piece of cardboard in front of his face. From behind, Jonas could see light from the film coming through a tiny hole in the cardboard, which the myopic old man was using to see the image more distinctly. After a few moments of watching the bald head, though, he put the card down.

The head on the wall was haranguing in that shrill and acrid voice distressingly familiar to Jonas from the television in Glaros and from the radio that had come through his jail cell walls on Corfu. Finally the head finished and a phoenix-cum-soldier was projected, accompanied by blaring military music. The music ended and the wall went white. The audience sat down with sighs of relief and Jonas saw Katsarida's assistant go into the shed. After several minutes a new film came on and the audience immediately became attentive. Half a dozen hole-pierced cardboard pieces unused during the bald head performance now popped up.

The film opened with a wide shot of a dry landscape, not unlike parts of Crete, and a lone horseman heading for a frontier town. Behind the Italian titles, the face came into view: Clint Eastwood. The audience murmured excitedly. In Italian with Greek subtitles, Clint ordered a whiskey in the bar, then matched antagonisms with the bad guys who held the town in their grip. Whatever Clint said caused the audience to hoot their approval, and when Clint humiliated the town sheriff, the basketball court crowd whooped with delight. Then the shooting started: face full of lather, Clint gunned down three bad guys in one swivel of his barber chair, and the audience cheered. But then a strange thing happened. Clint went into the street, where the townspeople were waiting passively to see who would win the gunfight. Clint lit a cigar and looked over the locals, then delivered a disdainful speech on the heels of which, with a disgusted expression, he turned his back and walked away. The audience sank back on the benches. Several people brought down their sight-cards. The basketball court became still. Clint went on shooting people and being cool but the audience no longer responded. Their faces were blank, their movements on the benches small and stiff. Before the movie finished, Jonas got up and left.

Back in Xhrimatos, outside the police station one of the cops was speaking with two foremen from the power station. As Jonas passed, one of the power station men made a remark to the others and affectedly ran his fingers through the long hair he did not have. Cloaked with the mantles of righteousness and belonging, the three men looked at Jonas and laughed.

The pathways of Xhrimatos were quiet. Dark clouds lowered the sky and pressed on the tin roofs. Jonas passed the cement box that housed the village barber and through the open door saw a man getting a haircut. Jonas felt his own hair, uncut since Corfu, since Liana had hacked away the knots of blood and filth he'd brought from jail. His hair was very long now, much longer than usual, longer than he liked it. Gave people, like the cop and the electricity men, an excuse to mark him. A meaningless excuse. What had happened to anonymity? He went into the barber's.

Two other men were waiting. Jonas sat down and the mirror looked back at him. The others' haircuts and shaves were far from careful and deliberate, but the length and vehemence of conversation—at one point the barber's thumb stopped a flow of blood while in his other, arguing hand the razor whizzed only inches from the customer's nose—made Jonas's wait a considerable one. He studied his face in the mirror. There was something wrong about it. Strange; distant. It made him uncomfortable. As he sat, the face in the mirror seemed less and less him and more and more someone he was watching, someone he had been watching for a long time. When his turn came, he didn't ask for a haircut. It had been ten years since he had seen himself without the moustache.

20

In the middle of the night, it rained. The metallic drum roll on the roofs of Xhrimatos turned Jonas over and over in his sleep. Early in the morning, he woke to the sound of automatic weapon fire; he found himself sitting up, pressed against the wall next to his bed, stroking the tender flesh of his naked upper lip. There was silence, an explosion, another silence, then the automatic weapon fire again somewhere near the road to Martissa.

Outside, the only battle he found was between the sun and the puddles that hadn't yet penetrated the hard-baked earth. The sky was a brilliant blue again, but a different blue, as if the gauzy cocoon of September had been silently stripped away in the night. It was warm, but people were wearing an added layer, and there was a different quality to the air: thinner, clearer, uncluttered by the spores of summer. The morning had a certain serenity. And a sadness. It was finally autumn. Winter-the-parent hovered just behind the sky, permitting the children a bit more play but announcing with its call of rain that it would soon be time to come inside. As Jonas walked to Martissa, he looked at the sea, a rugged, thick-muscled green, churning and restless. He realized that he had not swum since getting to Xhrimatos. And now the water would be turning cold.

Near Martissa he found the automatic weapons—merely two men with jackhammers. They stopped him from going any farther down the path: more dynamite about to go off, an extension to the main road that ended at Xhrimatos. People out to see if the rain had softened their fields enough for autumn plowing were now forced to come down from the hillside terraces, shoulders hunched, to the dirt path below. Women in trousers and high boots and white head-wraps, who had just managed to collect the goats that had scattered at the dynamite, now stood silent and resigned to the next explosion.

Shouts from the construction men, a universal silence, then a blast that grabbed the air by the throat and shook it violently, only gradually loosening its grip. When the rain of dust and pebbles settled, the construction men scurried up the hill while the goatherd women moved slowly after the animals that had run again in panic.

Jonas found Silly and Nemosia sitting in front of the school, with a view of the blasting. Instead of greeting Jonas, the schoolteacher continued speaking to Silly in a voice to calm a frightened child. After a while Silly began to nod and his drooping face reanimated slightly. He noticed Jonas.

"*Guten Tag*," Silly said with difficulty and no indication of ever having seen Jonas before. Nemosia gently explained that Jonas was an American, but instead of Silly's usual questions, he merely spoke a few words to Nemosia and got up.

"Do you stay near the road?" Silly asked Jonas distractedly.

"You mean in Xhrimatos?"

"Xhrimatos?" Silly looked to Nemosia for help, then recalled the name on his own. "Yes, Xhrimatos."

Jonas said yes, that was where he stayed.

"Maybe you come visiting to my trees. I'm Vasilly." He put out his hand. "You like bananas?" Silly again noticed the workmen on the hillside and a cloud of doubt crossed his face. "They are building some things," he looked to Nemosia, who nodded support. "But it's okay. Anyway," he brightened and began to sing, "Dream a little dream . . ." Still crooning, he went down the path.

"He gets confused sometimes."

"So do I," Jonas said.

"He forgets. But the forgetting releases him from . . . too much life." They looked out over Martissa, the dirt road, the sea. Silly was bouncing again, moving along toward Xhrimatos.

"At least they don't shut him away someplace," Jonas sympathized.

"Oh, they did, yes. But that was *before* his forgetting, not after. Once he became . . . confused, they let him out. He did have banana trees, you understand. All these were his." Nemosia gestured toward the multiple rows of trees that paralleled the road. "His grandfather planted them. From Africa. For many years the family traded the fruits all over Kriti. No one else had bananas.

"Then some people in Athens decided that *they* wanted banana trees. They can't grow in Europe, you see, so they bring quite much money. But even in Greece they only grow in very few spots. And Vasilly's grandfather had the best. The Athens people wanted to buy the land, and plant many, many banana trees. But the grandfather would not sell. Not the father either. And not Vasilly.

"Then six years ago came the new government." Nemosia paused. "May they think of themselves as I think of them, then live long and thoughtful lives. . . . They are friends to those who want Vasilly's banana lands, so they make a special law: bananas are a 'protected nation resource,' only to be sold from a new Greek Banana Council. This council, of course, sells to their export friends, who hire their ship owner friends, who sell to their north Europe friends, and so on. Each time one of them touches a banana, more money is made."

"But what does Vasilly . . . ?"

"Ah, yes. We were talking about Vasilly. Well, Vasilly would not sell his land or his fruits to this council. But since he only traded the fruits with local people and did no selling for money, he thought the special selling laws had nothing to do with him. Logic. Making sense. And foolish. He was arrested: 'Unauthorized Exchange of Bananas.' They let him go after a few days, with a caution not to trade more bananas. But still Vasilly would not sell his land to Athens. Instead, he said anyone who wanted could pick the fruits to eat. So, they arrest him again; also some people who had taken bananas to eat: 'Destruction of Sellable Goods,' they called it. . . . One cannot invent how ridiculous men can be, eh? Or, how horrible.

"But this time for Vasilly it was more serious. They held him for months. And while he was in jail, the State filed a claim on his land: Vasilly had 'abandoned' it, you see . . . by being in jail. Finally they released him, but by then his land, and his trees, were no longer his. Even the small place he built to storehouse his bananas—also 'abandoned.' Back there." She gestured toward the other end of the bay. "Before there was anything there called Xhrimatos.

"All of this, of course, made Vasilly a strange and angry boy. But still he had most of his head. Until the third time. After the poison. The trees, you see. A poison was put in the ground around all the trees; it did not kill them, but for years it is not possible to eat the fruit, or to plant any new trees. Beautiful fruit that you cannot eat. And perfect land that you cannot plant. They never see Vasilly do it, but they arrest him anyway. And take him to hospital near Heraklion. Only, by then it was not a hospital but an 'Education Center.' ... Those marks?" Jonas had seen the ragged scars on Silly's temples. "From 'the crown.' The one they make tight with screws. Vasilly—'the king,' with a crown." Nemosia spat: "What is there people will not do to other people?"

She struggled to her feet. "The blessing is he remembers none of prison or the crown. At least, not in the front parts of his memory. But not much either of yesterday or the day before. Most mornings he begins like it is the day before they take him away. Sometimes, though, his body remembers. Like when they light that big bird. That used to be his place, you see, his banana storing place. Taken now by the Kwik Stop shop of Katsarida."

"Katsarida? She ... I didn't think ... I mean, she seems nice enough."

"Nice enough? Yes, she is that. I know her all her life. And Vasilly does, too. Katsarida didn't want the bird. But if she wanted the place for a shop, she had to take the bird also. And a shop was what she wanted most. Then later, when they bring the power to Xhrimatos, they put the bright lights up on the thing. Nice enough, Katsarida? Sure, she is. All these worlds rest on people who are nice enough.

"Anyway, you can see how it is all very confusing for Vasilly." Nemosia looked at the school. "He and my Kalliope, they loved to make up crazy songs together..."

Jonas and Nemosia headed down the hill in silence.

"Why ... tell me all this?" Jonas finally said.

"Maybe, because I am a teacher." She looked around the deserted village. "And who else now can I tell?"

They turned a corner, and standing in front of Nemosia's house was a short, slight figure wearing an Australian flag T-shirt. His hair was now darker and straightened but there could be no mistaking the enormous moustache—it was Nosey.

"'Lo, mate," Nosey said to Jonas from several yards away. "All right?" He spoke in an exaggerated Australian version of his inimitable mongrel accent, and as casually as if he had just seen Jonas the night before. Jonas was stunned. And thrilled. Wanted to pick Nosey up in his arms. But Nosey stood with such restraint, his eyes darting so uncertainly between Jonas and Nemosia and up and down the lane, that Jonas held both his ground and his tongue. Nosey quickly introduced himself to Jonas: "Clive. You remember, from the tour group, down the road. Thought I'd have a look 'round on me own, for a change."

Nosey indicated no recognition of Kalliope's mother; Nemosia stood by quietly, evincing no interest in this Australian tourist.

"Oh, right." Jonas thought his voice must sound transparently false, but Nemosia did not react. Why were they playing this game? Jonas wondered. This is Kalliope's mother, for chrissake.

"Gonna leg it down the sea. Come along if you're a mind."

Jonas looked at Nemosia.

"Yes, you have listened to me enough for one day," she said.

Jonas and Nosey walked together toward the water. It was extremely awkward: Jonas was elated to see that he wasn't in prison. But he was constrained to show it by Nosey's shadowy reticence.

"So, you're all right."

"Fit as a butcher's dog."

"I mean, you're not in jail."

"Well, you ain't, neither, are you "

"Didn't they arrest you?"

"Don't get done if you don't get found."

"But . . . how did you get off Corfu?"

"Well, surrounded by water, innit? . . . Dead funny, you know." Nosey momentarily dropped his guard. "Same way I got on the bleedin' island goin' on thirty year ago."

"So, what, ah, what are you doing here?"

Nosey bristled. "Might be I could hear somethin' 'bout Kalliope, eh?" He didn't look at Jonas. "If there was somethin' to hear."

"She wasn't arrested?"

"Dunno, do I?" Irritation rose in Nosey's voice. "B'sides, what *you* doing 'round here, then?"

They walked without speaking for a few moments.

"What about Alekos?" Jonas finally asked softly.

Nosey's enormous brush of moustache trembled as he shook his head. He and Jonas both had a chilling idea of what Alekos must have gone through—must still be going through—in one of the regime's many political prisons.

"Has Nemosia heard anything? About Kalliope?" Jonas asked.

"Nemosia? Who's Nemosia?"

"But... *that* was Nemosia. Back there. Kalliope's mother."

"Ah, herself, was it?" Nosey said with only mild interest.

"I thought... since you were at her house..."

"Well, yeah, but... I ain't talked to her yet."

"Then what have you...?"

"Don't always do the right thing, do I?" Nosey snapped. "Anyways, *you* was talking with her—you tell me."

"Nothing to tell. She clammed up when I mentioned Kalliope; said she's in Germany. And I haven't got up the nerve yet to tell her about Corfu.... So, what are you going to do now?" Jonas asked when Nosey said nothing more. The words came out more sharply than he intended.

Nosey stopped abruptly. "And what about *you*? Just where have *you* got to, eh?"

When Jonas didn't answer, Nosey said he had to get back to Xhrimatos, had some things to take care of, but asked if Jonas would meet him for supper. Jonas was distressed by Nosey's shifting moods, by the surges of anger and distrust which choked him off from Jonas. He was relieved to let their meeting—their collision—cool off before trying again. Sure, Jonas said; supper. Nosey left him standing by the water.

The steel-and-glass-tube phoenix atop the Kwik Stop squinted down through the slanting autumn sun at the construction workers carrying dynamite toward another round of blasting. Silly was perched on a rock on the crest of a hill behind, watching them with all his senses, like a predator tracking a bigger, dangerous foe.

Jonas went to his room and lay down. Why would Nosey come all the way to Crete? And he's probably on the security police wanted list, so why risk showing up in the home village of Kalliope, likely also wanted by the police? And if Nosey had come all this way, why hadn't he spoken with Kalliope's mother? Come to think of it, hadn't Nosey resented the hell out of Kalliope's songs? So what was he doing here at all? And wait . . . hadn't Nosey left Korina's house that night in Corfu—Jonas became queasy with the recollection—*just before* the security police busted in? Just in time . . .

Jonas bolted up and out. He asked some Aussies sitting outside at the red restaurant if they knew where Clive was but no one had seen him. Jonas scoured Xhrimatos and then from the rear of the housing grid spotted Silly and Nosey up at Silly's Car Wash tree, talking. Jonas met Nosey as he came down the hill.

"Dead strange, that one. Face like the back end of a cart horse. And all this tosh 'bout bananas."

"He's Kalliope's old friend," Jonas said cautiously. "Since they were kids."

"Yeah? Well, still bleedin' strange."

They stopped at the rear of the Xhrimatos settlement.

"Not just strange, Nosey."

They looked at each other and Jonas could see that Nosey knew all about Silly. "*Kakourgi*—the bleedin' criminals!" Nosey spat.

"*Pyos einai?*"—Who is?—a voice demanded. Two policemen came out from among the houses; one cop slid over to Nosey as the other circled behind. The cop close to Nosey spoke Greek to him in a voice dripping with ill will.

"Sorry, guv." Nosey looked blank. "Don't speak the language."

"You see, captain, we were having a little argument." Jonas stepped up. "And I've been teaching him a few words I picked up. Like *kerata*! And *malaka*!" Jonas pronounced dramatically the words—cuckold! jerk off!—that Nosey himself had taught him on Corfu. "And *kakourgos*! That one he loves."

Nosey dissembled a smile behind his moustache and gave a shrug. A particularly Greek shrug, Jonas noted with a shiver.

"So, when he's pissed at me, I mean pissed off, because 'pissed' to an Aussie means drunk, which was another fight we had . . ."

"Australia?" the cop grunted at Nosey.

"Yeah. Sydney. You been there?"

The cop stared at Nosey as if trying to find the entrance to a secret passageway.

"This other time, see," Jonas jumped in again, "he tells me he was really pissed the night before, so I say, 'What the hell did I do?' and now I'm pissed off, see, so you can see what a problem language can be . . . even among friends."

Jonas smiled. The cop looked at him as if deciding whether Jonas was actually saying something or was merely being an American fool. The cop turned back to Nosey: "*Dthyavatirion!*" he barked.

Jonas felt a cold trickle down his arms. "That's passport, ah, Clive. Means passport. But we, ah, we don't carry them around with us, captain."

"Passport? Why didn't he say so?" He turned back to the cop. "Sure thing, guv."

To Jonas's astonishment, Nosey pulled out an Australian passport. The cop studied it and Nosey's face, spoke to his partner, then growled at Nosey. Jonas understood the last word, "Greek"—something about Nosey being or speaking Greek.

"So here's what the real argument was about," Jonas blurted, "why he said *kakourgos*! . . . It's, ah, on account of this."

Jonas pulled a closed fist out of his pocket and stared at it. The cops stared, too. Slowly Jonas opened the hand: his bandless watch. The cops looked at it, then at Jonas, and he knew he had to say something, fast. "See, it's his. I mean, it's mine, from the States. Well, from Japan, but from the States. Know what I mean?"

Jonas put the watch in the cop's hand.

"It was, ah, *tavli*." The cop blinked at Jonas's mention of backgammon, a revered Greek national pastime. "Playing *tavli*, see, me and him, and we're drinking a little, and he starts getting *methisos*, eh?"

"What d'you call me?" Nosey said.

"*Methismenos*—drunk. Hell, that one you oughta know," Jonas said with a show of irritation. "So he's getting drunk," Jonas continued to the cop, "and he wants to make a bet, you know, on the *tavli* game. So he's got this dinosaur thing from Australia"—Jonas grabbed Nosey's wrist to show the cops his watch—"and he says, 'Watches, let's play for watches.' So I tell him okay, mine's back in the room, and he says, 'Oh, yeah, sure,' but finally he says okay, let's play. And somehow—don't ask me—the guy wins the game. So just now I bring him the watch. But when I show it to him, he starts complaining because—you ready for this?—'It don't have no bleedin' hands on it.' I mean, do you believe it? No hands, he says. On a digital watch!"

"And no strap neither!" Nosey complained.

Jonas threw his arms in the air. "I mean, look at this watch, captain. And tell this dumb-ass Aussie how good it is."

"Who you calling dumb, you bleedin' Yank?"

"See? Calls me names, like *kakourgos*. 'Cause he thinks this piece of junk"—Jonas roughly pulled the watch off Nosey's wrist—"is better than my digital." He thrust Nosey's watch into the cop's hands, which now held two watches and the passport. "Backward fucking kangaroo-land, haven't made it to the modern world yet."

"Watch your mouth, son." Nosey poked a finger at Jonas. "You and your poncy digitals."

"Poncy? Who you calling poncy? Man, if you had half a brain you wouldn't need to hide it behind that stupid moustache."

"Right!" Nosey lunged and butted Jonas in the chest and in a moment they were grappling with each other and swearing.

"*Vlakes!*"—Idiots!—the cop yelled. Nosey and Jonas broke their holds. "You are stupid! And your clocks are stupid, too." The cop threw the watches at them, made a noise of disgust, and stalked away with his partner.

"I don't know what it is," Jonas said, exhaling, "but whenever you're around, I always wind up in some kind of shit."

Jonas meant it as a comradely remark, but hearing his own words resurrected his doubts about Nosey and the raid in Glaros.

"What say to a stroll a bit later?" Nosey asked abruptly as he brushed himself off.

Jonas didn't know what to make of this. But he wanted to find out whatever he could, and so instead of probing Nosey, he just accepted the offer. Nosey said he would come get Jonas later on.

"Well, at least we got them off our backs." Jonas nodded toward the police shed.

"Oh, yeah?" Nosey said. "Then why'd they keep my passport?"

⟵⟵⟶

A shyly smiling Silly stood at Jonas's door.

"You're Americo, eh? I saw you before."

"That's right."

"He said you're wanting to walk."

Jonas didn't understand.

"The small one, with the big *moustaki*. Say you walk with me." Silly was quickly becoming disoriented.

"The small one. You mean Nosey?"

The name didn't register; the side of Silly's face drooped more markedly.

"Okay. Sure," Jonas said quickly. "*Pamay*"—Let's go.

They went up the path behind Xhrimatos. Jonas expected Nosey to appear, but past Silly's tree and into the olive groves there was no sign of him. Silly bounced along to the music in his head; he carried a woven sack filled with fruit, a loaf of bread peeking from the top. Though listing to one side, he picked his way nimbly along the narrow path.

Beyond the olive groves, the hills became steep and thick with brush, the path more and more indistinct. Silly marched along steadily, humming, the walk itself a pleasure sufficient without words, here and there pointing for Jonas to a camouflaged bird, a skittering lizard or a mushroom which had sprouted with the rain. They headed into a ravine; both Xhrimatos on one end of the bay and Martissa on the other were blocked from view. A few steps more and the glinting sea swells disappeared, then the quiet lapping of the tide was gone, the sound one does not listen for until one can hear it no longer.

They continued to climb and twist through hills and ravines until Jonas thought they must be miles from the sea. Some moments he wondered what he was doing off trekking with Silly, and where Nosey was, but the afternoon was so beautiful and the hills so peaceful that he let himself be carried along in the silent sedan chair of Silly's company. Finally they ducked through a brush-covered natural tunnel and came out on a small plateau. Below them, opposite from where Jonas would have guessed, there again was the school with the basketball court, Martissa and the sea beyond. Silly and Jonas sat and admired a view that stretched in every direction save the sheer cliff behind them. Silly was at home and at peace here; obviously a favorite spot. He pulled from his pocket several dried figs but didn't touch the bulging sack of other food. He and Jonas stretched out and chewed the figs in silence.

Soon Jonas was dozing, and in his dream heard the sound of an *aulos* pipe.

"*Posso avere questo ballo?*" A voice from the heavens entered the dream. "I ask if you want to dance."

Heart pounding, Jonas opened his eyes to a figure moving behind a bush on a ledge above. Moments later she emerged through the tunnel and even a layer of grime could not diminish that wide ingenuous smile. She gestured for Jonas to come away from view, and they embraced. Kalliope.

As she attacked the food in Silly's bag, Kalliope explained that she had got away from Corfu in a small boat with Nosey. She asked about Jonas's jailing and appreciated the modesty of his brief reply. When Jonas asked if she knew anything about Alekos, Kalliope stopped chewing. She knew nothing. But what was there to know that they all could not guess?

After getting down enough food, Kalliope spoke at length. In Athens she had known of people to help them, but after several weeks in hiding she had become restless. She wanted to do something, and the best place for that, she shrugged, was the place you call home. With his Australian "Clive" passport as cover, she and Nosey had traveled as a tourist couple, and then Nosey had been able to sniff around Martissa. Kalliope did not know whether the security police were looking for her here, so for now she could not risk showing herself. She had been staying up in the hills, in the same caverns in which her father had hidden from the Nazis. She and Vasilly had played up here as children. Kalliope glanced at a silent, contented Silly. It was their secret, this place, hers and Vasilly's. "Until you are coming," Kalliope smiled.

The night before, Kalliope had slipped down for a rendezvous with her mother and Nosey. Nosey told her of having spotted Jonas, and of Nosey's suspicions: What was Jonas doing here? As Kalliope spoke, Jonas thought with chagrin and relief of his own doubts about Nosey.

"So, I am asking to him the same question." Around Kalliope's violet-ringed eyes there cavorted a litter of ironic wrinkles. "Nosey, why are *you* here?" The hand twirled upward in the same motion Jonas had first seen her make on the train, what seemed so long ago.

"Well, remember," he said, "you did invite me. 'Very special, Kriti,' you told me."

Kalliope laughed and gestured at the sea, at the hills, at the sun setting behind the mountains: "And so?"

Jonas waited as if making up his mind, then gave a shrug, and they laughed together. Silly did not follow the conversation as much as he did Kalliope's face, and now he laughed, too. But it quickly faded. As the daylight dwindled, Silly was becoming increasingly fidgety; his face was drooping markedly.

Jonas told Kalliope of the run-in with the police that morning and the confiscation of Nosey's passport. Kalliope became somber, then was lost in thought. She looked again at Jonas. "Your moustache. They are taking it from you in the jail?"

"No. No, I just decided . . . I don't know."

"They are doing that sometime, for making you ashamed. Pulling it out, piece by piece."

"Moo-stache, no moo-stache," Silly droned. He looked at Jonas's pants. "Cuffs, no cuffs. Cuffs, no cuffs."

One end of the bay suddenly glowed neon green: the Kwik Stop phoenix had been lit. Silly jerked his head away from the sight of it, cowering, trembling. Kalliope spoke to him in a low voice and after a minute Silly nodded. With a bit more encouragement and some difficulty, he got up. He no longer noticed Jonas. Kalliope walked Silly to the tunnel, keeping her hand on him until he lurched into the brush. Kalliope came back and sat down. "He wasn't like this before."

"Your mother told me." They were quiet for a few moments. "What's this thing about my cuffs, do you know?"

Kalliope allowed herself a little smile.

"When we are children, my mother is sometimes taking us to Chania. And the cinema there. Big thing for us, the cinema. American ones, we were crazy for them. And one time we are seeing this dancer movie, the skinny one, with the flat hair . . ."

"Fred Astaire?"

"Fredastaire, yes. And Fredastaire, he's going to be married. But right before, these friends are saying to him, 'You can't marry yet, you don't having any cuffs. Marriage trouser, it's got to be having cuffs.' So, they are taking his trouser away and he can't be married then. After, he's getting trouser with cuffs, but then these guys are telling him, 'No, no, cuffs no good.' And they are taking away his trouser again. So, again he can't marry. And going on and on like this because he is never having the right trouser. Me and Vasilly, we are thinking this must be some crazy place, America: cuffs, no cuffs; cuffs, no cuffs, and in the end Fredastaire marry a different girl because then the guys are not bothering him of the cuffs. And about this they are making a whole movie!

"Later on, sure, we are knowing it's a joke. But now, Vasilly is again remembering things . . . different." Kalliope's voice quivered. "Always he was playing music. He loved the jazz so much."

Kalliope took a minute to gather herself.

"So, you have been seeing Martissa. But now is enough. It is the best you are leaving now. Maybe coming back a later time, eh?"

"Well, I . . ."

Kalliope waved her hand to end the discussion. She drew a small jug from the sack, pulled the cork, and passed it to Jonas. "*Raki.*"

They drank and waited for the fire to spread through them. Kalliope stared at the neon phoenix glowing through the darkness.

"The chicken is very beautiful tonight."

21

Next morning, Jonas couldn't find Nosey at the motel or any of the three restaurants, at either of the tour agents, at the Kwik Stop or up at Silly's tree. Silly was in his chair, though, clarinet on lap, Car Wash sign leaning against the tree. A man and woman stood over him, their mud-splattered expensive car parked on the path. Silly noticed as Jonas came up the hill and showed a flicker of recognition but made no greeting. The couple were young, fashionably if casually dressed, and extremely exasperated; they spoke immediately to Jonas in a whining rapid French, the gist of which was that they could not get Silly to wash their car.

Silly peered at Jonas: "Australia?" he guessed.

Jonas shook his head: "New York."

"Hah." Silly smiled. "These peoples don't talk English, don't talk German, don't talk Greek. Can they talk to you?"

"I can try."

"Okay." Silly put on a stern face. "Please say for me I don't clean black cars."

Jonas suppressed a chuckle and translated. The French couple scoffed: "*Absurde*." In his retranslation Jonas substituted "very silly," and Vasilly smiled.

"Ain't nobody's business but my ooown . . ." he crooned. "Please say for me, no black cars *Pareskevi*."

"Friday?"

"Yes, Friday. No black cars Friday."

Jonas translated. The French couple wavered between incomprehension and outrage, the combination making for strange faces which Silly understood before Jonas retranslated.

"Dream a little dream..." Silly trilled. "Say for me please, the man to clean black cars is not here this day."

The French couple exploded: What did he mean, the man who washes black cars? What's the matter with him? Why won't he wash a black car?

Jonas condensed and translated.

"Black cars," Silly shrugged. "I don't know how."

At this the couple let out a string of abuse which Jonas synthesized for Silly as "This is no way to run a business."

Silly tooted a few chords on the clarinet, then answered: "If I clean their car when *they* want, it's not making me rich. If I don't clean their car when *I* don't want, it's not making me poor. So ask them, please: If they are me... and today *they* don't want to clean a car, what will they do?"

Jonas did his best to translate and succeeded well enough that the couple stormed off. Silly began to play the tune Jonas had heard him hum before when he was feeling particularly good. Jonas was trying to place it when he spotted Nosey scuttling along the road toward Xhrimatos. He said so-long to Silly and hurried down the hill. Halfway down it came to him: "Ain't nobody's business but my own"—Ella Fitzgerald. "Dream a little dream"... "A-tisket, a-tasket"—Ella. "You been before to Ella's? The place of Apollo?"—Ella Fitzgerald; Apollo Theater. And that strangely familiar face on the Black Madonna in the ancient bird woman's hut?—It was Ella. Ella. Ella. By the time Jonas reached the road, he was laughing out loud.

Jonas found Nosey coming back into Xhrimatos along the road to Martissa. He was nervous, didn't know what he should do. A real tourist would go to the police and ask for the return of his passport; if Nosey didn't show up, what would they think? But maybe the passport would just have been thrown on a desk and forgotten for a while and Nosey would only provoke unwanted interest by showing his face.

All in all, things were getting very dicey, in Nosey's turn of phrase. And as had Kalliope, Nosey now urged Jonas to leave. Because soon, he said, either leaving *or* staying could suddenly become much more difficult.

"And what about you? You could have gotten out with that passport. Out of the country."

"Don't I know." One part of Nosey was nettled that he hadn't left, but some other part of him hadn't allowed it. "Already left once before, ain't I?"

They detoured through the Xhrimatos houses to avoid passing the police shed.

"*Kerates!*"—Cuckolds!—Jonas growled toward the shed.

"Coo, listen to himself. Don't he love trottin' out his Greek, now. Not bad pronouncin', neither."

Jonas smiled: "Thanks. It's not so tough."

"Well, it's all them different letters we got, innit?"

"Yeah, but...not as many as learning English."

Nosey stopped: "What d'you mean, 'not as many'?"

"Well, nothing. Just... Greek has only twenty-four letters, English has twenty-six."

"We got twenty-six."

"You do?"

"Course we do! Maybe we don't... *use* 'em. But we *got* 'em."

Jonas tried not to smirk. "Sooo, the proud Greek today, huh?"

"Might as well do." They walked again. "I mean, if I ain't proud I'm still Greek, ain't I?"

They reached the *kafeneion* and ducked inside. It was empty except for the counter man.

"Listen, can I ask you something? You were making money in England and Australia, right? And that's what you left for, right? So...why'd you come back? I mean, with things the way they are here nowadays?"

They took coffees and sat down.

"Well, I'll tell you. First off, I were in England, see. Manchester. And I'm workin' for this bloke called Simkins. Only his real name ain't Simkins, it's Simiotis. Me uncle. Two other cousins workin' for him, too. Makin' pet furniture.... That's right, you heard right: beds for dogs, little settees for cats—the Brits, they love it. 'Them what has money and no brains...,' eh? So, these cousins and me was all kippin' down together in one freezin' little room, and workin' like dogs, pilin' up a bundle for old Simiotis. And himself, he was always saying how we was all family, all working together, and how we was all gonna be rich and proud. Course, the whole bleedin' time we was slavin', he were off doin' what-all in his back garden with these other naff old geezers. But Simiotis were a sickly old goat, see, and we was his only family. So, we was waitin' him out. Well, the old bugger hangs on and hangs on, and after two years I've had a belly full and I'm fixin' to pack it in, when, Boom!, old Simiotis goes and gets his self topped by a lorry on the Bolton High Road.

"So, finally we can stop makin' them bleedin' budgie bedroom suites. And we all go round to solicitor to hear him read out the will. Only, old man Simiotis's will don't say nothin' 'bout no family. Don't even say nothin' 'bout being no Simiotis. Nah, old man 'Simkins,' he ups and leaves every bleedin' penny to some lot called the Society for Protection of the Aylesbury Drake."

Jonas looked at him blankly.

"Some kinda duck. We was family, worked 'til our fingers was raw . . . and he leaves it all to a bleedin' duck!"

Nosey slammed his fist on the table.

"And for what? Just so's people'd keep thinking he's a proper Englishman. Even after he's stiff in the ground! Well, I could never feature bein' no Simkins like that. So I legged it down to Australia. They was a bit easier to suss down under, but even so, whenever things got down to the short bits, I was always a Greek . . . and they was always not. Know what I mean?"

Jonas thought it was a flash of her eyes, but it was probably the emerald green shirt that he spotted—that same green silk shirt she'd been wearing on the ferry to Corfu those many months ago. She was sitting outside at one of the Xhrimatos restaurants. Seemingly waiting for him to appear. As he sat down across from her, Liana's gaze came to rest where his moustache used to be.

"You know," Jonas struggled, "my wife always wanted to see what I looked like without it. I used to think that was an unreasonable request. . . . How have you been?"

"The long answer or the short?" Her voice was ragged.

"Both. But for now, whatever you can manage."

"I've been traveling. Perhaps you remember, though: I was tired of traveling quite some time ago."

"Yes. Yes, I remember."

They made love in order to bridge with their bodies the time and times they had spent apart, and to burn away quickly the layers of restraint which might stand between them. Liana might have said they were trying to get to "Alice."

She told him that she had found no trace of Aphinotis, her father, either in his home village or in Athens. The myriad police and military agencies all denied any knowledge of him despite neighbors having seen him taken away by a squad of government security men. And the British embassy had received her with far more questions about herself than answers about Aphinotis; over several weeks their various platitudes had amounted to utter silence. Of course, Liana said, they had been ever so polite.

Worn out and dispirited, she had come to Crete to get as far as possible from Athens without leaving Greece, and once here on the island she had remembered the name Martissa. She had known little about Kalliope, but Martissa seemed out of harm's way and if not a destination at least someplace to go. She had arrived here three weeks ago and after several aimless days—she didn't know Kalliope's family name— Nosey had appeared. Then, at last, she said, she had a real destination: Nosey and Kalliope had asked her to go to Athens for them. She had just returned that morning.

Liana was talking about destinations; Jonas found himself thinking about love. That itself was not entirely bizarre. From time to time Jonas did think about love. Sometimes thought about it hard. It was just that he had very rarely been *in* it. Whether as a hedge against his own inaptitude for it, or in response to failed expectations all around him, Jonas had come to consider the notion of romantic love as false prophecy. Love Saves, the romantics contended; just find the right love, give in to it completely, and the tasks of living will melt away under its grand enveloping marquee. To Jonas, this notion of love as salvation, and the mass pursuit of it, was a cultural pathology. And the failure to reach it a major source of modern society's pandemic depression.

Not that Jonas didn't believe in love. He knew it to be a powerful force. Love may not be everything, he once confided to his wife, but he was sure it could help. Help make *other* things possible, that is. Being in love is swell . . . but then it's time to *do* something . . .

Wait a minute, Jonas now caught himself. What does love have to do with this? After all, he barely knew Liana. And knew her not at all in any "real" life. So what is all this? The delusion of a man who fears so much his inability to love that he creates its graven image . . . in order to have something to pray to? And be saved? Then again, she is here, Liana. "Real" in that very real sense. True, she said nothing about having come here because she thought Jonas might be here. But she must have considered the possibility. It must have been at least part of what carried her all this way . . .

He gazed at Liana lying quietly next to him. She looked up, and in the shifting tones of her face he could see that whatever her thoughts about him, she had others as well.

The next morning Jonas and Liana walked together to Martissa. Just inside the village, near the tiny ancient woman's hovel, they heard faint music. Jonas recognized Kalliope's singing and an *aulos* pipe. But Nosey suddenly appeared and steered them away from the hut. Too many people together can be dangerous, he said. The police sometimes watch Martissa from the promontory; if they see several people together, they might investigate. And in the hut they were "busy" just then. Nosey led them back out to the edge of the village and strongly warned them to stay away from Martissa that day. In fact, he said, it was time for them to leave the area altogether. Because after tonight, after the movie . . . He said no more, but faced with his grim insistence, Jonas and Liana reluctantly agreed.

"Got to get on with it sometime," Nosey encouraged them, "know what I mean?" He looked long at Jonas, then embraced them both warmly and darted away.

Back in Xhrimatos, Jonas and Liana picked desultorily at some blue restaurant food. Several Australians were there, tanned, relaxed, laughing. Jonas and Liana felt foolish amidst the joviality and sought refuge in Jonas's room.

"That was the other reason I came here," Liana said as soon as they closed the door. "I had the songs, you see."

"Songs?"

"On that bit of film. Kalliope's and Alekos's songs. When you came out of jail on Corfu, I found the film. In your shoe. And I couldn't bring myself to get rid of it. Do you recall that strange little icon from your room in Glaros? With the two heads?"

"John the Baptist?"

Liana pulled the small tin icon from her bag. "Korina made me take it. To protect me, she said, when I went to the police to find out what had happened to you. And the film fit just so, inside the body. After that, I just . . . had it with me. So, when I got to Crete and remembered Martissa, I thought perhaps it might be useful to someone. It wasn't a terribly bright thing to do, I suppose, carrying it with me, considering the nuisance I made in Athens the first time."

"Yeah, Athens. So why did Nosey and Kalliope send you back there?"

"Tape recorder. If you're a Greek, you see, it takes all kinds of permits to get one. Apparently in Greece a tape recorder is a dangerous thing. But a British tourist like me, with a story about recording old village *bouzouki* and *lyra* players, and my own machine breaking, well, they can allow it . . ." She sank back on the bed and covered her eyes with her arm. "I'm so tired now. . . . Would you know when there is a bus?"

The same words, the first words, he recalled, that she had spoken to him that long-ago day in Glaros. Jonas smiled inwardly at the memory.

"Maybe I'd better find out."

It was Saturday, market day, and Jonas was told that there was an evening run in addition to the usual morning bus. As he walked back to the room, he thought about the fact that Liana hadn't asked him anything about his time since they had parted on Corfu. She had found him in Martissa, doing nothing. Did she assume he'd been doing nothing all along? No, in order to understand where he had gotten to now, she would need to know where he had been. If she wanted to know. But what, exactly, did he have to tell her?

She was asleep when Jonas got back. "No room on the bus tonight," he whispered. "What do you say to a movie?"

The sun had fallen behind the mountains and could do no more about the onrushing clouds than to brush their thunder-gray with violet. The crows had left the power line and were perched on the tin roofs of Xhrimatos, waiting. Jonas and Liana moved through the scores of people who had come from the region's villages and mountain hamlets for the weekly market. Some sat at the three restaurants, with goods they had bought or had not sold; others dipped in and out of the Xhrimatos *kafeneion* to pick up and disseminate the week's bits of gossip.

Jonas and Liana headed for Martissa. There they found Nemosia sitting in her courtyard, stringing tobacco leaves. "I have to dry as much as I can"—she glanced up at the darkening clouds—"before the rains come again." Restrained but angry voices came from deep inside the house. Nemosia shook her head wearily and went back to her tobacco. Jonas and Liana went in and found Kalliope and Nosey in a rear room; a length of electric cord and a tape recorder lay on the floor.

"Kalliope!" Jonas said with surprise.

"Who you think, Jackie Onassis? But no talking now; you must be leaving. Right now it's no good here for company."

Nosey snapped at Kalliope in Greek, then finished in English: "Don't make no bleedin' difference no more, anyways, does it?"

Kalliope and Nosey growled at each other again in Greek, then moved apart.

"The film tonight," Kalliope told Jonas and Liana, "Peoples are coming from all over. And before the film is finishing, they are having big surprises."

"Yeah, great surprise all right—watchin' us two get lobbed into the slammer."

"Vasily," Kalliope said to Jonas, seemingly by way of explanation.

"Haven't seen him all day," Jonas said.

"Nah, us neither," Nosey snarled. "That's the problem."

"Vasily, he is helping tonight. Bothering to the police so they don't be bothering to us. Later, you see, it will be little problem for him because they think he is too strange to be knowing anything."

"Yeah, no problem 'cept he started knowin' nothin' a day early. We ain't seen him since sunup this morning."

Kalliope grumbled and Nosey gave a surly reply in Greek. The two began to argue until Nemosia appeared at the door to quiet them.

"Go on, my friends," Kalliope said, slumping against the wall and sliding down. "It's the best you are going."

"Yeah," Nosey agreed, "this cock-up's all ours."

Jonas wanted to say something, but nothing he knew would reach where they were. Liana touched his arm and they left the house.

It was getting dark and much of the market crowd from Xhrimatos was flowing along the dirt road and up the path toward the schoolyard movie. Jonas and Liana followed them up but stopped outside the school and sat on a rock overlooking Martissa. They tried to pick out Nemosia's house through the closing darkness. Behind them, at the school, Kwik Stop Katsarida and her husband assistant were collecting admissions.

"Listen," he turned to Liana after watching Katsarida for a moment, "you don't really want to see this stupid movie, do you? I got a better idea. More romantic. What do you say?"

"Romantic . . . ?"

"Yeah, I know. But people are always telling me you got to work at romance. So, we'll just call this practice."

Jonas took her hand and led her scurrying down the hill. Liana waited at the edge of the village while he hurried back to Nemosia's house. Kalliope and Nosey were sitting dejectedly against opposite walls.

"What is it Silly's supposed to do?" Jonas said as he barreled into the room.

"What do you say?"

"He's supposed to do something, you said. The police . . ."

"Yeah." Nosey sat up. "When things get funny up the cinema, someone's bound to call 'round the law. But if the law's busy somewheres else, we might have us enough time to finish our business and maybe slip off without them twiggin' who was what."

"But what about the Kwik Stop people? It's their movie."

"No problem. I am watching for weeks," Kalliope said. "Soon as she is having the money, Katsarida is going back to Xhrimatos. And the other one, the husband, he runs away if we are just saying Boo!"

"So, okay, but what is it Silly's supposed to do?"

"Dunno 'xactly. Couldn't rightly suss it. Kept natterin' on 'bout bananas." Nosey stared at Jonas. "Listen, mate, whatever it is you're thinkin' of, forget it. If they tie you up to what all we're gonna get on with at the picture show, they'd be dead stroppy with you. I mean diabolical . . ."

"Hey," Jonas smiled, "I'm just a tourist, remember? All they do is cut my holiday short, right? And what the hell, it's going to start raining anyway."

Jonas raced with Liana toward Xhrimatos. They passed the police shed; a light was on but Jonas couldn't tell if anyone was inside. He clambered up to his room, came down in a moment, then pulled Liana toward the water. At the deserted dock he quickly untied one of the identical, numbered rental dinghies.

"Wait a minute." He stopped and held the rope. "You ought to know what I'm up to."

"There is a first time for everything."

"Hey, I'm talking serious, here. This is sort of...a diversionary expedition."

"I've had that notion for quite a while."

Jonas had no time for her allusions.

"If it works, they're going to come out and get us." He indicated the police motor launch. "Could be a rough time."

"I'm the one who went for the tape recorder, remember?"

"We'll have some explaining to do."

"Carried away by love." She jumped into the boat. "Do you think they'll believe us?"

Jonas rowed until they were out far enough to see Martissa past the promontory. A flickering blue light licked the heavy clouds behind the hill: the movie had begun; bits of the soundtrack floated out to them on the rising breeze. Jonas pulled out two packs of cigarettes and began to empty tobacco into a pile.

"Smoke signals."

"How American."

"Yeah, we use 'em all the time in Brooklyn."

The neon phoenix sputtered to life and spread its pestilent glare over Xhrimatos and much of the bay. Jonas rowed out farther to stay clear of the light, to avoid premature notice by anyone on land, then pulled from his back pockets a packet of rolling tobacco and the tattered paperback copy of *Alice in Wonderland*.

"Ah, she's come a long way, our Alice," Liana said.

The light and sound at the school suddenly shut off. Jonas ripped out a few pages of the book, laid in some tobacco, and rolled it into a sort of torch.

A steady white light now came on behind the school; a moment later the sounds of an *aulos* pipe and singing drifted down, reaching the bay.

"Kalliope and Silly," Jonas said.

"What?"

Jonas listened for a moment. "That's Silly on the pipe. Playing Panastakis. And Kalliope singing. Yesterday, at the shack in Martissa, remember? They must have been making the tape then, with the recorder you brought.... '*Axion esti to timima*'—'Worth it is the price we must pay,'" Jonas repeated the words drifting down from the school. "They're showing one of the poems, from the film strip," Jonas said. "Ready?"

Liana nodded. They lit the first roll of pages and Jonas stood up and waved it over his head. Jonas could see people outside the restaurants and milling about the lanes, but the phoenix so brightly lit the main road, the housing grid, and the Xhrimatos side of the Martissa dirt road that no one noticed their makeshift flare.

Liana lit a second roll of pages and they waved the two mini-torches more briskly, hoping the motion would attract attention. As they did, Jonas explained his plan to her. Lovers taking a boat out may be illegal, but innocent enough to be taken lightly. And if they did manage to draw out the cops into the bay, they'd conveniently "lose" an oar over the side as excuse for their distress signals.

The Panastakis song began again at the school, and this time other voices rose with the refrain "*Axion esti to timima*." With each chorus, Jonas and Liana could hear more voices join in. It was only a matter of time before the banned music was overheard in Xhrimatos, or someone left the school to report things to the police. And given how quickly their little flares petered out, Jonas and Liana still hadn't managed to draw anyone's attention.

"The fucking chicken!"

"What?"

"The bird. The phoenix. It's so goddamn bright they can't see us out beyond it."

"Well, let's make some noise, then. Sing something."

"Sing? Sing what?"

"I don't know. Something loud. Something from the US. Lord knows you people make enough noise."

"Yeah, all right. Okay." He lit another flare and held it high: "Oh-oh say can you see-ee ... ," Jonas howled, "... by the dawn's early light ..."

After "The Star-Spangled Banner" they lit two more flares and Jonas joined Liana in an exuberant "Rule, Britannia." But even if people in Xhrimatos heard them, the way sound traveled across water would give them no idea where the sound was coming from. And since no boats went out at night, they might not think to look out beyond the phoenix's neon glare. Besides, no one paid attention to drunken singing in English: package tourists had been coming to Xhrimatos for two years now.

Jonas noticed one of the local cops bring out a chair and take up a position next to the police shed door, taking the evening air. On the other side of the promontory, Jonas spotted four or five people hurriedly leaving the Martissa school—soon either they or the sounds of the songs would reach the police.

"Jesus fuck!" Jonas slammed the oars into the water and rowed desperately toward shore but they were going nowhere: the tide that had so easily carried them away just as easily now held them back. They tried singing again but the northerly breeze that rode before the storm refused to let their voices reach the land.

Jonas stopped rowing to see what was happening on shore. A shadow moved across the Kwik Stop roof, briefly blocking a part of the neon. A few moments later, the air was shattered by a thunderous explosion. Flames shot out through the Kwik Stop's shattered windows; the phoenix on its roof sparked wildly, then was swallowed in billowing smoke; metal, glass and plaster soared and fell in a wide arc while bits of cardboard and paper fluttered jaggedly in the smoke like birds just released from a cage who don't yet know which way to fly.

When the echoes subsided, there was an innocent moment of silence in which Jonas could hear the tape continuing to play Kalliope's singing of the verses from the film strip being projected on the school wall: "*Axion esti to timima.*" Then all hell broke loose. Across the road from the Kwik Stop, restaurant patrons howled with shock and terror and people came swarming out their doors in the housing grid. The cops ran toward the main road carrying automatic weapons. And after a minute, the clouds opened up with a pounding percussion on the tin roofs of Xhrimatos.

No one noticed when Jonas and Liana finally managed to bring in the dinghy. All the villagers and market visitors were gathered, standing in a steady rain, in front of the hissing shell of the Kwik Stop. The two policemen were paralyzed, not knowing whether to grab and interrogate people or to enter the smoldering building. People huddled in small, fearful groups, talking guardedly; Jonas was surprised at how quiet and subdued they were. Then he and Liana came around the front of the shop and saw why: hanging on the twisted wreckage of the phoenix was Silly's rent and blackened body. Jonas stared, and the rain came down harder, drowning out the voices around him.

22

Steam rose from the hood of the morning bus; moisture clouded the inside of the windows. Waiting was agony, terror: Jonas expected that at any moment a Xhrimatos cop would lead several soldiers onto the bus, survey the passengers, lock his eyes on Jonas and Liana, and point. Jonas tried not to look outside.

During their sleepless night, Jonas and Liana had heard through the rain the rumble of jeeps and a truck. The hours before dawn they had spent weaving in whispers their story to tell the soldiers who would soon burst through the door. Even when it seemed they had covered every detail, Jonas kept Liana talking so as to hold at bay recurring images of his jail cell, of other men's cries, of hideous laughter and the voice which had offered him *phistikia*—pistachios.

But no soldiers came. Heads down, he and Liana had padded toward the few people who huddled with their parcels next to the morning bus. Other than tourists readying to leave the motel, the main road and the paths of Xhrimatos were empty. People stayed indoors. Waiting. Jonas and Liana waited, too. The Kwik Stop rubble was still smoldering.

The other people on the bus were also silent and fearful, although Jonas barely noticed. Nor did he feel the pain in his arms from the night's frantic rowing, nor the chilled sweat that ran down his back. He looked toward the power station: an army truck in front, the entrance patrolled by two soldiers, the dynamite hut manned by two others. Standing apart in the mud and rain next to the police shed, a dozen people were being guarded by still more soldiers; under a makeshift canvas awning, two military officers conferred with the local cops. Jonas sucked in his breath to see Kalliope's mother, Nemosia, among the detained. But if Kalliope herself had been captured, or even recognized, her mother would not now be merely one of many usual suspects to be questioned. The idea of Kalliope still free in the hills gave Jonas a small boost of courage.

The bus driver and his helper appeared and approached the boxes and bags waiting to be loaded. They were joined by three soldiers with automatic weapons and an army officer with a sidearm who directed a search of the baggage. The soldiers poked here and there, peered into boxes and sacks, but the rain was coming down hard again and the officer seemed disinclined to spend much time amidst the soggy cargo. Occasionally he raised his eyes to the misted bus windows. Jonas kept his head down.

The helper opened the luggage compartment in the side of the bus and began to load the baggage. It took forever. Finally the driver got in and Jonas heard the blessed sound of the engine. Passengers crossed themselves, the drenched helper hopped in, the driver closed the door. But before the bus could pull away, there was a bang on the hood; the driver opened the door and up stepped the officer, hand on his holstered sidearm. He walked slowly up and down the aisle. Jonas was afraid to look but afraid to look away. The officer stood and glared, fingered his gun, stood and glared some more, until Jonas realized that rather than looking for anyone, he was simply making everyone look at him. Finally he growled at the driver, turned to give a last glare, and got off the bus.

They were moving. The bus pulled out of the mud and onto the main road. As they passed the husk of the Kwik Stop and its twisted rooftop wreck, Jonas wondered what they had done with Silly's body. And wondered if Kalliope knew.

The bus climbed away from Xhrimatos. Jonas and Liana realized they were gripping each other's hand and slowly untwined their fingers. Moments before the bus disappeared into the hills, Liana nudged Jonas and pointed: they could just make out the school, standing alone on the hill behind Martissa. And on the ridge between, the soothing sight of olive trees bathing gratefully, leaves glistening silver and soft in the rain.

They rode along in silence, the noise of the laboring engine covering everyone's reluctance to speak. In the mountains, a car honked at the slow-climbing bus, tried to pass on the narrow road, fell back, honked, tried again, fell back. With a burst, the car finally drew alongside; an Australian T-shirt was squeezed into the middle rear seat, and as the car went past he looked back. The windows of bus and car were fogged and the distance between was lined with rain. Still, squinting with his green eye, Jonas thought he saw a huge moustache close behind the glass.

The bus stopped at a small mountain village and another damp half dozen people crowded on. An enormous woman squeezed her way into the aisle, from her old woven bag the smell of fresh garlic wafting over the passengers. The driver lurched the bus away; only the woman's great girth against both sides of the aisle permitted her to maintain her balance. A man at the back called to her and after a protracted struggle she made it to the seat he offered and hoisted herself up. The driver's assistant was collecting money from the other newcomers toward the front and yelled at the big woman about not having paid. She opened her arms, looked down at her tremendous bulk, and snapped back what Jonas did not need to translate much of to understand: "What? You think I could hide?" The testy exchange did nothing to lessen the already overbearing tension. The bus rumbled on, swollen, steamy, sullen.

After a few minutes, the big woman began to hum. At first Jonas could not hear the tune over the noise of engine and rain, but her voice gained purpose and soon Jonas and the others could not help but recognize the familiar, forbidden Panastakis melody. Eyes grew wide, some with reproach, others with weary discomfort. People sitting near the woman tried to inch away.

The cross-mountain road finally emptied into a broad plain crossed by several larger roads, and the bus stopped at a junction town. Jonas wiped the mist from his window and read the name on another waiting bus: Kissamos—Crete's northwest port, gateway to the western coast but the opposite direction from the ports with ferries that left the island. Liana saw the bus, too.

People got off to stretch their legs; several went into a *kafeneion*. Jonas and Liana scurried under a trellis out of the rain, then Liana ducked into a small ticket office.

"The Kissamos bus," she reported back, "leaves in an hour." He said nothing. Their bus helper was unloading some baggage. Liana had him pull off her bag; she brought it to dry ground.

"I think the truth is I also came to Crete for another reason," she said slowly. "Do you recall, I told you about a cave, my mother and ... my father? The west of Crete? Well, when I was in Athens trying to find him, I thought, what if he were on the run again? Where would he go? Or perhaps he'd been arrested but now finally had been released, and gone there in retreat? Or . . . to recapture something?" She turned to Jonas. "My mother described it so often. And I've come this far. You see, they were happy there. At least for a time. . . . And besides, that way is sort of the way home, wouldn't you say?"

"I suppose," Jonas replied, "that depends on what direction you're going."

Liana stared at the raindrops hitting a puddle.

"I think I'll see if they sell candles," she said, nodding toward a village shop. "Always a good thing, a candle."

Jonas stared at her for a long moment, then nodded: "Especially if you're in a cave."

He stood and searched her face, noticed how fitful were the colors in her eyes. After a moment, when he said nothing more, she turned and walked through the rain to the little shop.

The driver returned. He and his helper loaded baggage as several new passengers and most of the original ones mounted the bus. The driver started the engine. Jonas got on. As the bus rolled away, he could see her at the window of the shop, looking out.

When the bus had been moving for a few minutes, the big woman at the back again began humming the Panastakis music. And soon she added words. But Jonas had been told there were no words to that song. None, that is, except the poem Jonas had unwittingly smuggled into Corfu, that Kalliope had sung onto a tape, and that she and Nosey had shown on the wall of the Martissa school. The woman's singing reached the front of the bus. The driver and helper turned, appearing both angry and distressed, but made no moves. No one else breathed a word.

The big woman reached the final chorus, "*Axion esti to timima*"— Worth it is the price we must pay—and sang with redoubled emotion. Three times she sang the refrain, looked around at the silent passengers, then crossed her arms and sat perfectly still, defiance fixed on her face, until the bus came to a stop in a small mountain village. There the woman gathered herself and her garlic and struggled through the crowded aisle to the rear door. She turned and surveyed the other passengers with an expression which simultaneously disdained and beseeched. Most of them avoided her gaze. She got off the bus.

The driver quickly closed the doors and pulled out of the village, exchanging loud remarks and contemptuous gestures with his helper at the expense of the departed woman. No one took the seat she had vacated; it yawned huge and imposing. The odor of garlic clung to the moist windows, to the damp seats, to wet clothes, wet hair, wet skin. Finally, a tiny wizened old man edged his way back and took the empty rear seat, filling only half the space the big woman had. Several people grinned to see the ancient child in the grown-up's chair and soon, for the first time since the bus had left Xhrimatos, there began normal if subdued conversations. Within moments, though, a small voice climbed its way over the talk, the engine and the rain. At first the old man's voice could barely be heard, but as people recognized the song, their chatter stopped. He reached the chorus, took a breath, and summoned all his frail strength. "*Axion esti to timima*," he sang out, "*Axion esti to timima*."

The driver and the helper heard him, conferred for a moment, then the helper started back through the crowd, a determined, threatening expression twisting his face. The old man saw him coming but sang the refrain once more. When the helper had made it halfway back, a woman's voice joined the song. Jonas turned to see who it was but couldn't locate her in the crowd. The helper stopped in surprise at this second voice, then kept moving back toward the old man. Now another voice at the back joined the song, then a voice from the front, then another, and another. The helper stood in the middle of the aisle while voices rose all around him and "*Axion esti to timima*" soared over the drumming rain and the noxious growl of the engine.

When they finished the song, there was stunned exhilaration among the passengers. The feeling of fear overcome left them speechless, enthralled. The bus rolled into the next stop, a larger town, where the driver and helper leapt off and dove into a building across the square. The tiny old man got up from his rear seat. People made room for him and, with several others, he stepped down into the rain.

Two disheveled local policemen crossed the square with the driver and his helper. The cops came around the bus and accosted the tiny old man, ordering him to the side. Then the policemen confronted three other passengers who were waiting for their bags. Soon two men wearing suits and city hats arrived and took charge. They instructed the cops, who shoved the old man and the other three against a wall and held them there in the rain. But there were still more people on the bus. Jonas and everyone else.

About the Author

Joseph Matthews was born in Boston and raised there and in California. For a number of years, he was a criminal defense lawyer in the San Francisco Bay Area. He is the author of the novels *The Blast* and *Everyone Has Their Reasons*, the story collection *The Lawyer Who Blew Up His Desk*, and the post–September 11 political analysis *Afflicted Powers: Capital and Spectacle in a New Age of War* (with Iain Boal, T.J. Clark, and Michael Watts).

ABOUT PM PRESS

PM Press is an independent, radical publisher of books and media to educate, entertain, and inspire. Founded in 2007 by a small group of people with decades of publishing, media, and organizing experience, PM Press amplifies the voices of radical authors, artists, and activists. Our aim is to deliver bold political ideas and vital stories to people from all walks of life and arm the dreamers to demand the impossible. We have sold millions of copies of our books, most often one at a time, face to face. We're old enough to know what we're doing and young enough to know what's at stake. Join us to create a better world.

PM Press
PO Box 23912
Oakland, CA 94623
www.pmpress.org

PM Press in Europe
europe@pmpress.org
www.pmpress.org.uk

FRIENDS OF PM PRESS

These are indisputably momentous times—the financial system is melting down globally and the Empire is stumbling. Now more than ever there is a vital need for radical ideas.

In the many years since its founding—and on a mere shoestring—PM Press has risen to the formidable challenge of publishing and distributing knowledge and entertainment for the struggles ahead. With hundreds of releases to date, we have published an impressive and stimulating array of literature, art, music, politics, and culture. Using every available medium, we've succeeded in connecting those hungry for ideas and information to those putting them into practice.

Friends of PM allows you to directly help impact, amplify, and revitalize the discourse and actions of radical writers, filmmakers, and artists. It provides us with a stable foundation from which we can build upon our early successes and provides a much-needed subsidy for the materials that can't necessarily pay their own way. You can help make that happen—and receive every new title automatically delivered to your door once a month—by joining as a Friend of PM Press. And, we'll throw in a free T-shirt when you sign up.

Here are your options:

- **$30 a month** Get all books and pamphlets plus a 50% discount on all webstore purchases

- **$40 a month** Get all PM Press releases (including CDs and DVDs) plus a 50% discount on all webstore purchases

- **$100 a month** Superstar—Everything plus PM merchandise, free downloads, and a 50% discount on all webstore purchases

For those who can't afford $30 or more a month, we have **Sustainer Rates** at $15, $10, and $5. Sustainers get a free PM Press T-shirt and a 50% discount on all purchases from our website.

Your Visa or Mastercard will be billed once a month, until you tell us to stop. Or until our efforts succeed in bringing the revolution around. Or the financial meltdown of Capital makes plastic redundant. Whichever comes first.

The Blast

Joseph Matthews

ISBN: 978-1-62963-910-9 (paperback)
978-1-62963-911-6 (hardcover)
$20.00   416 pages

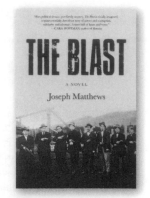

San Francisco, 1916. The streets roiling: pitched battles between radical workers and the henchmen of industrial barons, and between a vibrant, largely Italian immigrant anarchist milieu and the forces of state and church. All in the looming shadow of Europe's raging war, and of a fierce struggle over whether the US should commit its might, and human fodder, to the slaughter in the trenches.

Into this maelstrom arrives Kate Jameson, a novice envoy from Washington tasked to secretly investigate the tenor of support for war entry among San Francisco's business elite. She's also hoping to glimpse her wayward daughter, Maggie, whose last message to Kate had come from there. And, too, she's seeking the ghost of her husband, Jamey, who fifteen years earlier had landed there upon his return, shattered, from his part in the US occupation of the Philippines.

Arriving back in the city at the same moment is Baldo Cavanaugh, a Sicilian-Irish son of San Francisco whose militant beliefs and special skills have led him time and again to the violent extremes of the city's turbulent history. And who now must confront the doubts and demons of his own character, which he'd sought to escape by fleeing the city three years before.

This stunning tale explores how these two seemingly disparate characters become engaged with the city's and nation's turmoil, and with the complexities of their related pasts in Boston, Dublin, London, Cuba, and the Philippines. A vivid picture of a city and a moment, the novel brilliantly reveals the explosive admixture of the deeply personal and the deeply political.

"A novel full of heart and verve. Strikers, spies, propagandists, anarchists, immigrants, suffragettes, and provocateurs—schemers and dreamers all—converge in this portrait of turbulent pre–World War I San Francisco. Part political drama, part family mystery, The Blast *is vividly imagined, a quintessentially American story of power and corruption, solidarity and sabotage."*
—Cara Hoffman, author of *Running*

*"*The Blast *is quite simply a tour de force. Matthews brings to life a lost world of radicalism, in a riveting story that ripples out across multiple continents, with the entanglements of the personal and the political squarely in his sights. He has a keen ear for the passions, large and small, that impel women and men to take matters into their own hands. This is a novel for our troubled times."*
—Sasha Lilley, author of *Catastrophism*

Everyone Has Their Reasons

Joseph Matthews

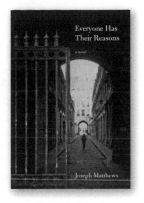

ISBN: 978-1-62963-094-6
$24.95   528 pages

On November 7, 1938, a small, slight seventeen-year-old Polish-German Jew named Herschel Grynszpan entered the German embassy in Paris and shot dead a consular official. Three days later, in supposed response, Jews across Germany were beaten, imprisoned, and killed, their homes, shops, and synagogues smashed and burned—Kristallnacht, the Night of Broken Glass.

Based on the historical record and told through his "letters" from German prisons, the novel begins in 1936, when fifteen-year-old Herschel flees Germany. Penniless and alone, he makes it to Paris where he lives hand-to-mouth, his shadow existence mixing him with the starving and the wealthy, with hustlers, radicals, and seamy sides of Paris nightlife.

In 1938, the French state rejects refugee status for Herschel and orders him out of the country. With nowhere to go, and now sought by the police, he slips underground in immigrant east Paris.

Soon after, the Nazis round up all Polish Jews in Germany—including Herschel's family—and dump them on the Poland border. Herschel's response is to shoot the German official, then wait calmly for the French police.

June 1940, Herschel is still in prison awaiting trial when the Nazi army nears Paris. He is evacuated south to another jail but escapes into the countryside amid the chaos of millions of French fleeing the invasion. After an incredible month alone on the road, Herschel seeks protection at a prison in the far south of France. Two weeks later the French state hands him to the Gestapo.

The Nazis plan a big show trial, inviting the world press to Berlin for the spectacle, to demonstrate through Herschel that Jews had provoked the war. Except that Herschel throws a last-minute wrench in the plans, bringing the Nazi propaganda machine to a grinding halt. Hitler himself postpones the trial and orders that no decision be made about Herschel's fate until the Führer personally gives an order— one way or another.

"A tragic, gripping Orwellian tale of an orphan turned assassin in pre–World War II Paris. Based on the true story of the Jewish teen Hitler blamed for Kristallnacht, it's a wild ride through the underside of Europe as the storm clouds of the Holocaust gather. Not to be missed!"
—Terry Bisson, Hugo and Nebula award-winning author of *Fire on the Mountain*

RUIN

Cara Hoffman

ISBN: 978-1-62963-929-1 (paperback)
      978-1-62963-931-4 (hardcover)
$14.95/$25.95   128 pages

A little girl who disguises herself as an old man, an addict who collects dollhouse furniture, a crime reporter confronted by a talking dog, a painter trying to prove the non-existence of god, and lovers in a penal colony who communicate through technical drawings—these are just a few of the characters who live among the ruins. Cara Hoffman's short fictions are brutal, surreal, hilarious, and transgressive, celebrating the sharp beauty of outsiders and the infinitely creative ways humans muster psychic resistance under oppressive conditions. RUIN is both bracingly timely and eerily timeless in its examination of an American state in free-fall: unsparing in its disregard for broken, ineffectual institutions, while shining with compassion for the damaged left in their wake. The ultimate effect of these ten interconnected stories is one of invigoration and a sense of possibilities—hope for a new world extracted from the rubble of the old.

Cara Hoffman is the author of three *New York Times* Editors' Choice novels; the most recent, *Running*, was named a Best Book of the Year by *Esquire*. She first received national attention in 2011 with the publication of *So Much Pretty*, which sparked a national dialogue on violence and retribution and was named a Best Novel of the Year by the *New York Times Book Review*. Her second novel, *Be Safe I Love You*, was nominated for a Folio Prize, named one of the Five Best Modern War Novels, and awarded a Sundance Global Filmmaking Award. A MacDowell Fellow and an Edward Albee Fellow, she has lectured at Oxford University's Rhodes Global Scholars Symposium and at the Renewing the Anarchist Tradition Conference. Her work has appeared in the *New York Times*, *Paris Review*, *BOMB*, *Bookforum*, *Rolling Stone*, *Daily Beast*, and on NPR. A founding editor of the *Anarchist Review of Books*, and part of the Athens Workshop collective, she lives in Athens, Greece, with her partner.

"RUIN is a collection of ten jewels, each multi-faceted and glittering, to be experienced with awe and joy. Cara Hoffman has seen a secret world right next to our own, just around the corner, and written us a field guide to what she's found. I love this book."
—Sara Gran, author of *Infinite Blacktop* and *Claire Dewitt and the City of the Dead*

The Colonel Pyat Quartet

Michael Moorcock
with introductions by Alan Wall

Byzantium Endures
ISBN: 978-1-60486-491-5
$22.00   400 pages

The Laughter of Carthage
ISBN: 978-1-60486-492-2
$22.00   448 pages

Jerusalem Commands
ISBN: 978-1-60486-493-9
$22.00   448 pages

The Vengeance of Rome
ISBN: 978-1-60486-494-6
$23.00   500 pages

Moorcock's Pyat Quartet has been described as an
authentic masterpiece of the 20th and 21st centuries. It's
the story of Maxim Arturovitch Pyatnitski, a cocaine addict,
sexual adventurer, and obsessive anti-Semite whose epic
journey from Leningrad to London connects him with
scoundrels and heroes from Trotsky to Makhno, and whose
career echoes that of the 20th century's descent into
Fascism and total war

It is Michael Moorcock's extraordinary achievement to
convert the life of Maxim Pyatnitski into epic and often
hilariously comic adventure. Sustained by his dreams and
profligate inventions, his determination to turn his back
on the realities of his own origins, Pyat runs from crisis
to crisis, every ruse a further link in a vast chain of deceit,
suppression, betrayal. Yet, in his deranged self-deception,
his monumentally distorted vision, this thoroughly
unreliable narrator becomes a lens for focusing, through the
dimensions of wild farce and chilling terror, on an uneasy
brand of truth.

God's Teeth and Other Phenomena

James Kelman

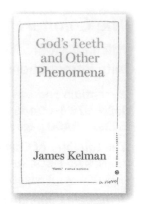

ISBN: 978-1-62963-939-0 (paperback)
978-1-62963-940-6 (hardcover)
$17.95/$34.95   384 pages

Jack Proctor, a celebrated older writer and curmudgeon, goes off to residency where he is to be an honored part of teaching and giving public readings but soon finds that the atmosphere of the literary world has changed since his last foray into the public sphere. Unknown to most, unable to work on his own writing, surrounded by a host of odd characters, would-be writers, antagonists, handlers, and members of the elite House of Art and Aesthetics, Proctor finds himself driven to distraction (literally in a very tiny car). This is a story of a man attempting not to go mad when forced to stop his own writing in order to coach others to write. Proctor's tour of rural places, pubs, theaters, and fancy parties, where he is to be headlining as a "Banker Prize winner," reads like a literary version of *This Is Spinal Tap*. Uproariously funny, brilliantly philosophical, gorgeously written, this is James Kelman at his best.

James Kelman was born in Glasgow, June 1946, and left school in 1961. He traveled and worked various jobs, and while living in London began to write. In 1994 he won the Booker Prize for *How Late It Was, How Late*. His novel *A Disaffection* was shortlisted for the Booker Prize and won the James Tait Black Memorial Prize for Fiction in 1989. In 1998 Kelman was awarded the Glenfiddich Spirit of Scotland Award. His 2008 novel *Kieron Smith, Boy* won the Saltire Society's Book of the Year and the Scottish Arts Council Book of the Year. He lives in Glasgow with his wife, Marie, who has supported his work since 1969.

"God's Teeth and Other Phenomena *is electric. Forget all the rubbish you've been told about how to write, the requirements of the marketplace and the much vaunted 'readability' that is supposed to be sacrosanct. This is a book about how art gets made, its murky, obsessive, unedifying demands and the endless, sometimes hilarious, humiliations literary life inflicts on even its most successful names."*
—Eimear McBride, author of *A Girl is a Half-Formed Thing* and *The Lesser Bohemians*

"James Kelman is an extraordinary writer—smart and incisive, witty and warm, with prose so alive it practically sparks off the page. God's Teeth and Other Phenomena *is one of the wisest, funniest and most brutally honest books I've read in ages. I loved it."*
—Molly Antopol, author of *The Unamericans*

"James Kelman changed my life."
—Douglas Stuart, author of *Shuggie Bain*

The Cost of Lunch, Etc.

Marge Piercy

ISBN: 978-1-62963-125-7 (paperback)
     978-1-60486-496-0 (hardcover)
$15.95/$21.95   192 pages

Marge Piercy's debut collection of short stories, *The Cost of Lunch, Etc.*, brings us glimpses into the lives of everyday women moving through and making sense of their daily internal and external worlds. Keeping to the engaging, accessible language of Piercy's novels, the collection spans decades of her writing along with a range of locations, ages, and emotional states of her protagonists. From the first-person account of hoarding ("Saving Mother from Herself") to a girl's narrative of sexual and spiritual discovery ("Going over Jordan") to a recount of a past love affair ("The Easy Arrangement") each story is a tangible, vivid snapshot in a varied and subtly curated gallery of work. Whether grappling with death, familial relationships, friendship, sex, illness, or religion, Piercy's writing is as passionate, lucid, insightful, and thoughtfully alive as ever.

"The author displays an old-fashioned narrative drive and a set of well-realized characters permitted to lead their own believably odd lives."
—Thomas Mallon, *Newsday*

"This reviewer knows no other writer with Piercy's gifts for tracing the emotional route that two people take to a double bed, and the mental games and gambits each transacts there."
—Ron Grossman, *Chicago Tribune*

"Marge Piercy is not just an author, she's a cultural touchstone. Few writers in modern memory have sustained her passion, and skill, for creating stories of consequence."
—*Boston Globe*

"What Piercy has that Danielle Steel, for example, does not is an ability to capture life's complex texture, to chart shifting relationships and evolving consciousness within the context of political and economic realities she delineates with mordant matter-of-factness. Working within the venerable tradition of socially conscious fiction, she brings to it a feminist understanding of the impact such things as class and money have on personal interactions without ever losing sight of the crucial role played by individuals' responses to those things."
—Wendy Smith, *Chicago Sun-Times*

Men in Prison

Victor Serge
Introduction and Translation by Richard Greeman

ISBN: 978-1-60486-736-7
$18.95   232 pages

"Everything in this book is fictional and everything is true," wrote Victor Serge in the epigraph to *Men in Prison*. "I have attempted, through literary creation, to bring out the general meaning and human content of a personal experience."

The author of *Men in Prison* served five years in French penitentiaries (1912–1917) for the crime of "criminal association"—in fact for his courageous refusal to testify against his old comrades, the infamous "Tragic Bandits" of French anarchism. "While I was still in prison," Serge later recalled, "fighting off tuberculosis, insanity, depression, the spiritual poverty of the men, the brutality of the regulations, I already saw one kind of justification of that infernal voyage in the possibility of describing it. Among the thousands who suffer and are crushed in prison—and how few men really know that prison!—I was perhaps the only one who could try one day to tell all . . . There is no novelist's hero in this novel, unless that terrible machine, prison, is its real hero. It is not about 'me,' about a few men, but about men, all men crushed in that dark corner of society."

Birth of Our Power

Victor Serge

ISBN: 978-1-62963-030-4
$18.95   256 pages

Birth of Our Power is an epic novel set in Spain, France, and Russia during the heady revolutionary years 1917–1919. Serge's tale begins in the spring of 1917, the third year of mass slaughter in the blood-and-rain-soaked trenches of World War I, when the flames of revolution suddenly erupt in Russia and Spain. Europe is "burning at both ends." Although the Spanish uprising eventually fizzles, in Russia the workers, peasants, and common soldiers are able to take power and hold it. Serge's "tale of two cities" is constructed from the opposition between Barcelona, the city "we" could not take, and Petrograd, the starving capital of the Russian Revolution, besieged by counter-revolutionary Whites. Between the romanticism of radicalized workers awakening to their own power in a sun-drenched Spanish metropolis to the grim reality of workers clinging to power in Russia's dark, frozen revolutionary outpost. From "victory-in-defeat" to "defeat in victory."